The Accomplice

The
Accomplice

Elizabeth Ironside

All the characters and eveÎnts portrayed in this work are fictitious.

THE ACCOMPLICE

A Felony & Mayhem mystery

PRINTING HISTORY
First UK edition (Hodder and Stoughton): 1996
First paperback edition (Hodder and Stoughton/Coronet): 1996
Felony & Mayhem edition: 2006, 2007

ISBN 978-1-933397-50-4

To
Michael and Sylvia

The icon above says you're holding a copy of a book in the Felony & Mayhem "British" category. These books are set in or around the UK, and feature the highly literate, often witty prose that fans of British mystery demand. If you enjoy this book, you may well like other "British" titles from Felony & Mayhem Press, including:

Death in the Garden, by Elizabeth Ironside
A Very Private Enterprise, by Elizabeth Ironside
The Killings at Badger's Drift, by Caroline Graham
Death of a Hollow Man, by Caroline Graham
Death on the High C's, by Robert Barnard
Out of the Blackout, by Robert Barnard
Dupe, by Liza Cody
King and Joker, by Peter Dickinson
Death in the Morning, by Sheila Radley

For more about these books, and other Felony & Mayhem titles, or to place an order, please visit our website at:

www.FelonyAndMayhem.com

or contact us at:

Felony and Mayhem Press
156 Waverly Place
New York, NY 10014

Contents

The Daunsey and Loftus Families

The Daunseys

Zita Daunsey—an attorney
Tom Daunsey—Zita's son
Oliver Daunsey—Zita's ex-husband, Tom's father
Valentina Guilfoyle—Zita's mother

Lynne—Zita's and Tom's "nanny, housekeeper, driver and nurse"

The Loftuses

The Present

Jean Loftus, at one time known as Yevgenia Konstantinovna
   Chornoroukaya—Zita's client and friend
Marcus Loftus—Jean's step-son
Naomi Loftus—Marcus' wife
Rosie Loftus—Marcus' daughter, Naomi's step-daughter
Al—Rosie's boyfriend
Ivo Loftus—Marcus' son, Naomi's step-son

Xenia Chornoroukaya—A Russian student

The Past

Baron von Korff—Yevgenia's father
Princess Marina Yurievna Chornoroukaya—Yevgenia's mother
Prince Yuri Alexandrovich—Princess Marina's father, Yevgenia's
   grandfather
Princess Zoya Chornoroukaya—Prince Yuri's sister, Yevgenia's
   great-aunt
Prince Yegor—Brother of Prince Yuri and Princess Zoya,
   Yevgenia's great-uncle
Alexander Chornorouky ("Xan")—Yevgenia's cousin, grandson
   of Prince Yegor, and great-nephew of Princess Zoya and
   Prince Yuri
Nikolai ("Lai")—A childhood companion to Yevgenia and Xan

The Accomplice

Part One

ZITA

Chapter One

She had made all the arrangements for her own funeral. She had interviewed the undertakers and ordered her coffin. She had chosen the hymns and seen to the printing of the service sheets, as if she were deciding what clothes to wear. She had decided who would be buried

ЕВГЕНИЯ КОНСТАНТИНОВНА ЧОРНОРУКАЯ

1917—1992

Zita Daunsey, seated in the second row, moved her eyes from the coffin, resting in the entrance to the chancel, to the Cyrillic letters on the sheet she held in her hand. Who was Yevgenia Konstantinovna Chornoroukaya? Who here knew her?

The organ died away and the congregation rose to its feet. The service began. The beauty of the words, familiar even to an unbeliever, distracted Zita only momentarily from the other questions that her mind persistently formed. Since she had given up her job in the City and become a partner in a provincial law firm, she had been to many funerals; it was the sort of attention still given to and appreciated by clients in a small town. She had often observed the comfort of ritual to those in the first bewilderment of loss. The calming words covered the rawness of individual grief with a soothing sense of inevitability. Death comes to us all, they said, we are part of a process. And so they smothered rather than answered the inevitable questions, why? why now? why her?

In this case the questions were not to be denied. She resisted them. There was nothing, she told herself, nothing at all, to indicate that Yevgenia's death was anything other than a tragic accident. She was elderly, crippled, in pain, and in the last three months she had been tormented by memories that she had successfully suppressed for most of her life. Zita rehearsed the words that survivors use to console one another, to convince themselves as much as others. *It was a merciful release; she was glad to go at the end.* All the old untruths. *We* cling to life, in pain, misery and defeat; but we are different. The dead one let go; she died because, secretly, she wanted to. The logic is that as long as we maintain our will to live, we can fend off the darkness, live for ever.

And yet...and yet. There was something wrong. It was more than an accident: there was a pattern there, if she could only see it for a moment, like a rose window in a turning kaleidoscope. She stared at the stained glass above the altar which, as if her thoughts had received a sharp jolt, seemed to re-form in a new pattern.

She was, of course, mistaken. No one else saw anything wrong. Dr Flowers had issued the death certificate. She would have died rapidly and without pain, he had assured Zita, a confidence she had passed on to the family. Her view, one pew back, comprehended them all. Marcus, as correct as always in his black suit, and Naomi, whose flowing garments made no concession to the conventions of grief; Rosie, whose exotic neatness in a tight black dress studded with silver was almost a parody of mourning; Al, whose dark suit and tie were only extraordinary to those who knew him well; and, last of all,

Xenia, seated beside Zita in her old Russian skirt and cardigan. The question of appearance and what it signified was only one strand in the tangle of Zita's mind. There was no one who could answer her questions. She should not voice them. It was all settled: Accidental Death. She could do no good; besides, she had no proof.

They were singing the last hymn, "To be a pilgrim". Zita fixed her mind on the words. Yevgenia's pilgrimage had been short and violent, like a rebirth. She had journeyed from one world into another in her twenties; thereafter, it seemed she had eschewed all adventure. She had made her metamorphosis and there was no going back. Or so it had been until this summer, when the past had raised itself again, releasing in her mind memories that had long been hidden. Zita had been appalled by the reliving of the past, the emotions of love and pain re-experienced with all the freshness of the original, but with the bitterness of hindsight, so that knowledge and regrets cancelled out all the careless optimism of the first run. She had heard Yevgenia's cathartic recall with horror. It was better, surely, for some things to remain buried for ever than to endure such painful purgation.

The past killed her, Zita thought. An embodied past? I have watched and said nothing. What does that make me? An accessory after the fact? The accomplice to a murder?

Chapter Two

The body buried beneath the roses was not uncovered until later. On the day Asshe House changed hands, when Zita brushed against the flowers and pierced the grass with her heels, she released no more than a fall of petals onto the lawn and a faint scent into the air. No odour of the past or taint of death touched her nostrils. She had been unconscious of the past buried beneath her feet; everyone was self-consciously thinking of the future. It was a moment when time, instead of moving forward imperceptibly, makes a sudden lurch, shifting power between the generations. Asshe House was being handed over from mother to son, or, more accurately, from stepmother to stepson, and Jean Loftus, who had recently moved herself and her possessions out, had arranged to mark her departure by inviting her stepson and his family and a few friends to the deserted house for a farewell drink.

As Zita had approached, she admired, as she always did, the red brick façade of Asshe House. It was a house a child might draw, with a door in the middle and two windows on either side; on the first floor five long windows looked out over the gap-toothed green space of the churchyard that formed the centre of the square. This was the heart of the town and Asshe House was the only building that had not been turned into shops or offices. Its paved front garden, loosely hung with honeysuckle and clematis behind its railings, looked human and informal in contrast with the bright colours and stiff borders of the council's hanging baskets and beds.

She climbed the dipped stone steps to the front door which stood open to invite her through the echoing house to the garden beyond. The air was thick with the heat of the late afternoon, with the scent of the roses which hid the walls behind the scaffolding of their branches.

Jean Loftus was seated with her stepson and his wife at the far end of the garden in front of the gothic summer-house, a bottle of champagne and a tray of glasses placed before them on a rusting metal table. Zita had known her since moving to the town six years earlier. She had taken over her file from a retiring partner and had since then acted for her on a number of occasions, including the conveyancing for the recent purchase of her new house. This was only one element in their relationship and, in some ways, a peripheral one, for Marcus Loftus and his first wife, Susie, had been friends of Zita's own parents and she was reputed when little to have played with their eldest child, Ivo. Zita thus came into the category of family friend rather than just family solicitor. She had been welcomed as such by Jean on her first arrival in Broad Woodham, cast up there like a piece of jetsam after a traumatic period in her own life, when only work had offered any shape to her existence. Jean's kindness, her evening telephone calls and weekend lunches, had been the first manifestation of returning normality.

Now it was Jean who was in need of some support. She had been driven out of her old home by arthritis which made the daily negotiation of the flights of stairs, the uneven floors and dark basement kitchen an impossibility for her. She had at the end been confined to two rooms on the ground floor and had been forced to recognize that she must move. She had bought a modern property next door to Zita's own on the outskirts of the town and, if she regretted the architectural exchange of the vertical lines, faded bricks and flower-filled garden of her old home for the horizontal and grey banality of a bungalow surrounded by mown lawns, she did not permit herself to show it.

As Zita approached, Marcus rose to greet her and to pour her a glass of champagne. He and his second wife Naomi lived in Hampstead and it was not clear to Zita what they would do with the gift of a large, beautiful, listed Queen Anne house with a very small garden, cramped in the middle of a prosperous Sussex town. Although it was out of London, it was not a country retreat, and not, surely, what they would have chosen for a second home. However, those lucky enough to be given a house must suppress their natural desire to complain that it is not what they wanted. In Marcus's and Naomi's case, the gift was simply an anticipation of Marcus's inheritance, although Jean had, as yet, done nothing about transferring the property. Marcus handed Zita her glass and sat down cautiously on his ancient chair.

"Here's to Asshe House," he said. "May we live here as long and as happily as you have done, Jean."

They all looked across the garden to the house; this hidden façade was as crooked and asymmetrical as its front was elegantly balanced. No window was level with any other; a huddle of extensions and additions of different heights and widths clung to it, trailing off in a hovel of a coal house. "How many years is it?"

There was a pause. "Forty-three," Jean said at last, as if she had been counting every one of them. "Kenward and I bought it in 1949."

"You'll have a job to beat that, darling. You'll be a hundred and two if you hand it over to Rosie or Ivo after forty-three years."

"Oh I'll make it. I don't feel any older than I did when I was twenty-five, younger sometimes." Marcus leaned back, causing his seat to creak warningly.

The three women gazed at him assessingly. He had thick grey hair which he wore rather long and the contrast with his features, which were remarkably youthful, made him, in some way, appear younger, because of rather than in spite of his greyness. Marcus was a cosmetic surgeon. He rarely admitted to his branch of the medical profession because women would immediately begin to ask about face lifts and men to eye him with humorous or half-admiring contempt. He resented having to rebut unspoken assumptions about the nature of his work by explaining what could be done for flesh melted by fire or sliced by flying windscreen glass.

"Will you be living here?" Zita asked.

"Only at weekends at first; but perhaps when I retire..."

"There's work to be done before that," said Naomi. "Woodworm in the roof and wet rot in the cellars."

"It's nothing serious," her mother-in-law protested. She was a tall woman, bent by arthritis. Her long face had an air of weariness, because of the dark skin that encircled her eyes, or because of the pain of her condition. She was smoking a black cigarette which she waved dismissively. "People nowadays make too much fuss about houses. This one has stood up for three hundred years; it's not going to fall down just because of a little rot in the basement."

"I've never had the chance to renovate a house or to design a garden before. I just moved into Marcus's house when I married him." Naomi had married Marcus soon after Susie's death. She was a good fifteen years younger than he, but because her principles of life would allow no make-up or dyeing of her wavy dark hair, streaked with grey in the heavy bangs on either side of her high forehead, the difference in their ages was not noticeable.

"Are there going to be major works here?" Zita asked.

As the new mistress of Asshe House began to describe what was to be done to the interior, Zita leaned aside to smell one of the roses nearest to her; it was so dark a red as to be almost black. She lived in a modern house which was equipped for function and nothing else. She had never endured the renovation of an old house and would never do so; the account she was half-hearing had, therefore, neither the resonance of recognition nor the interest of anticipation. She thought instead about the extraordinary garment that Naomi had chosen to wear. The sleeves ran seamlessly into the body and hung down in a V shape over her waist, as if she were wearing a camouflage tent. Zita clenched her stomach muscles and smoothed her skirt over her thighs. Whatever else, it was well cut, she thought, with the complacency that only expensive clothes can produce. Jean Loftus was not paying full attention either, for she interrupted her daughter-in-law with alacrity when she saw a figure framed in the doorway of the house.

"Rosie, at last," she said, struggling to pull her body up from her chair.

Marcus got up. "Don't move, Jean, I'll find another bottle."

"No, I shall come in. I have something I want to give Rosie."

Naomi and Zita, too, were standing by now, but did not follow the others into the house. Naomi pursued her account of the planned alterations as she stood between the rose beds. She kicked the sun-hardened lawn.

"And all this will go."

Zita turned her eyes from Jean's painful progress across the grass. The old woman walked on two sticks, leaning forward on them, heavily, so her gait was rather like that of a great ape, walking on its extended arms.

"What do you mean? You can't knock down the summer-house. I'm pretty sure it's listed as well."

"No, no, the garden, I mean. It is going to be redesigned. I have a wonderful plan for a little Queen Anne parterre to match the house, very formal, with box hedges and bay trees and statues and water."

Zita could barely conceal her horror. She was no gardener; her own bare plot aspired to no more than suburban neatness and the overflowing roses and lavender of Jean's garden had always seemed to her the height of horticultural beauty. "But what's wrong with it as it is?"

"Oh, Zita, look at the lawn, there's no grass. It is all moss and daisies and bald patches and these terrible concrete paths which must have been put down in the fifties, all crumbling to pieces. No, no. It's all got to go. In fact, we're starting with the garden; the builders are going to dig the pool next week."

"A pool? A swimming pool?"

"Of course not. It'll be a little strip of water, a sort of mirror for the summer-house. Don't you think it will be delightful?"

Marcus and his stepmother, accompanied by Rosie and several other guests, had by now re-emerged from the house. Rosie came swiftly across the lawn to greet Naomi and Zita. Naomi continued to talk to Zita as she nodded in acknowledgement of her stepdaughter's arrival. Rosie, Zita always thought, could not have been less appropriately named; it was fortunate that her parents had not called her Hope or she might have turned into a manic depressive. She was slight and pale with skin of a transparent whiteness that revealed a mesh of blue veins on the inside of her wrists. It contrasted with her short dark hair cut in a rough urchin style that made her vulnerable to being talked of as a girl, even though she was twenty-five. Zita rarely saw the two women together; whenever she did she was aware of the undercurrent of mutual irritation that flowed beneath the surface of their determined respect. She noticed that Naomi, as she continued to talk, drew herself up fractionally as Rosie approached. Naomi was a handsome woman, tall, five foot ten or eleven, Zita estimated, and she made the unconscious assumption of many tall people of the association of height with moral worth and physical attractiveness. However, in spite of her fragile appearance, Rosie was in no need of sympathy; in her covert game with her stepmother the scores were fairly even, Zita reckoned.

Naomi, conscious now Rosie was listening of the insensitivity of her choice of subject, suddenly abandoned her planned improvements to Asshe House and said to Zita, "Did I hear that Valentina was coming back this summer or did I dream it?"

The remark had the effect of the beam of a torch in darkness and Zita's attention came sharply into focus. The subject of her mother was not one she could talk about with half her mind elsewhere. "Yes," she said. "She is. She arrives this weekend."

Valentina, Zita's mother, was an extraordinary woman; so extraordinary that Zita often felt weak speaking about her, for how could a woman whose life, hewn by nothing but her will and intelligence from the unpromising rock of her circumstances, have produced a daughter so ordinary as herself? Once she had tried to express this feeling to a friend who knew them both well, who had said comfortingly, without any attempt to convince the daughter, that she did, or even one day could, equal her mother. "It's called regression to the mean: geniuses tend to produce children less brilliant and idiots children cleverer than themselves." Then she had stopped, as if wondering where that placed Zita in relation to her own child.

"It must be years since she was last in England. Years and years. Is she going to be here long? I hope she'll have time to come and see us."

"She's planning to stay until Christmas, so I'm sure she will."

"What is she going to do? With Valentina it is impossible to imagine that it is just a holiday."

"No. She has a sabbatical from Caltech and has agreed to give a series of lectures in Oxford. Since she's here anyway, she has accumulated a mass of other invitations to lecture while she is in Europe. And she will dash round and see all her friends."

"That sounds just like Valentina. She makes me feel old with her inexhaustible energy. When did you last see her? When did she go to America?"

"It must be six years ago now that she left. I saw her about three years ago. She was in Germany and I went over for a weekend. The truth is, in spite of everyone saying that the world is getting smaller, California is still a very long way. And I can't leave for long."

"How *is* Tom?" Rosie asked.

"Fine, thank you."

Naomi stuck to the subject of Valentina. "Valentina hasn't been back to Russia, has she, even since Gorbachev?"

"No, you know what she was always like about Russians. She says things about them that even the fiercest cold war warriors in the fifties would never have said and she only gets away with it because she's Russian herself. There's been no sign that she regards them differently. She just complains more because there are so many of them in the West now."

"So strange that she doesn't go back. You would think that she would see all the events in Eastern Europe and Russia in the last few years as a vindication."

"Valentina doesn't think that she needs vindication. And she has never been very interested in politics."

"That's true." This was Marcus who had rejoined them. "Valentina has the sublime selfishness of genius. Life has arranged itself so that she could work and nothing else has ever counted."

Naomi's train of thought took no account of these interventions. "When you think of the amazing things we have seen in the last few years. I wept when I saw the Wall coming down in, which year was it, Marcus? It was just after we got back from staying with the Cookes in Sicily. And in Russia: the dismantling of the Communist Party, the ending of the Soviet empire, the emptying of the camps. It seems almost perverse that Valentina doesn't want to see it."

"Valentina has been heading west all her life," Marcus stated. "Now she is installed in California she has got as far from Russia as she can go and I imagine that's how she likes it. Wouldn't you agree, Zita?"

"Anyway, you must let me have her address, so we can ask her to dinner in London. I wouldn't want to miss her while she is over here and time always rushes past."

"We are to have our own Russian visitor this summer," Rosie remarked. "At least, she is to stay some of the time with Dad and Naomi and some of the time here with Granma."

"Oh yes." Naomi took over the subject. "Have you heard about this from Jean, Zita? A Russian student is coming to stay. She claims to be some connexion of Jean's, though Jean insists that she is an impostor. However, this seems to me to be quite irrelevant. Whether or not she is of the same family, she is a very enterprising girl. She wrote a charming letter to me to say that she would do any menial job that was available if she could have the chance of spending four months in England (the home of Shakespeare and Dickens, she called it), which she had always dreamed of visiting."

"One has to add," Marcus put in, "that the conditions of her visa don't permit her to take a job while she is in England. We have given our word to support her while she is here."

Naomi waved this aside. "That is bureaucratic nonsense, darling. She will do some baby-sitting and child-minding in Hampstead and when she comes here she will do for Jean what Lucia normally does. None of that counts as a job. It will give her some pocket money and some independence."

Lucia was Jean's Swiss au pair who attended a language school in the town and did the shopping and other errands that the old woman's lack of mobility made impossible for her. An au pair had been the first solution to the problem of Jean's health and it had worked well. Lucia was the fourth in a succession of girls who recruited their own successors from among their friends in their Italian-speaking canton of Switzerland. She was going home for a month's holiday in the summer, returning in the autumn.

"The letter was wonderful. It was written in very correct English and so full of enthusiasm and reverence for English literature and culture, something from another century."

"It sounds phoney to me," Rosie said. "What she thought you would like to hear, but hadn't the skill to express more subtly."

"No, you're quite wrong. It was certainly nothing that you or Ivo would have written at her age. Young people here are much too streetwise and cynical to write, or even think, such things. What she wrote rang true. It was perfectly genuine."

"It will be amusing to bring her face to face with Valentina," Marcus said. "We must arrange it."

"Only if you think she is very tough, otherwise Valentina will eat her alive." Zita rose. "I must get back to Tom," she said.

"You must come round the house and give me your advice about moving the kitchen," Naomi objected. "And Ivo hasn't arrived yet."

Zita said her goodbyes and began to walk back to the house; she found that Rosie was accompanying her.

"I'm not really a good person to ask for advice on decoration," Zita said as if to explain her decision to leave.

"She doesn't want advice," Rosie replied. "It's all pretty much decided. It's been a game for years, driving back to London after Sunday lunch with Granma, what would *we* do with Asshe House to make it habitable. Though there was never any idea that they would get the chance to put the plans into action. I don't think Ivo and I ever joined in because we thought it was perfection. I'm still hoping that Naomi will decide to leave my little room as it was and not turn it into yet another bathroom."

"Making a formal garden seems so unlikely in Naomi."

"Authenticity is the thing. Naomi might be all for unrestrained nature but it would be anachronistic with a Queen Anne house."

"Marcus says he might retire here. Will that be soon?"

"Hard to say. Dad would like to eventually but Naomi might want to stay in Hampstead. More neurotic people and broken marriages there."

Naomi was a therapist and counsellor specializing in marriage guidance, with a lucrative practice in Hampstead where her skills and reputation were passed on by word of mouth; at the first hint of marital discord in any couple, concerned friends would telephone to recommend Naomi's services, so she always had a waiting list for consultations.

"Oh, we exist everywhere nowadays, don't we?" Zita asked. Although her life was one long regret, she could not imagine that things would have been any different if she had subjected her problems to the probing silences of Naomi's demanding common sense. They stood together for a moment on the top of the flight of semi-circular stone steps that descended into the front garden. For a second Zita had thought that Rosie was about to say something; then she had realized that the hesitation was due to pity. Zita turned abruptly away. She found it easier to be with people who did not know the details of her past, people for whom she would not always be "poor Zita". It was, in part, to escape such reactions that she had come to Woodham in the first place. In theory, she could acknowledge that Rosie had been moved by sympathy; in practice, it was easier to deal with those whose egotism forgot the troubles of others, or with those who did not know of them at all.

The square was now quiet, all the tourists and shoppers of the daytime hours had left. One side was occupied by the church, the others by a not disagreeable mixture of old buildings: several runs of Georgian terrace, in one of which Zita's firm had its offices, a half-timbered pub, some early Victorian artisans' cottages. One corner was occupied by the main post office, an isolated example of post-war building. Zita often wondered if they had deliberately pulled down an eighteenth-century house in order to include the twentieth century. She took one of the alleys that ran between the houses to reach her firm's car park. As she manoeuvred the car into the one-way system that kept traffic out of the square, she glanced, as she always did on leaving work, at the dashboard clock. It was 7.50. She had told Lynne that she would be home at eight. She would make it easily. When she had come here six years ago she had chosen her house in part because it had been specially built for an elderly couple and was therefore already adapted for a wheel chair; and in part because she could reach it from her office in ten minutes, even in the rush hour.

She parked in the car port next to the minivan. Through the thin hedge she could see the bungalow into which Jean had just moved. In the kitchen all signs of Tom's supper had been cleared away, though there was a pile of carrier bags on the kitchen table. She could hear the sound of the television in the little sitting room. Lynne was crouched on a low stool, her fingers in her mouth, watching her programme with total absorption. It was almost certainly a soap, although whether a new episode or an old one was impossible to know. Zita's video machine was set to record every episode every evening. Lynne would watch them whenever a moment presented itself the following day and sometimes put on old ones to revise her extensive knowledge of these alternative worlds. Zita sometimes felt that the house was more Lynne's than her own when she found Lynne's shopping strewn on the kitchen table, her sweatshirt hanging over the back of the sofa, her video cassettes lying on the floor. Zita, who was fanatically orderly, had long ago learned to suppress her irritation at Lynne's untidiness. She was far too conscious of her dependence on her.

She had found Lynne in her first week in Woodham and had hired her as a cleaner for two mornings a week, for three hours a time. The rate in those days had been about three pounds an hour. Only after a year of disaster after disaster with Tom's nannies had Lynne turned herself into nanny, housekeeper, driver and nurse. The previous nannies, one a Norland, another a trained nurse, another a New Zealand treasure handed on from a friend, had each stayed a few months and then taken their leave, their declared love of babies rapidly blunted by the reality of Tom. Lynne had stayed and assumed an ever more important role in Zita's life. It was she who normally drove the minivan with its electric lift to take Tom and his wheel chair to the Centre, to go to the supermarket, to drive herself home every evening. Only rarely did Lynne stay overnight; she lived three or four miles away with her brother and her detested sister-in-law. The feeling was reciprocated. The brother's wife had said scornfully to Zita once, "Is it safe to leave your baby all day with Lynne? She's not all there." And indeed she was not. Zita was unaware of the correct definition of her employee's mental state; once she would have been called slightly educationally subnormal. A strict village school had taught her to read and write and her devotion to Tom did the rest.

"Had a good time?" Lynne asked. She removed her fingers from her mouth, her eyes never wavering from the screen. The sound was, as usual, very loud as she was slightly deaf.

"Yes, thanks. How's Tom-Tom?" Zita was changing her shoes in the hall, putting on a pair of velvet mules with turned up toes that she had bought years ago with Oliver in Istanbul.

"He was worn out, so I gave him his shower and put him to bed. I took him swimming; that always makes him tired."

Zita left her bag and briefcase on a chair and went out into the hall at the far end of which was her son's bedroom and bathroom. His curtains were drawn and behind them the blackout blinds were lowered so that the strong summer light did not penetrate. The night light, a small steady glow, was on. All these details, arranged for Tom's comfort, had been devised by Lynne. She asserted that Tom did not like to go to sleep in summer when it was still light and that was why he tossed and screamed until midnight and that he needed a night light to comfort him if he awoke in the dark. How she knew these things Zita could not imagine; she accepted the empirical proof, his peaceful sleep, that Lynne's interpretations of Tom's desires were correct.

Quietly, she approached the centre of her life. Tom, now seven, slept in a sort of cot, an old wooden bed with balustraded sides, which she had found long ago in a junk shop. Even in sleep his contorted limbs did not relax. He was firmly tucked in, lying on his back like a crusader on his tomb, his face half-hidden, only the top of his head showing. The pucker between his brows, which she was convinced he had been born with, was not eased. He ground his teeth and his arm jerked. She ran her hand over his silky blond head and pulled the cover straight. A bald rabbit, its button eyes glinting dimly in the half light, was lying between his arm and his chest, held in place, as was Tom himself, by the tight embrace of the sheet.

Lynne's programme had finished and an advertisement filled the screen. She was still watching, although she had risen from the stool and was picking up her sweatshirt.

"Oh, your mum rang," she said, not moving her eyes from the television.

Zita halted on her route back into the kitchen. "Yes?"

"She said she was arriving tomorrow and she would phone you from Oxford. Is that right?"

"Yes, it would be."

"American is she, your mum?" Lynne and Valentina had

never met because Valentina had never visited her daughter in Woodham.

"No, not American. She was Russian originally. She's lived in America for some years now."

Lynne pondered the combination of Russian and American connexions in Zita's parent and then said, "Well, that accounts for her accent then."

"Did she have anything else to say?"

Lynne sniggered. She turned the television off now that real life offered more interest. "When I said you were out, she said, 'What time is it with you?' and when I told her, she said, 'No hope it's a man?' and I said, 'Fat chance.' "

"Thanks, Lynne."

"I'll see you Monday then. Doing anything nice tomorrow?"

"Oh, just the usual. Goodbye, Lynne."

"Goodbye, Zita."

Chapter Three

When Naomi rang on Wednesday morning, Zita was in her office. Her desk was placed across the corner of the room farthest from the door and if she looked over her left shoulder through the tall windows she could see the balanced face of Asshe House beyond the corner of the churchyard. She was looking abstractedly in that direction when her telephone buzzed.

Zita Daunsey seated at her desk gave an impression of competence and authority. Size had something to do with it: she was large, the legacy of her Russian genes, and her solidity engendered confidence. No flightiness here. Fat people make excellent confidants, too; at least, that is what others think. Zita had found that she had often been told more than she needed to know about the details of her clients' cases and their lives. She never protested, just listened, for sometimes an odd detail is important. Her age (thirty-two) was difficult to estimate; she had never been thought too young to handle their business by middle-aged men or elderly women.

The phone recalled her thoughts from her mother's imminent arrival. She looked back at her computer screen and picked up the receiver at the same time.

Naomi's rather high, normally reassuring tones sounded anxious. "Zita, I'm sorry to disturb you. I'm sure you're frightfully busy, but we need your help. It's nothing to do with Jean; it's, well, it may be professional help."

"Yes?"

"Look, well." Naomi's calm grasp of affairs had slipped. "I don't know quite how to put this. Could you go across to Asshe House. I mean right now. It's quite urgent, I think. I've just had a call from the builders..."

Zita had long ago written Naomi down as a ruthless exploiter of friends and contacts, but this was going too far. Surely the architect was the professional to call in when the builders had a problem. She was preparing to give a crisp answer to whatever small service of "nipping" or "popping" across was going to be requested.

"They say...I couldn't get a very clear statement from him, Mr Wilson, that is...I know it sounds incredible. They say they've found a body."

Zita adjusted her response. "A body?"

"Yes, he says he's called the police, so I expect you'll find them there too."

"What is it? What sort of body? And where? Did he say?"

"No. He said it was all a 'bit of a shock, like' and I know what he means. He didn't find it himself. It was his two workmen who are digging. You know, the pool I told you about. I think *they* phoned *him* and *he* phoned *me*. He was rather indignant, as though I had deliberately let him in for all kinds of problems he hadn't expected." Naomi was now more relaxed and her customary fluency returned. "Such a cheek, when you think normally builders ring you up to tell you with great satisfaction that they've found new and expensive problems."

"I'll go over at once and see what's happening."

"Would you? It would be so kind. I hope it's nothing. Perhaps it's a pets' graveyard or something like that."

"I'll phone you later."

The two young workmen who had made the discovery were squatting, naked to the waist, on the pile of rubble that they had just excavated, Coke cans in their fists. The pit itself was about twelve feet long and six feet wide and occupied the end of the garden with only a few feet between its edge and the steps descending from the summer-house. She recalled standing on that spot, between the roses, only four days earlier. Now there was a void. She stepped forward to the brink of the hole, cut as precisely as a surgeon cuts flesh, to reveal the layer of top soil, like subcutaneous fat, rich and black. Below, in the muscular belts of the subsoil, the colour of the earth faded to paler brown, streaked with chalky white stones marking the layers of the years, like tree rings, counting down the past. Out of the sheer edges of the trench roots projected, thick veins showing their white pith where they had been sliced open. The bottom of the pit where the men had been digging with pick and shovel was stepped. Standing in there, four feet down, was Mr Wilson. Legs straddled, hands on knees, he was peering at what Zita recognized instantly as a human skull. Whatever else, the men had not revealed a pets' graveyard. No more of the body, if there were more, was visible beneath its earth covering. The head was tipped forward and the curve of the cranium was smooth, stained brown by the soil, the seams of the fontanelle strongly marked, as if sewn in place with a darker thread. Then she saw the place where the skull was broken, behind, just below the crown, and she understood that he had been placed like that, tenderly, with his head up so that he should not rest on the damaged place and lie in pain. Something in the bed-like shape of the pit made Zita imagine lying there herself, face to the sky, soil filling her eye sockets, yet still able to see the tendrils of roots thickening as they receded into the matting of the grass, out of which legs, stems, trunks thrust upwards into the light.

One of the workmen was explaining to Mr Wilson, who had evidently only arrived minutes before Zita herself, how he had been loosening a strip of earth with a pick when a clod had detached itself in a neat cap-shape and revealed beneath it the upturned bowl of the skull.

"We're digging behind it, d'you see what I mean? and a lump of earth just falls down like that, so you can see the back of the skull, like. Then I lift off the top and there's no mistaking it. It's a body."

"Then we called you."

Zita continued to gaze at the skull as they talked. The way

the head was tucked into the earth, as if reluctant to emerge from under its quilt, evoked the image of Tom lying under his tightly stretched bedclothes.

"And stopped digging." She spoke sharply to cancel out the momentary vision.

"And stopped digging. I'm not going to touch nothing. Like, it's for the police to move it, not us. Besides, you never know what you could catch from a corpse. The plague or sommat."

"This one never died of the plague. He came to a sticky end." Mr Wilson pointed to the fracture of the skull. "Someone coshed him from behind. You don't have to be Sherlock Holmes to see that."

"You have called the police, Mr Wilson?" Zita asked. The builder continued to peer at the head, caught between the same suspicion and fear that his young workmen felt and the fascination of the skull itself. He lifted his attention reluctantly. "Yes, I called Mrs Loftus in London and I called the police. They'll be sending someone right away. I'm surprised they're not here."

The horror of the moment of recognition of the skull had passed for Zita now. She had been reassured, she found, by the young labourer's reference to the plague. He, the skull, whoever he had been, clearly did not die of the plague, but he was probably very ancient. The house was old and the body had been in the ground for a very long time. She had no idea how long a corpse took to reduce itself to bone: she thought that it varied according to conditions. In any event, that body had not been buried yesterday, or even last year.

"I'll wait until the police come," she remarked to the builder, "to find out what they intend to do."

Their arrival, some ten minutes later, at first reinforced the reassurance that the apparent age of the body had given her. The first to make his appearance was a uniformed constable who had barely finished radioing a description of what and whom he had found when a party of four entered, all in plain clothes. They did not introduce themselves, disposing themselves rapidly, without conversation, each evidently knowing his task. One of them brusquely hauled the builder out of the trench and told him to wait with his two men. They walked around the pit, viewing the skeleton from various angles. Their voices and gestures seemed to register disappointment; they had expected something more demanding than a very ancient skull. Not much for us here, they felt. Zita, relieved, seeing them thus occupied, began to walk back to the house, when she was arrested by a shout.

"Hey, where do you think you're going?"

She turned. It was the senior of the four men, his status indicated by his sports jacket; the others were wearing jeans and sweaters.

"We'll need to interview you. You can't leave."

Zita strolled back towards him. She could see he was about her own age. His light brown hair flopped forward onto his brow. He did not look as fierce as he tried to appear. "You make it sound very serious."

He looked sheepish. "Sorry, I didn't mean to be overdramatic. But we will need to interview you, all the same. It won't take long."

"I'll be in the house, then," she said and continued on her way. She was trapped. By arriving before the police she was required to give an account of her presence, and questioning her and the builders had evidently a lower priority than setting up the examination of the scene. Inside the house she discovered that the builders had made themselves at home, with an electric kettle, mugs, tea, coffee, sugar, milk, biscuits and sandwiches. She boiled the kettle, poured herself a mug of instant coffee and carried it upstairs to the drawing room on the first floor from where she could watch the police at their work, as if in mime.

They stood on the edge of the pit and conferred, laughing. The sports jacket jumped down into the hole and, like Wilson, straddled the corpse, bending over to look it in the face. Finally, he turned round to find a way out without breaking down the sharp edge of the grave; he pulled himself neatly over the rim with a display of agility and stood up, brushing dry earth and grass off his jacket. Zita suspected that he had caught sight of her watching them from the house.

There was a sudden ripple of activity in the garden, as if a pause button had been released. The faces of the five policemen all turned towards the house. Someone new had arrived. Zita could not see him; he was evidently standing immediately below her, in the doorway, viewing the scene from a similar vantage point to hers. The sports jacket had evidently received orders; his gestures to the scene-of-crime officers had a new abruptness. The meaning of his swathing arm became apparent a little later, when tarpaulins were brought through the house and unrolled in the garden. The photographer was now setting up his camera. Zita could hear the telephone from one of the ground-floor rooms. The battered metal table and chairs that had been in use on Saturday evening were carried across from the summer-house to serve as an impromptu desk.

Mr Wilson was called in for his interview. The two workmen sat on the steps of the summer-house, drinking their Coke and watching others working with the ease of men who have an unexpected paid holiday. Zita fretted, thinking of the pile of papers waiting for her which she had thought she was leaving for thirty minutes at the most; she would end up taking it home this evening. She took her phone out of her bag to call her secretary and saw that one of the workmen was being led round the trench into the house. She was to be last.

The officer whose arrival had changed the tempo of activity in the garden had installed himself in the room looking over the garden which in recent years had been Jean's bedroom. There was still a faint scent of Jean's Black Russian cigarettes in it, Zita noticed. It was now empty of furniture, except for the garden table and chairs. The newcomer was large and his air of authority explained the effect on his men. His head, massive and square as a sculpture, was naked, as hairless as the skull lying in the ground and much the same colour, tea-stain brown. Yet it was not skull-like, shiny, smooth, or bony. Its covering skin, subtle and tactile, moved in folds and creases around his neck and face. It was impossible to tell whether it was disease or some wayward vanity which had produced his bizarre appearance. His voice was impatient and unfriendly; a shaved head is always threatening. Yet as she faced him, Zita had the impression less of aggression than melancholy. He reminded her of one of the breed of Chinese dogs called Shar Pei, with folded faces like W.H. Auden.

He introduced himself as Detective Superintendent Stevens, the sports jacket as Detective Constable Neville. She was invited to seat herself on one of the rickety ironwork chairs and to state her name and her business.

When she had explained that she was the lawyer acting for the owners who had phoned her as soon as they had heard from the builder, she gestured to the photographer and the scene-of-crime officers in the garden. "That skeleton must have been here for centuries. What do you have to do if you find a pile of old bones when a bulldozer is excavating the foundations of a multistorey car park or a new road? You don't have to call an inquest every time?"

The dismissive impression given without any words by the police that they had been called to investigate history was suddenly cancelled. When Stevens did not reply at once, she saw that his attitude was quite different and that what she had said was being interpreted as a desire to minimize the find, to write it off before an investigation had been made.

"No," he said flatly. "We don't have an inquest for every odd bone that is found, but when we find a body neatly buried in someone's back garden, we have to establish who it is and how long it has been there. It could be only ten or twelve years. A corpse can rot down very quickly; that one could have been put there a very short time ago. And there's no cut-off point for murder. It's not like tax where if the Revenue forget about it for six years, it's forgotten. If there is a possibility that a crime has been committed and the perpetrator is still alive, we have to pursue it."

In the garden the scene-of-crime officers were now pulling the tarpaulins over the frame they had erected, hiding the pit from view. Jean had lived here for forty-three years, so she had said on Saturday. A long time.

"Of course," Stevens added, "We have to be reasonable. There could be other explanations, apart from murder, I mean. We start with the pathologist and the archaeologist."

"So you agree it could be very old, the skull?"

"It could be. The archaeologist, Reskimer, will tell us. He's at London University. He's not a forensic specialist but his laboratory can do a lot that ours doesn't. We've used him before; he's very co-operative. Likes doing it. Makes a change from neolithic flints or Sumerian pottery or whatever his speciality is."

"So you can't begin until he gets here?"

"We can do our bit. It'll be tomorrow or the day after, I guess, before he comes. But as you said, it's been there a long time. It can wait."

Zita rose, assuming the interview to be at an end. She had learned as much as she could hope for now. "If you need me again," she said, "you know where to find me."

"We do. And I'm sure we'll come back to you. But I haven't quite finished for today. I want to know a bit more about the owners, Mr and Mrs Loftus of Hampstead. Still the same Mr and Mrs Loftus, is it?"

"The same?"

"I remember there used to be a Mr and Mrs Loftus living here a long time ago; or was it Dr and Mrs Loftus?"

"The same family. Dr Loftus is dead. It's his son and daughter-in-law."

"And about old Mrs Loftus? What's happened to her? Died, did she? Gone into a home?"

"No, neither. She's moved to the edge of town, to a bungalow. She's very arthritic, but neither dead nor gaga." Even at the time it occurred to Zita that Stevens' knowledge of the inhabitants of Broad Woodham was extraordinarily detailed.

"And she gave the house to her son? When did she do that then?"

"Her stepson. Just recently. That's why the house is empty

and the garden is being dug up. He and his wife are renovating it. There's going to be a new garden with an ornamental pool in front of the summer-house, which is why the hole was being dug in the first place."

"And how long was she living here, Mrs Loftus? Many years?"

Zita was becoming more and more uncomfortable with the line of questioning. She recalled Jean's slow reply to Marcus's query. "How long is it?" Forty-three years.

"A long time," she said vaguely. "Since the fifties."

"Forty years. That's a long time. And she's handed the ownership over to her son?"

"Stepson," Zita repeated. "Not formally. She is still the legal owner."

Stevens was tapping the metal of the table with broad-nailed, blunt-ended fingers. "And what was the garden like before they began digging?" he asked. "They're really giving it a going over, aren't they? *They* certainly didn't know there was anything there."

"How could they? It was beautiful. There were roses every-where. Two rose beds there, just in front of the steps and a path between them, lavender along the walls, a rather moth-eaten lawn..."

"The rose beds came out as far as where the body lies?"

"Yes, though the path between them leading to the sum-mer-house would have crossed it." She looked out at the tar-paulin. "It's very neat, isn't it? The grave, I mean. Whoever put it there, and lined it up to lie parallel with the summer-house, had an orderly mind."

Stevens looked a little surprised, and then nodded, as if acknowledging a useful insight. "I'll let you get back now," he said.

As soon as she entered her office Zita rang Naomi, who said irritably, "I suppose they won't be able to get on with the work for the time being."

"I forgot to ask when they could restart." Naomi had the ability to make you feel that whatever you had done was not enough, so that you owed it to her to do a little more to make up for the shortfall. "It depends on how long the archaeologist takes."

"Who is the archaeologist?" Naomi demanded. "I'll ask Al about him." It was Naomi's assumption that there was always someone they knew who would be able to do something about any problem that troubled her. In this case she was referring to Rosie's boyfriend. "Al's an archaeologist, didn't Jean tell you? Or at least he was; he read archaeology and anthropology at Cambridge. Now he writes." Naomi rang off abruptly, saying that she had a client whose hour was about to start. She had not taken in the implications of what Zita had told her: only the inconvenience had struck her so far. Probably not until Marcus came home in the evening and she began recounting her day to him would it occur to her that a corpse in the garden posed some difficult questions.

Chapter Four

Jean was really more involved than Naomi, Zita thought, driving home that evening. She ought to tell her about what had been discovered. She parked in Jean's drive in order to avoid being seen by Lynne and Tom and disappointing them by not coming in at once. The door bell's light, two-toned chime had none of the sonorous importance of the great lion's head door knocker at Asshe House. She waited a long time for Jean to make her way from her sitting room on the other side of the house to unlock the front door, and then followed her slowly back to her seat.

The old woman had established herself in her new surroundings as if they were the old ones. Her customary wing-chair with its pile of cushions was positioned so that she looked out over the empty lawn to a thick wall of cypresses which separated her garden from that of the house beyond. Beside her was the small table with its neat piles: books and spectacles, pad and pencil, cigarette box of Black Russians and matches, just as it had stood at Asshe House.

"Pour yourself a drink, my dear, and one for me too, if you don't mind." Zita pottered about finding ice and soda for Jean and wine for herself, wondering how to begin. Her hesitation cost her the initiative, for no sooner had she sat down than Jean said, "The Russian girl arrived yesterday, I think."

Zita looked puzzled; the only Russian in her mind at that moment was her mother.

"The one who is going to stay with Naomi and Marcus. They want me to have her when Lucia is on holiday. She is called Xenia Chornoroukaya." This was the first time that Zita had heard the name and she suddenly recalled a conversation which she had had with Jean months ago, at Asshe House, before the move.

"Chornoroukaya? I didn't realize...Is she the same one who wrote to you?"

Jean was lighting a cigarette. She had once been a heavy smoker; now she had five a day, carefully rationed. "Yes." She sighed. "I made a mistake. After I had shown you the letter, I told Naomi and Marcus about it. I should have known better."

The occasion Jean referred to, the arrival of the letter from Russia, clearly marked in Zita's mind, had taken place before Christmas. Jean had called her at the office to ask her to come to see her at lunchtime. It had been during the early stages of the plan to move house and, although she could see no reason why the business could not be dealt with on the telephone, Zita had assumed that her summons had to do with that. When she had arrived, knocking and pushing open the front door of Asshe House, she had found Jean seated in the same chair that she sat in now, although then her view had been over the railings to the daily movements round the square, filled with office workers out in search of lunchtime sandwiches.

Jean had gestured to her to sit down opposite her and had said, "I wanted to show you this." She held out an envelope, addressed in a distinctively foreign hand.

A little surprised, Zita had taken the airmail paper and extracted a letter, written mostly in Cyrillic script. "Do you want me to translate it for you? How curious to get a letter in Russian."

"No, it's not a translation I need. I've read it already. It is...It's advice...Not even that, an opinion, your reaction."

The letter had no longer held Zita's attention. "Do you

read Russian? You never said." She had recalled that there was supposed to be some Russian connexion in the Loftus family. She had never related it to Jean.

A pause. "Yes, I read Russian; indeed, in some senses, I am Russian."

"You are Russian? You don't sound…"

"No more do you, my dear. I am exactly as Russian as you; my mother, too, was Russian. It may have been my mother tongue, in the sense of being my first language. Of that I am not absolutely sure, because I grew up speaking so many languages, I am not certain whether Russian or English or even Latvian had priority. I am more Russian than you, however, because I was born in Petrograd in 1917 and at that time my parents were Russian citizens. So you see, it is no wonder I speak Russian."

As Jean had talked, Zita had listened attentively for those sounds that mark the native Russian speaker, the liquid vowels, the strong stress, that characterized her own mother's English. Nothing was to be detected. There was no trace in the voice that this was other than an elderly upper-middle-class Englishwoman speaking. Nor did she look in any way Russian; she had none of the features that Zita associated with Russianness: the solid body, the round head with its massive forehead and blunt nose. Jean had been tall; she was now bent and angular; her forehead was broad and her face tapered down to a small rounded chin. Her hair, the fine hair of the aged, was smoothed into a knot at the base of her skull, held severely in place by combs. Her colouring must once have been very fair, for she retained under the cobwebbed lines that covered her face a translucency of skin; her eyebrows and eyelashes had almost disappeared.

"But never mind that. I have been English for almost fifty years now. The bit before was a mistake, a false start. I deliberately put it behind me a long time ago. Read now; read the letter."

Zita had opened the paper and read,

Respected Yevgenia Konstantinovna,
I hope you will forgive this approach from an
unknown member of your family who wishes to re-
establish links that have been broken for so long. I am
Xenia Alexandrovna Chornoroukaya, your cousin. I am
twenty-one years of age and a student in the Faculty of
Languages at Moscow State University. My parents are
both dead and as I never knew my grandparents I am
not very well acquainted with my family history. It is a
sad thing that in the past in Russia so many families
have been broken up and have not been able to main-
tain contact with one another. It has been particularly
true of families like ours, split between the emigration
and our homeland, where our name alone has been a
disadvantage to us. All this is to explain to you that I
do not know how we are connected. What I do know is
that we must be of the same family, for the accusation
of being a Chornorouky was one that followed my
father all his life. About myself I can tell you. I was
born in Siberia in 1971 in a small town called
Novoleninsk where my father was teacher of languages
at the Technical High School. My father died in 1989
and in that year I came to Moscow State University
where I study English. Here she abandoned Russian.
Now I write in English, so that you may see that I
already know English and that what I am about to ask
is not an unreasonable request. I would like to come to
England. I can work. I will work at anything. I shall
clean, or teach or look after children. This would be for
the summer vacation. I have some money and the pos-
sibility of obtaining a ticket. However, I am told that
for my visa I must have an invitation from someone in
England. As I know no one there, when I discovered
this I was in despair, as I could think of no possibility.
Then, one day, I visited the Club of the Nobility in
Moscow and there someone told me of you and gave me
your address in England. She returned to Russian here,

as if to the natural language of emotion. *I was over-joyed, as I suddenly saw it was fated that I should go to England after all. I write this, dear Yevgenia Konstantinovna, to implore you to help a cousin and to invite me to your country.*

The letter had finished with very business-like instructions about the phrasing of the invitation in order to make it acceptable to the bureaucrats, Russian and British, issuing passports and visas.

Zita had folded up the sheets and looked at the disturbed face of her friend. "Well, what are you going to do? Is there any reason why you shouldn't write a letter of invitation for her?"

"She is an impostor. There are no Chornoroukys left in Russia or elsewhere. You can tell she is not a real Chornorouky: she has no idea who her father or her grandfather were. She has no idea about the family at all. It is inconceivable that a child should be born with the name and not grow up knowing about its ancestry. That is the essential thing about old families: estates and titles and possessions don't really matter; even great deeds in the past do not matter beside the vital question of birth which carries you back to the Chornorouky, Slav princes before the conversion."

She had looked a little embarrassed at her own vehemence, and laughed. "Does it sound strange to hear me say that here in England at the end of the twentieth century? Of course, it does. I've abandoned such ideas myself. I'm just telling you how it was."

"Did you tell Marcus about this when he was a child?"

"No," tetchily, as if Zita had not understood what she had been saying. "Of course not. In the first place, Marcus was not my son. He had no blood link with me or with Russia. It had no relevance to him. And in any case when I came to England, I put all that behind me. I wanted to become an Englishwoman, safe, with no family and no past."

"Perhaps Xenia's father, too, wanted to shed his history. He had even more reason than you to conceal it. It's not really surprising the girl knows nothing about her family."

Resistance had appeared on the old woman's face. "No, no," she said again. "You don't understand these things in England now. There are no Chornoroukys left. This girl knows nothing. It's a sign that she is not of the family. I know every Chornorouky of my generation, in my mother's, in my grandfather's. They are all dead. It is my mother's family we are talking of, by the way. I wasn't even born a Chornorouky, yet I know every branch."

"Well," Zita had said soothingly. "It's easy then. She can't be a member of the family. She just has the same name as you. I know that serfs, when they were liberated and moved to the cities, used to take their former master's name, or the name of the estate on which they were born. Perhaps that is how she came to have the name."

Jean had remained silent, unplacated by this historical exegesis. Zita had tried a different tack. "In which case," she went on, "the question really is, do you want to help an unknown Russian student of English to come to Britain for her summer holidays? It looks," she consulted the end of the letter, "as if you have to sponsor her in a sense, but she could get a job as a waitress or au pair or something."

"But why should I? Why should she reach out of the past and demand services from me? There are hundreds, thousands, millions of young Russians who want to come to the West. I can't write invitations for them all."

"Don't. Forget it. Forget the letter. There is no need to let it upset you, Jean. Just put it aside, leave it. Don't even answer it." Zita could see no reason why such an invitation should not be made. The girl had shown plenty of enterprise in her attempt to visit the West; Jean's insistence on her not being a relative seemed beside the point. Zita had been finally cornered into saying not what she thought, but what Jean wanted to hear and the tension in the room relaxed.

"I must get back to the office," she had said. "Really, Jean, don't let it worry you." She had stood up and put the envelope on the little table, as if to signify that it was not necessary to hand it back to Jean to deal with it. "How did she find out about you in the first place?" She had asked suddenly. "No one here knows that you were once Yevgenia Konstantinovna Chornoroukaya. How did she?"

"I was not born a Chornoroukaya. My name was von Korff. It was my mother who was a Chornoroukaya."

Zita had waited to see whether Jean was going to answer her question. At last, the reply had come, reluctantly. "I read in *The Times* a while ago, after the coup last year, that a Club of the Nobility had been established in Moscow. It isn't really a charitable organization; it is a truly self-referring aristocratic one. However, since I had its address from the paper, I sent some parcels of clothes, asking the Club to distribute them to anyone in need. And I wrote a letter. I happened to ask if any Chornoroukys were registered with them. I didn't know where else to start. They don't even have a phone book in Moscow, you know; citizens cannot cope with so much information. No proper street maps either, only ones that are deliberately falsified. What a society."

"So you did think there might be some members of your family still in Russia?"

"No, no, not at all. I knew there could not be. I just asked. To hear them say no. To hear them say that a family that was first recorded in the barbarism of the ninth century was wiped out in the civilization of the twentieth."

Now, seven months later the old woman's voice was plaintive. "I should have listened to you, Zita, and forgotten about the letter. Instead, I told Naomi and you can imagine what happened next: she simply took everything over."

Zita felt ashamed. She remembered very well how she had been manoeuvred into advising Jean to do nothing. And Naomi, seeing that Jean was reluctant to act, had decided to do so herself. Jean's own unwillingness to involve herself with a stranger had been no reason for Naomi to fail in an act of kindness that had not even occurred to her, Zita.

"I regretted it as soon as I had done it." Jean's voice was

stronger now, no longer victimized. "But at first I thought, if they want to do it, let them. I shan't have to see her. Now they want me to have her for a month when Lucia is away and they are bringing her down for lunch on Sunday for me to meet her."

"Is it really such a bad idea?" Zita asked. "If you don't like her, you can tell Naomi it's not on. But it seems quite a sensible plan to me. And a kindness on Naomi's part to want to help her."

Jean appeared to consider this idea as if it were original and striking. "Kindness? Yes, in effect, it may be a kindness, though that is not why she has done it. She invited her because she likes to interfere. She is interested in people and the ways in which they like and dislike one another—that's why she has that curious profession of hers. In short, she is interested in power. And, though she would die rather than admit it, she is fascinated by aristocrats. There is something about inherited title and birth which, she thinks, is palpable in their possessors."

Jean had never before shown her powers of dispassionate analysis of the people who surrounded her. Zita wondered how she was assessed.

"Is that what you think, as an aristocrat?"

"Certainly not. I abandoned all that a long time ago."

"So Naomi thinks Xenia really is a Chornoroukaya?"

"Yes, though I have told her she is not. She cannot be. There are none of us left."

This statement was the end of Jean's complaints about both the Russian girl and her daughter-in-law. She said as Zita left, "You must come on Sunday and meet the Russian. Who knows, her English may be so poor that we shall need you to speak to her."

Chapter Five

Only after Zita had said goodbye to Lynne and was engaged in putting Tom to bed did she realize that she had not told Jean about the skull. The memory came sharply at the moment when she bent to kiss Tom, neatly tucked into his cot, his arms by his sides. On school days the physical efforts he was put through always tired him out and he went gladly to bed. It was an instant of pleasure that Zita and Lynne competed for. Zita was usually able to insist on it as her privilege and Lynne only took the task over if Zita was late, in order to inflict on her employer a penalty that she would feel. The sight of his hair slicked down from his shower, moulding his skull, his little bony face breaking the surface whiteness of the sheet and pillows, jolted her memory. She had been distracted from her task of telling Jean about the skeleton by the Russian girl. She would phone at once. And then decided not to. She would call Naomi instead, to tell her that Jean did not yet know and to wait until tomorrow, when more definite news of what the builders had found might emerge. There was no point in worrying Jean if tomorrow they were to be told that it was a two-hundred-year-old grave that had been opened.

Later, when she had turned on the night light and half-closed the bedroom door, she went into the kitchen to make herself something to eat and found a note on the table in Lynne's large, illiterate hand. *Youre Mum Rang.*

Phoning Valentina, who had arrived in Oxford four days ago, seemed even more daunting than phoning Jean to tell her there was a grave in her garden. She ignored the duty implied by the note; yet she could not refuse to answer the phone when it rang.

Valentina's voice was forceful, faintly Americanized by her years in the States. She wasted no time on asking about her daughter's or grandson's health, attacking her purpose straightaway.

"The flat I hired is impossible. I had forgotten, Zita, about English houses and Oxford houses in particular. It has an Ascot boiler. Can you believe it? You might as well be in the Third World. And the carpet, full of damp and dog hair. I shall have to move out."

Zita made sympathetic murmurs about the difficulty of finding another flat.

"No, that is not a problem. I rang everyone I could think of this morning and they have found me somewhere in a new building belonging to one of the colleges, I forget which one. After all, I am here to give their lectures; there's no reason why they shouldn't find me a flat. No, all that is perfectly OK. I visited it this afternoon. It's small, but light and modern. Altogether much better. No Ascot boilers. No, the problem is this. It's not available until next week and I certainly cannot remain here another day. So I thought I would come to stay with you. I should have to come some time and it may as well be now. So I shall arrive tomorrow. After lunch."

Zita could only express delight and welcome, give directions about how to find the house and how to obtain a key from Jean, as Lynne and Tom would be at the Centre until mid-afternoon. She replaced the receiver with a sense of dread. Valentina had not seen Tom since his christening, which had taken place on the last weekend before her departure for America. Zita and Oliver had still been married, just, and Oliver had insisted on a christening as something babies in his family always had. Valentina had attended with the air of a Victorian lady explorer and ethnologist, participating in an unusually obscure and interesting native ritual. How was she going to cope with Lynne and Tom now?

Zita's admiration for her mother was unbounded, to the extent that she recognized it as one of the problems of her existence: a problem that had been resolved not so much by her escaping from her mother, as her mother leaving her. It was hard, anyone would acknowledge, to be the child of not one but two Nobel prizewinners; it was even harder when one of those laureates was Valentina, whose life had been as romantic, and even as dangerous, as it had been brilliant.

When, in the late seventies, ten years after her husband, she won the Nobel Prize for physics, Valentina Guilfoyle had suddenly become famous. Not for her work on quantum physics, which was incomprehensible to anyone outside her own field, nor even for the glory of her prize, nor for the fact that she was a woman, nor that she was married to a Nobel prizewinner. She became famous for her love affair and marriage. A television play had been made about her life which had told the story of her perilous love for John Guilfoyle, a Cambridge physicist. Zita's knowledge of her parents' lives before her birth was based on the stories of her childhood which had taken flesh as television drama. She had once tried to make Valentina separate fact from fiction, to strip away the glamour bestowed by the camera's framing shots, without success. Valentina, who cultivated a sceptical view of most subjects, had been perfectly content to accept what the film said about her, even insisting to her daughter on its "truth".

Valentina Panteleimonovna Pankratova was born in Moscow in one of the apartment blocks overlooking Patriarch's Pond. She liked to say that every day on her way to school she passed the spot where the devil met Berlioz and Bezdomny at the start of *The Master and Margarita*. In those days the flats were still communal, with bathroom and kitchen shared between ten families. They were overcrowded and the occasions for pettiness and spite, selfishness and minor cruelty were manifold. When deliberate maliciousness did not enter into it, simple squalor, the tyranny of the laziest or least fastidious, made life as physically unpleasant as possible. For the Pankratovs the situation was exacerbated by Valentina's mother's being Jewish, which made her and her daughter a target for in-discriminate insult and accurate saliva. Her father, wholly Russian, had been a minor bureaucrat on the railways and had survived the upheavals of the Revolution and the twenties because of his technical expertise which had been harnessed in 1929 to the building of the Moscow Metro. He was a scholarly man, interested in literature and philosophy and art. It may have been these subversive studies which caused him to be denounced; or it may have been random chance that he was picked up on the Red Line of the Metro, his own creation, late one night in 1938. Before he disappeared from Valentina's life, he had shared with his wife her passionate devotion to the cause of her child's education. It had taken all Lena's skill to ensure Valentina's enrolment in the best primary and then the best secondary school in Moscow. But from the time that Valentina was about twelve encouragement was no more necessary than a child's pedalling a bicycle downhill. Valentina had her own momentum: she won prize after prize, passing into university at the age of sixteen; the hardships of the war caused many disruptions to the family, but not to Valentina's progress. Her achievement was not without a psychological price, for the disappearance of her father and her mother's Jewishness were facts to be suppressed at all costs. Valentina made no secret now of her early life, and she would speak with wondering scorn of the silent, secretive, hard-working child that she had been.

The culmination of that period of her existence came on 6th March 1953, the day of the announcement of Stalin's death. Valentina was by then adult, a doctoral student, yet with the rest of the country she had wept hysterically at the loss of the man who had protected her country and killed her father. It had been cathartic, a sloughing off of her childhood, she would say later. In June of that year she had accompanied her professor to an international conference in Rome and there met John Guilfoyle of Cambridge, England.

On the television film Zita had watched an actor as John Guilfoyle and an actress as Valentina meet and fall in love at the physics conference under the oblivious eyes of her KGB minders and the disapproving ones of the British security services, scenes of erotic charge intensified by prohibition and danger. They had touched hands and exchanged glances as they passed coffee cups in the breaks in the meetings. They had arranged to meet and had escaped for an hour one evening to walk, to embrace, in the dark streets of Rome. They parted. The camera had indicated the passage of the long years of their separation with shots of Valentina sitting at a bench in her laboratory, scribbling notes which she slipped under pages of calculations. The actress's voice-over, with its attractive foreign accent, recited the passionate words that she was writing. The letters' itinerary was shown by the hands of colleagues, by the letter boxes of the Western cities to which they were allowed to travel. John's replies were seen passing from hand to hand until, weeks later, they reached Valentina and were tucked into her briefcase until, in the privacy of the corner of a library, she was able to open them and John's voice was heard as the camera roamed over the dusty scholars and the overarching dome.

After seeing the programme, Zita said to her mother, "But what language did you use, Mama? Did you learn English at school?" For she knew that her father had never spoken Russian, or any other foreign language for that matter.

Valentina had said only, "We managed, we managed." Then with a little embarrassment, "When we met I did not really speak English, though I had taught myself a little, enough to read scientific publications. And Dad knew a bit of German."

"German? You made love in German?" Thus Zita realized that the relationship had begun essentially without language, and had been more mysterious, more passionate and harder to convey than anything the film had depicted.

The danger to Valentina had been enormous. She, who had lost her father to the camps, who was half-Jewish, knew what she risked all those years. Finally, in 1957 she was once more allowed to go to a conference in Helsinki. This time, on the second night, after she had delivered her paper, she had put on her raincoat, padded with all her latest calculations, and with nothing else in the world had walked round to the British Embassy in Skarpogaten. She had refused to move from the chair in the interview room there until Guilfoyle's mobilization of friends in London had finally persuaded the bewildered diplomatists that they had to take her. Zita had doubted if the Foreign Office had been quite as bumbling or her mother quite as Joan of Arc-like as the film showed; yet Valentina had insisted it had been "just like that".

The next morning Zita warned Lynne that Valentina was arriving that day. She telephoned Jean about the key and set off for the office in a state of anxiety which she kept at bay while she concentrated on her work, but which threatened to overwhelm her as she returned home in the evening. She found Lynne sulkily preparing Tom's supper. The television was turned off. Valentina was in the drawing room with Tom in his wheel chair, his computer open in front of him. Zita could hear Valentina talking and Tom's voice synthesizer answering. He had a choice of voices and had selected the man's, a sign that he was interested in what was happening on his computer screen. Zita stood in the doorway, with Lynne just behind her, using her as a shield, and saw that Valentina was inscribing figures on a piece of paper and passing it across to Tom who was doing calculations, his head nodding as he used the switches on his head rest. Zita had just time to think, of course, Tom will like that, why have I never thought of numbers for him, before her mother turned to greet her. Lynne, muttering, "He's had too much work today already," darted round Zita and seized the wheel chair, triumphantly recapturing her charge.

Valentina looked older. Her hair, which was cut like a helmet, was now entirely white. She had an American air about her, though her Russianness was ineradicable. She was tall, with broad shoulders, and was clearly meant to have been a babushka by now, a barrel of a woman. Instead she was lean and stringy, exercised almost to gauntness. She kissed her daughter with a kind of exasperated affection.

"Zitushenka."

"Mamochka."

The reproaches that Zita knew to be inevitable, that she dreaded, did not come for twenty-four hours, which was an act of considerable restraint on Valentina's part.

Zita was preparing dinner, arranging slices of aubergine in a grill pan. Valentina was sitting at the kitchen table and, in the act of pouring herself a second glass of wine, said, as if she could contain herself no longer, "Zita, you must put the past behind you, you know."

Zita concentrated on the flames above the aubergines. "What do you mean, Mama?"

"Why do you live like this? Do you ever ask yourself, why am I living like this?"

Zita stirred the lemon sauce that was to be poured over the chicken. She did not look at her mother. "I live like this because of Tom. My life is very well organized. I don't know why you say, why do I live like this? How could I live better?"

"In fact, everything is for the best in the best of all possible worlds." Valentina picked up the bottle of wine and offered to pour some for her daughter who moved her glass away. A red trickle of liquid splashed onto the table. Neither made any effort to wipe it away. Zita was calm. She was pleased with herself. It was her mother who was behaving in a childish and unreasonable way, not she.

"If you can tell me what I should do to live better, I am quite prepared to listen."

Valentina held her glass in both hands, dangling it so its stem swung gently, like a pendulum. "I don't speak about your doing law in the first place, instead of something creative; the child of your father a lawyer."

"His father was a lawyer, Mama, a judge."

"Exactly. Anyway, I don't speak of that. I don't speak of you working in a little provincial town doing the papers for the sale of bungalows. I don't speak of that. I accept what you have chosen and what fate has given you. What I am speaking of is Oliver."

Zita took the grilled aubergine from the pan and put the slices carefully on the pile of onion in a dish, and placed it on the table. "Do help yourself, Mama. It'll get cold if you talk too much."

Valentina ignored the proffered spoon. "You are living in the past, Zita. You grieve for him. You hope he will come back. You cannot accept that is over, finished, *konyets.*"

Zita sat down and began to pile food onto her plate. There was no need for her mother to speak; she understood what she felt. In Valentina's opinion, to become a lawyer was almost as bad as becoming an accountant or a civil servant; they were worthy professions to make society work, but not ones to be done by anyone of originality or independence. Zita's reading law at university had been an act of real rebellion; rebellion which had brought down no curses on her head. Her liberal-minded parents made no protests about her decision. They took up a new position: whatever she did, she should do to the utmost. Her entry into a big City firm was applauded and fêted. Then came the disaster of her marriage.

Oliver Daunsey was also a lawyer, already a QC, some seventeen years older than Zita. The force of his charm had worked on Valentina, who made no objection, at the time, to his age or Zita's youth and professed herself delighted with her son-in-law. He might have been a lawyer, but he was at least a highly talented and successful one. For Zita, Oliver was supreme. Even years later, after conflict and disappointment, she could not cancel her first passionate admiration. Oliver was not exceptional in appearance; even she had to acknowledge that. He was tall, with a long face and expressive features; he lost his hair early which aged him and gave him a philosophical dome. Lanky and graceful in youth, he had begun to thicken out by the time Zita met him. Yet none of this diminished his attractiveness of person and personality, which operated equally powerfully on both men and women. He was funny in a quiet, droll manner, which blunted the sharpness of his remarks, at least until afterwards. He was always remembered, after even a brief meeting.

Zita had adored him. The first rift was nothing; no more than a hairline crack. Oliver wanted children. He was one of five and wished to reproduce his happy childhood in his own family. Zita wanted children, but not yet, not yet. However, if they were to have a large family, it was better to begin earlier rather than later and they agreed that she would continue to work, to aim for her partnership and they would employ all the nannies and housekeepers that might be necessary. So Tom was conceived; the hairline crack became the rift valley.

Tom's handicaps were so severe that they were evident very soon after his birth. Zita, who up to that point had maintained an attitude of detached interest in the matter of her offspring, fully intending to return to work within weeks, fell entirely and wholeheartedly in love with her son, a love which was compounded by the guilt that she felt towards him, at having somehow allowed him to be born so horribly defective. Tom was the watershed. Oliver could not accept a child who was malformed and Tom's oddly floppy limbs, his violent and uncontrollable movements repelled him physically. He could not bear to look at him after the first few weeks, as the extent of the damage became evident. He could not bear to look at Zita either, as she identified so fiercely with her child. Zita had very quickly realized what Oliver's reaction meant. She had hung on for a time, hoping that the father would become accustomed to his son, although without conviction.

Just after Tom's first birthday she had moved out. She had

done her research and had discovered the Witte Centre in Woodham, whose work with children with cerebral palsy was both new and controversial. Her faith, her willingness to change her life to bring Tom to them, got him in and while she was directing the bulk of her energy to persuading the Centre to take him, she was scouring the vicinity for a legal firm in need of a partner. Oliver was not ungenerous: his contribution made possible the setting up of a life based on Tom's needs. His return was that he should never have to be involved beyond the pecuniary level. Tom, and Zita with him, were cancelled from his existence. For Zita, there had never been any question of choice. She had not contemplated a solution that somehow abandoned Tom and left her with Oliver. Nevertheless, she lived every moment with regret for her husband, with his image which never lost its humour and attraction, with his memory that was never clouded by their separation.

In this Valentina was right. She had uncovered the false premise on which Zita's life was based. Zita knew that reconciliation with Oliver was impossible. Not only had he never made any attempt to see her or Tom again, he had remarried. This apparently conclusive evidence was, in fact, a secret comfort to her. For Oliver's second wife was undeniably like Zita, whose Russian-Jewish grandmother had bequeathed to her black hair and an aquiline nose which were curiously similar to Shobana's glossy Persian colouring and features and her wide pale-eyed gaze. Shobana was a television presenter and journalist who had successfully penetrated the masculine world of political and economic commentary; only the most unjust of her rivals implied that her beauty was as important to her success as the acuity of her judgement. As a stepmother, she could not be faulted. Tom's birthday and Christmas presents arrived ahead of time: thoughtful, well-chosen, always accompanied by a note for Zita from Shobana herself and a card for Tom, signed, in Shobana's handwriting, by Oliver. Shobana had, it seemed, no wish for children; at least none had appeared in the four years of her marriage.

"You must give up the past," Valentina was saying. "Look

at me. I ran away from Russia and I gave it up. I became English. I did not think about the past. Your father died. I moved to America. I have given up the past. You must let it go, abandon it. If you live with it as you do, it will corrode your life."

For a moment Zita felt the swelling of the membranes of her nose and eyes and was afraid that her mother was about to exercise her ultimate power and make her do what she had never done since she had left Oliver: cry. If once she began to weep there would be no end to the flow of sorrow for Tom, trapped inside a jangling, disobedient body, unable to speak or move, although as able as anyone to think and reason; for herself, trapped on a treadmill whose alternating steps were her work and Tom; for Oliver and his loss; for what might have been.

She breathed in sharply and looked at her mother whose eyes beneath her white fringe were speculative as well as concerned, as if she had spoken not merely out of affection, but also to gauge her daughter's reaction on some scientific scale of sensible behaviour. It was Valentina's strength that she combined a detachment of observation with a passion of purpose; it was Zita's weakness that she had never been able to determine whether detachment or affection predominated in her mother's attitude to her. No tears fell. She considered all the things she could say to her mother's just reproaches. She would give up the past if she could, but it was beyond her will to blot it out. It was an addiction which she was not willing to give up.

"You're right, Mama. I should."

Valentina, who was still Russian enough to enjoy meandering discussions that covered the ground without actually reaching a conclusion, put down her glass in displeasure.

"What's more, Zitushenka, you should lose some weight, fifteen pounds at least. You take no exercise; you drive everywhere."

This time Zita did protest a little. "I have so little time that I have to take the car. Anyway, I enjoy cooking and I like eating."

"That's all very well, but what's the point? Tom can't eat anything except purées and Lynne prefers hamburgers. You should just eat salads, then you would gain time to go to a health club or jogging or something."

Valentina always went the whole hog, Zita thought. When she decided to become American, she became American; she had never exercised when she lived in England. "You're right, Mama," she said again.

For Valentina, Zita had always been the most exasperating child and even worse as a teenager. She had never disputed with her parents; she had just quietly gone on doing or not doing whatever seemed best to her. Valentina sighed and changed the subject.

"Yevgenia is an unexpected neighbour to find in deepest Sussex," she said.

Zita looked at her in surprise. The worst was over now; she was going to be able to eat the chicken in lemon without more accusations. "How did you discover she was Russian?" she asked. "I have known her ever since I came here and only found it out myself a few months ago. Or did Marcus tell you?"

Valentina smirked. "I wish it was my perspicacity that had uncovered it, the innate Russianness that spoke between us. No, it wasn't Marcus either. She spoke to me in Russian right away. It's a long time since I used the language. It felt quite odd. I think I shall enjoy it. I shall go and see her again tomorrow. Of course, she isn't really Russian."

"She isn't?"

"No. Her father was a Baltic German. I think he was a justice minister or education minister under the last Tsar. Her name, von Korff, rings a bell to me. Not that I would have learned about him when I was in school in Russia." Valentina's scorn comprehended not only Russians foolish enough to have stayed in Russia after she had left, but all Russian institutions. She gave the impression she had arrived in the West with her bare genius and no other education at all. "She was only born in Petrograd. Her parents took her to Latvia when she was a baby and she lived all her early life on an estate not far from Riga. So she only became a Russian citizen after 1940 when the Baltic States were forced to join the Soviet Union." Valentina presented these historical details approvingly, as if it showed that Yevgenia's Russianness was an oddity of fate and nothing innate.

Zita smiled. "You've learned more about her today than I have in all these years. She has always maintained your attitude to the past: she barely admits that it happened."

And she suddenly remembered that she still had not told Jean about the skeleton buried under the roses.

Chapter Six

Zita realized that she must tell Jean before Sunday when Naomi and Marcus were coming to lunch with the Russian girl and when speculation about the body could not be avoided. She was uncertain why she had postponed telling her or why it was with such reluctance that on Saturday afternoon she wheeled Tom round to her neighbour's with Valentina walking by her side. On the face of it, there was no reason to expect that Jean would react any differently from Naomi, who had displayed curiosity and a proprietory interest in the corpse, even a hope that what was revealed would be particularly startling, if only in a remote and academic sense. Why should telling Jean be more difficult?

The lunch on Sunday had grown into a large affair. To Jean's original guests, Naomi, Marcus and the Russian girl, had been added Rosie and Al, Rosie's boyfriend, and Valentina and Zita. Lucia would be there in charge of the kitchen and Ivo, Marcus's son, had said he might come too. Tom did not count as an eating guest, as he only consumed purées that were laboriously fed to him in private. Zita had volunteered to help Lucia by preparing a walnut tart. It had been agreed that she would do this in Jean's kitchen on Saturday afternoon, and this was the last opportunity to mention the subject that she found so hard to broach. The two elderly Russians, Valentina and Jean, sat on either side of the kitchen table, watching Zita at the far end with her hands in a bowl of flour. Tom sat strapped into his wheel chair opposite her. They were speaking Russian.

"I remember our cook in Latvia," Jean was saying. "She

was rather thin and pale, stringy and energetic, not the traditional fat and rosy cook at all. She mostly used ingredients
which we produced ourselves on the farm. We had to buy some
things, of course, but as little as possible. Her newly baked
bread was like...I can't say what it was like, far better than
caviar or foie gras or any delicacy that you can imagine.
Plunging your teeth into that firm, sweet-smelling bread was
the most delectable thing in the world."

"We used to buy *Rizhki chleb,* Riga bread, in our bread
shop in Moscow," Valentina said. "It was more expensive than
Moscovski." It was the first time that Zita had ever heard her
mother reminisce about her Russian childhood.

"Not the same at all," Jean was contemptuous. "Industrial
bread bears no relation to what we used to eat. Perhaps I shall
get Ivo to recreate it."

The elusive Ivo, Marcus's son, Zita had not met since childhood. He was a chef, a profession which, she gathered, had
been hard for his parents to accept at the moment that he had
turned down a place at university in order to go to a hotel
school in Lausanne. Now that he was a television personality,
with two starred restaurants to his name, the family had forgotten their rage at his choice.

"I think you will find there is an essential ingredient that
Ivo is not able to supply," Zita suggested. "The taste of the past
is always better than anything which can be cooked now."

"It has always seemed to me," Jean went on, "that attitudes
to life, to people, to marriage and sex—of course, nowadays
these are not necessarily the same thing—can be deduced from
people's attitude to food, more particularly, from women's attitude to cooking and to the raw materials of cooking. Maris, our
cook in Latvia, was so thin, wiry, energetic. She was rather
rough with us children, and she had a sharp tongue. Yet she
had this feeling for ingredients, for the cheese and milk and
eggs from the farm, the vegetables that we grew. And though
all the time I knew her I thought of her as old, she was obviously tremendously sexy. She never married, but she had a
series of lovers who were utterly in thrall to her. Then, look at

Naomi, all theory and no practice, of cooking, I mean. So she buys expensive gourmet things, pre-cooked, all dished up. Like that strange job of hers, all high-minded theory, applied ready-made to the human condition."

"Yes," said Valentina, "and look at me. I don't cook any more. I have given up completely since John died."

"This theory isn't supposed to reflect the circumstances of people's lives," Jean protested, "but of their natures. I have always been squeamish, myself. I never really like cooking meat. I hated the texture of raw flesh, that soft, moist cling-ingness. I couldn't bear the stickiness of making pastry and dough, as Zita is doing now."

"Ah, Zita..." Valentina said.

Zita had seen this moment arriving as soon as Jean had started the conversation. "And Lucia," she interrupted. "She cooks wonderfully, with clinical cleanliness and exact measurement. So Swiss. How I wish I could be as organized as she is in the kitchen."

"National characteristics are crude, but they are real observations," said Valentina, not to be diverted. "Zita is truly Russian; she cooks with passion and emotion."

Zita glanced at her reflection in the black glass door of the oven. She could see that she had flour in her hair. "When my mother says something is Russian," she remarked to Jean, "she means it is bad and to be regretted."

"She is right that you love cooking."

"I do because it's relaxing to do and pleasurable in its outcome; it is creative and yet always needs to be renewed."

"What does this tell us about the waste of her life, with no one to cook for?" Valentina demanded rhetorically.

"Mama," Zita did not want to quarrel with her mother in front of Jean, but she was sometimes too exasperating to be borne. "That you, of all people, should imply that a man is necessary to a woman's life; let alone that a woman should be cooking for him.'"

"I don't imply it, I know it," said Valentina. "All right, I did not cook much for your father. But what would I have done without him? I met him when I was still very young and I did not know what I was doing. There was someone before him, but he did not count. Once I met your father what could I not do? I escaped from Russia, I became English, I had you, I did my work, all because of him."

Zita was now rolling her pastry with heavy-handed fury. She knew that the tart would be ruined. "In that case, Mama, you know how difficult it is to manage without him."

"Yes." For a moment Valentina's voice was sad. "It was very hard for me after he died, I missed him every day. But one cannot give up. You have to forget the past and start again." Zita resisted the impulse to shout at her mother and her insufferable rightness.

"I hope Ivo won't come tomorrow. I am afraid this tart will not be up to his standards." This was the point to tell Jean of the skeleton. Anything was preferable to allowing Valentina more opportunity to comment on her life.

She began her account as if what she had to tell was of a minor snag in Naomi's building works. Jean listened, at first with perfect detachment; the tearing out of her roses was something that had no power to touch her. Even the description of the revelation of the skull by the workmen did not elicit any disturbance in her normal expression. Zita was relieved that her task had been so easily achieved and began to talk with greater ease of the archaeological aspect of the excavation, the calling in of Dr Reskimer of London University who had come with several students to dig out the skeleton.

"I saw the body myself when I went over there yesterday afternoon. It had been completely uncovered. It was rather strange because when I first saw the skull I had not taken in anything about its size. When I saw it this time, it gave me a shock because it was immediately clear that it was the body of a child. I don't know whether it is of a boy or a girl. They spoke of it as 'he', but I can't see how you can tell the sex of a skeleton."

"I'm no biologist," Valentina said, "but you don't need to be a pathologist, Zita, to work out that the structure of the bones will be different: the female skull is smaller than the male; there will certainly be a difference in the pelvis. Overall, the male is larger than the female."

"Yes, yes," said Zita, irritable that Valentina thought she could not work that out for herself. "Of course, that would be obvious if you were looking at the skeleton of an adult; but if you are looking at a child, before you do laboratory tests, how do you know whether this is the skull of a large six-year-old boy or of a small nine-year-old girl?"

"I am sure an experienced eye can tell by the size and proportion," Valentina asserted authoritatively. Zita suppressed a sigh. Why, she wondered, how, did she and her mother get into these entirely pointless wrangles over details which meant nothing to either of them. There was no reason, intellectual or emotional, that they should take issue with one another on such a subject.

It was only then that her attention came back to Jean. Clearly the bickering of mother and daughter was distressing to her; she was looking shocked, as though she wished to remove herself from what was going on around her.

"So I learned very little yesterday. Perhaps Al will have more news for us tomorrow."

"We shall be ten tomorrow, if Ivo comes," Jean said with an effort. Her voice trailed off. Valentina gave her a sharp regard.

"It's years since I saw Marcus and Naomi, Yevgenia," she said. "I hope they have changed. I don't like to come back to England and find everything is the same. It's like coming back to the past. I want to come back to the future, or at least the present. I hope I shall see that they have both aged considerably."

Jean laughed. Her expression changed once again, her face transformed by amusement. It was as if she had shut a door on something and by an act of will refocussed her consciousness. She shifted in her chair, looking for her walking sticks. Zita thought, of course, she lives in pain. No wonder she sometimes seems troubled.

Part Two

XENIA

Chapter Seven

"Xenia is some kind of avenging Fate as far as Jean is concerned."

Naomi was reflecting on the arrival of the Russian girl in London, talking to Marcus as she prepared dinner in the large, open-plan kitchen-dining-living room on the ground floor of their ugly Hampstead house. Xenia was baby-sitting for a neighbour, so there was no danger of her overhearing her benefactor's thoughts.

Marcus was sitting with his back to his wife, sunk into the old sofa that served to cut the cooking from the eating areas of the room, leafing through a loose pack of papers on his lap. For Naomi, discussing human relations and their implications was a way of life. She never told Marcus the details of her clients' problems, although she sometimes recounted funny stories that she had heard during the day, without attribution. The staple of her accounts was her friends' lives; she had a real interest in human affairs, those that involved the emotions and could be unravelled, in row after row of cause and effect, spanning time and generation.

"Do you mean one of the Furies?" Marcus asked. "They were snake-haired, dog-faced and bat-winged, I believe. Not a very accurate depiction of our little Russian, who is really not unattractive. Anyway, since you believe in Fate, it will amuse you to watch events."

It was true that Naomi had a very deterministic view of life for someone who was dedicated to helping people change. This was partly due to her training as a psychologist. Once human behaviour was gathered into a huge enough heap and then sorted into different piles, it had a reassuring predictability. She often felt that if you knew enough about someone: about their parents, childhood, education, upbringing; if you ran all the personality tests that there were on them, you would know enough to predict their careers, marriages, divorces, breakdowns, age at death, even cause of death, with a high degree of probability. Naomi liked ranging her world into such impersonal and tight categories; it gave her the democratic comfort of finding that, in certain things, the rest of the world acted as she did, and the elitist affirmation that, in others, she was in the ninety-ninth percentile of the population.

She emptied a bag of ready-washed salad into a blue pottery bowl that she had nursed on the aeroplane returning from Greece where they had spent their honeymoon eleven years earlier.

"Yes, to say she is one of the Furies makes her too fierce. You are quite right; she seems a very quiet, gentle little creature. What I meant was that she represents the past that Jean has tried to repress for all these years, living as an English housewife. That is why Jean is so unwelcoming. You would think that she would be interested in what is going on in Russia. It is a great historical event, like watching the French Revolution. Yet she tries to pretend it isn't happening."

Marcus scribbled a note in the margin of the form he was reading. "She's old, darling, why should she bother with revolutions? She won't live to see the outcome."

"In the long run, nor shall we."

"She has no children whose future concerns her."

"Marcus, what rubbish you talk about people." She was shaking dressing from a bottle onto the salad and then began to turn it, vehemently, enjoying the brilliant green of the various leaves against the blue glaze. "*You* are Jean's child. Ivo and Rosie are her grandchildren. She idolizes Rosie, would do anything for her. How can you say she has no concern for the future?" She put the bowl on the table, letting it clash on the wooden surface with unnecessary noise. "You say that because you think that a woman who has no children cannot feel for anyone as a mother does."

Marcus put down his papers and advanced towards the dining table, putting an arm around his wife's shoulders. "No I don't, darling. I think whatever it is we are going to eat must be ready. It certainly smells like it."

Naomi's own childlessness was the result of a decision they had taken at the time of their marriage. She had her career; they had the motherless Ivo and Rosie to care for; another child was simply unnecessary. As years passed, Naomi began to voice her regrets: the idea of the mother became more potent to her in her work. However, her disappointment was never sufficient to persuade Marcus to reconsider, or for her to take unilateral action. But, the subject was the point at which her companionable ramblings over the doings of their friends would sometimes break down into a personalized commentary. This time she was not truly upset and was easily diverted into serving out the spicy, ready-cooked meal that she had sent Xenia out to buy in the middle of the afternoon.

"One of the nice things about having Xenia here," she said as they sat down after rescuing the chicken from the oven, "is that it is a bit like having a grown-up daughter living at home. She is so willing and helpful and it is so nice having someone to chat to at lunchtime after a morning of really horrendous appointments. I shan't mind at all if Jean refuses to have her for the last month when Lucia goes to Switzerland. She will be very welcome to stay here."

"We'll be in Tuscany. It won't matter to you where Xenia is." Marcus forbore to comment on the real grown-up daughter living at home: Rosie in the basement flat. He had already begun to fork up the Indonesian-style chicken.

"We are so lucky," she was saying. "Sometimes when I look at all the misery and fear around us, my clients, even Jean who has always seemed so tranquil, I marvel at our luck. I think…"

The door bell rang with piercing insistence. "Who can that

be at this time? I do hope poor Andrew has not muddled up day and night again. Last week he came at nine thirty at night for a morning appointment."

Marcus did not speculate; he went to open the door, returning a moment later with Al.

Rosie's boyfriend shared the basement flat and was in many ways a more acceptable member of the family, as far as Naomi was concerned, than her stepdaughter. He was an eye-catching figure; his most striking feature was his hair, reaching beyond his shoulders and tied in what could legitimately be called a pony tail, so thick and black was it. Although he lacked the ash that would have adorned his head, he looked like a Hindu holy man or a Muslim saint; his face had an austerity which fitted such a calling. It was long and narrow with a sharp, high-bridged nose and unexpectedly pale hazel eyes. He wore jeans and a denim shirt, neither of them clean or pressed.

"Sorry, Naomi, I'm disturbing you. I came to ask Xenia for a drink, but Marcus says she's out."

"Al, come and join us. Have you eaten? Have a glass of wine." Al refused food or drink, yet did not leave. "Xenia'll be back soon. Where's Rosie?"

"At one of her evening seminars. She won't be home till late." He turned reluctantly to go. "We'll send her down to you when she gets in," Naomi called. "The more conversation practice she gets the better."

But when Xenia returned she pleaded tiredness and refused to descend to see Al, preferring to sit between Naomi and Marcus on the old sofa and watch the ten o'clock news. Pushkin, Ivo's elderly Burmese cat, who had been left with Marcus when Ivo moved out, even though he detested Naomi, curled up on her lap, raising his round face to hers in adoration.

"Even the cat loves her," Naomi said later, as she discarded her skirt. Marcus was in his dressing room. He dropped his cuff links into the brass inlaid box on the chest of drawers and made one of his infrequent contributions. "A good thing she didn't go down for a drink," he said. "Rosie might not have liked it."

"Rosie? Why ever not? I think Rosie is grown-up enough to cope with Al and Xenia having a drink together. If Rosie wants to be jealous, and she isn't, if you ask me, she could give herself hell about many other aspects of Al's life before that."

Marcus said no more and Naomi, having, with great magnanimity, disposed of his accusation, gave no further thought to her husband's attribution of interest to Al, or to why such a motive might have occurred to him.

"I do think we are doing such a good thing with Xenia. Good for her and a pleasure for us."

All Naomi's thwarted maternal instincts had been aroused by Xenia when she arrived. She was, in any case, well disposed towards her: we all want the object of our benevolence to be worthy of us, and when she saw the forlorn figure disembarking from the taxi in Gayton Street her heart went out to her. She had anticipated a strapping girl with a physique to match her force of character. What she saw was someone much slighter and frailer than she expected of any Russian. Xenia had a broad face with wide cheeks and large pale eyes. Her light brown hair was unattractively scraped back and tied at the nape of her neck, which was long almost to the point of exaggeration and was perhaps the element in her appearance which most emphasized her fragility, giving the impression of a twig that might be snapped at any moment. Her clothes were hideous; she was not pretty. She clearly needed looking after.

Naomi's warm-hearted care and generosity were immediately repaid by Xenia's gratitude and admiration. She had arranged for the Russian girl to go to language classes for a couple of hours every morning at a nearby school of English. She had already found two people, one a neighbour, one a client, who would employ Xenia as a child-minder. She had put flowers in her room and a pile of books and brochures about London beside her bed. She had bought her first week's travel card for her. Everything she had organized was received with fervent thanks. The pleasure of giving and the power of doing good are strong and Naomi enjoyed them both. And yet...and yet...Was there something wrong, even at this stage, an unplaceable dissatisfaction with herself or with Xenia?

Even in Xenia's first week in England, an unease had made itself felt. Naomi had telephoned Zita to ask news of the skeleton. They had decided, in unspoken agreement, to call the body the skeleton: it made it seem much older, an archaeological specimen rather than a murdered child. In the course of the call, she recounted Xenia's first visit to a supermarket. It had been a good story. Xenia's astonishment at the high temple of Western consumerism had been all that could have been desired. Her foreknowledge of the copiousness, the extravagance of choice, could barely contend with the reality of aisle after aisle of jars, tins, packets, of snacks, crisps, biscuits, cakes, fruit and vegetables, meat and dairy products, chilled and frozen and dried. In front of the breakfast cereals, as Naomi wandered up and down looking for Marcus's favourite muesli, Xenia said suddenly, "But what are they all for?" She was walking along reading the names and attributes of the packets and their contents.

"For breakfast."

"No, I mean, why so many? Who needs so many different breakfasts? And how do you choose?"

"I don't know really. It's true I've never tried even a quarter of them. What I'm looking for is Luxury High Fruit Muesli With No Added Sugar. Here's High Fruit, High Fibre, but I think there must be sugar in it. The packet I want is green, can you see it?"

"This one?"

"Yes. Clever you. I can never find anything."

Xenia turned away. "I cannot discriminate," she said. "I do not see how you choose."

Even then, beneath the gratitude Naomi sensed disapproval and resentment. Xenia was quite right, she told herself, interpreting the wordless criticism in her own terms. We are far too materialistic. Russians, deprived of the endless things which we create to sell and buy, are able to concentrate on ideas, which are truly enriching. But what was really eerie was not silent disapproval of consumerism; it was rather the idea that underneath that agreeable exterior was someone else, another Xenia whom she had not yet encountered.

"She is a bit unsettling," she had said to Zita. "So sweet and useful to have around. But suddenly one starts to see everything with her eyes. I keep feeling apologetic and wanting to explain and excuse."

Chapter Eight

If Naomi sensed a faint odour of hostility emanating from Xenia, it represented merely the vapour escaping from the crater of a dormant volcano. In her first week in England the Russian girl was in a turmoil of resentment and fury which she only hid because she had been trained since childhood in the suppression of her true feelings and the demonstration of acceptable ones. Her alienation from everything that she saw around her was made more distressing because she had no loyalty to what she had left behind.

She had been brought up with a sense of injustice by her father, who had educated his daughter in the idea that, although it was necessary to conform in order to survive, she must never submit her inner self to the values that she saw around them. An utterly defeated man himself, he nevertheless imbued in her the belief that the preservation of independence and self-respect lay in the secret hatred, and even, if it were possible, subversion of authority. His rebellion lay in an internal monologue of mockery and criticism of Soviet life, a monologue which, when he was drunk, more and more often towards the end of his life, he spoke aloud. His attitude of mind had, necessarily, to be hidden, and the cultivation of a compliant façade was one of the skills of life to be learned at an early age.

Xenia, although she detested and feared her father, had accepted his view. She had never outwardly rebelled. She had been a docile student in a school system which always discriminated against her. She could not win: that was something she and all her teachers knew. Yet she accepted the conditions that life laid down, apparently without demur. And the system came good for her. When she won a place at the Language Faculty at Moscow State University, the teachers at her Siberian high school marvelled as they congratulated her. They wondered where the *blat,* the influence, had come from to make such a translation possible, for they knew from their own careers that being clever, as Xenia was clever, was not enough. To gain the good things of life one had to be one of the elect, a high Party official with influence in the workplace or local region or with favours already performed, to be paid off by the more powerful. How the daughter of someone who had come to Siberia as a prisoner, and a political one at that, and had remained as a mere high school teacher, could have won such a sought-after prize was incomprehensible. That there was something more to it than merit went without saying. What they did not reckon with was the operation of luck.

Xenia was lucky. She had noticed it when she was very young. One of her earliest memories was of the misery of her nursery school, where she was the victim of persecution. The dominant children would mock her. There was always something indefinably wrong about her that could be used to destroy the glory of any success she achieved. The teacher was their accomplice, awarding a star for her excellence in spelling, while permitting the taunts, her acquiescence acknowledging their justice in another scheme of things. Xenia could remember hiding in the sparkling Siberian winter sun behind the concrete wall that separated two sections of the playground, unwilling to emerge and run with the other children. The cold air froze her tears to her cheeks and she felt ice shards forming in her nostrils and between the inside of her lips and her teeth, piercing her skin like knife tips. She wished her persecutors dead, that some great power would sweep down and destroy them, gathering her up for reward and comfort. No miracle happened. She had to run out to face her tormentors. But the very next day, in an administrative rearrangement, she was removed from her class and placed in another school.

No other explanation but organizational convenience, a quota for the region to be fulfilled, could explain how she got to Moscow University in the first place. Once she was there, she applied herself to her first goal of never having to return to Siberia. It was a difficult task to get her internal passport marked with Moscow residence and she knew that when her course finished she might still be forced to go back to her birthplace. However, with the political changes after the coup in August 1991, her horizons had widened and whereas her first hope had been to travel to the Baltic States, the western window of the Soviet Union, she now hoped to go to Europe itself. Her father, a teacher of languages at the Technical High School, had taught her to speak and read English and French, beginning when she was very young, and those languages had been the verbal expression of her resistance to the Soviets. Her success in them, deriving from her father's knowledge and teaching, had been a secret pleasure. The discovery of the Club of the Nobility in Moscow had suggested that his name, which had always been a handicap, might now work in her favour. Her father's death meant that she lacked the proofs necessary to register herself. But this did not matter. It would have been a dangerous thing to do and her caution would have held her back.

Her visit there had been lucky. She had gone on a day when a letter had arrived from a Russian of the emigration, married to an Englishman, enquiring about the Chornorouky family. She had been shown it by a friendly clerk who had searched for it among the piles of paper on her desk, and found it weighed down with a glass of cold tea. As Xenia read it slowly, she could already see herself in England. She had copied down the name and address and handed the paper back to the clerk, without giving the slightest sign of the vision she had had or the excitement she was feeling. She knew almost nothing of the

West or, more particularly, of England than could be learned from the pages of nineteenth-century novels, which, though teaching her many profound truths about the people they depicted and their way of life, hardly prepared her for London in the 1990s.

So, to find when she reached England that, in spite of the warm welcome, the generosity with which she was met, she still felt that she was on the outside, was a rejection by the place where she had hoped she would at last feel at home. Xenia was, however, always adaptable and the method of existence that had served her in Siberia and in Moscow still worked well in London. She listened and smiled and thanked and thanked. She attended the language school every morning and applied herself diligently to her classes, thanking Naomi for arranging them, although she had no idea of the cost they represented. Whatever else was difficult about a Russian university, the cost of classes was not a problem and it never occurred to her that the lessons were not free and that Naomi had not simply used influence to obtain her a place. She was, however, already aware of the expense of life in London. She could see that the three pounds fifty an hour that she earned baby-sitting would not buy much, even when her basic living expenses were met, and would certainly never support her.

All these things told her that she had much to learn and that she must set herself to comprehend. She listened and watched in the streets, in the houses where she worked, in her classes, in the shops, above all in the house in Gayton Street. She was fascinated by the Loftus family. She noticed their contempt for possessions and their wealth; their carelessness and their consumerism; the volume of their things spread over a space that would house five or six families in Moscow. She saw how practical problems, the impossibility of moving from one place to another, the difficulties of papers and passports and permissions, the trials of housing, of buying things, even of acquiring food, simply did not exist for them. The minor annoyances of a car refusing to start or the immersion heater not working were solved at once by a telephone call and a cheque. You paid and things worked again. Which left other problems; ones you talked and talked about, but did nothing to change.

She began to listen outside the door of Naomi's consulting room to find out what went on there. Naomi had explained to her what she did. She had become expansive over dinner one night, delivering one of her lectures on the benefits of therapy in helping to create the integration of the personality, to become a whole being. The problems of the personality, of its being whole or fragmented, appeared irrelevant to Xenia and she had listened with a blankness which Naomi did not notice, but which clearly struck Marcus, who intervened on several occasions to tone down his wife's claims, as if defensive of her self-exposure before Xenia's critical gaze.

Sometimes, during the day, while she crouched on the stairs outside the door of the sunny, first-floor room which was Naomi's office, she could hear nothing. There were long periods of silence, followed by indistinguishable murmurs, then more silence. On Thursday evenings Naomi held an adultery encounter group and this was a noisy and interesting session for Xenia. She was sitting in her usual place on the stairs, listening so intently to what was being said behind the closed door that she failed to hear Marcus return from work. He mounted the stairs and, turning on the landing, came face to face with her. His surprise was so great that she began to laugh and they had to smother their noise by a rapid descent, to avoid disturbing the encounters that Naomi was supervising.

In the living room Marcus said, "What were you doing there on the stairs? I wasn't expecting to find you there."

Xenia looked a little shamefaced. "I was listening. I wanted to understand what they did in Naomi's group."

"You mustn't do that. It's very confidential. We're not allowed to hear. Even just passing on the stairs, you must close your ears. I know it's rather bizarre to you, but you must never tell Naomi you have overheard anything. She would be most upset."

Although Marcus and Naomi had been good to her, Xenia felt no attachment to them. They assumed, she thought contemptuously, that their generosity made them likeable. She, on the other hand, could think of no reason why she should like them, when their hypocrisy and self-deception were so glaring. She acknowledged to herself that she would probably resemble them if she lived as they did. She would, in fact, like to live as they did and envy played a part in the impatient contempt that was growing up under her grateful exterior. That she, too, was hypocritical, she recognized freely. But she had the excuse, which she readily accepted on her own behalf, of being powerless. Camouflage is the protection of the weak and she knew at least what was her protective covering and what was her real self. They were free, rich, independent, powerful, yet they concealed themselves and their motives from themselves, as if they were ruled, as she was, by poverty, necessity and impotence.

Rosie was different, had more perception. Xenia had observed her less, for she and Al led a separate existence in the basement and so she had not worked out what Rosie was hiding from herself, if anything. She only knew that Rosie had seen something in her of the rage at unfairness and animosity towards those who were established with all that she lacked. She respected her for that. As for Al, she paid no attention to him, for she could not see him as a person of significance. He was Rosie's lover, a hanger on, a black. She was not even sure what he did. Her first concentration in fascination, in envy, was on Naomi, Marcus, Rosie.

As she became more used to the household during her first week, she became bolder in occupying the spaces, invading its private places. At first, her own bedroom on the top floor, once Rosie's when she had been a school girl and still decorated with the Laura Ashley sprigs she had chosen when she was eleven and now despised, had seemed a haven. She had retreated there, lying on the bed under the sloping ceiling with Pushkin beside her, purring like a powerful motor, looking out over the roofs of the neighbouring houses descending the hill. She had never had such a vast area to herself in her life. In the *obshezhitiye* on the Lenin Hills in Moscow she had shared a room smaller than this with two other girls; in Siberia her father had slept in the living room and she had had a little bed that she put up each night in the hall.

In the quiet mornings, when Marcus had left for the hospital, when Naomi was already ensconced in her consulting room, before the cleaning woman arrived, Xenia began to venture out and explore the house. She started in the more public areas. In the kitchen she opened cupboards and looked thoughtfully at Naomi's random stacking of jars and tins. She would take out a packet and read its label carefully, *Funghi Porcini Secchi; Easy Blend Dried Yeast, Best Before See End,* replacing it exactly where it had been before. In the drawing room she fingered the objects with which Naomi decorated the shelves and tables: curiously shaped items from the Far East or India or Mexico whose original purpose was hard to guess. In Marcus's study-cum-dressing room on the second floor she spent a long time taking books out of the bookcases and browsing through them, before she began on the desk. Marcus kept here hundreds of detective stories; opening them, Xenia sometimes found old bus tickets or laurel leaves, used as book marks. She pondered them with the same attention as an archaeologist gives to an ancient bone from which he can deduce a mass of evidence about the way of life of a mysterious, vanished people. The roll-top desk lay exposed to her view; no picking of locks was called for. She simply pulled open the drawers, pushed her fingers into the crevices of the pigeonholes to look at Marcus's scribbles on his cheque stubs, at the folded series of American Express statements, where the sums she read seemed to be of unimaginable size. The desk was endlessly rewarding, with boxes of cigars in its central cubbyhole and paperbacks of near-pornography stuffed right at the back of the bottom drawer, along with a bundle of letters from someone Xenia eventually decided must have been Marcus's first wife, written from the hospital where she was dying of cancer. Naomi, who strictly respected a right to privacy within marriage and who had never done more than enter the dressing room to turn off a light (Marcus was expected to put away all his own ironed shirts, socks and underwear), had never so much as glanced at the telephone pad on the desk. Xenia opened all the cupboards and stroked the sleeves of what seemed to be hundreds of suits in shades of grey and black. She counted twenty-five sleeves one morning. Who could need twenty-five different suits? She slipped her hand into a pocket and found a pound coin and a still-folded, slightly dusty handkerchief. She held them both in her hands for a moment; sniffed the handkerchief on which lingered a pleasant perfume; then thrust both of them into the pocket of her cardigan.

This act somehow broke a taboo; the closet became a regular visiting place, and she began, too, selecting certain coins from the papier mâché bowl into which Marcus emptied his change. She took, ritually, three 1p pieces every day as she finished her browsing, an activity that became more and more prolonged, so that it was often the turning of the key in the door at ten o'clock, announcing the arrival of Mrs Vokins, that called her attention to the time. She would then slide shut the drawer, select her coins and pad upstairs with the silence and speed of an experienced thief.

From the house she ventured out into the streets of Hampstead, at first just to watch and to learn. The blatant openness all around her shocked and amazed her: the lovers entwined on the Heath with no attempt at hiding or discretion; the goods in the shops displayed with the same lascivious inducement to desire and to possess. She would, all the same, have probably not have done more than look, run her hands over the glassily smooth cover of a book, or lift the tail of a silk blouse to her cheek, if she had not seen two girls of no more than school age, stealing a dress from a little boutique in the High Street.

She had been standing by the entrance, gazing abstract-edly at the models in the window. The girls had entered a moment or two earlier, two slim English teenagers, each with blonde hair tied in a rope at the back of her neck, good-look-ing, respectable. She only became aware of what they were doing when she saw the flash of a dress sliding off its hang-er into the taller girl's shoulder bag. Xenia looked in startled disbelief to authority, to the sales assistant, whose back was turned as she attended to the questions of the other teenag-er. A moment or so later, with thanks, without haste, the two thieves left.

As if in a dream, when you know what you have to do without being told, Xenia entered Waterstone's, walking slowly round the stacks of books. With an unlearned skill, she picked up a large volume and, bending below the display table, put it into her bag. Her heart, she discovered, was rac-ing; her breathing was rapid and shallow; with a sudden, cold shudder she realized that her back was drenched in sweat. Not until she was safely in her bedroom did she look at her booty: *The Pasta Cookery of Northern Italy*. She turned the pages curiously, not to look at the contents of the book or the quality of the recipes, rather to examine what it was her risk had acquired. She rubbed a page between her fingers, as if she were testing the thickness of a cloth. Finally, when her heart rate had returned to normal, she carried the book downstairs and placed it carefully among the cookery books on the jumbled shelves in the kitchen. A sudden wave of nausea overcame her. She ran to the ground-floor lavato-ry and wrenchingly threw up the bread and cheese that she had eaten for lunch.

After that she took something almost every day. She fol-lowed no plan; she never chose an object beforehand. Her only rule was never to steal twice from the same shop. It was as if an object would jump towards her or place itself in her hands. She knew it was about to happen only when the now familiar rapid breathing suddenly warned her. Some of the things she stole she hid around the house; some she threw away at once, stuffing them furtively into public rubbish bins, or depositing them in a waste-paper bin at her language school. Once she pushed a full bottle of wine into a bottle bank, heard it crash and imagined the gush of red wine over the pile of green glass. She kept nothing.

Chapter Nine

For Xenia the lunch at Broad Woodham on the Sunday after her arrival in London was significant for two reasons. It was the occasion of her first meeting with her cousin, who called herself Yevgenia Konstantinovna Chornoroukaya. It was also the moment when she decided she must stay in England.

Yevgenia Konstantinovna had been the person with whom she had first made contact in her enterprise to come to England and she had never really understood why, once the plan had been accepted and she had obtained her letter of invitation, it had been arranged for her to go to Hampstead rather than to Broad Woodham. Seeing Naomi had explained what had happened, at least to some extent. Naomi herself had said that her mother-in-law was elderly and crippled, as if these facts, in themselves, accounted for Xenia's not staying with her. Naomi's discursive explanation went on to relate the details of Yevgenia's relationship with Marcus, of Marcus's father, first wife and children. Naomi's free flow of information was astonishing to Xenia, who was used to people who only admitted such confidences to those they had known for many years and trusted absolutely. She, in particular, had always had to be extremely guarded in what she said about her family and to whom. She felt some contempt for Naomi's carelessness; how could she know that Xenia was to be trusted? However, Naomi's open speech revealed a deeper level of explanation for how and why she had achieved her ambition.

Naomi liked power, the power that came from meddling in others' lives, in "making a difference", in "doing good", and from the allied power of binding people to you with the bonds of admiration and gratitude through the giving of presents, making of telephone calls, bestowing of hospitality. Xenia was acutely sensitive to power and always studied what counterposing force she had. In the main, it was simply the will to resist it, even when obeying, and on her first arrival this was the only way she could avoid being overwhelmed by Naomi, a detachment that separated her from the poor, appreciative student she appeared to be. Then she discovered that Naomi was interested in her, not simply as a recipient of her benevolence, but as a Chornoroukaya.

"Tell me about your family," she had said in the car on the way to do some shopping. They were driving on the complicated tangle of roads in North London that links the Edgware Road with the North Circular. Naomi drove with cautious confidence, always correctly signalling her change of lane, accurately choosing the exits and slip roads to bring her through the maze to the car park of the shopping centre. "Jean tells us nothing about the past and all I know comes from bits of research I've done myself. Marcus is not really interested in this sort of thing, though he sometimes dredges up bits from his childhood about Jean's aristocratic family."

Xenia's own knowledge of this subject was almost as limited as Naomi's. It derived from her father's rambling and drunken monologues. He would sit in their bleak room, fifteen floors above the wind-scoured Siberian plain, as if he were an ancient Slav chieftain beside his fire, chanting the exploits of his forebears. For Xenia his stories had little coherence. The history she was taught in school did not permit her to place the anecdotes of her parent into any factual context. From his tales she was hard put to distinguish between her grandfather and the earliest pagan Chornorouky prince who had ruled in the time of the Grand Princes of Kiev. Most of her father's sagas were, in any case, about the feuds of the gulag. Tentatively, she had produced one or two of these stories for Naomi, vague, generalized, their theme being the immense antiquity, power and riches of the Chornorouky. She could see that Naomi was disappointed by such impersonal stories and with an immense effort told the story of her father's terrible end. It was the first time she had ever recounted her version of the episode to anyone, apart from the police. She was astonished at herself for having done so. Her halting description had been a great success. She saw that Naomi interpreted the story as an act of intimacy and her evident pain in telling it as signifying the revelation of deep emotion. So, even though she had had no information about her family's princely past, she felt that the confidence she had forced herself to make had been worth while.

For Zita, Jean's lunch party only became important in retrospect. A death focuses the attention of the living; and a death, especially if it is doubtful, unexpected or violent, casts the mind back to the past to sift through the soil of everyday events for tiny, fateful shards of truth. Zita only selected the elements of the explanation—or an explanation—later. At the time, the events pointing back to the lunch, or even further to the evening in the garden of Asshe House, were only a part of the normal pattern of existence: work, Tom, no-Oliver, music. She was a believer in significant detail. She had begun her career as an observer as an only child in a household that did not pander to childish things. She had spent many hours at lunch tables, watching the adults who argued and gossiped over her head. Their topics might range from a Feynman formula recently published to Cambridge politics: the subjects were of no interest to her. Her attention had always focused on a detail from which she would extrapolate meaning. Although the fantasies of her childhood had been discarded and the rules of evidence had imposed boundaries to her ideas, she still found importance in small things.

At the lunch that Sunday she noticed how recently Jean had become Yevgenia, and in the abandonment of her English name she seemed to have begun the journey in reverse that had made Yevgenia—Genya—Jean, a Baltic-Russian aristocrat, into a middle-class Englishwoman. At the time she put the change down to the influence of her mother, who, in deciding to speak Russian again, was instrumental in returning Yevgenia to her past. However, the significant detail of the name led Zita to overlook something which she later saw as even more important: Yevgenia's first meeting with Xenia. She did not really remark on it because of Valentina, who was seeing Marcus and Naomi for the first time in six years, whose presence attracted all attention, allowing other activity only as an eddy of the main flow.

As they walked next door for lunch Tom was making the low, rushing noise in his throat which indicated he was annoyed. Zita could not bear to think of the frustration that he suffered. His consciousness was shut up, like Ariel in the cloven pine, in a body that he could not move, even to speak. The computer by which he was learning to communicate was his passion and he was vexed that Valentina could not play with him any longer. Valentina embraced Naomi and Marcus, remembered Rosie as a teenager, was introduced to Al. Watching, Zita saw that for each of them Valentina was exceptional, meeting her was a memorable event. And it was not simply that an encounter with the famous is always interesting; Valentina's personality imprinted itself on everyone she encountered. She led the way into the garden where chairs had been arranged in the shade and where champagne was waiting for Marcus to pour.

"It should have been Russian champagne, Jean," he said, handing Valentina a glass.

"A revolting idea."

Marcus countered Valentina's contempt for all things Russian by appealing to Xenia. She had been introduced to everyone except Zita, arriving late from the kitchen, but her presence had made no impact. She was standing on the edge of the group, marginal, although perfectly self-possessed. She was not a striking figure; there was no reason why anyone should have noticed her, Zita thought. Her hair was fair, like a dun horse; her eyes were pale, too, yellowish-grey. She was astonishingly badly dressed, in a reddish cardigan of some nasty synthetic material, which was clearly, on such a fine day, going to be too hot for her, but which she could not discard as she wore no T shirt or blouse. Her skirt, in an incoherent pattern of muddy tones, hung loosely on her frame. Her legs were bare and her feet were shod in a pair of battered trainers. Zita realized with a shock that these were the garments of poverty. Even in Russia, surely, where supply was limited, no one would have put on such clothes, in such a combination, if their choice had not been decisively determined by lack of money. Even Naomi, who made not thinking about her appearance part of her creed, was today rather attractively dressed in a natural-coloured linen skirt and blouse. Zita dragged her mind back to the conversation. She paid far too much attention to clothes, lavishing time and money on the purchase of material to be made up by Wladzia, an elderly Polish dressmaker, now retired, who shared her passion for colour and texture and shape.

"Is Russian champagne that bad, Xenia?" Marcus was asking.

"I have not tasted it so often. I should say it is not as good as this." Everyone laughed at this judicious reply, as if she had said something witty.

"I don't expect it is. This is vintage, I see, Jean."

"I found it in the cellar when I was clearing Asshe House. And some other wines as well. I have put a couple of cases out for you, and another two for Rosie, to take back to London, Marcus. You drink more of it than I do."

Zita left them to park Tom in the shade. "Will you be all right there, Tom?" she asked him. He had recovered his good humour and cast up his eyes, his method of affirmation. The conversation reached him across the lawn, very loud and cheerful, fuelled by the champagne and the presence of Valentina.

That at least was how Zita saw it at the time; later she wondered whether other mechanisms were already at work, whether Xenia's deceptively unobtrusive personality was already having an effect.

Lucia was calling them to the table, Yevgenia directing them to their places. Where was Ivo, Zita wondered, noticing for the first time the preponderance of women. Was he not supposed to be joining them? She found herself between Lucia and Xenia, opposite Rosie, while the other end of the table was dominated by Valentina, who held Marcus and Al captive in her conversation, so that Naomi was almost defeated. Lucia, a very competent cook, was setting down cold soup in front of each of them. Zita picked up her spoon and listened to the surge of voices.

"What are you doing here, exactly, Valentina?"

"Reskimer is very well thought of."

"Where *is* Ivo?"

"I went yesterday to see *Richard III* in the park."

"A wonderful exhibition."

"I am looking at a very interesting subject: the effect of the future on the past in quantum situations."

"He did two years of medical training before he turned to archaeology."

"Did you understand it? I mean the language is not exactly what you hear on the street."

"Some crisis at one of the restaurants, he said. He phoned this morning."

"You see, some of the equations seem to suggest that a quantum particle acts or makes its decision to act, one could say, on the basis of information it does not yet have, that is, it is receiving knowledge from the future as well as from the past."

"I bought a little sculpture."

"He uncovered an eighteenth-century graveyard and did some work on the bones."

"I expect he was in bed with his girlfriend and did not want to have lunch with his family."

"Yes, of course, not every word, but the sense."

"It was very expensive."

"Doesn't that rather bugger up the arrow of time? And what about free will?"

"Ivo used to creep around doing imitations of Olivier as Richard III."

"No, I don't think so. Or he is a very good actor. He sounded sorry."

"I, that am curtail'd of this fair proportion,
Cheated of feature by dissembling nature,
Deform'd, unfinish'd, sent before my time
Into this breathing world, scarce half made up..."

"Well, it does in a way. But it's rather like predestination if one is a Calvinist, we are free to make any decisions we like, the past already knows about them and has taken them into account."

"How much was it, Naomi?"

"I can't tell you, darling. I have forgotten myself by now."

"The thing I can't take about that play is the idea that being maimed or crippled or a bastard is an outward and visible sign of inward moral turpitude."

"So there is both forward and backward causation, but we can't see it. Except at a quantum level."

Zita sat listening to the lapping of conversation around her. Yevgenia, at the head of the table, took little part, once she had defended Ivo's right to be absent. Al and Marcus were engaged by Valentina, who was not someone who assumed that her world of quantum physics was too abstruse for the ordinary person. The exposition of work in progress by some academics might be numbingly boring. In her it was fascinating, flattering to her listeners, who thought they understood the science of a Nobel prizewinner. Zita also attributed Naomi's display of affection towards her husband to Valentina's presence. As Naomi moved around the table helping Lucia to remove the soup plates and to put vegetable dishes at either end, she paused behind Marcus, on one occasion resting her hands in a proprietory manner on his shoulders, on another listening to what he was saying and dropping an approving kiss on his thick grey hair. Only later did Zita recognize that, although Valentina's charisma was great enough to disturb her daughter's equilibrium, her power was not so influential on others. The cause lay elsewhere, in the other new arrival.

However, even at the time, Zita was struck by a conversation that grew out of Lucia's visit to the theatre, to the extent of losing track of who was gaining the upper hand at the other end of the table.

Xenia, who had been listening to Lucia and Rosie, said suddenly, "He does this because it is true."

"True?" Rosie was so surprised at the intervention that she seemed momentarily to have forgotten what she had said.

"That physical disability shows moral distortion."

"You think it does?" Rosie flicked a glance at Zita, whom she saw was listening, and quickly averted her gaze.

"Of course."

Rosie reacted as if she had found someone who asserted that the earth was flat, with a kind of exasperated contempt, which came in part from her consciousness of Zita's attention. "You can't believe that; it's patently untrue."

"Not at all. Look at Stalin."

"Stalin?"

"Yes. He was like Richard III with a withered arm. It came from being dropped as a child, I think."

"Possibly. But one can counter that with innumerable casesßof tyrants who were physically fine specimens or alternatively of handicapped people who were saints."

"For example?"

"Well, I don't know. Attila the Hun, perhaps—or Hitler."

"Attila," said Xenia with some defiance now. "How do you say it? He had a funny foot. Club-footed? Yes. And Hitler, you have only to look at him to see he was unsafe and insane."

Al had given up his conversation to listen to the row that had developed between the Russian girl and Rosie. It seemed to amuse him. He began to hum, *"Hitler, he only had one ball..."*

Zita was thinking of Tom. She was a believer in childhood's innocence. Tom's condition could not be a statement of his moral condition; he had no power to act, for good or evil. He could only be, according to Xenia's thesis, a reflection of the state of his mother's soul. Zita suddenly realized that this was not so far from an idea that lay at the base of the rationalization of her life, that Tom was in some way a retribution for a failing in herself which she could not identify, but of which she was always guiltily aware. Her attention returned to Rosie and Xenia who were both by now furious with one another.

Rosie was faintly pink with annoyance and contempt, exacerbated by Al's indirect support for Xenia. The Russian girl was flushed in an uneven, mottled fashion. The stupidity of the argument (Zita was convinced there was some linguistic misunderstanding at the bottom of it), bore no relation to the passion of hostility that it had evoked. Xenia was speaking, fumbling for her words. "You have only to look around you to see how a person's soul is shown in their outside." She hesitated for a moment.

Lucia, placatory, said, "I understand in the play it is symbolic."

Xenia continued as if she had not spoken. "Even clothes show you. A person's soul is shown in the colours they choose, in the way they are."

The tension drew Yevgenia's gaze; Zita saw her watch her granddaughter lean over and say with the cruel triumph of someone who has been dealt a winning card, "If honesty is shown by appearance, who will they believe, you or me?"

Xenia recoiled. Her humiliation was so acute that Zita felt a sympathetic pain. Comparing the two of them was like pitting a glossy-coated house dog against an ill-fed but combative mongrel. She could smell the sharp, repellent odour of sweat emanating from the Russian girl, physically underlining what Rosie had just said.

Zita began to speak to cover the rift that had been torn in Yevgenia's lunch party. "Perhaps the English tradition of identifying with the underdog had not developed then."

Lucia, bewildered by the antagonism that her carefully practised English had aroused, got up to fetch Zita's tart. She placed it in front of Yevgenia who was still looking abstractedly down the length of her table at Xenia who was sitting in silence, her face a mask, and at Rosie who had turned away to listen to Valentina's conversation with Al. Lucia touched her arm to recall her. Yevgenia took up the knife and handed it to Valentina, inviting her to help herself.

Xenia's encounter with Yevgenia did not come until after lunch. After their initial handshake, her hostess had more or less ignored her, making no attempt to speak to her alone. There was none of the warmth which, however self-referring, had been present in Naomi's welcome. Yevgenia showed only reserve. Xenia was not disturbed by this attitude, for she did not find it strange. It was how she would behave, until all suspicions were allayed. She had already decided that she must break down Yevgenia's hostility; she was not yet sure how she would do it. Yevgenia presented a very different problem from Naomi, who, for all her love of power, was complacent, easy to please, contemptible. She began to think, as the day wore on, that she would have no chance to speak to the old woman. Only towards the end of the afternoon, as she sat in a deck chair on the edge of a conversation, was her eye caught by Yevgenia's beckoning finger. She rose and stepped into the empty drawing room. Yevgenia sat down heavily and dropped her sticks beside her.

"Come and tell me a little about yourself," she said in English. Xenia seated herself opposite her. The afternoon light fell full on her face, making it difficult for her to see Yevgenia clearly, who, with her back to the french window, was in shade.

"I am Xenia Chornoroukaya," she said, also in English. "I

am in the third year of the Faculty of Languages at MGU, Moscow State University. I study English and French." She could quite well use longer and more complex sentences, but she had already found it useful with Naomi to simulate a younger, less fluent self. It gave her time to react; a means of concealment; a reason not to understand.

"So you said in your letter," Yevgenia remarked. "Where do you come from? Were you brought up in Moscow?"

"No, I was born and brought up in a town in Siberia, you will not have heard of it, called Novoleninsk. I only saw Moscow for the first time when I went to university there." It was only as she saw some tension ease in Yevgenia's dimly discerned face that Xenia realized that the old woman had been strained as she asked these questions. Her replies so far had been satisfactory.

"So you came from Siberia."

"My town is rather far east. It is very, very cold. Often in the winter we had thirty-five degrees of frost for months on end. It is difficult to describe such cold. Moscow seemed to me to be a very warm place when I went there. My father used to say…"

"Your father. Who is your father?"

"My father is dead. He was Alexander Alexandrovich Chornorouky."

"Alexander Alexandrovich?" From the small table beside her chair Yevgenia took a packet of black cigarettes and selected one, lighting it with a match held dangerously in her quavering hand. "Well," she said, as if explaining something to herself, "it is a common enough name. What did he do, your father?"

"He was a teacher of languages. It was he who taught me French and English himself at home when I was very young. He taught at our Technical High School."

Xenia censored her descriptions of her origins as much in England as in Moscow. She had no intention of explaining that her father came to that desolate town not as a highly paid volunteer from European Russia, but as a former camp inmate.

He had been released from the gulag which lay in the hinterland of the town and of the consciousness of all its citizens, released, but without the means or influence to return whence he came. She was waiting to hear something from Yevgenia that would tell how to slant her history, to make the links that she wanted to create.

"He taught you well. I have always understood that the Soviets were excellent in their language teaching methods."

Xenia made no protest at her father being called a "Soviet", an epithet to which he would have vehemently objected; she was building up a sense of Yevgenia's prejudices. Yevgenia had been relieved at hearing of Siberia; she had tried to discount the significance of the name Alexander; she had called him a "Soviet". Xenia suddenly understood. Yevgenia did not want them to be related. It was not just that she was suspicious of a claim of relationship; she wished actively to discredit it.

"My father spoke very fluently; he would often use English or French in preference to Russian." She did not add, because he thought our apartment was bugged.

"Presumably he learned them in a Soviet school, rather than in Paris or London."

Xenia did not contradict this. Her father had sometimes spoken of Paris, but it was hard to know if he had ever been there or whether he was talking of what he had read in books. She did not wish to quarrel, she wished to soothe. She tried another tack. "My father used to talk of his family and of its great past. He spoke of the Prince Chornorouky who built a convent in the bend of a river, with white walls all round, where the Empress Anna was imprisoned."

"Yes, Prince Vsevolod Chornorouky in the eleventh century built the Convent of the Annunciation; the Empress Anna was imprisoned there in the seventeenth century. Both are well-known characters in Russian history." Yevgenia spoke dismissively, putting out her cigarette; she struggled to rise from her chair, indicating her sticks for Xenia to hand to her. Xenia picked them up and gave them, one by one, to her hostess.

She is running away from me, she thought. Then, she is afraid; she is afraid of me. This conclusion, so unlikely, intuitive rather than reasoned, became stronger in Xenia's mind as she thought over the way that Yevgenia had reacted to her letter and her coming to England. She had something to hide, or to fear from Xenia. The girl could not imagine what it might be; at this stage her nostrils simply scented an unease amounting to terror. For some reason Yevgenia did not want her to be a Chornoroukaya, at least not a real one. Xenia built no structure of speculation upon what she sensed; she did not attempt to reason with it. She held it in reserve. She had no idea whether she and Yevgenia were related. Nothing her father had ever told her referred to relatives in England or anywhere else abroad. If it were in her interest not to be related to Yevgenia, Xenia would renounce her claim; she could not care. Her only aim at the moment was to stay in England.

The conviction that this was what she must do had come to her during that painful day as, from the margin, she had watched the family, talented, various, amid all its riches. She hated them all. She was filled with fury at everything she saw, yet she knew she must find a place here. Immediately, her mind began to search for ways of achieving her permanent escape from Russia. Influence was always needed to gain anything from the authorities. Nothing was ever given as a right, only as a favour, which would one day have to be repaid. But repayment was for later. For the present task Marcus was going to be the key. Yevgenia was too hostile to hope for help from her. Naomi's active, meddling benevolence might very well be used for her purposes, but she was sure it would have to be Marcus who would deal with the authorities. Naomi worked at home; only Marcus, who went out into the world, would have the influence to fix what she wanted with those irrational powers who rule lives, bestowing or withholding stamps of residence. She had observed, like Zita, that Marcus had been more animated than usual among his family. Unlike Zita, she did not attribute it to

Valentina's presence. She had recognized the interest, quieter, less demanding than Naomi's, that Marcus had shown in her, and knew it for what it was. She had done nothing to acknowledge it, seeing no use for it, yet she had encouraged it in an oblique fashion, always preferring his company to Al's. Now she could see what must be done.

Part Three

ZITA

Chapter Ten

The day after the lunch party Zita returned home from work to find Valentina and Yevgenia sitting together under the horse chestnut tree at the end of her garden. On a table between them were two glasses containing the dregs of tea and lemon and two saucers in which several wasps were paddling in the remains of raspberry jam which had evidently been eaten with spoons. As she crossed the lawn towards them, Zita heard the sound of Russian. If you suppressed knowledge of the modern house behind, of Tom and Lynne, the videos and the electric wheel chair, you could imagine you were looking at two old Russian women exchanging gossip in the garden of a dacha somewhere near Moscow in the summer of 1929, she thought. Valentina had transformed herself into a Russian grandmother, talking about family to a contemporary.

"Who is Al, by the way, Yevgenia?" Valentina was asking. "Explain him to me."

"Naomi told me about him a year ago, when he first appeared on the scene. He is the son of an enormously rich Indian family who is doing his best to annoy his parents. He is a bit old for such behaviour, I would have thought. But that must be the reason for all that hair, and his clothes, and for Rosie too. He went to a good school and to Cambridge to read archaeology. Then when his family wanted him to do an MBA and enter their business he refused."

"Poor Rosie," Valentina remarked. "So difficult to be someone else's act of rebellion."

Yevgenia nodded. "You're right. My poor Rosie. Although you are so much younger than me, Valya, you are developing that horror of old age, the Cassandra syndrome. You see the disasters ahead with such clarity that it is painful not to call out. But, of course, you must say nothing."

Perhaps because her insight was associated with old age, Valentina reversed her opinion. "Sometimes extraordinarily unlikely relationships based on most unpromising premises work out. Who can tell? Look at John and me, meeting as we did, hardly knowing one another at all when we married. One disaster I foresee is with Xenia, who is doing everything she can with her Russian charm to make herself beloved by her benefactors, I noticed."

"She certainly does not get on with Rosie and Al."

"That is pure racism, of course. Russians are the most prejudiced people in the world. I shall never forget coming to England in 1957 and being shocked by all the black men on the buses, not to mention at dinner tables at Cambridge. Do your Cassandra-eyes foresee trouble there? I think she'll have driven Naomi and Marcus mad within a week."

Yevgenia paused for so long before replying that Zita looked at her in surprise. "No, on the contrary, she will have chained them to her: they'll be her slaves, both of them. Then they'll send her here to work on me."

Valentina looked sceptical. "I saw no sign of her power of attraction. She struck me as ugly, difficult, badly dressed and awkward."

"It's not power of attraction, just power."

"Why do you say that?"

"Zita, you saw that ridiculous argument between Xenia and Rosie? It took me back suddenly to my childhood. I remembered an incident, so small at the time, but so important. It was a quarrel between two of…of my friends. And that made me think. What is 'tape recorder' in Russian?"

"Tape recorder?"

"*Magnyetofon.*" Valentina supplied the answer.

"Yes, that is what I need. I shall ask Lucia to get me one

tomorrow. I need a little one, that I can hold easily, and lots of tapes."

"And what's it for, the tape recorder?"

"I have to record the past. I can't write or type because my hands can't cope, so I shall record it. It was that argument between Xenia and Rosie, I couldn't sleep last night for thinking of it, or rather of the memories it evoked. Or perhaps it was earlier. After I had written to the Club of the Nobility in Moscow, I began to have nightmares. I don't sleep much anyway nowadays and when I do I dream about when I was a child in Latvia, or worse, about when I was older, during the war. I have read that the only way to rid yourself of these dreams is to write everything down."

"Do you dream of the past as it was, or is it just the setting for ordinary nightmares, frustration dreams like missing trains, or punishment dreams of being trapped by a wall of water?"

"They are not ordinary nightmares, but whether they happened or not, the horrors I dream of, I can't remember. There were so many it's difficult to distinguish between the nightmare and the reality. That's why I want to write it down. From the beginning, to make it straight."

The nightmares, it seemed, had no bearing on Woodham and the corpse of the child in her garden. It was curious, Zita reflected at the time, with what she came later to see as exceptional obtuseness, that Yevgenia had so little regard for the skeleton under the roses. Valentina had seen at once what was involved and she had a cruel way of speaking aloud what others would not say, unfolding the implications that they preferred to leave until time or need unwrapped them.

"What's the news of the child's body?" she asked Zita when Yevgenia had left them. "Is it a murder?"

"Who knows? It could have been an accident, that hole in the back of his head, but there is no doubt it is very odd to find a corpse in someone's back garden. The assumption is that the explanation is not an innocent one."

"How cautious and pompous you lawyers are. How long was she living there, Yevgenia? Forty years, did you say? It'll have to be pretty old, the corpse, not to involve her. It looks as if Naomi has been digging up the past for her."

The problem expressed so bluntly by Valentina nagged Zita all night. If the body was less than forty years old, there would be very unpleasant questions for Yevgenia to answer. The quiet resident of a country town, an elderly widow, and a corpse lying four feet down in her garden made an improbable juxtaposition. Yet Yevgenia would certainly be asked to explain the riddle and it was hard to see how any innocent answer could link the two of them. Having thought the unthinkable, Zita reverted to her original position: the bones were very old, with no relevance to the recent owners of the house. Naomi's building works had turned up an ancient tragedy that would be of more interest to Reskimer, the archaeologist, than Stevens, the policeman.

The following day she rang Stevens. His tone was not helpful, but he imparted quite willingly the information, which she knew already from her conversations with the archaeologists at the house the previous week, that a body in its entirety, not just a skull, with some metallic remains, had been found under the last thin covering of earth.

"What happens next?" Zita enquired.

Stevens' voice changed, took on more force. "It is a murder investigation. An incident room has been set up and a couple of officers are working on the case. They'll be interviewing the owners and the former owner very soon."

"Murder?" Zita repeated.

"How else would you explain a child with its head staved in, buried secretly in an unmarked grave? I've got the pathologist's report here in front of me. There's little doubt that he died from a blow on the back of the head."

Zita remembered the seams of the skull which had had the appearance of being sewn together with strong brown stitches, the way that the head was tenderly propped up. She decided to get hold of the forensic scientists to see if they could tell her anything more. "Who's the pathologist?" she asked. "Did he have anything to say about the age of the skeleton?"

"Not much that is useful at the moment," Stevens replied. His voice had still that combative edge which she had noticed at Asshe House. However, he made no difficulty about passing on the name and phone number of the pathologist before ringing off.

"Poor Yorick, is it?" he said when she telephoned Dr Pigot and explained what she wanted. "I've just finished my report on him. Do you want to come and have a look this afternoon?" he added unexpectedly. "We're just off the Brighton Road; I'm free about four."

She found her way easily. It was on the route to her dressmaker's and she recognized immediately the sprawling complex of local authority administrative offices. Dr Pigot, waiting for her in the reception area, was the model of an old-fashioned country practitioner rather than the modern forensic scientist. He was dressed in what Zita thought of as mouldy green: ancient green-brown corduroy trousers, brown-green tweed jacket in spite of the warm weather, Tattersall check shirt and a green woollen tie. She recalled descriptions of operations performed in morning dress by Victorian surgeons and wondered whether Dr Pigot, too, ever bothered with a white coat or rubber gloves. He led her down lengthy corridors to a room whose chill immediately struck the skin.

She had been asking herself why she had come and why he had invited her; all the information she needed could be supplied by telephone. When they entered the laboratory she realized why she had wanted to see for herself and not simply hear the results of Dr Pigot's researches. The skull lying on its pillow of earth under its duvet of soil had reminded her of Tom, his bony face, with its huge eyes and sharp little chin. She wanted to see the rest of the body, uncovered; she wanted to know who it was.

Although Pigot conjured up the earthy, more careless medical past, there was nothing primitive about his laboratory, which was scrubbed and bare. On one long table lay the skeleton, a collection of unconnected bones, arranged like a puzzle successfully completed. Pigot was walking round to the far side, already talking with enthusiasm. He was dealing with points in an orderly manner as though ticking off numbers on a standard questionnaire that he had to fill in.

"There was no doubt at once that it was human and one corpse." He was spreading his hands in the air above the body as if officiating at some arcane ritual. They were broad and fleshy, very white with silky black hair between the knuckles and first joint. "And that's not always obvious, I can tell you. We have people bringing us animal bones, thinking they're human. And I've had times when I've been faced with a grave-ful of bones and I've had to work out how many individuals there were. But this was very straightforward. It was laid out very nicely for the archaeologists to do their excavations and it was evident at once that it was a human child. After that things got trickier.

"Sex. Almost impossible to tell in a child. This is the manubrium," another pass of the palm, "which is propor-tionately larger in males than females. The formation of the pelvis is the other area which is conclusive, in adults. But here we have to look at other factors, to give us the answer on that one. Age at death is the next question. Size and age go together in a general way. What would you think?"

Tom never stretched out like this full length, the tension in his limbs bent and contorted them; only for moments in the swimming pool did he ever attain some kind of relaxation for his body. Then his long, skinny body was just this length. "Seven," Zita said decisively. "He was seven."

"Do you think so, now? Interesting you should say that. At first, I'd have said older. Measuring what we've got here (and we've got almost everything) we have one metre thirty-one or, if you're old-fashioned like me and still work in feet and inches, that's four foot four. Now that's a little bit above average for a seven-year-old, even today when children are bigger than they used to be. At first, I put him at about eight and a half or even nine. I checked the height, by the way, on several other tests, not just reassembling him. Best to try everything. One rough and ready method is the outstretched arms, you know, like the Leonardo drawing. You'll find that putting your arms like this..." He formed his body into a crucifix. "...gives you the same measurement as your height. Except with this one they didn't. A bit less. And there are formulae for applying to the long bones to give you an estimate of height. I used the femur and tibia and both came within a centimetre of what I'd reconstructed, so the height is right. But I digress. Because you're right about his age. When I started on that, I found he was definitely younger than I thought. For age we look at ossification, the fusion of the epiphyses of the bones to their shafts. This occurs in a given order, and when I examined this child I found considerably less ossification than one would expect in a nine-year-old. And, of course, teeth. He had only four permanent teeth. Both lots of markers indicate a lower rather than greater age. So, a tall seven-year-old, and the combination of size and age make me think we have a boy here. It's not conclusive, but I would put my money on its being a boy. Whether he was English I am not absolutely sure. There are certain features that suggest that, though he was Caucasian, not Asian, not African, he was not necessarily English. I'm still thinking about this: it's all to do with the proportions and shape of the skull, but when you're talking about a child you haven't got the final result as it were. Dental data are very good." He bent his head as if to look in the mouth. "No fillings. Strange, that, for the days before fluoride. Perhaps he came of a very strict family, or was alive during the war when sweets were a rarity."

Zita looked at the hand nearest to her, lying on the table, the bones of the thumb curved in under the very slight angle made by the arrangement of the metatarsals and phalanges. She resisted an impulse to lift it, to take it in her own hand. "I suppose," she said tentatively, "the really important question is how long has it been there."

Dr Pigot was now standing at the foot end of the table, his hands in his pockets, his conjuring of information from bones was over. "That's easy," he said. "A long time."

Zita waited for an elaboration. "How long is long? How long does it take for a body to decay to a skeleton?"

"Well, that depends, as scientists always say. It depends on the conditions of burial, as you can imagine: the length of time the body is in the air between death and inhumation, whether there is a coffin or not, whether there is a shroud or clothes, all these things have a bearing. A coffin with plenty of air and woodshavings or vegetable matter, straw or hay, makes for faster putrefaction. The flesh liquefies and the bones are freed very quickly, in say a year. If, on the other hand, a body is put into the ground without a coffin and with clothes on, it will be preserved for a surprisingly long time, especially if the ground is free draining and well tamped down: no oxygen, no water, you see." He was leaning with the heels of both hands on the edge of the table, bending slightly over the skeleton as he talked, a man thoroughly at home.

"Shall I tell you how I know all this? It is all real experience, y'know. Not book learning. We had National Service in my day and I did mine straight after the war in Germany. It was what decided me to go in for medicine, and for pathology at that. I was part of a team investigating war crimes: not finding the criminals; finding the crimes. We dug up bodies to investigate illegal deaths of various sorts. Strange, isn't it, that after all that mass slaughter, the Blitz, Auschwitz, Dresden, Katyn, there were teams of people going meticulously round to find out how and why the crew of a Polish bomber or a troop of partisans lost their lives."

Zita noticed how much more fluently he talked as he relived his youth, losing the habitual hesitation of English professional speech. The past spoke through him; he became its mouthpiece. She could see a thinner, more youthful, Pigot, still essentially the same, applying the same enthusiasm and dispassionate interest to the dreadful task he had been given, able to abandon thought of the human beings who had been shot, tortured, murdered and betrayed, in order to observe the rates of decomposition and what accelerated them. She could imagine the group of English squaddies digging in the sandy soil of the north European plain, uncovering the pits of bodies, neatly stacked like a log pile, or tumbled untidily where they had fallen, shot, into the graves they had dug themselves. She recalled news items that she had read some years ago about the most famous of those mass forest graves, at Katyn. The victims there had been Polish Army officers, thousands of them, shot in the back of the neck by the Russians. She imagined an overview of Europe, a sort of moral satellite photograph of the fields and forests from Berlin to Moscow with the secret graves burning red, like the aerial photographs used by archaeologists to make the earth reveal the past buried below. And where had the Balts been in all this? Had they been the instruments, the accomplices, of the Germans, or had they been victims too?

"We spent our time digging up the war. Mass graves of Jews and Poles, buried in thin German coffins with rhomboid lids. They had almost entirely gone, melted away. The single grave of a British pilot buried in woodland in all his clothes with a bullet hole in the back of his neck. Now *he* was in a remarkable state of preservation. Two and a half years on and his friends would have known him at once, no problem. The clothes protect the corpse, you see, prevent the entry of insects, absorb water, encourage good saponification, adipocere formation. You know what that is?"

Zita confessed that she did not. "Very little criminal work," she explained, when he looked as if everyone ought to be familiar with adipocere.

"It's the transformation of the water and fat of the body into a wax-like substance of fatty acids. The hydrogenation takes place on the fatty parts of the body through the action of enzymes." Pigot seemed pleased with the opportunity to talk about a subject which he still found fascinating forty years on.

"And had adipocere formed on this child?"

"This one? No, or at least if it had it was all rotted away.

Strange, that, because it was buried directly in the earth. There was no sign of a coffin or a box that had rotted and collapsed around it. Adipocere can only form if there was sufficient body fat in the first place: women and obese men are best. Perhaps this was a skinny child. Many prepubertal children have a very low ratio of fat to body weight, especially boys."

Zita thought of Tom's twig-like limbs and his torso with its scaffolding of bone visible through almost transparent skin. He was so thin because he could not eat normal food, living on puréed pap which he swallowed with resentment and difficulty.

"So," she summarized in her orderly fashion, "it is a child, possibly a boy, about seven years old, of Caucasian origin." She hesitated. "When was he buried?"

Pigot rubbed his head behind his right ear, roughly. "There you have me. I couldn't say at all. The skeleton was very well arranged, to judge from the photographs that the archaeologists took. No bone tumble. The bones are not much worn, you can see that. But whether we are talking about ten years, twenty years, fifty years, I couldn't say. Skeleton cases presented to us like this are relatively rare in police work, y'see. Usually we are looking for a body or signs of a body. Bits of flesh and blood stains, OK, but a complete corpse with no meat, that's another matter. I don't think I've seen one like this since I was in Germany in '46. There are several lines to follow. Reskimer and I will share them out. A very good fellow, Reskimer. I worked with him once before, about five years ago. We can take cross-sections of bone and look at the development of fungal growth. That could tell us something. There are other tests too, thin-layer chromatology and ultra-violet fluorescence may help. I hope Reskimer's excavations may give us something from the earth levels, root growth, that sort of thing. We'll have to find out very straightforward facts, like when the rose bed was planted. Reskimer may come up with something simple and conclusive from the debris, like a button or a bit of metal off the clothing that is easily datable. Otherwise, perhaps carbon dating, which is a bit out of my field. The thing about these tests is that one by itself is not going to tell you anything conclusive, but running several should give us a ten- or twenty-year time frame."

Zita could not imagine Stevens being satisfied with this scientific reluctance to prejudge the facts. "And what have you told the police? Presumably, the age of the skeleton is crucial for them. Either it falls into the category of a crime to be pursued or not."

Pigot's fluency had dried up again. He spoke once more with the mumbling of the educated Englishman. "Well, as to that, Stevens seems pretty sure, from other evidence, that it is a recent case."

"Recent? How can it be? You've just said that a body without a coffin and dressed in clothes decays more slowly than most. That must put it, what, fifty years back?"

"Oh, no," said Pigot unhappily. "I couldn't say categorically fifty years. It could be much less."

"Did you give him a figure?" Zita persisted.

"No, I wouldn't commit myself. But I had to agree, when he said could it be thirty-two years, that it could. It's very difficult once you get to arguing about twenty or thirty years. I can tell you straightaway this child is not a hundred years old. Bones that have been in the earth that long have discoloured much more than this; and their texture is quite different, they lose their mineral content and become lighter, more friable. These are too sturdy to be that old."

Zita let it go at that. "We've been talking as if it were a crime we were dealing with. There is no possibility that this is a plague victim or accident or something else?"

Pigot would be no more definite on that subject. "The cause of death of a skeleton is not always obvious, but that hole in the back of the skull makes a fairly convincing claim. It must have been done with some heavy, pointed instrument, but whether it was deliberate or accidental, pathology won't reveal."

"But if it was an accident, why was he buried where he was?"
"Exactly, so the presumption remains murder."

That evening was Zita's quintet night. Lynne was able to go home at her usual time and Valentina stayed to baby-sit. Yevgenia was to come round after dinner to spend the evening with her. Zita left home thankfully. She ought to have cancelled this evening's meeting, but rearranging was always difficult and unpopular with her fellow players, and she often found that problems that had entangled themselves in impenetrable knots during the day, loosened themselves as she played and that, the following day, they were more easily disentangled. There was something about a strings ensemble, she thought as they were tuning their instruments at the start, that was physically as well as emotionally releasing. Violinists and cellists toss and sway in unison, like tree tops or waves in the wind, the music or their instruments carrying them with them into motion, so that in the more vigorous or romantic moments of Tchaikovsky she felt as if they were all five of them in a little boat in a storm at sea, their music the wind that sang in their ears and swept the air and water around them. When eventually, more or less successfully, they reached the end, she felt as if she had been rescued and was climbing ashore, at the same time purged and healed.

The most important thing she had learned that day, she realized in the car on the way home, was of Stevens' conviction that the skeleton was thirty-two years old. Why thirty-two years? What had happened thirty-two years ago that he could be so specific?

Chapter Eleven

Valentina left the following day to return to Oxford to install herself in her new flat and to immerse herself in academic life. She departed professing that the holiday had done her a great deal of good, that she felt refreshed and renewed. Her daughter, on the other hand, felt diminished by the visit and said goodbye with a feeling, she hoped well enough hidden, of relief. Valentina had made no more reproaches about her way of life and the overshadowing past, although Zita was conscious that her opinion had undergone no change during her stay. She had half-hoped that Valentina would say something more on the subject so that she would be able to voice the angry responses that she had thought of, later. But she did not feel so secure of her innocence of the charges against her that she could reopen the debate herself.

However, she was softened towards her mother, touched by her efforts towards Tom, who had enjoyed her company. She had wondered, a little unkindly, whether they had been made partly to annoy Lynne. For whatever reason, Valentina had spent several hours each afternoon with her grandson and his computer. Zita was not sure what they did together, though she could see that it stimulated Tom who had enacted none of his thrashing rages during the visit. Valentina had made no comment about him, apart from saying that he was much more numerate than Zita had ever been. With his grandmother's departure Tom withdrew into frustration.

"It'll take a long time to settle him down again after *her*," Lynne said with gloomy pleasure.

Tom refused to exercise his normal methods of communication, the eye-signals that conveyed yes and no, the eye-pointing in answer to questions that allowed him to indicate his choice of food and clothes. In the evenings he would not sleep and he and his mother were often locked in wordless wrangles which exhausted both of them. Zita wondered whether her obsessive interest in the discovery of a child's body, buried secretly in a garden, was a case of wish fulfilment.

She was wearing her co-respondent shoes when she went to see Stevens later that week, pt on to cheer herself up after an early morning battle with Tom. If she had realized then how much he disliked her, she thought afterwards, she might have chosen a different pair. She gave clothes an importance that was almost superstitious. She rationalized this by saying to herself that what one wore delivered messages subliminally, that even the most obtuse, unintuitive of people picked up, without knowing it, and translated into associations. The trick was to know yourself the message you were conveying, otherwise you were like Tom, relaying misconstrued messages. She had chosen the shoes for herself; she had not thought of their significance to a policeman. She was sure that it was the co-respondent shoes that did for her with Stevens. Or perhaps they were simply a magnet, drawing out his general dislike of women? of lawyers? of women lawyers? of dark-haired women? or his particular loathing of Zita herself.

She had telephoned to make an appointment which had been conceded, but only grudgingly, so she was not surprised to be told that the Superintendent was out when she arrived at his chosen time. She settled herself to wait, which she was obliged to do for some twenty minutes or so until he arrived in a flurry of papers and assistants, and for a further ten minutes until he was ready to see her. Once they were seated opposite one another in his box-like office he went straight to the point.

"You want to know about the body at Asshe House and what we are doing about it? I told you on the phone that we have set up an incident room and have assigned two officers to work on the case under my supervision. They have already interviewed Mr and Mrs Loftus, your clients in London, and we are seeing the previous occupant very soon."

"I understand from Dr Pigot that poor Yorick, the skeleton, could have been there for a hundred years," she said.

Stevens' eyes were cold and grey, unfriendly in his massive, hairless skull. The texture of his scalp looked like suede; Zita wondered what it would feel like to the finger tips.

"I follow your literary references, Ms Daunsey, there's no need to translate for me." Zita, who detested being called Ms, registered her error and his sneering response without displaying any reaction. She tucked her feet under her chair and cursed Pigot whose foolish nickname she had taken over. "Yes," he went on, "it could be a hundred years old, that skeleton; it could be thirty and the person who bashed the child's skull could still be walking the streets of Broad Woodham."

"I simply wondered whether police time and money were being used in what might well be a wild goose chase."

"What would you rather we do with police time, investigate a murder, albeit an old one, or chase parking offenders?"

She did not shift her gaze and their eyes locked. He was in his mid-fifties, she reckoned, a blunt, irritable man, not stupid, with a slow-burning anger that fuelled his energy. Underpromoted, unfaithful wife, unreasonable boss, ungrateful children, overwork, money worries; she wondered what it was that gave him the air of melancholy. Or perhaps it was not ingrained; perhaps it was she who provoked it. The silence lengthened while she debated whether her ends would be best served by being aggressive or placatory. She did not have to choose, for he said suddenly, "In 1988 a child's body was discovered in Yorkshire, or rather a child's skeleton, dug up by a dog. The father was convicted of murder more than twenty-five years after the crime was committed. You may have heard of the case."

"Yes," said Zita reluctantly. She remembered something about it: the use of archaeological evidence had set a precedent for British courts.

"There is no reason why a murder thirty years old should not be solved and properly solved with a conviction and sentence in the courts. The past should have its justice." He paused, staring abstractedly at the floor in front of his desk, at her co-respondent shoes. "In any case, it is not such a random search as you imply. This body may be a child I've been looking for for thirty years and more."

"You mean you've known all along who it is?"

"No." His humour had improved. "No, I don't know. I just have a case in mind." He shifted some papers on the desk, leaving the pile marginally more disorganized than before.

"What is this case? Could it really have anything to do with Asshe House?"

"A Saturday evening in October 1960. A small boy went to buy some sweets and a comic from the newsagent in the corner of the Square, St Michael's Square. *Dandy* or *Beano* were the comics they used to sell then, or *Eagle*. And the sweets, you're too young to remember them, liquorice Catherine wheels, sherbet fountains, love hearts. He went to buy them on his bike, though he didn't live far away, in a row of cottages in Ormond Street; they've been pulled down since. We like to think it was a safe world in those days; kids could ride their bikes, walk the streets, go to school, to the shop and no harm would come to them. But it wasn't a safe world, not for this child. He set out about five; it was getting dark, cycling along the pavement under the street lights. He got to the sweet shop all right. It's gone, that shop. It's the travel agent's now, do you see, on the corner with Flood Street, opposite your offices. He bought a *Beano* and a packet of sweets, Refreshers I think they were, and set off home. But he never arrived. And we never found his body. The bike was found in the river. Eddie Cresacre was his name. Seven years old, a well-grown lad, open, chatty, not timid. He would talk to anyone and he clearly did."

Zita fixed her eyes on his face as he talked, not allowing their glances to meet, taking in his expression. He did not seem particularly moved by the story he was recounting in such detail, but even as he was speaking she wondered why he was able to tell the story so vividly. In part it was because he wanted to shock and disturb her. And he was, to an extent, successful. She had not imagined that there was a case which corresponded so neatly both in time and place with the skeleton under the roses. Clearly, to establish a connexion between the two was not a waste of police time. The implications for Yevgenia were not agreeable. By 1960 she had been living at Asshe House for over a decade. Zita hoped her face did not convey her dismay. He was subtler and perhaps even crueller than his bluff exterior admitted, and she felt she was being manipulated.

When he finished speaking, she said, "Thank you for being so frank with me, Superintendent. I had no idea that there was a particular child to be matched to the skeleton. I suppose, with dental records and that sort of thing, it should be quite easy to establish whether it is the skeleton of Eddie Cresacre."

Stevens hesitated. "There may be a problem there. The records of the investigation should in theory have supplied us with that sort of check, but it seems there were no dental records for Eddie Cresacre. There was a fire at his dentist's a few months before the kid's death. At the time we weren't particularly bothered as we didn't have a body to compare them with. However, there are things we can do nowadays, even without dental records and if necessary we shall do them. For the time being at least, it's just a question of waiting for more input from the archaeologists. Nothing in Pigot's report eliminates Eddie Cresacre. If the archaeologists produce nothing conclusive against such an identification, we shall do some intensive work to check the hypothesis."

He rose to indicate that Zita had had enough of the time of a very busy man. She stood up too and was making her ritual thanks and farewell, as she made her way to the door.

"So you can tell your clients that's where we are at the moment. Nothing for them to worry about. They'll even be able to start work again soon on that fancy pool they're making. I'll let you know when, tomorrow or the next day, I think." He held the door for her. The gesture, even though he was a middle-aged man to whom the action might have come naturally, had a parodic quality to it. "And you can tell the former owner, too. She's your client, as well, isn't she? The Russian woman."

Zita drove back to her office thoughtfully. She opened the cupboard in the alcove beside the fireplace and looked at the dozen or so pairs of shoes which she kept there. She kicked off the co-respondents and selected a pair of loafers. A change of shoes was always conducive to clear thinking and her thoughts were now much occupied by Stevens, who need not have told her what he had, nor told it in such a way. He was trying to make her see that the body under the roses was more serious than she would admit. But not just that; his purpose was not aimed primarily at her. He meant her to pass this on to Yevgenia.

He had appeared unmoved by the story he told. Yet there must have been some explanation for the clarity of his memory. He must have taken part in the Eddie Cresacre investigation all those years ago. It had occurred to her as he had been speaking and she had held herself back from asking him. Only that could explain the rapidity with which the association was made. It had not been a question of searching the records; it had been in his head. Thirty-two years ago. He was in his early fifties, say; he must have been a very young police officer. Perhaps it had been his first case, his first experience of the disappearance of a child, with all its concomitants of distraught parents, clamorous press, fearful neighbourhood. It had etched itself sharply on his memory, so that it remained when subsequent cases, years of actual bodily harm, murder, attempted murder, manslaughter, dangerous driving, battery and assault merged into one another, the normal course of criminal life. That would account for it, or part of it. She was still uneasy about something, however. She felt she had missed the significant detail of the meeting, which was not the co-respondent shoes. There was an excess of zeal in his treatment of the case that she could not understand. And then it struck her that Stevens knew that Yevgenia was Russian, a fact she had spent over forty years hiding from everyone else in Broad Woodham.

Part Four

YEVGENIA

Chapter Twelve

I was born in Petrograd in 1917 in the last days of the Russian empire. My father was Baron Konstantin Kirilovich von Korff and my mother was Princess Marina Yurievna Chornoroukaya. I was their first and, as it turned out, their only child. I never knew my parents, so what I say about them is only what I have been told. I have never checked in history books or in memoirs to see if what I believe is true. Everything comes from my memories of the stories of my aunt, Zoya, who brought me up. For her, family and religion were the two pillars that held up the world and so her tales of saints and ancestors would become entangled in my mind. I am sure for many years I regarded the story of the deaths of my parents in the same light as the martyrdom of the saints Boris and Gleb.

Aunt Zoya was my mother's aunt, my great-aunt, a Chornoroukaya, and her interest centred chiefly on her own family. My father was a good and worthy man, ennobled by being the choice of a Chornoroukaya, but in no way an equal. This fact defined my status in the household. I was only half as good as my cousin, Alexander Chornorouky, with whom I was brought up; and, in any case, I was a girl. So I shall begin with my poor despised father. He was well over forty when I was born and came of a very ancient German noble family, that had been established in the lands of the eastern Baltic for many centuries. This area, which is now Latvia, had been ruled in succession by the Germans, the Lithuanians, the

Poles, the Russians. The local aristocracy was German, the local people Latvians. Under Russian rule from the eighteenth century onwards, the Baltic Germans turned to the imperial court at St Petersburg to make their fortunes; they became a sort of *noblesse de robe,* a service nobility for the Tsar. My father, grandfather and great-grandfather were all jurists and ministers of the Tsar at some point in their lives. They tended to be liberal-minded, westernizing, progressive. My father was a member of Nicholas II's State Council and Minister for Education. I am not really sure about the dates and duration of these offices. Aunt Zoya felt his service to the Tsar was worth mentioning, although she was not precise about the details.

She was far happier telling the history of her own family. These stories would range from our distant ancestor in the eleventh century, the Prince Yaroslav Yurevich, great grandson of the Monomakh, Grand Prince of Vladimir, to the court triumphs of my mother, her beloved niece. My mother was much younger than my father, by fifteen or twenty years. She was an only child, very beautiful, with a strong will which allowed her to dominate her father, Prince Yuri Alexandrovich, Aunt Zoya's second brother. He, a widower from her birth, was his daughter's slave. She was very similar in looks and manner to her grandmother, Xenia Vassilievna Orlova, another strong-minded woman, whom her son Yuri had also adored. She, my mother that is, was very intelligent and interested in art. She painted quite seriously herself, but she saw her role as the traditional one of her caste, the patron. She bought many modern paintings, silly things, Aunt Zoya thought, and encouraged her father to buy them too. She was evidently reluctant to commit herself to marriage. She travelled widely with her father, not just to the usual places that Russian aristocrats used to go, like Nice and Rome and Egypt. She went, too, to America and India. Aunt Zoya did not altogether approve of the way my mother had been brought up. She certainly gave me the impression that it was no bad thing for my moral welfare that my childhood was so different. Aunt Zoya attributed to my mother's extended education and travel, her "spoiling" as she called it, the fact that when the time came, rather late, for her to marry, she had to settle for a Baltic baron. However, when she was feeling more charitable, she admitted that my parents were devoted to one another. My father passionately adored his beautiful wife; she, inexplicably to Aunt Zoya, warmly admired her middle-aged, bureaucratic husband. This is how I like to reconstruct them. They died before I have any memory of angry words, maternal sulks, paternal harshness, so they are preserved for me in the two years of happy marriage with the high point, my birth.

They met and married in Petrograd during the war and almost immediately my mother became pregnant. For this reason, when revolution broke out in Russia in February 1917, there was no question of her moving, as other families did, out of the capital to the relative safety of their country estates. Aunt Zoya was torn between her wish to be with Marina at the birth and her duty to her great-nephew, Alexander, whom she had already adopted when his mother died in the first year of his life. In the midsummer of 1917 there was a lull in events in Petrograd, so Aunt Zoya left with Xan for the Chornorouky estates in Livland, the ones closest to the capital. She was never to return to Russia. My mother was unwell after my birth and was not thought strong enough to risk the journey to the country, so she and my father, who was deeply involved with Milyukov and Kerensky and the Provisional Government, delayed and delayed until the worst happened in November and the Bolshevik coup took place.

Their journey from Petrograd to Kornu, the Chornorouky estate near Riga, was always referred to by Aunt Zoya in epic terms. It was one of the stories of my childhood that I asked for time and again. I suppose it was a fascination with my own earliest history, a sense that I very nearly didn't escape, that made me demand to hear how my parents, accompanied only by a young nursemaid and a manservant, set off by coach, how they were stopped by soldiers, walked for miles, hired a cart, slept one snowy night in a barn, all lying together in straw with me tucked between them, before they arrived in Dorpat and were able to get messages to Aunt Zoya to send transport to bring them at last to Kornu. It may have just been the reassuring sense of danger evaded that I liked so much, of hearing how, after all risks and tribulations, I arrived safely into Aunt Zoya's arms. I think it was also a kind of prefiguring. If I had not had the tale of that journey to sustain me, I might never have survived the later one, which I had to endure for much longer, under much worse conditions.

There was great rejoicing at the arrival of the von Korffs at Kornu and for a short period the remnants of the family were reunited, for my parents found my grandfather, Prince Yuri, and his elder brother, Xan's grandfather, Prince Yegor, also there. The only missing Chornorouky was Yegor's son, Xan's father, Alexander, who was thought to be with his regiment somewhere in the Caucasus. They had all somehow survived the upheavals of world war and revolution. But if they congratulated themselves, they did so too soon. After the Orthodox Christmas of January 1918 my parents moved to my father's estate which was about twenty miles away, where they rested and took stock of a world which had been turned upside down.

The Baltic nobility had made themselves useful to the Tsars; now they were necessary to no one. That's how it was in the long run, something that became apparent in the twenties and thirties; at the time, I think, it was all less clear. The point about change is that it's so fluid. The flow is not all in one direction; even if you're about to be washed into a backwater, you don't know it at the time. You still expect that things will alter again, to your advantage. Civil war broke out in Russia in 1918 and my family hoped for the restoration of the Tsar, with modified powers, developing the country on Western lines. I don't think my father made any active efforts to promote the return of the Tsar. He did not join the

White Army which was advancing on Petrograd. He was content to live with his wife and child on his estate and to wait and see.

And this is what happened. The events I describe come from Aunt Zoya. I was witness to them, but as I was not two years old I do not have a coherent memory. Yet there are echoes in my mind even now which, I sometimes think, may be uncomprehending recall of the night when my father's estate was sacked: flashing lights, roaring noises, a high-pitched scream that went on and on in a rhythmical sawing sound. Or are these memories, which I suppress as soon as they arise, early in the morning, in the moments between sleeping and waking, ones from a later time, or even worse, are they acts of imagination of what another child suffered years later?

In the summer of 1918 my father's house was attacked by a gang of Latvian Bolsheviks, patriots ridding their country of its oppressive foreign rulers and landowners. They broke in and looted. A trail of booty dropped in haste was found on the track leading to the woods: silver forks, a gold and tortoise-shell inkwell, things that had been seized at random. My father, woken by the noise, went down to investigate and was shot immediately. His body was found in the hall, blood lying in a circle round his head, like the halo of a martyred saint. Xan and I were later shown where the same bullet that killed him entered the panelling of the hall, gruesome information which we cherished. My mother, hearing the shot and the commotion, emerged from her room and someone fired at her as she came down the stairs, but failed to kill her. A ribbon of blood traced her path as she fled up again to hide in her sitting room. She was pursued by her killers who took an ancestral sword from a display of such things in the hall. Many blows, some with the flat of the blade, some with its edge, no longer sharp, were beaten on her head and shoulders. The weapon was thrown on top of her when her assailant, in weariness or horror, had had enough. Whether she died then or only sometime later during the course of the night, Aunt

Zoya never knew, though she dwelt on her niece's end for many years, speculating how long it had taken her to bleed to death.

What she did not tell me, because she did not know it, was that my mother was also raped, probably between being shot and finally belaboured to death by the sword. Years later I had gone back to Jamala to visit my nursemaid who had come with me to Kornu and then married and returned to her home village. It was during the war and I went to gather news and a little rent which was paid in kind, honey, ham, cheese, from some property I still held there. It was only then that Inna told me. We were sitting in the kitchen of her little wooden house. Through the open door we could see her two white-haired children playing among the untidy rows of potato flowers. She had been explaining to me about the empty shops and houses in the central square, once occupied by Jewish families. There had been a round up in the town a week earlier. Some had come out with docility and stood in meek rows while others, defiant, were hunted like rats from the cellars and lofts of the houses nearby.

"I might as well tell you. I thought it was the worst thing that had ever happened in the world at the time which is why I never said a word to Princess Zoya. It would have killed her. Nowadays, we see and hear horrors every day. What's one more from the past? Then, the rape of a Princess Chornoroukaya was like an attack on a holy object, blasphemy almost. But it wasn't the sacrilege that was the most shocking; I couldn't believe a man could rape a dying woman, bleeding to death before their eyes. And it was *their* eyes. Several of them raped her, there was no doubt." And the rhythmical sawing scream suddenly came into my ears, suppressed until that moment, and I recognized it as the sound of my nightmares.

"But now," Inna said, "I saw what they did here only last week. And these weren't aristocrats, like you, that they were beating and shooting and raping; they were ordinary people of the town, like us." And I saw then how she made an exception of me, because she brought me up; but in her mind an attack on aristocrats was understandable, they were people apart, but ordinary people should not do such things to one another. And I saw too that it just depends where you draw the line; those on the other side of it can be killed and raped with a good conscience.

At some stage, perhaps even before they began to ransack the house and before they murdered my parents, the attackers had set fire to one wing which, built of wood, had burned quickly. The flaming roof woke those few servants who still lived with us. (I say few, of course, in comparison with the numbers that used to be employed in the old days. There must still have been some forty people in residence even in the depleted days of 1918.) They were fully occupied in trying to control the fire and, very sensibly, made no attempt to stop the attackers who ran off into the forest. It was only after dawn, when the fire had burned itself out, that the extent of the devastation of another kind was revealed in the main house. It was assumed that I, too, had been killed with my parents and it was not until some hours later still that I was discovered in my mother's sitting room. The place had been looted, the furniture smashed in the joy of destruction and in a fierce and unsystematic search for valuables. My cradle had been turned over and I had been captured within, unnoticed by the raiders. I wonder if I crouched behind the bars, watching my mother repeatedly raped, bleeding to death, listening to her cries and groans. Did I cry and wail too, or, muffled in my overturned bedclothes, did I sleep through it all? I have no memory of the events I witnessed. It is as though it happened to someone else. And it did happen to someone else. It is that child, a witness of other horrors, whose cries of terror, stifled, never uttered, that I have heard for fifty years, not my own.

I was found in the daylight by the distraught Inna and the other servants, oblivious of the danger I had survived.

Messages were sent urgently to Kornu and Inna and I were transported there to spend the rest of my childhood with Aunt Zoya and Xan.

As I have said, Xan, too, was an orphan and we had a ghoulish rivalry about the nature of our parents' deaths, the more violent the better. Here I scored over him for both my parents had died horribly, while his mother had merely expired of some kind of puerperal fever a few weeks after his birth. However, Xan, a fiercely competitive male supremacist, insisted that his father's death, actively fighting the Reds in the Civil War, counted for more than my parents' passive victim-status as murderees. I would retaliate with my own unremembered experience as witness of events. His father might have died fighting, but Xan had seen nothing of it himself. Superiority on this was close but unclear. We were both, however, leagues ahead of our childhood companion, Nikolai, whose parents were both still alive. He may often have wished his rich and devoted father and mother dead of a thousand bizarre tortures in order to compete with Xan and me. In this he simply foresaw their ends.

The turmoil of the former Russian empire gradually subsided during the early twenties. The Russians had retreated from the western provinces; the occupying German forces, defeated on the western front, returned to their own country, leaving the Slavs and Balts of the intermediate lands to establish their own states. None of this was a matter of rejoicing for my families. In Latvia the great estates of the German and Russian nobility were confiscated and handed over to the peasantry. The old landowners were allowed to retain a house and a farm of a few acres. The ruins of my father's house were taken over by the state and I was assigned a smaller house and some land which had previously been let. I never lived there, for my home was with Aunt Zoya and Xan at Kornu. The Chornorouky lands in Latvia had never been extensive; their riches had come from huge estates in the Ukraine which were now lost for good. Aunt Zoya settled in Latvia because it was close to Russia; she could lead as Russian a life as was possible, but she was not under Bolshevik rule. So we lived an existence salvaged from the past and from the confiscation of the Chornorouky estates, and a very odd household we must have made.

The core of it was Aunt Zoya. Her two brothers, our grandfathers, the Princes Yegor and Yuri Alexandrovich, also stayed with us from time to time. My grandfather, Prince Yuri, spent the winter months in Baden-Baden or Berlin, only coming to Kornu for the summer. He chose German cities because he had had some money in Berlin which had been frozen there at the start of the war in 1914. This, at the time, according to Aunt Zoya, had been regarded as typical of the combination of bad luck and bad judgement that characterized my grandfather, because the sums had been so considerable as to be noticed even in my mother's fabulously wealthy family. But by 1918 Prince Yuri was seen as one of the lucky ones. His money in Germany was nothing in comparison with what the Chornoroukys had lost: the palaces in St Petersburg and Moscow, the summer houses near Pskov, the villas in the Crimea, the endless tracts of the black earth lands of the Ukraine. Nevertheless the money in Germany would permit my grandfather to live still as a man of means. However, Prince Yuri was as unlucky in this as in everything else. All his remaining wealth was wiped out by the terrible inflation of the early 1920s; he watched in astonishment as his money disappeared in value like our lake at Kornu in the December frosts, until the whole expanse of water was transformed into a snow-covered field, as if it had never existed. In 1924, when I was seven years old, my grandfather, ruined for a second time, returned to live with us in Latvia. He was a gently complaining presence in the background of our lives. Aunt Zoya organized the household to give him great respect and to allow him an almost entirely nocturnal regime, spending his waking hours of the night reading by the fire in winter and in the summer sitting on the verandah in the white light that is never completely extinguished at that time of year. Occasionally some real money must have materialized from somewhere, for Prince Yuri would leave once or twice a year to visit friends and fellow exiles in England or France, returning with tales of Yousoupoff luxury in Paris and Vyazemsky penury in London.

Xan's grandfather, Prince Yegor Alexandrovich, to whom Kornu belonged, did not live with us in Latvia, but made his home in London. He came home to us in the summer of 1925 or '26 to die. I remember the two old men sitting on the verandah, dressed in immaculate suits of white duck or cream linen with waistcoats and bow ties, playing chess with a crude wooden set with which Xan and I learned the game. They talked and talked, drinking glasses of tea and eating redcurrant jam with spoons. They would go over the events of the last decade, what he, or she, or they should have done to fend off the catastrophe that had overwhelmed them all. If only at that moment the Tsar had appointed X, or sacked Y; if a certain policy had been abandoned earlier, or another adopted sooner. If only the Tsaritsa had not been so religious, nor the Tsarevich so ill. If only, if only...The alternative worlds proliferated indefinitely in their talk of what might have been.

At that time, just before he died, Prince Yegor wrote the note about his English will, which he gave to Aunt Zoya, who told Xan about it in the summer of 1940, just before she died. Xan mentioned it to me, casually, by chance, one afternoon, lying in the undergrowth in the forest when I visited him in hiding in the woodcutters' hut. And so the last remnants of the Chornorouky fortune reached me in England after the war. With what Prince Yegor left me I bought Asshe House. I chose it carefully; it was old and beautiful, but not grand, the house of a bourgeois in a small provincial town, not the home of an aristocrat.

As a child, I knew we were poor. I didn't look too closely into the question of wealth; I simply knew that there were very many things to be had for money and money was what we lacked, although the farm provided us with all that the household of some twenty persons needed. Aunt Zoya worked ceaselessly to bottle, to pickle, to preserve, to smoke, to salt our own produce so that there was always a satisfying array on the shelves behind the locked doors of the storerooms. But there was very little in the way of cash. Nikolai, in contrast, was rich. During the summer holidays he lived in a large modern house near the village; his father rented my property at Jamala and many other farms, taking all the milk and butter, eggs and wheat to sell in Riga where he owned houses, which he let to the people who flooded in from the countryside. Nikolai had pocket money and could afford books and coloured pencils and little pads of paper made in England from the stationers on Marijas iela in Riga, things that Xan and I craved for but could never hope to purchase.

Xan and I were brought up by the old who had known the Golden Age, who had witnessed the Fall and who had been ejected from Paradise. The assumptions on which our lives were based were that the good days, the great days, were over. *Everything Gets Worse.* This was the fundamental law of life, a scientific principle, which had been empirically tested. We heard only obliquely about the magnificence of the past, for the old men did not speak to us about their palaces and their wealth. Aunt Zoya told her tales, which were like fairy stories, with the same indirect relationship with reality. They taught us about our family and our past, about human relations, love and betrayal, but they said nothing about the future, about how we were to live, Xan and I, when we grew up. We knew there was a world beyond Latvia, a world where power and fortune lay. The message from Aunt Zoya and the Princes was that it was not for us. We were dodos, young dodos, unfitted for the new world that had been born out of the war; indeed, they implied that our being unfitted for the modern world was a sign of moral worth, for it was a world of random violence, inhuman cruelty and arbitrary intolerance, without order, faith, reason or feeling.

For Xan this induced a fascination with the Bolsheviks which he had to hide from Aunt Zoya.

"There has to be a reason for their victory," he would

say. "It's not a question of if the Tsar had done this or that or if some tiny thing had been different. Russia was a dodo; the whole empire was doomed. It couldn't go on. The communists could see what was happening. They have the future with them." He liked to read about communist achievements in Russia, the building of factories, the creation of the Metro, the Stakhanovite overfulfilment of the production targets. Photographs in months-old magazines which we sometimes saw, showed rhythmic views of factory chimneys, pumping machinery, railway lines. Xan admired all that. I could not share his admiration, though I loved him above everyone, for I was afraid. I accepted the old people's belief that there was no hope for us in the new world. We had to avoid attracting attention in order to be allowed to live at all.

I have to say that, although I knew we had been ejected from Paradise, wrongfully too, I thought we had not ended up in too dreadful a place. Of course, I had never known the true golden age; yet Kornu in the twenties seemed like heaven to me. The house, originally a hunting lodge in the forest, was large and rambling, yet, because it was low, of wooden construction, it appeared simple and unpretentious. Standing on a little hill, it faced south and a long verandah ran the whole of its length, looking out over the lake below to the forest beyond. Through the trees could be seen the tip of the onion-domed church built by the Orthodox Chornoroukys. Its gilding was now blackened and damp mottled the paintings on the iconostasis within. Yet it still retained a gaudy exoticism in comparison with the sober white churches of the Protestant Latvians. My ideal landscape has always been that flat northern plain with its low horizons and huge overarching sky, and at one's back the forests of birch and larch. Xan and I rode, walked, cycled for miles around Kornu. We bathed in the lake in the heavy afternoons of summer, swimming, weightless, in a blue globe of sky and water. We punted among the bulrushes at dawn in the spring, watching the birds through a heavy pair of German field glasses, passed back and forth between us. We built snow houses in winter, carefully forming bricks to create large structures that would endure from Christmas to March, a period when the temperature never rose above freezing, even during the still, clear days of February when the sun shone fiercely and we would take off our jackets and tie them round our waists, radiating the heat of energy as we swooped along the forest paths on our skis, leaving behind us the criss-cross tracks of truly fast skiers. Such a different childhood from Hampstead children's, like Ivo and Rosie. They never had the freedom that Xan and I had at Kornu because their parents feared for them. Aunt Zoya never worried about the dangers we might meet: the terrors of the forests, the secret shootings, the murder of children, the hunting of men lay in the future.

The world outside was hostile to our species, so we were lucky to have a little reserve where we could live in peace. I rarely left Kornu. My greatest adventure was to go to Riga to see Xan when he went away to school, to collect him for the holidays, or more sadly, to deliver him for the start of term. I did not attend school, ever. I was taught at home by Aunt Zoya and then by students, very often young graduates, who came to stay with us for shorter or longer periods and who, in return for their board and a very small salary, spent three hours every morning with me in the school room, teaching me anything they cared to impart. I learned languages from Aunt Zoya: I spoke Latvian and Russian and English every day; German and French were rotated by the week. On Monday Aunt Zoya would declare, *"Une semaine française,"* and all conversation at meals would be in that language. A novel would be read, bits of it aloud by the fire or on the verandah, and had to be finished before next Monday's announcement of, *"Deutsch, bitte."* This ramshackle way of learning was not good enough for Xan who was sent to school when he was ten, boarding in the home of Nikolai and his parents and only returning to us at Kornu for Christmas, Easter and the endlessly long summer months with the great celebration of the festival of St John's Day, Xan's birthday.

Nikolai made the third person of our trinity, the necessary balance and counterweight. The relationship between the three of us has, throughout my life, made me think, in spite of everything that happened, that the triangle not the pair is the fundamental grouping. Since I had no parents, the trinity of Alexander, Nikolai and me, Xan, Lai and Genya, was the basic unit of the world, the family, for me. And, like more ordinary families, it was full of tension as well as a source of security. Perhaps the tension held it together.

Nikolai was the son of a Latvian doctor. His great-grandfather had been a peasant, not much more than a serf, on the Chornorouky estate, a fact of which Nikolai's father made no secret, of which he was proud. His son had become rich through the farming of sugar beet, buying land, building sugar mills, exporting the sugar to western Europe out of the port of Riga. He had diversified into timber and other products and had established himself in fine style in Riga, in a grand new house. Nikolai's father was educated, first at St Petersburg University and then in Paris. The grandfather was a peasant; the father was a businessman; the son was to be a scholar and administrator. However, he chose medicine, not law, as his subject and when he set up his plate in Riga, he became a fashionable doctor whose large clinic had two doors: at one entered the comfortable Latvian bourgeoisie, who paid for those entering the other door, the peasants and working people of the town. Nikolai's parents were Latvian nationalists, hostile both to the Baltic nobility, such as my father's family, and to the Russians like the Chornoroukys. They were the winners in the break up of the empire, where Alexander and I were the losers.

Nikolai was brought up to speak Russian and German as well as Latvian; with us he insisted on speaking his own language which remained always the one we spoke naturally among ourselves. It began when we were very little. Then we spoke Latvian to him in the same way that we spoke

Latvian to the servants, because he spoke nothing else. Later on, it became one of the ways in which he maintained his torsion on the strings that bound us together. Although he knew our languages, he made us speak his. Lai needed to exert his power where he could because it was acknowledged between the three of us that Xan was our leader. His dominance was, in the first place, physical. He was tall and slim, dark-haired and grey-eyed, a handsome boy. He ran faster than we did; he climbed higher in the trees, swam farther; he was fearless, where I was timid and Lai reasonable, in the face of risk. He maintained his leadership through personality as well as strength. He had a charm that could win round the most obdurate of adults and it was exercised ruthlessly over Lai and me. Xan's displeasure was a real threat. On the whole, however, Lai and I were de-voted subordinates, each of us recognizing our place in the natural order of things. Lai's characteristics, overshadowed by Xan's, were those of persistence and endurance. They were borne out by his appearance. He was stocky with a round skull which seemed bald when he was small because his hair was so silvery fair. Later it thickened into a pile of straight fine gold which grew into a long fringe during the summer months and from under which peered light blue, frowning eyes.

I'm talking a lot about who we were and what we looked like. What did all that matter to three children growing up on an isolated smallholding in one of the remotest corners of Europe? A great deal. We did not articulate any of these things, but everything I have tried to express was known to us, our relative social, racial and financial positions, our individual appearance and character and each element was a factor in the play, the tension, between us. If Xan was the leader, Lai was the best friend, Sir Lancelot, the loyal lieutenant; I, of course, was the one, younger, female, they could both feel superior to. I heard their complaints and praise of the other. I sustained them both. My loyalty was one of the spoils that had to be shared, justly, though not evenly. Nikolai did not claim equality with

Xan, yet he knew his worth and demanded his due. The trouble came when what Lai thought was his right was more than Xan was prepared to give.

When I saw Rosie and Xenia in battle on Sunday I suddenly recalled Xan and Lai, as I have not remembered them for years and years. I remembered the act of independence that precipitated everything.

Nikolai and I made a secret expedition without Xan, creeping out of the house in the siesta hour when we were supposed to be resting on our beds. It was done wilfully, that is we knew that Xan would resent it, although we did not know how deeply. It was not much as a rebellion. We walked through the forest that stretched for kilometres behind the house. The strong summer sunshine was filtered through the green cover of birch and pine into a pure greenish light. We had no particular purpose and wandered along the woodcutters' rides, sometimes wading into the thin undergrowth to investigate something that attracted our attention. Crouched under the bracken, we enjoyed the sensation of being hidden from Aunt Zoya, the maids and from Xan, too. Finally we crept back to the house for tea, carrying with us a handkerchief of myrtles and wild strawberries to placate Xan's displeasure. We were never to do it again because Xan's revenge was so terrible. And from his point of view it was right, for we might well have made a habit of it, if he had not punished us so dreadfully. We found that a companionship of equals is peaceful and happy; there was none of the fierce competition, the striving for supremacy, that characterized our games with Xan. When we returned, Xan said nothing and we thought at first we had escaped without reproach, that what we had done was not so bad after all.

In the summer we used to bathe in the lake below the house. It had been created originally as an ornamental lake by the damming of the river and was part of the *parc anglais* laid out by some unhappy Chornorouky princess, abandoned at Kornu at the end of the eighteenth century. By the early thirties everything was neglected. Reeds grew all round the edge of the lake and the little temple which had served as a landing stage for the voyage to Cythera was marooned among the bulrushes. There was a sinuous, wooden jetty projecting into the water used as a diving board and bathing raft. We were sitting there after our swim the following evening when Xan began to taunt Lai. His mockery played on all Lai's characteristics that we, with unanimous and arbitrary certainty, rated lower than their counterparts in Xan: his being Latvian, non-noble, shorter, slower of speech and thought. Even as I sat listening, shamed and horrified, I admired the cleverness of Xan's punishment. I realized at once that he had chosen deliberately to avenge himself on Lai in this way. The two boys could have fought one another in the woods, when I was not there, but that would have been no good. The whole point was to humiliate the victim in front of a witness who, by seeing and saying nothing, becomes the accomplice: shamed like the victim, implicated like the bully.

What Xan said was true, but wrong and cruel and I knew it to be wrong and I said nothing and I did nothing. Psychological violence is not worse than physical violence, I found that out later. Nothing, nothing compares with real pain, but the effect of psychological cruelty lasts longer. You forget physical pain; it is impossible to recall the excruciating suffering of the body, but mental cruelty you never forget. I suffered with Lai and I was joined in guilt with Xan.

Nikolai did not resist; he seemed to accept that what Xan was doing was necessary. He let him finish speaking, then he dived into the water and swam away. He left his clothes and did not come back. I gathered them up and took them home with me. And next time we met nobody spoke of what had happened. Each of us thought the others had forgotten. But none of us ever forgot.

Part Five

ZITA

Chapter Thirteen

Who was Eddie Cresacre? The image of the dome of a skull lying under its blanket of clay, gazing through its blank eye sockets at the roots of the roses had imprinted itself on Zita's imagination. Now that she had been told of a real child she pictured the digging of the grave, the spade slicing into the soil like a knife into meat, the placing of the boy's body in the grave, tenderly, his limbs geometrically aligned, the heaping of stones and earth on his chest. She was sufficiently self-aware to observe that her interest was not entirely rational, in the same way that Stevens' interest seemed more intense than the circumstances warranted. She could no more account for it in herself than in him, and made less effort to do so.

When she went to see Yevgenia that evening to warn her to expect a visit from the police, she found her sitting in her customary wing chair, one of her Black Russian cigarettes in her bent fingers. Zita noticed the tiny tape recorder that Lucia had bought for her lying on the table beside her with her cigarette packet, spectacles, books and note pad, seemingly now one of the items necessary to her daily existence. She looked old and ill, more haggard than usual.

"Is your hip very bad today?" she asked sympathetically.

"My hip? No. No worse than usual. I rattle with all the pills Dr Flowers gives me. One doesn't die any more, as people used to do, of violence or disease; one just rusts away. All the moving and non-moving parts slowly seize up. Terrible process. No, no, I am very well, my dear, and you?"

Zita sat down without bothering to define her state of health.

"I've made a start on recording the past," Yevgenia said. "I still can't decide whether it is a good thing to do or not. All I know is that now I can't help it. It is very painful, at times, remembering what I had forgotten. I marvel at what it is possible to forget, moments of amazing happiness and of the most dreadful pain which I have not thought of for years, not allowed myself to think of. So when they come back, you relive them twice, all the emotion, the horror and the joy of the first time, but with an added element that can only be a sort of intensifier, that comes from having survived, a sadness that the love could not last and a relief that the pain finally ended. So I escaped the first time, but now I can't escape."

"It was about the past that I wanted to talk to you." They were still speaking in Russian. "I wanted to ask you about a child; there was a child who disappeared..."

Yevgenia, shaking her head, interrupted. "No, no," she said. "No."

"I wondered if you could remember about him. It was a little boy..."

"No." Yevgenia repeated, loudly, persistently. She was scrabbling around on her side table, knocking a paperback book and some pencils to the floor. Zita bent down to collect the fallen items. "I haven't got there yet. It'll come back eventually. I've spent all this time not thinking about it."

Zita rearranged the table. "What'll come back?" she asked. "What happened?"

Yevgenia had resumed control. "Remembering a past as long and horrible as mine is what I imagine undergoing analysis must be like. Such terrible things come out. I wake in the night with sudden new memories of how things were, why things happened."

Zita tried again. This time she did not use Russian. "The child who disappeared in 1960, Eddie Cresacre was his name. Do you remember anything about him?"

Yevgenia looked at her rather oddly. Finally, she said, in English, "In 1960, 1960. What happened in 1960?"

"Well, I was born," Zita said frivolously.

"As long ago as that? Yes, that's right. Ivo was a baby. Marcus was married to poor Susie. I have to mark the years in England with events like the grandchildren's age or where we went on holiday, because for Kenward and me, life was so...not monotonous, so even, that's it, even. In 1960, a child disappeared? Who is this child, Zita, I don't follow what you're talking about."

Zita started again, by explaining that she had been to see the police about the skeleton in the garden of Asshe House. "The man I spoke to, a Superintendent Stevens, seemed to think there might be some connexion with a child who disappeared in 1960. He was called Eddie Cresacre, apparently, seven years old, and lived in a cottage on Ormond Street. He wants to come to see you about it."

Yevgenia considered for a while. "I do remember. I knew Eddie Cresacre. It was so upsetting for everyone, a child vanishing into thin air in a little town like Broad Woodham. There was a terrible outcry. The local paper was very excited about it, naturally. I'd forgotten that his body was never found." Her tone of detached reminiscence suddenly sharpened. "How could the child's body have got into our garden? What nonsense." She was now making a strong effort of recall. "The man who did it, I forget his name now, how could he have got in? The idea's absurd."

"The man who did it? You mean they found the abductor, but not the child?"

"Yes, didn't he tell you? It comes back to me now. There was tremendous pressure on the police to find the child and the murderer (we all assumed it was murder), and eventually they arrested someone, who then confessed. There was lots of circumstantial evidence, I suppose, and finally the confession. But the body was never found. It was one of the things that aroused great hostility towards the accused man, that he wouldn't reveal what he had done with the body."

As Zita listened, she reassessed her interview with Stevens which became even more incomprehensible. Why had he not mentioned the murderer? Why had he implied that the mystery of the child's disappearance was unsolved? She recognized now that his air had been vaguely menacing, as if suggesting that she and her clients knew something which they would wish to hide and that he had the means of knowing what it was, if they did not reveal it themselves.

"What happened to the murderer?" she asked.

"Petre," Yevgenia replied. "That was his name, Petre. He was tried, of course. I seem to remember Kenward saying that the evidence against him was rather weak, but that he never stood a chance after the way he behaved. About three times he said that the child's body was hidden in a certain place and great searches were made and nothing was found. You can imagine what that must have been like for the parents. I remember them now. I remember the little boy, too. They were Kenward's patients, though I don't think he knew them well; they were obviously a healthy family. And then afterwards they moved away from the town. Who could blame them for wanting to escape such memories? The death of a child is the most awful loss there can be, one that can never be filled. And it's not just the loss. There is the constant wish that you could have been taken instead. If only you had not failed in your care, if only you could have exchanged your life for his. You live with it for ever and ever."

Zita was thinking of Tom's fragile babyhood, the innumerable infections, the ambulance screaming its way to the hospital. She had fought for him and fought against herself, for the thought had often intruded, what if he died?

"And what happened?" she asked.

"He was tried. I said that, didn't I? I think his defence must have been insanity, for he was put into Broadmoor."

"He could still be there."

Yevgenia looked surprised at this, as though she did not welcome the past still having a living presence. "I suppose he could. What age would he have been? Not old, not young, and it's more than thirty years ago. Well, I am still here, so he could be too."

"Do you remember anything about the police enquiry? I don't mean local talk or newspaper articles. I mean, did the police interview you?"

"Well, you know, they did. I imagine they interviewed everyone. I remember it was very unpleasant. I had ideas in those days, like a foreigner, about British justice and the British bobby and these people had a way of making you feel guilty from the start. It was a horrible shock. It reminded me of the war, the terror of the police, the plain clothes ones, the Gestapo or the NKVD, the knock on the door in the night." She returned abruptly to the present. "So how does he think this Petre got into our garden and dug up the lawn and buried the child there without our knowing?" Her voice was high, almost petulant, with indignation.

"I agree," said Zita. "It does all seem a bit odd. And when were the roses put in? You said, 'dig up the lawn'."

"Kenward developed a passion for old roses. But that was quite late on, after he retired, so it would have been in 1970 or after. Charles de Mills, Tuscany Superb, Reine des Violettes. He loved all those very dark red and purplish roses. But when you plant a rose bed you don't dig four feet down. You dig to a spade's depth and you mix in lots of well-rotted horse manure. It's nonsense," she said with more force. "It can't be that child."

Zita walked back to her own house. On the face of it, Yevgenia must be right; but she was regretful that she had demolished Stevens' strange hypothesis. She had seen the story of Eddie Cresacre as a threat; however, if Eddie Cresacre's murderer had been found and convicted, the identification of his body as the one in the garden, however inexplicably it got there, would tidy up the problem of the skeleton, a problem that Stevens had seemed very eager to make as annoying as possible. If it were Eddie Cresacre, tests of his DNA or comparison of photographs of the child and the skull would show this. The conversation with Yevgenia had made her less concerned; the question that remained was why Stevens was so determined to make a link between Eddie Cresacre and Asshe House. He was playing a game, she was now sure of that, and only revealed as much of what he knew as he wanted, to achieve the effects that he desired.

Part Six

ZITA

Chapter Fourteen

Zita awoke to thoughts of Oliver, a second before she remembered there was no Oliver. This trick played by her mind, the minuscule but definable splinter of time which it took for the present to catch up with the past, the delay in recalling what she did not want to believe, still happened occasionally. The past ran its continuing existence, somewhere else, beyond her control.

She rolled onto her back and, with her eyes still closed, she rehearsed his faults. He was not a generous man. Although he was good at finding little treats for himself—a second-hand book, a new silk tie with spots on it, a good bottle of wine—he rarely gave presents. He was impatient and easily bored and had neither the politeness nor the self-discipline to appear interested when he was not, so he often went to sleep at other people's dinner parties, leaving his wives to excuse and explain. He had the unpleasing habit of cleaning his ears with his finger tip as he read the paper at breakfast. But it was no good. No connexion flew between the disagreeable facts she could list about him and her feelings for him.

She could hear sounds from next door that showed that Tom was awake; uneven rattling suggested that he was lying in frustration, waiting for her to get him up. He took after his father in his impatience, she thought. She sat up in bed and called, "I'm coming, Tom." Her bedside clock read 6.15.

She had to spend the day in London, a chore which she

always mitigated with a visit to a shoe shop. The thought of returning on the crowded evening train with the cords of a shoe bag in her hand made the programme of meetings and visits not just more bearable, but something to desire. There was the pleasure of planning to which shop she would order her taxi after her last meeting, for, unfortunately, interesting shoe shops are not found around the Old Bailey or the Inns of Court. Whether it would be Wigmore Street or Old Church Street or Amwell Street, she sometimes did not decide until the moment that she slammed the taxi door and leaned forward to instruct the driver. However, on this day, as she sat in her aisle seat on the 8.32 from Broad Woodham to Victoria and took her day's programme out of her briefcase, she thought of Reskimer. It was an ideal opportunity to see him, if he were free in the afternoon. She was determined to shadow Stevens' enquiry, to understand what he was doing. If Reskimer could show without doubt that the skeleton was more than fifty years old, he would free Yevgenia from all concern and Stevens, too, presumably. The police could not be in the business of solving ancient crimes; they had enough unsolved in the present.

During the morning, between her first and second appointments, she telephoned the archaeology department and asked for Professor Reskimer. She waited for the inevitable disappointment of his not being there and so was surprised when a voice, younger than she expected for a professor's, with a faint Scottish burr, answered. She explained who she was and her interest in the Broad Woodham skeleton.

"There's a terrible lot of impatience about this burial," he said. "I never thought the law was renowned for its haste; it seems that archaeology moves even more slowly. I haven't much to say, but come by all means, if you're here and you want to. I'm teaching until three thirty; then I've got someone else. So shall we say five? That's not too late for you?"

Zita thanked him and accepted the suggested time. She had hoped to see him in mid-afternoon. She would have to ring Lynne and warn her she would be late. But she might now fit in a shoe shop after all. She thought, later, that her interviews that afternoon were affected by the fact that her lunch meeting finished promptly and, faced with a two-and-a-half-hour interval, she had set off to Wigmore Street with a pair of suede court shoes, discreet and elegant, in mind. When she left the shop an hour later, she was carrying a pair of sandals which consisted of not much more than a thin sole, a high heel and a couple of fine strands of brilliant gold patent leather. They had cost a lot for so little; not much, though, for so much daring and beauty and quite enough to leave her feeling reckless.

She was outside Reskimer's door thirty minutes early. There was nowhere to sit; no sign of a secretary's office and no voices from within to indicate the continuation of his previous appointment. She knocked and a voice called, "Come." She opened the door to find herself in a poky modern office, of which one side was made of glass and the other of books.

"Ah," he said as she entered, "it's you."

"Yes, I'm a bit early. Would you like me to wait?"

"No, no, on the contrary, I'm very glad you're here. I didn't know, when you knocked, whether you were the last appointment late or the next early. He's had his chance, now you're here."

Zita threaded her way between the columns of books and papers to the chair opposite the desk and sat down facing the professor. He was older than his voice, by a good ten years or so. He had thick grey hair and a determined, muscular face, that gave no impression of flabbiness.

"And what can I do for *you?*" he asked. Zita noted the odd stress, as if he were contrasting her with someone else. She began to reiterate who she was, when he interrupted her.

"Yes, it's about the skeleton in the Broad Woodham garden." He lifted a folder which lay in front of him already open. "I don't have so many cases of modern bodies from the police that I confuse them."

"Is it a modern body?" Zita asked.

"Modern in my terms. My current interest is Caucasian burials of the fifth century BC, so this looks like yesterday to me."

"The dating is for me the crucial thing. Dr Pigot was extremely vague about how old the remains were. That they were less than a hundred years old was as much as he would say. He suggested that you might be able to be more accurate."

"He's passing the buck. We haven't run many tests yet. As I understand it, the police are approaching it from the other end, which is probably easier to deal with, that is, they are going to give us some data and ask if it fits. It's much harder to begin with the bones and work out from there."

"According to Pigot, it is impossible to tell the age of the child, or its sex or how long it has been dead with any certainty, all completely fundamental questions. Can archaeology help?"

"He's exaggerating a bit. A very cautious man, Dr Pigot. There's DNA testing; we can do that and so can the Metropolitan Police laboratory. If we have a relative, we can compare his DNA with that of the skeleton and say whether the bones belong to a member of the family and, even if the result is negative, we can discover whether the Y chromosome is present. If so, we have a girl, and from that other things will follow. Not with certainty, but with some statistical probability."

"And what about the time elapsed since death?" Zita persisted. "Can carbon dating help?"

"You lawyers want everything so cut and dried," Reskimer grumbled. "You probably want me to give you the day of the week and the phase of the moon when the child died and I can't do it. We can't establish dates, not unless we have an inscription or something like that to anchor us. We can only produce time sequences, runs of years, cycles of seasons, which we have to tether somewhere to fix them to human time. The sorts of inscriptions we are looking for in this case are not carvings in stone; we are hoping for a wrapping paper or a tin can, a shoe print, a zipper stud which by the date of manufacture of the artefact would give us a fix, to which we could tie things like the rate of growth of the rose trees."

"And carbon dating?"

"Too recent, too wide. It could say whether it was over seventy to a hundred years old, but it would give us a spread as wide as our guess work."

"Your guess would be?"

"Fifty to sixty years."

Zita felt a lightening of her spirits; the sandals had been a good omen. "The police think thirty to thirty-five."

"And it may be the difference between the two, say forty to forty-five. Unless we have something to give us a co-relative, we have no way of telling."

"Did you come across anything in the area around the grave, anything to help with the dating?"

"We may have. I'll show you. There may have been more in the gravefill, but most of the soil from the upper levels had gone. If we had excavated the grave ourselves we could have done something by looking at the root growth. The way plants have grown into graves can be useful for dating. But the builders had done all that for us. We got the last few barrow loads of soil out of the skip and the students sieved it. They retrieved a number of items and we're examining them now, but whether they relate to the body is another question."

"What sorts of things?"

"Pieces of metal, wood, cloth. A link will be very hard to make. A garden of a house which is at least three hundred years old, on a site which may have been in continuous occupation for a thousand years, it's a midden tip. Chicken bones, oyster shells, kitchen rags, old implements. If you dig it out, you'll find the lot. Now where is it?" Amid the apparent chaos, Reskimer could find the photograph without effort. It was a black and white print and showed a clod of earth into which a coarse basket-weave pattern was etched.

"This came from the rubble removed by the workmen earlier on the morning of the find. It could be the print of some unrelated rag or it could be the fabric of what the child was wearing."

Zita, the clothes lover, looked at it blankly. "Does it help?"

"Not much, I admit. We'll be able to tell you something about the fabric, the number of threads to the inch on warp and weft, if anyone's interested."

She could not think this information would advance either her or Stevens.

"And then there's these." Reskimer opened a little plastic bag and tipped two small round objects onto his palm. "What would you say these were?" He handed them to Zita who took them curiously.

"They're buttons surely?" They were round, black, domed, and on the flat underside of each one was riveted a metal eye.

"Yes, one would say so. They were found under the ribs on the left side. It's odd that there's only two of them. I don't know many garments that have only two buttons."

"A polo shirt?" Zita suggested.

He shrugged. "Well, I've never worn a polo shirt with this sort of button on it. I've set a student to investigating when and where they might have been made, assuming they are of English manufacture of about fifty years ago. A hopeless task, but systematic attention to detail is the foundation of good archaeology." He looked at his watch. "I'm glad you were early." He took back the buttons. "It means I can get home sooner than I hoped." He was already pushing back his chair. "It's the dating that concerns you mostly, if I've understood you right. Give me a ring next week sometime and I'll let you know if we've come up with anything more definite." He ushered Zita out of his office, letting her step over the obstructing piles of books and reach the door, before placing his own large feet in the same spaces. He locked the door behind them and shook hands hastily.

"I'll just catch the 5.54 if I run," he said and set off at a jog down the corridor. Zita watched him punch the lift button. The door opened immediately and he stepped in, calling for her to hurry, but was immediately carried away, disappearing behind the scissoring doors. She waited for the return of the lift, touched the call button a second time, at last abandoning her wait and taking the staircase. As she descended, she heard someone coming up fast with laboured breathing. She reached a landing and, as she turned to make the next stage of her descent, she encountered Stevens.

They passed one another, and each had taken the hand rail of the next section of stairway when they simultaneously swung round. Stevens' surprise was greater. Zita knew at once that he was going to see Reskimer and was the missed appointment preceding hers. They stared at one another for a moment, Stevens' expression now registering suspicion as well as astonishment.

"He's left," Zita said, trying to conceal her amusement. "He was obviously dying to get home. You just missed him in the lift."

"Bloody British Rail," Stevens said. "The train was twenty minutes late and then we sat outside Victoria for half an hour. Would you believe it."

"Yes," said Zita. "The rule is: always take a book and the earlier train."

"Ach." He did not appreciate good advice. "Fine, if you have the time to live your life like that." He hesitated, as if he suspected that Zita might be trying to prevent his meeting Reskimer, then rejected the idea. He moved alongside her.

"Going back to Woodham now?"

"Yes."

"There's a train at 6.14. Would you like to share a taxi?"

Zita had not expected such a proposal. "OK, we might just make it."

In the taxi they sat in silence. She felt she could almost hear the clockwork of his brain working, calculating what to ask her and when. At Victoria, he said, "You've got a ticket, I hope," as he banged the taxi door. They both thrust money at the driver, who was left with a double fare as they galloped onto the concourse towards platform fifteen. The barrier was down and the board above the entrance said succinctly, *1814 cancelled.*

"The 6.44 is the next," said Stevens, as they looked disconsolately at the empty platform. "We'll have a drink." Zita was thinking about Lynne and Tom. Now that they were fellow victims of British Rail, she felt more sympathetically towards Stevens. They queued together at the station buffet, placing their cups of tea on a shared tray.

"What did he have to say, Reskimer?" he asked when they had settled at the table Zita had spotted.

She summarized; she could see that he was not chiefly concerned with what she said. He could check everything with one telephone call. It was her motives, not her report, which were exercising him. He poured two sachets of white sugar into his cup and stirred it thoughtfully, barely paying attention to what she was saying. When she had finished speaking, she picked up her cup and sipped the lukewarm, faintly bitter tea. Stevens took a gulp and made a faint grimace.

"She's worried, is she?"

"Who is?"

"Mrs Loftus. You're acting for her presumably."

Zita was uncomfortable; she had not expected him to be so blunt, to go immediately for her weak point, the fact that she was acting on her own initiative, on the pretext of her clients' interest.

"No," she said precisely, setting down her cup in the circular indentation in the centre of the saucer. It was too small and swam uneasily in its pond. "If you think I am acting on specific instructions from Naomi Loftus, you're wrong. I have received only the most general watching brief from the owners of the house. I just happened to be in London on business and had a moment to spare at the end of the afternoon."

"I didn't mean the London Loftuses. I meant the old woman, the Russian."

"No, not for her either."

"So why all this activity? Unusual for a lawyer to display all this unpaid energy."

"Oh, I don't know." Zita was not unused to displays of male rudeness and had trained her temper. "A duty of care, you might say. It's disagreeable for the Loftuses to have a corpse discovered on their property, especially when the police insist that it is not, as it seems to me, well over half a century old, but a recent case."

"We've been through this already. I have a duty, too, and that body is certainly recent enough for the killer still to be alive."

Zita went onto the attack. "My question to you is, why all this activity by the police when you've got the murderer already? Petre was arrested and convicted."

"Convicted? Who told you he was convicted?"

"Wasn't he?"

"No, he was not, not for Cresacre." Stevens was oddly triumphant, as if he had scored her off in some way. She could not understand why he, a policeman, should be so pleased by the failure of a prosecution of thirty years ago.

"So what happened?"

He was caressing the bland, hairless skin behind his ears. She could not see, even at such close quarters, any sign of hair regrowth. Perhaps he didn't shave his skull after all. "Petre was a nutter. He was picked up quite early on and eventually he was persuaded to confess, but he couldn't find the body. The case was a real shambles. Two children disappeared that year, Eddie Cresacre in October and Peter Gilling earlier, in about March. Petre confessed to that one too. We never found his body either, but for that case there was enough circumstantial evidence which, along with the confession, convicted him."

"The murderer's been brought to justice, whatever you think about the matter. The case is closed."

"There's a lawyer speaking. We need to know; to get things straight. If this body is Eddie Cresacre's it'll make an enormous difference to his family. They'll at last know where he is. They can give his remains a proper burial. They can have a focus for their grief after thirty years. That means something, you know."

What he said was correct, Zita acknowledged to herself.

But it just did not ring true. It came out too pat, as if he had it prepared, ready for the press. She picked up her cup again and held it in front of her, like a shield.

"You were involved in the Eddie Cresacre case, weren't you," she said. It was a statement, not a question. "A young constable on your first murder case. Your feelings got involved; something happened to churn your stomach, which you never forgot."

Stevens' whole head turned crimson with rage, the colour suffusing the back of his neck and his skull. "Keep your cod psychology for your clients and don't apply it to me," he said furiously. "What do you know about people's feelings? It is a question of duty; there are no feelings involved."

Zita watched him calmly, raising her cup with both hands in front of her mouth. It was amazing, she thought; couldn't he see the contradiction between what he said and the way he said it? "Sorry, sorry." Her tone was not apologetic.

He swigged the dregs of his tea, unmollified.

"Does that mean you weren't in on the Cresacre case in 1960?"

He got up abruptly. "The train leaves in four minutes," he said, picking up his leather folder from the table. Zita stood up more slowly and followed him out of the buffet.

They got onto the train together. Zita was glad to find it crowded, so they would be forced to sit separately. In the end, they found two places on either side of the aisle. She sat facing the engine, he the rear of the train. She put her new shoes under her seat and her briefcase on her lap. She took out some papers to disguise her wish not to converse. She was interested to see how intensely her dislike was reciprocated. Whereas she had taken some trouble not to give way to her antipathy, he had by now given full rein to his. There was a difference in the sources of their mutual antagonism. She found him physically repulsive and all her liberal instincts told her to resist prejudice based on appearance. She thought briefly of Xenia's crudely expressed opinion at Yevgenia's lunch: no liberal instincts there. Stevens, on the other hand, was not concerned with appearances. It was what she was, not what she looked like, that he loathed. She was an overeducated, affected, patronizing bitch. In which case, there was nothing she could do, no change of appearance or behaviour, that was going to modify his opinion, so she had nothing to lose. It seemed that Stevens had come to the same conclusion about her.

They both got off the train at Broad Woodham and crossed the bridge over the line, not together, not separately, in a gaggle of other passengers. Outside the station he stopped, waiting for her to draw level with him. Most of the returning commuters had flooded past them. They were the last in the entrance to the station. Stevens spoke with suppressed violence.

"You're right," he said. "I expect you're used to that. I worked on that case. I remember it very well. She did it, you know. She killed Eddie Cresacre." He waited for Zita's reaction and whatever her features showed it was evidently enough for him to go on with equal force, "I know she did it and I'm going to get her after all these years. There's no escape from the past. You can tell her that." He walked off down the hill, his trousers rumpled by the gritty breeze that always blows around railway stations.

Zita unlocked her car. He was mad, mad and obsessed. She noticed that her hand was shaking as she fumbled to introduce the key into the ignition. She had meant to phone Lynne from Victoria, but Stevens had distracted her. Her mind was pulled back immediately to thoughts of Tom, anticipating her conversation with Lynne on her arrival. What evidence could there be against Yevgenia that he should, thirty years later, still be convinced of her guilt? She pushed the question to the back of her mind to enable her to greet Tom.

The phone was ringing with so much emphasis as she stepped through her front door that she knew at once that it must be Valentina. She called a greeting to Lynne and picked up the receiver.

"I'm going to Milan for a week," Valentina announced. "I thought I'd better let you know." She was speaking Russian, as she always did now.

Zita who had lived for years without knowing where her mother was, beyond the geographical concept of "America", simply said, *"Da,"* and then, as an afterthought, "Have a good time."

"I was invited to a colloquium there a long time ago." Her mother seemed determined to explain all the details. "But I didn't see how I could fit it in and so I turned it down. Then last week someone showed me the programme and the list of participants. It is not a very big affair or very prestigious, but there are some interesting papers on the list. So, I thought, why not?"

"Well, why not, Mama?" Zita repeated encouragingly. "Though I don't think Milan is very beautiful."

"I'm not going for tourism, Zita."

"No, well, good. It should be fun." She tried to rouse herself to be a better daughter. "So, you'll be back, when? Why not come the weekend after next? Or we could meet in London. Would you like to see a play or an opera?"

"That would be very nice. See what you can arrange, Zi-Zi. You know I like opera best."

Zita, who had not been called Zi-Zi since she was eight and who detested opera, agreed to arrange something and Valentina rang off. It was very wearing having Valentina in England, much more so than she had expected. She could not understand why her mother had wanted to tell her so much, about the papers, the list of participants, the place. Was she lonely in England? Noises from Tom's room indicated that he was still awake and had heard her arrive. She abandoned thoughts of her mother to go to say goodnight to her son.

It was not until she lay in bed that night that she allowed herself to think again of her sporadic conversations with Stevens. Lying there in the dark, she remembered him saying what she had been refusing to acknowledge. Yevgenia had killed Eddie Cresacre.

It was impossible. She could not contemplate a woman, a friend, killing a child. Or even wishing his death. She refused to recall those nights sitting in hospital waiting rooms while Tom-Tom struggled for breath, when the thoughts came, unwilled, what if he died? She put aside those alternative lives that presented themselves, as seductive as a photograph of Oliver, as the temptations of St Anthony. It had reached a stage that more was needed than to watch what was going on. She must resist. Stevens was a man obsessed (why? why?) He was not interested in truth. For some reason that she could not understand, in rejecting Petre, he had fixed on Yevgenia as an alternative. She began to make lists in her head. DNA tests might show that the bones were not those of Eddie Cresacre. Even if they were, Stevens still had plenty of work to prove that Yevgenia had anything to do with them. The tests would take time. The child's relatives would have to be traced, samples taken; extracting DNA from old bones might not be a straightforward procedure. Science, as Professor Reskimer had said about archaeology, moved slowly. In the meantime she could look at alternative explanations. If the bones were as old as she wanted them to be, they must relate to earlier owners, before the war. And Stevens himself, why was he doing this? What lay behind his duty? Or hers?

Part Seven

XENIA

Chapter Fifteen

"**D**arling, you haven't forgotten that we are taking Jean to the opera on Sunday?"

"On Sunday?"

"Yes, it's this weekend. I told you months ago to put it in your diary."

"Ah."

"We'll have to leave early to get to Woodham for lunch, load her into the car and reach Glyndebourne for 4.30. It starts early on a Sunday."

"What are we going to see?"

"*The Queen of Spades.*"

"Ah."

Taking Jean to Glyndebourne was an annual ritual. She had once gone several times a season with her husband; now she was so crippled that the visit took on the nature of a major expedition and, because of that, was a great event in her life.

Naomi and Marcus were eating peaches. Xenia was sitting with them, watching their conversation with a care which only Naomi's lack of self-consciousness could tolerate with ease.

"Such a shame," Naomi was saying, "that I didn't know you would be with us, Xenia, when I ordered the tickets. I should love you to see Glyndebourne. It's so English."

"You could phone to see if there is a returned ticket."

"Of course. I'll try in the morning, when I have a gap. In

any case, Xenia, even if I can't get one why don't you come to Woodham for the day? We can have lunch together and then bring you home in the evening. Lucia may be there, or Zita and her poor little boy. It might be more amusing for you than staying here alone all day."

Xenia acquiesced in the suggestion with the gratitude she always showed. The incoherent rage that had held her in its power, uncontrollably, in her first couple of weeks in London had dissipated somewhat. She still prowled the house, first thing in the morning, reading the letters in Marcus's desk, sniffing the cosmetics on Naomi's dressing table. She still ritually took the three coins from Marcus's bowl. She still, occasionally, made desperate, undiscriminating raids on shops, now having to go farther to avoid those which she had already attacked. Such irresistible events were always followed by the same revulsion, the same retching, the same rapid disposal of the booty, usually in the cupboards of the house in Gayton Street, so that it was enveloped by the Loftuses' possessions, becoming one more item on their inventory. However, these episodes were now much rarer, as the bewilderment that produced them was replaced by a sense of purpose.

The terrible, orderless injustice of life preyed on her. She could not stop thinking of her own brief past and that of her parents: her much-loved mother who had left when she was eight; her father, punished and rejected for no more than being who he was. She thought of the barren grid of tower blocks in the middle of Siberia where she had grown up, a place without beauty, or hope. Why even her detested father should have been condemned to such a life, while Marcus and Naomi and Yevgenia lived surrounded by plenty, she could not begin to understand. She walked around the streets of Hampstead, counting the huge houses, the cars, quantifying affluence; and she watched the bag ladies in their cast-off trainers, no laces, shuffling from bin to bin, scavenging with the grim persistence of the stray dogs in Siberia.

There was no fairness, so it was up to the individual to take what she could for herself: that much was clear. For her, taking what she could did not mean merely three 1p pieces from Marcus's bowl, it meant taking London. She was going to stay; she was never, never going back to Russia. She had seen that here she could be free from the poverty of life in Moscow, from the fear of being returned to Novoleninsk, from the burden of her name, and from the tyranny of the security people. She had fallen into *their* hands (like her father, she could never bring herself to articulate even in her head the acronym, Kay Gay Bay) when she arrived in Moscow. They had seen her fear of return to Siberia and used it to trap and make use of her. She only operated at a very low level: no more than a little reporting on her classmates in the modern languages faculty. Once or twice she had been told to meet a foreign student, to make friends with him or her. Those assignments she had enjoyed; tickets to the theatre or ballet were made available, and she was paid her expenses. Her conscience did not reproach her for what she had done; nonetheless, she hated it. It was a submission to the authorities which she would have preferred not to make. She had not dared to refuse their requests and had to conceal her loathing of them under her habitual willingness. They had given her her reward, enabling her to have her passport, exit visa and hard currency without difficulty. It would be a pleasing irony if they had thereby given her the means to liberate herself for good.

The naivest plan, of simply staying on without papers, followed by most would-be immigrants, she did not entertain. Since she was used to an all-compassing, bureaucratic state, she imagined the authorities had almost supernatural knowledge about her. However, she was convinced that what she wanted was not impossible to achieve and her evidence was the presence of Al within the family. Al was a foreigner, but he lived in London, had a job, was at home here; and he was not merely a foreigner, but a black and eccentric one. It is true that Al now appeared less disturbing than when she had first met him. Indians and Afro-Caribbeans, she had now discovered, were numerous in London. She saw them everywhere. And Al's style of dress, his long hair, his black jeans and T shirt, were also common enough to be an alternative to the grey suit which, to her, signified respectability and power. It was her assumption, made on the basis of her Russian experience, that Marcus must have obtained permission for Al to live in the country. He must be made to do the same for her.

The following evening Naomi reported that she had, miraculously, been successful in her attempt to obtain a returned ticket for the Sunday performance. Xenia had expected nothing less. In Moscow, although seats in the opera were not easy for ordinary people to obtain except by luck or barter, anyone with enough influence or money could always apply to the administrator, who would hand over the tickets that he retained for such a purpose with greater or less readiness, according to the status of the supplicant. Or you just went to the entrance of the Bolshoi Teatr at the beginning of the evening and bought a ticket for dollars. The face value of a ticket in Moscow was minimal, its rarity valued in other ways than by money and it never occurred to Xenia that no influence but an enormous amount of cash had been expended to ensure her company. This ignorance saved her from the regret of thinking what she might have done with the money if she had had it to spend as she liked.

"We'll have to find you something to wear. I'm afraid part of this bizarre ritual, which includes a picnic as well as singing, involves dressing up. We shall have to see if Rosie has something suitable that would fit you."

Naomi had already taken Xenia's appearance in hand. The sight of the Russian girl so out of place at Jean's lunch at Woodham had decided her to intervene. It was an article of her creed that outward appearance was to be ignored. (She had not heard Xenia's disagreement with Rosie on this very subject.) A civilized person would always try to penetrate beneath the surface of another, whether it was crystalline smooth or pebble-dashed, to reach the real character beneath. Yet seeing Xenia so badly dressed, the vile combination of colours, the poor quality material, made her decide that she must be given new clothes. Her own were too large and would only look too clearly like cast offs. Rosie might be persuaded to part, with ill grace, with something from her wardrobe, although Xenia might well refuse to accept such a gift. So Naomi went to The Gap and bought two pairs of jeans, four T shirts, a sweater and a jacket.

When they were presented to Xenia, she seemed overwhelmed by this generosity. She struggled with emotion and embarrassment to express her gratitude. She kept making promises to pay for the new clothes out of her earnings for child-minding. Naomi waved away both the thanks and the repayment and felt herself rewarded by the sight, next day, of Xenia emerging, transformed, from her bathroom which Naomi had stocked with shampoos, soap, deodorants. The skinny jeans and clinging top did not make her into anything glamorous in Naomi's eyes; she looked like a Western teenager, both younger than the Russian Xenia and tougher. Her hair, newly washed, radiated from her head in a huge mane-like halo, surrounding her pale, unmade-up face. She had obviously been studying what she should wear and how she should wear it, even when she was enclosed in her Soviet nylon blouse and skirt. She blushed with pleasure as she skipped down the stairs towards Naomi, and smiled. Naomi was very touched; Xenia looked almost pretty, her eyes were suddenly a very attractive pale blue; the colour of the jeans and sweater had been well chosen.

Marcus, from behind his wife's shoulder had said, "You're a Westerner now, Xeni."

Naomi turned, not having realized that he was behind her.

"It is thanks to Naomi," Xenia had said fervently. "These jeans are wonderful."

"It's marvellous," Naomi remarked, making for her office, "that young people like such practical clothes—jeans and boots and T shirts are their idea of finery. Working jeans, playing jeans, court jeans, it's all you need."

"I cannot say thanks enough," Xenia repeated. "I am so happy with them."

But jeans would not do for Glyndebourne, still less the discarded Russian skirt and cardigan. Xenia, as usual, seemed little concerned about her dress. She had noted something which was of far greater importance to her than the invitation to go to an opera which she had already seen once in Moscow, although she had not admitted as much. It was Marcus who had made the proposal to fulfil Naomi's vague wish that she should be with them. Naomi, after her efforts on the telephone, took the credit and accepted the thanks and seemed to have forgotten that this time the idea was not hers. It might be that this act fell within the compass of Marcus's general benevolence. It might rather have been that he actively wished for her company, which would give him a pleasure that going to the opera with his step-mother and wife would not normally hold for him. Xenia inclined to the second explanation. The conspiracy, into which they had entered when he had discovered her eavesdropping on Naomi and her patients, had not been strengthened or continued in any overt way. Yet Xenia was aware of the interest that she held for him. It was her belief, derived from her life in Siberia and Moscow, that the weak often exaggerate the power of the strong and the strong often do not know the extent of their power. In the past she had used this observation to give her courage for some demand that she knew in theory she had no chance of gaining, and had found that her position was better than she thought and those in power less determined to deny her than she was to gain her ends. The time would come to persuade Marcus of what he had to do and in that persuasion the attraction that he felt for her would play its part. In the meantime, she felt a contented contempt for Naomi who had so much and saw nothing, who gave so generously and understood nothing.

Chapter Sixteen

The problem of what Xenia should wear at Glyndebourne, a matter which concerned Xenia herself not at all, was solved by Naomi, who early one evening made a rare visit to the basement and returned half an hour later with a short plain black linen dress belonging to Rosie.

"With a belt and some earrings it will be ravishing," she said, laying the garment over the back of a chair for Xenia and Marcus to admire. Xenia thanked and praised and then praised and thanked once again, Naomi in person and Rosie *in absentia*. Naomi accepted for both of them with equal grace, failing to mention that Rosie had not been at home and that Al, with an unusual show of interest, had helped her choose something from Rosie's wardrobe. He had declared that he was sure she would not mind, had opened cupboard doors, selected several possibilities and urged the final choice on Naomi. She had been glad of his co-operation. Kindness fully justified what she was doing, she was sure, and it was bad luck that Rosie was not there to share in the act of benevolence. Al's help diluted her unease that Rosie might not like what was being done on her behalf.

Naomi did not much like opera. She was tone deaf and could only recognize the most obvious and often repeated melodies, so she always greatly enjoyed Glyndebourne where the drive, the company of friends, food in the form of a messy and time-consuming picnic composed so considerable a proportion of the performance that the music, like her guilt about the dress, was diluted. Taking Xenia as well as Jean doubled the pleasure.

Xenia accepted the dress as she accepted everything, displaying the emotions that were expected of her and suppressing her own confused resentment. She controlled impulses to screw the linen slip into a ball and thrust it into a rubbish bag, and took a perverse pleasure instead in wearing Rosie's dress and taking Rosie's place with Rosie's parents and grandmother. She went through her part for the evening feeling as if she were disembodied, watching what she was doing. From the outside she fitted in as perfectly as the dress fitted her; no one looking at their group, seated at Yevgenia's feet on a rug by the ha-ha, would have known she was an impostor, an audience of the performance of the English at the opera. Her distanced self both rejected what she saw and desired it all at once. She wanted it for herself, of right, so she could refuse it, and not have to accept and admire without choice.

Naomi, who was wearing a trailing dress of several different tones of pink, looped up her shawl and handed Yevgenia a glass of champagne that Marcus had just poured. They had half an hour before the performance to sit in the afternoon sunshine.

"I don't know," Naomi said, as she rummaged in one of her baskets, "why we don't just order dinner rather than bringing a picnic. It would be so much easier. But, somehow, for me, the food and wine in the sunshine is the whole point of the expedition. Why else go to the country in summer if not for a picnic?"

"I don't know why you don't, either," Yevgenia said, disagreeably. "What we eat is really immaterial. It's the music we come for."

And when the music began, Xenia had to agree. She had had no expectation of enjoyment from the opera, her thoughts having been entirely engaged in the wearing of Rosie's dress and the watching of the audience. In the dark of the auditorium, isolated, the social bonds cut at last, she found herself unexpectedly moved by the performance. It was, to her surprise, sung in Russian and what she had expected to be a period of private reflection turned into intense concentration on the singing and on the characters, well known to her, Tchaikovsky's palimpsest of Pushkin's story, the old woman holding her secret and her power, the young girl with her helplessness and longing for love.

When she emerged into the dark green shadows of the garden, still immersed in what she had seen, she found it difficult to resume life outside. Her silence was not remarked on; it was covered by Naomi's flow of comment as she handed out plates and smoked salmon. The sharpness of desire, for money, for power, for love, Xenia could feel piercing her heart; its expression in music and drama concentrated her own passionate need. Suddenly conscious of her role, the necessity to conceal herself, she looked up. Naomi, her grey-brown curls falling forward over her brow, had her hands deep in a picnic basket searching for lemons lost or mislaid, talking as she did so.

"Is it because it's Russian or because it's opera that there is such an extraordinary level of emotion? I try to imagine what one could say to each of them, because it's certain they need therapy, an extended course, I should think."

Xenia found that Marcus was watching her; she caught his eye and her own shied away quickly to focus on the steep hill on which sheep grazed like cut out toys. Marcus was necessary to her. He was her means of entry to England. Her eyes moved back to his, held them, unsmiling for a moment, moved on.

Yevgenia, seated on her folding chair, watched her stepson and Xenia. Her expression was thoughtful. She neither smiled nor relaxed as Xenia's glance met hers. Xenia found she could not look away. The old woman's comprehensive gaze held her. She could hear Marcus's movements, caught the flicker of Naomi's hair and scarves, while she stared at Yevgenia. She had a long face with pale, hooded eyes and creased swags of skin around the mouth and jaw, a delta of deep lines that ran into the lips. You could see that she had been a countess in the old days. Xenia gazed back. She would not be outfaced.

"Here," Naomi was offering a plate and they simultaneously turned to her.

Xenia remained conscious of Yevgenia throughout the last act of the opera, in the same way that she was conscious of the fabric of Marcus's sleeve against her bare arm. The memory of Yevgenia's unsympathetic gaze overlaid the determination of the old Countess on the stage. She did not allow herself to speculate on what Yevgenia saw; she abandoned herself to the music. Only in the darkness of the car as they drove in silence towards Broad Woodham did she wonder what Yevgenia had understood. Yevgenia had not wanted her to come to England, did not want her to be a Chornorouky. Yevgenia was afraid of her.

At Woodham they deposited the old woman at her house, Marcus accompanying her to the door, while Naomi went ahead to unlock the house, to turn on lights.

Then they resumed their journey to London, Naomi now seated in front beside Marcus.

"I thought Jean was in rather bad form this evening," she remarked.

Marcus pulled out to overtake and changed gear as the car surged forward. Xenia sank back in the seat behind, stilling herself into invisibility, watching the arrows on the dashboard blink right, then left.

"She was quiet," Marcus said. "But I think she enjoyed the music. It was a very fine performance this evening. The Lithuanian was superb."

"She was distinctly grumpy," Naomi insisted. "I wonder if being a Pushkin story and in Russian didn't stir painful memories."

"I don't think Jean was ever a poor, dependent relative."

"Marcus, don't be so literal. I mean, the Russianness of it all. What was she thinking of when she was speaking just now about how she came to England after the war? She's never mentioned the past in all these years, then she suddenly starts talking about your mother. Do you think she's blaming herself for your father's divorce after all these years?"

Xenia had wondered what Marcus had made of the conversation Naomi was referring to; perhaps he had not understood. She was still suffering from the shock of it, of understanding very well the words that were puzzling Naomi. She pulled a shawl around her arms to take away the chill that penetrated her.

Thinking about the reworking of Pushkin's characters, she had not been aware of how Yevgenia had begun her remarks. She only began to listen closely when she heard the smoke-hardened voice saying, "Of course, today, no one can come to live in England as I did. They simply don't let people in."

Marcus had said, "You can still get in by marriage, as you did. Wives, spouses I should say, and children and dependants still come in. And a few refugees."

"I didn't come in by marriage. I didn't marry Dad until 1947. I came in as a displaced person, as a European volunteer worker under the Balt Cygnet Scheme, it was called."

"I don't remember that. I thought you came in to get married." Marcus's voice was surprised.

"You don't remember the details because you didn't know them. I did come in to get married. There was just one problem. Your father was still married to your mother, Marcus. So I had to come another way. In fact, Kenward fixed it. He found me in a refugee camp in Germany. I had been picked up fainting on the street and sent to hospital in the camp as I had nowhere to go. I had pneumonia and weighed forty-five kilos. I was one of the fat ones. I suppose that is why I survived. I had spent the war on a farm in Latvia and had some reserves. Still, it is hard to see what my attractions could have been for your father. At the time that never occurred to me, though I have often thought about it since. Whatever they were, they worked. Kenward wanted me badly enough to bring me to England, even though he could not marry me. He arranged for me to work as an auxiliary in a TB sanatorium. That's what you imported people for, to do your dirty work. Kenward got me out of the camp and onto a list to enter the country. I was here long before he divorced your mother because divorces took so much time in those days. But you can't do that now."

"Can't do what?" Her stepson now sounded faintly exasperated, as if he could not understand the purpose of her remarks.

"Fix things, get in on influence."

"Well, no, probably not."

"Kenward would have had to come back to Germany to marry me. Would he have done it, I wonder, if the present rules had been in existence then?"

"I'm sure he would. Your power over Dad was absolute, I'd say."

"I doubt it. The power of sexual attraction is in the present and in the presence. Don't you think, Naomi? And, if I hadn't come, your mother, Marcus, would have stayed with you."

"It's no good playing 'what if' with the past. Meaningless."

"It's the only thing to do with the past," Yevgenia said. "All the alternative worlds, the choices you refused, the roads you didn't take."

Xenia thought of her father, the vodka that used to speak before it felled him. For him the alternative worlds of his imagination were vast. What if Kerensky had defeated the October Revolution; what if Trotsky had outmanoeuvred Stalin and sent him to a camp; what if Hitler had been assassinated in 1936? But it did not matter; however he rewrote history, he ended up in the gulag. The real miracle had been that he had survived to be a teacher of languages in a Siberian technical school, that he had survived at all.

"She's old." Marcus was replying to Naomi's question. "She's aged a lot recently. Old people think about the past."

No, Xenia contradicted him in her head. No, she's not thinking about the past. She's thinking about the future and she's talking to me. The message was given in no friendly spirit either, of that she was sure. You're going back, Yevgenia had been saying. I didn't want you here and you'll have to go back. Don't think you can stay. How had she seen what Xenia wanted? Xenia made the obverse identification. Yevgenia had come here as a refugee forty-five years ago; she would enter instinctively into the mind of a girl from Russia, in a way that Naomi and Marcus could never do. She would know that the imperative was to stay, to keep heading away from the wastes of Siberia. Xenia cursed the old woman who had read Marcus's interest in the web of obsessed glances in which he entangled her. She cursed herself for permitting herself to look at him. And she thought furiously, all to no purpose. He couldn't save her, anyway. His power did not reach to visas and work permits and rights of abode. She didn't doubt the truth of what Yevgenia had said. It was too clearly aimed and had found its target.

The next day she was still depressed about what she had learned. The only positive thing she had heard was that she could stay if she married an Englishman. This did not seem, in itself, an impossible solution, but it was annoying that she had not known it to start with and had wasted time on Marcus. The idea of marriage was not one she found particularly agreeable: she was naturally solitary and could hardly imagine a life truly shared with another person. However, ultimately, divorce was the solution to incompatibility and, in the short run, with life in London the prize, anyone would be tolerable, a drug addict, a cripple, a black.

The door bell rang. She glanced at her watch. It was two thirty. Naomi's clients changed on the hour so it was unlikely to be one of them. Marcus was at the hospital. Mrs Vokins had left before lunch. She opened the front door to find Al standing on the top step. His hair, not tied back in his customary pony tail, lay glossily over his shoulders. He was wearing a torn pink T shirt and black jeans.

"I could hear you moving around from downstairs," he said, "so I knew you were back from school."

Xenia stood aside to let him in. Al often came up in the afternoon to have coffee or tea with her; she always let him loaf around, grind coffee and boil water, making no effort to help as she did with Naomi. She would sit with him politely, watching guardedly, saying little. She never betrayed that she found his long black hair particularly effeminate and repulsive; that she disliked his casual clothes and his loose-jointed style of movement and his affectation of idleness. She knew his visits were motivated by an attraction like that suffered by Marcus, but which, unlike Marcus's, she had never encouraged. So when she said, "Al, where do you come from?" it was the first time she had ever shown any interest in him personally.

Al was pouring out two minute cups of thick Turkish coffee, a substance which he declared necessary to enable him to work in the afternoons. He replied with deliberate obtuseness, "Here, London. I'm a cockney. Or at least I am if the sound of Bow Bells reaches to St Mary's Paddington."

Xenia had no idea of what he was talking about. "No, I mean, where were you born."

"Here in London."

She absorbed this information. Her question had been an idle one, born of a moment's identification with him, like her a stranger in the land. "Were you? But what's your nationality?"

Al relented at last and explained. "I'm British, by birth and by nationality and so are my parents. If you mean what is my racial origin, which I agree is a tricky question to put tactfully, my answer only shows how complicated these things are. My family is North Indian Muslim. They must have moved to India from central Asia sometime in the fifteenth century. In terms of nationality, some of them are now Pakistani; some are Indian; some American; we are British."

Xenia did not allow her astonishment to show; she said, "So you're not Indian. I thought you were," as she adjusted her mind to this new perspective.

When he had gone she took the two little cups from the table and carried them to the sink overlooking the paved garden at the back of the house, thoughtfully running the hot tap over them. She must stop dreaming and act decisively, she told herself. She remembered she had been through the same process before her father's death. There had been a period of fantasy of what life would be like if he were no longer there, with his drunkenness and violence. Then the moment had come when she knew she must act to transform the imaginary into the real. Yevgenia's words last night had been the catalyst; Al had suddenly given her hope.

Equipped with a pen and a notebook, she left the house and strode into the High Street. She walked past the boutiques and bookshops which she had previously raided and made for the library. Her researches quickly established the truth of what Yevgenia had said. It was impossible to come to England permanently except by marriage or with money. Even to come temporarily as a student required a guarantor that she had sufficient money to pay her living expenses and her fees. She was amazed by this; she had always regarded learning as something, like the air, that came free to all those who wished for it. She walked slowly towards the Heath, considering her possibilities. Marcus was a potential guarantor, but where was the money to come from to pay her fees? She could imagine manipulating Marcus and Naomi into permitting her to live with them, to guarantee her to the authorities. But she could not see how they could afford to pay the thousands of pounds necessary or why they would be willing to do so even if they could afford it. To be a student would only give her three or four years in any case. She rejected the idea. Of the alternatives the choice was obvious: between marrying a British citizen and finding £750,000 to invest in the country only one was feasible. It was truly feasible. Xenia could see no reason why she should not marry, or arrange to marry, someone before the time came for her to leave England. She would prefer an Englishman, a real one, but it would probably have to be Al, since time was short and she had already wasted a month in reaching this point.

The next day she did not wait for Al to ring the door bell. After lunch, when Naomi had once more ascended to her consulting room in the company of Andrew, who had got the time of his appointment right for once, she telephoned the basement flat. Al was out. She waited impatiently for his arrival, sitting at the dining-room window with her English books. She had to go out to baby-sit for the evening at six; she willed his return. Al came home just after five. She did not have to call him again because he saw her as he was about to go down the area steps; he waved and came up to the front door instead.

Xenia was careful that her attitude to him should show no sudden unwarranted warmth. She allowed him to prepare the coffee as he always had done, as if she were the visitor to his home. She did not respond more or more positively to his conversation. But she ceased to resist. Her resistance was the internal monologue that she maintained against all of them. As she smiled and acquiesced in all that went on around her, the inner eye and inner voice viewed sceptically and spoke scathingly of everyone she confronted and of their motives. In Al's case she suspended her second voice. She treated him as she had done her father, not permitting herself to notice or criticize. She observed with interest that Al was becoming more attractive. She no longer found his black pony tail affected and effeminate.

One evening that week, when Naomi was at her adultery group and Rosie at her evening seminar, Xenia, Al and Marcus ate dinner together. After their meal, as the two men were stowing plates in the dishwasher while Xenia was replacing food in the refrigerator, she found herself observing approvingly the contrast between Al's height and lankiness and Marcus's stocky, middle-aged body. It was power, of course; Al had the power to give her what she wanted and that power transformed him. It was not just that she now began to approve his appearance; she longed to see him. Their moments together during the day, coffee after lunch, a picnic on the Heath, dinner with Marcus and Naomi, were ones she looked forward to. She knew that she was making progress, that what had been casual encounters were now purposive ones on Al's part. As for Marcus, she saw that he understood what was happening, at least to the extent that he recognized that her interest had shifted from him to Al, and accepted it. Naomi noticed nothing.

Xenia knew that she could not hope for the same security under Rosie's eyes, so she carefully avoided any occasion in which she would be with Al in his girl-friend's presence. This was, on the whole, not difficult to contrive: Rosie was out at work all day, while Al worked at home. When Rosie was free she did not choose to spend time with her father and step-mother, still less with Xenia. The confrontation would come one day; Xenia preferred it to be in her own time and at a stage when she had somehow enticed or forced Al much further down the road of commitment to her, a path he perhaps did not yet know he had taken.

Like most men, she thought, like Marcus, he wants every-thing, Rosie and me, Naomi and me. Then she relented towards them both; she was not a feminist and had no training in gender warfare. It was tough on poor Al who would have to choose.

She decided that though the moment of real decision could be postponed until quite late in her stay, she must establish some intermediate tests to tell her whether she was likely to succeed in her enterprise and began with Al's hair. She had grown used to it now and was no longer repelled by it. However, in spite of her recent exposure to London, to Western magazines and television, she could not think that long hair in a pony tail was proper for a man. She began a war against his hair, determined to get him to cut it. Her success in this would be a sign that she would succeed in her main enter-prise. One lunchtime, after they had eaten their sandwiches together in the little courtyard of the basement flat, she rose and stood behind him. She took his pony tail in her hand and with two fingers scissored it at the band that held it.

"Snip, snip."

Al removed her hand and pulled it over his shoulder in his. "Sneep, sneep," he imitated her. "Do you want it as a trophy? Or do you see yourself as Delilah, bringing me to my knees?"

Xenia slid her hand out of his, took the plates and went up the steps towards the kitchen. References to the Bible were wasted on her. Christianity was like the classics, a mist of meaningless fairy stories that for centuries painters had used as the subject matter for their art, only remembered now in order to read the paintings.

"Snip, snip," she would say, holding the swatch of hair in both hands; he would take her hands and kiss them.

The time scale for her new enterprise, cutting Al's hair and marrying him, stretched in Xenia's mind up to the date of her return to Russia in mid-September. She was reminded one night that her plans might be disrupted by their separation. Naomi was sitting at the big dining table with piles of correspondence in front of her. Her reading glasses were perched on the end of her nose and she was talking as she tore up paper and wrote cheques and lists. Al and Xenia were watching the ten o'clock news while Marcus prepared some herbal tea for his wife.

Naomi raised her head to remark, "We must find out when Lucia is going on holiday and whether Jean wants Xenia to go to Broad Woodham in August. Has she said anything to you about it, Marcus?"

Marcus, pouring boiling water onto dried camomile flowers and watching Trevor Macdonald at the same time, did not respond. Al looked round at Naomi. "Is Xeni going to Jean's?"

"That was the original idea. Marcus and I are going to Italy in two weeks' time and the plan was that Xenia would go to help Jean when Lucia went back to Switzerland for a month with her family. Thank you, darling." She took her tisane and held it in both hands. "It wouldn't be strenuous." She was addressing herself to Xenia now. "Lucia does her shopping. There are usually errands to do every day, but there is a cleaning woman, so it is not a question of housework or nursing. It's really just being about, in case she falls or has an accident. And preparing meals, or opening jars and tins and things like that. Jean really manages very well and is very independent. Oh, here's Rosie."

The front door opened and Rosie came in. "You weren't downstairs, so I thought I'd find you scrounging dinner up here."

"He's not scrounging, Rosie," Naomi said. "I think he may have actually made dinner, with Xeni's help. It's wonderful for Marcus and me, like having a couple: a butler and housekeeper."

Marcus was aware that remark was not likely to please his daughter. "Have you eaten?" he asked. "Can we give you something, a drink at least?"

"I'll have coffee, no, is that tea? I'll have a tisane like Naomi's."

He refilled the kettle and said, "To go back to what you were saying, Mimi, Jean has mentioned nothing to me. You'll have to ring her, or if you don't want to ask her directly, ring Zita."

Naomi tore more paper and threw the pieces into her recycling bag.

"Not that it matters," she said. "Xeni can always stay on here while we're away if Jean doesn't want her. She won't be lonely. Al is always around. You won't be going away until September, will you, Rosie?"

Rosie perched on the edge of the table to watch the advertisements. She took the mug proffered by her father. "We go on 5th September. God, I can't wait."

On Rosie's arrival Xenia, who had been sitting beside Al, got up and went to stand behind Naomi, on the edge of the group around the television, where she remained while Rosie drank her tisane. Finally, Rosie put down her mug and said, "Al, we must go down. There's a load of stuff to do before tomorrow." She led the way to the door; Al followed.

"Are you in tomorrow afternoon?" he asked Xenia, who nodded. "I'll see you then."

"You don't mind going to Jean's, do you, Xenia?" Naomi asked belatedly when they had gone.

"No," Xenia replied. "Not at all. I don't mind. I'll do whatever."

Xenia would go or stay according to Jean's wishes, Naomi thought. On the whole, she would prefer her to go. Not that she distrusted the Russian girl for a moment, but one of her momentary flashes of unease had come over her, the suspicion that there was something more to Xenia than the biddable child she appeared to be. If Jean refused point blank, there was little to be done. She had often in the past shown independence in the face of Naomi's attempts to organize her life for her good.

"You'll like it," she said authoritatively. "It will be a nice change from Hampstead. You'll get to see another aspect of English life. And there are young people around. What's the name of the girl who looks after Zita Daunsey's poor little boy? She'll introduce you to everybody."

"Yes," said Xenia.

"It should mean more money," Naomi went on. "Lucia works for so many hours a week and of course she is paid for them. I don't know what the rate is but Jean can certainly afford to pay properly." She leaned back from her papers and pushed her spectacles into her hair. "Jean's money..." she said, distracted to a new subject. "Jean's money was Russian money, wasn't it, Marcus? I mean, your family never had any serious money."

"My family has been downwardly socially mobile for at least three generations," Marcus said with relish. "The only thing I know about them is that my great-grandfather lost the bulk of whatever they had, and my grandfather finished off the rest. My father never had a bean."

"What was the story about Jean's money? Her family were White Russians, but she didn't come here until after the Second World War and then there was money here waiting for her. Such a well-organized family, I've always thought, to be so rich that you leave small fortunes around the world in case you should ever be a refugee."

"It's quite a common arrangement, if you live in a politically unstable part of the world, to have money stashed away somewhere in case of need. Swiss banking is built on it," Marcus commented. "Anyway, it wasn't quite as straightforward as that in Jean's case. I don't think I ever knew the details, but I think there was some legal process to establish that co-heirs were dead and eventually Jean got everything."

"She said the other night at Glyndebourne that she came to marry your father." Xenia had been listening, though Naomi and Marcus had almost forgotten her presence.

"Oh, she did," Marcus turned to face Xenia. "In fact, I remember now, she did not know that the money was here. It was my father who made enquiries for her and discovered it."

"There was money for her in England, family money?"

"Of course, I was forgetting, it's your family too. You must ask Jean about it."

"I don't really see how she can do that, Naomi."

"Well, no, perhaps not. Now, I must finish this, Marcus. I'll leave Jean to you."

Both Rosie and Xenia had heard and seen things to concern them that evening. Rosie was to take action while Xenia could only debate matters with herself. The revival of the project for her to go to Broad Woodham was unwelcome. It had been mentioned in letters in the early stages and never been developed in any concrete way. Xenia had allowed herself to forget the idea, especially since she had been concentrating her attention on Al, who needed to see her every day. Even though she could telephone him from Woodham, such a link would have none of the intensity of their afternoon meetings in Gayton Street. She was helpless, as she had so often been, her plans lying in the control of others. She could only wait to see what Yevgenia would decide. She was reasonably optimistic that she would be allowed to stay in London. She knew that Yevgenia disliked, even feared, her and so it seemed improbable that she would consent to have her at this late stage.

However, as Naomi was ruminating on the sources of Yevgenia's money a new idea had flared in Xenia's mind. She had already seen parallels between her own life and Yevgenia's and she now saw a new one. Yevgenia had found money in England, family money. Xenia had been as doubtful as Yevgenia as to whether a connexion really existed between her father and Yevgenia's branch of the Chornorouky family. She had now decided that there was. It would be annoying if she was removed to Sussex for four weeks, but there were openings to be explored there and she would have to do what she could to maintain her link with Al until she returned to London.

Part Eight

YEVGENIA

Chapter Seventeen

When I was a child Kornu was a place of enchantment. Even when I was a young girl, though the magic had disappeared, it was still a beloved home. By the time I had reached twenty, however, it had become a prison. Aunt Zoya was elderly now and becoming very frail. Her poor health and dependence on me meant that when Xan left, I could not do so. For Aunt Zoya this was nothing strange for girls always stayed at home until they married. There was no question in her mind of my leaving, of earning a living as a nurse or a secretary, even of going to stay with distant cousins in Paris or New York in order to meet people. I had become aware of the world outside Kornu; not just Riga, which for me was a great metropolis, but even greater ones, Paris, London, Berlin, and I had no hope of reaching them. Not only did Aunt Zoya need me, but I had no education, knew no one, could do nothing useful. I remember there was a huge and ancient typewriter that weighed so much that it took a man to lift it, given to me by Lai from his father's office. I taught myself to type, copying tracts from poems and novels in English and French. I must have been hoping for Aunt Zoya to die, for in no other way could I escape. Yet when the moment came for me to go, when Aunt Zoya herself begged me to leave, I refused. I did not want to, I was afraid of what lay beyond.

In the summers Xan came home, and Lai too, and their stories of their lives in the real world would drive me mad with longing. Lai had started his studies in medicine. His father, like all fathers, wanted him to be a lawyer, but Lai had insisted and the older man found he could hardly refuse to permit his son to follow his own career. He went to the university in Riga and it was intended that he should go to Edinburgh later to complete his studies.

Xan was in Paris, although what he was doing was unclear. He had gone there to study and had enrolled at the Sorbonne. He was not a good student. Chornoroukys never went to university. In early life they went into the army or travelled; later, they administered their lands and developed their estates if they were serious-minded; or drank Château Yquem and bought jewels for their mistresses if they were not. A whole way of life was closed to Xan and he could not find a new one. Worse, he could not decide if he was a serious-minded Chornorouky or a frivolous one. In some respects he wanted to be serious, like one of the great scholar-patrons of the eighteenth century, such as Prince Pavel Fyodorovich Chornorouky, the historian and dramatist. The Prince wrote an encyclopaedic *History of the World,* which Aunt Zoya made us read, and maintained a troupe of serf players who performed his pornographic plays, which Aunt Zoya banned. He married his most talented serf actress and killed himself when she died two years later. Such extravagant possibilities didn't exist for Xan. He belonged to a group of left-wing artists and thinkers, fellow travellers some of them, others paid-up Party members. I am not sure whether he joined himself; sometimes he claimed to be a communist, sometimes he denied it. He undertook studies of working conditions in Latvia during his summer holidays and would sit in the kitchen asking Maris about her life, noting her answers in a little book. He wrote theoretical articles, published some journalism and managed to supplement the very little that Aunt Zoya was able to send him from Latvia. This was the serious Chornorouky; but the old aristocrat lurked there still, so that he passed his days in conversation and drinking, a fainéance born of the belief with which we had been imbued, that we had no place in the new world.

In the summer of '39 he came back from Paris, as usual. He could not afford to stay there during the months when everything closed down and everyone went away. Lai, too, was on holiday, although he worked at his books during the mornings. In the heat of the afternoons we swam in the lake, as we always did, or lay beside the water in the shade with a picnic basket beside us. We were no longer the childhood trinity we had been, or as I imagined we had been, in the days before Lai and I had rebelled and Lai had been punished. The contrast between Lai and Xan ran through everything. It never broke out in open antagonism; it was simply and intrusively present in every opinion, discussion, decision. I came to prefer seeing them separately, rather than endure the tension of waiting for the flashpoint, the moment when the provocation of one by the other, usually, but not invariably, of Lai by Xan, would become unbearable.

Xan still had the upper hand; the glamour of Paris showed up all the provincialism of Riga. He was interested in ideas, which he would express with the fluency and abstraction of the French speaker; Latvian medical students did not articulate many ideas, beyond a fierce Latvian nationalism, which Xan, an internationalist, scorned. Latvian culture, expressed in folksong, looked very unprobing beside French philosophy. I longed for what Lai did and admired to appear as significant and as interesting as what Xan stood for; but however much I wished to protect Lai, to allow him to win sometimes, I still thought that Xan's life was more exciting and important. Perhaps I am making too much of the contrast between them at this stage. If they were so antagonistic, why did they spend so much time together? Or perhaps their differences were more obvious and more painful to me, who loved them both, than they were to each other.

I have no memento of my life in Latvia. Even the two or three photographs which I carried in my purse when we ran away in 1944 were stolen from me in Berlin. So my memory is not influenced by visual reminders in the present. I don't remember this period as a film, but as snapshots. I can see Xan and Lai sitting in the shade of the verandah at Kornu. Xan is lying back in his chair, his body as relaxed as a cat's; he is smoking; his dark hair is rather long. Lai is leaning against the verandah rail, with one leg drawn up, his foot resting on the back of a chair. I can see Xan just after he has flung down his mallet in bad temper during a game of croquet; and Lai drawing himself out of the waters of the lake onto the jetty, wearing a black bathing costume with straps over the shoulders. Did I see these things? Did I once photograph them and so fix them in my memory or have I made them up?

In England they call the period between the outbreak of war in 1939 and the fall of France in 1940 the phoney war. For us it was a time of phoney peace. The Molotov-Ribbentrop Pact, by which the Germans and Russians agreed on the partition of Poland, left us isolated while the Russians moved forward to retake areas of eastern Poland which they had not held since 1920. It was clear that one day soon the Soviets would turn their attention to us. Lai was fiercely anti-Russian, but he never considered leaving the country. Latvians are reeds, not oak trees; they cling to their soil and lie down under the storm. Xan might have left; he was already in exile in Latvia, so why should he not move on to safety in America, if he could get out through Norway or Sweden? He did not go, for complex and simple reasons. The complex one was that, although he knew it would be wiser to leave, given who he was, his curious admiration for the communists, the destroyers of his class and culture, and his feeling that he should not be better off than other Russians, prevented him from doing what was sensible. The simple reason was that he would not leave without Aunt Zoya and me and Aunt Zoya was too old and too ill to travel.

She urged me to go with Xan, but I could not leave her. Had I known what was to come, I would have gone, even though leaving an elderly woman unprotected seems a heartless thing to do. Had I known what even worse things I was to see and to do in the years that followed, I would have gone with Xan to Sweden, leaving her to die alone. But I did not know and could not imagine. I was as naive as it is possible to be if you have read all the classics of Russian, English, French and German literature. Of love and hatred, murder, torture and rape, I knew from a variety of sources. Yet I persisted in believing that none of the vileness of war would reach us at Kornu; we were so far from life. Not even the history of my family, the deaths of my parents, convinced me that we should run away. I think all these things, the violence of Aeschylus, Shakespeare, Racine, Goethe, Scott, my parents' murder, were all in an imaginary domain and I could not yet connect them with reality. So I insisted it was my duty to stay with Aunt Zoya and in my turn begged Xan to leave, and he, held back, not by lack of contact with reality, but by his perverse admiration for the impending violence, insisted on staying with me. I used to examine the reasons for his decision to stay, which had to be renewed each day in the face of the daily invitation to leave. Was it because of his open admiration for communist modernity, which he would welcome if it came to Latvia? Was it because of his care for his great-aunt who had brought him up and was the only mother he had ever had? Or was it because of me?

I had adored and admired Xan when we were children. When he returned from Paris as a young man, I fell entirely in love with him. It was inevitable, of course. I knew no one and the compulsion of the young to love makes them susceptible to almost anyone remotely lovable in their immediate environment. I could have loved Lai, but he had always been the second, and he could not compete with a man who returned from Paris with all the brilliance of a great capital reflected upon him. When Xan arrived in June 1939, I was no more to him than his little cousin, almost a sister, but as the world closed in on us during the winter of that year he began to notice me.

The trap for Xan was set with the signing of the Molotov-Ribbentrop Pact and sprung on 1st September with the invasion of Poland. These dates are a matter of history. I do not need to verify them, they are noted in every history book about the war. At the time there was nothing to mark the day. It would have been possible, if Xan had not been there, for Aunt Zoya and me not to know what had happened for some days. Xan, however, always listened to the news and that evening he came running out to where we were sitting in the shade of a great chestnut, looking out over the lake, to tell us that the Germans had invaded Poland.

Aunt Zoya was filled with fear at the thought of the forward movement of the Red Army. Poles are figures of fun for Russians, the Irish of eastern Europe, but she remembered the miracle on the Vistula in 1920 when the Polish Army had defeated Tukhachevsky and beaten the Reds back into the Ukraine; the Poles were guarantors of our safety. Now they were gone, who was left to defend us? Xan was excited. He saw no personal advantage in what was happening; simply the idea of military movements, of fighting, the breaking up of Europe stimulated him. He welcomed what Aunt Zoya dreaded, the Soviets reclaiming Latvia as they had just reclaimed Poland. So, the combination of the difficulties of going anywhere else and the excitement of staying, kept him at Kornu through the autumn.

I think now, I am sure, that if we had not been brought together by those circumstances, trapped by the icy Baltic winter at Kornu, with Aunt Zoya as our only companion, that he would never have thought of me. As it was, my passion was so powerful that, with no counter-attractions, he succumbed to it. If Aunt Zoya heard the murmur of our voices, our laughter beside the fire late in the evening, or even later, the creaking of the wooden floors as he moved between his room and mine, she gave no sign. But her wish that we should marry was made known, at first in hints, finally as open statements. As I wished for nothing more, I was in a delicate position: I had to feign carelessness, at least until the moment that Xan decided that, all things considered, he might as well marry me.

And so in the spring of 1940, 12th May to be exact, Xan and I were married at Kornu. I wore a dress of my mother's, dating from before the Revolution, of cream silk embroidered with butterflies, and some old lace that Aunt Zoya salvaged from somewhere. This magnificence was for the benefit of Aunt Zoya and the maids and a few elderly aristocratic Baltic neighbours. And Lai.

Because I had been so self-absorbed, or Xan-absorbed, during the phoney peace, I had paid very little attention to the political events of the time, which held everyone in Europe in the tension of an indrawn breath of terror. For me, my marriage allowed a release, in a gasp of joy, and with that new breath, events began to move with a speed that was horrifying to us in our fastness at Kornu, listening to the news in several languages on our crackling steam wireless.

The first event in the unfreezing of our war was the death of Aunt Zoya. We found her sitting in her chair in her bedroom one morning, still in her nightdress. The oil lamp burned in front of the icon in the corner of the room and the early light seeped through the cracks in the shutters. She was already rigid and had probably sat down to die after saying her prayers the previous evening. Her ancient face was crumpled like tissue paper, her skin darkened by her years of work, running the house and garden at Kornu. She looked like what she had become, an old and toil-worn peasant woman, rather than what she held herself to be, above all a Chornorouky princess.

Immediately afterwards France fell and Xan's thoughts were even more with his friends in Paris. He was married and with me at Kornu, but he wished he were not. Then the Russians tightened their noose on Latvia, demanding to take over the country. In mid-June, just a month after our wedding, the government was reconstructed under Soviet auspices. New elections with only one list of Soviet-approved candidates were held in July and the new Parliament voted at once to join the Soviet Union. The Red Army which had been lined up on our borders, marched in, and behind them came the NKVD. Prominent Latvians were arrested and deported, never to be seen again. Banks and shops were nationalized. The remains of my father's estate were confiscated. Lai's father was arrested as a prominent intellectual and a capitalist in these early months of occupation.

In terror, I persuaded Xan to go into hiding. At first we had exercised a rather cursory form of secrecy. If any outsider was seen approaching the house, Xan hid in a barn or an outhouse and the

maids were instructed to say that he had left. The savage snatch-
ing of Lai's father in the middle of the night by the NKVD, the
arrest of his mother ten days later, recounted to us by Lai, fright-
ened me so badly that in September I resolved that Xan must really disappear. We told nobody where he was, feeling that such
knowledge would constitute a danger to them and a source of con-
tinual worry to us. The maids were told that he had gone to Riga
and would not be coming back. I told Lai, who often came out
from the city, hiring a bike at the station and riding twelve miles to
Kornu on a Saturday afternoon, the same thing. He looked me in
the eye, waiting to hear the truth; but I said nothing.

During the autumn of 1940 and the winter that followed,
Xan lived in the cellar, in the dark, behind a door which was
hidden by piles of wood. As a prisoner he was very comfortable. He had books, writing materials, a wireless. I went every
night to see him, to supply him with food, to talk to him, to
make love to him. But he hated his imprisonment and, I think,
hated me for insisting on its necessity. Living such a life decided him to leave. To be captured and killed was better than to
live as a voluntary prisoner. We spent hours in passionate,
whispered argument, as we debated the alternatives of escape,
hiding, or coming out into the open. In the spring, with the
warmer weather, things improved in one sense, because I
moved him out of the cellar, where he had been warmed by the
house stove, and into a woodcutters' shack in the woods. Here
he lived above ground, for the forests were vast and little fre-
quented; during the day he was there alone, reading and writing. If he ever saw or heard signs of hunters or soldiers or even
partisans, as he did once or twice, he retreated into his lair
where we had constructed a hiding place for him beneath piles
of brushwood. At night he often walked the seven miles or so
to Kornu. At a pre-arranged signal I would let him in and later,
before dawn, he would return to his bothy in the woods with a
knapsack of food and books on his back. In the daylight of the
forest his morale improved. He was convinced he would not be
there for long because he hoped, through communist friends in
France, to be able to make his peace with the regime in Latvia.

He agreed now that he was in the open air that the decision to hide had been correct. Communists, he said, with some admiration, shoot first and ask questions later and there were no satisfactory answers we could give, even afterwards. Xan was a Chornorouky, a Russian in exile, an aristocrat, a landowner, even worse, an intellectual. There would have been no mercy for him on any of these counts. No protestations of sympathy for the communist cause, no waving of CP membership from Paris would have arrested the finger on the trigger of the tough Ukrainian who visited us with his troop of soldiers late one afternoon in January 1941.

They kicked in the door of one of the storehouses, helping themselves to potatoes out of our barrels, to jars of pickles, to smoked hams, to anything they found. It was my first of many such encounters. The maids shrieked and wept as much then for the thefts of our winter supplies which represented a significant loss, as for the later rapes and murders they were to witness. And their cries, I saw, both terrified and incited the soldiers in their violence. Such men would have shot Xan out of hand.

Our next visitors, from the NKVD, would have taken him away politely, with every appearance of legality, with warrants and correctly stamped papers, but the result would have been the same. Xan's loyalty and admiration found excuses for them. This was just how things were, he explained, amid the upheavals of war. In reality, these men were representatives of the fairest society yet instituted on earth. Because of this loyalty to his principles, Xan did not wish to join the partisans. After a while he began to despair of ever finding credentials to present to the Soviets and began to think of escape. He wanted to get into Germany where he had contacts in the army and Diplomatic Service, men of old families who were less than enamoured of Hitler and the Nazis and might be willing to help him get to Sweden. Later, he would arrange for me to follow by the same route with the baby, since it was only too clear that I could not travel with him at that time.

My pregnancy did not really become visible until about February 1941. I advanced it a little, by letting everyone know that the baby was expected in June, which allowed clear time for conception before Xan was supposed to have left. I could see them all counting the months backwards and forwards as they eyed my not very thickened waistline. They all must have suspected that what I said was false, but no one wished to know the truth, except Lai.

He was bitter towards the Russians. He lamented his country's lost independence, his parents' disappearance to almost certain death in the camps. He hated the new regime at the university. I knew he would have liked to run away to join the partisans, of whom we began to hear that winter, tiny bands of outlaws living in the woods, demanding food and cash from remote villages and farmsteads. I knew too why he did not go. He thought he could not leave me alone, pregnant, as Xan, so egotistical and selfish, had apparently done.

I wanted Xan to go because I wanted him in safety. I thought, as he did, that a woman and child were less vulnerable in their helplessness and might escape unnoticed, while he would always be targeted, by the Soviets as an aristocrat, by the Nazis as a left-winger. But I feared the dangers of his journey and the thought of the months without news which would follow depressed me. There was the contrast, too, with Lai, whose loyalty to me Xan was going to make use of. He decided he must talk to Lai before he left and early in June 1941 I told Lai what he had already guessed, that Xan was in hiding nearby and wanted to see him.

One night, in the early hours, under a sky which is never really dark at that time of year, we set off together from Kornu, Lai and I. Normally, Xan came to the house, but since we intended to talk, we decided that we must make the journey to him. I knew the forest paths well, but I cannot say I made my usual speed along them. I was eight months' pregnant, though not large; we had too little food for me to balloon up or to be indulged in cravings. We met on one of the rides leading up to the woodcutters' hut and sat to talk on a fallen trunk. I could sense that Lai disapproved of Xan's hiding and his running away.

However, he listened to the plan and only added, "When

you get to Sweden you must tell them what they have done, the Russians, the fixed elections, the deportations. Two or three hundred people every month arrested and shipped east by the NKVD, the confiscations, the impossible quotas placed on the farms. Genya knows all about that; she will have told you."

I hadn't, of course. I knew it would be of no use. Xan began to argue.

"This is just the initial stage. Since the country voluntarily joined the Soviet Union, it will quickly adapt itself. It's simply a question of the adjustments that have to be made in the change to a planned economy. Of course, the kulaks will resent it. There are always losers in a historical process like this."

He was as unconscious, as I was distressedly aware, of Lai's recoil. Lai had expected that Xan's views would have changed with experiences of the last year. He had not realized, and I had not been able to prepare him, that Xan's beliefs had hardened during his isolation. Xan had had no contact with Soviet reality; he had only listened to the propaganda on the wireless. He lived in a world of ideas.

"Hasn't Genya told you what has been going on? It's not just expropriations of banks and big manufactories, it's real oppression of the peasants, much worse than in the old days when you lot ruled us. I can understand their taking away my father. According to them, he was a capitalist and a bourgeois intellectual and I suppose we are as much class enemies as you aristos, but why take away the sons of peasants, impose enormous quotas on the farmers, lengthen hours at the factories? It is simple national oppression. It is not socialist revolution at all."

"Lai, you will never understand," Xan said impatiently. He did not want even to discuss the subject with him, not because he knew that their minds were so fixed at the start that there was no possibility of understanding, but because he did not think Lai was worth debating with. I could read his feelings as if they had been written on a banner flying over his head: *You are a jumped-up Latvian peasant: you have neither the breadth of culture nor the range of historical view to see that this is inevitable. Only an intellectual can see past his personal, class and national interest to recognize the necessary, impersonal forces of history.*

In later years, I learned more of the psychological phenomenon of the victim's identification with the bully, the admiration the loser feels for the winner, even for the unjust winner. I see now that I myself adopted the same strategy in becoming English: I was one of the defeated; I made myself into one of the winners. This was what Xan was doing with his allegiance to communism; it made him feel he was not one of the dodos; he had joined history's winning side. Lai was not like us; he and his people had been losers for so long that they could wait. They waited until last year.

"Lai, you will never understand."

What Xan did not say was written on his face. I could see it there, and so could Lai. It was like that moment a decade earlier beside the lake, when Lai had dived into the water to escape from Xan's mockery. I didn't know whether Xan was conscious of the pain he was causing, of his injustice and cruelty. Then, I didn't want to believe that he knew what he was doing; now, I think he probably did. Just like that earlier moment, it was a deliberate act. He did it because he believed he was right, the most powerful motive for inflicting suffering. But the greater blame lies with me. For I saw he was wrong and I saw what he was doing to Lai, but I said nothing. I averted my eyes in order not to see, and not to have to see Lai see me seeing his humiliation. I chose the side I was on; I chose to be Xan's accomplice, rather than Lai's defender. But I was punished for it, later.

They abandoned the discussion of politics and began to make arrangements for Xan to go. A date was set, a week away, a route was chosen. Lai promised to make certain enquiries and to return the answer to me in two days' time. Eventually Lai rose to leave. He and Xan shook hands. Xan kissed me, on the mouth, which he would not normally have done in front of others—we were very discreet in those days—so I knew that his antagonism to Lai reached as far as marking me clearly as part of his possessions. He could not bring himself to ask Lai to look after me or the baby. There was to be no sharing of that responsibility. I would look after myself. Lai and I walked away and Xan watched us go from under the trees.

Two or three days after this last meeting of the three of us there was a great round up by the NKVD, the last, as it happened. A troop of soldiers, marching through the woods with a gang of prisoners, searched the woodcutters' shelter and found Xan. They took him away with them. He was being loaded onto a train for the East with other prisoners, when he was involved in a fracas with a guard and shot. A week later, on 22nd June, the Germans invaded the Soviet Union, sweeping through Latvia by the end of the month.

I've described Xan's capture and death so quickly because to tell how I went to the shelter to see him and found it ransacked, how I searched for news, how I heard of his death on the platform of the station would still pain me after all these years. I shall never forget walking up the ride towards the hut in the moonlight, expecting every moment to see Xan, whose watch I told myself must have stopped. But even as I made explanations for myself, fear already anticipated what I would find. I could still weep to think of the story I heard from the wife of another deportee who had been present, of how she had seen Xan's body flung into the cattle truck just before the train moved off, as the guards could not be bothered to deal with it. I imagined the doors being opened to put in more prisoners, or to water them, like beasts, somewhere on the line into Russia and his corpse being tossed out to lie and rot beside the track in the summer's heat.

But worse than the pain of loss, the certainty of his death, was the suspicion I lived with, no, more than a suspicion, a conviction, that he had been betrayed by Lai. How else could the Russians have found him? Why was he discovered just a few days after Lai was shown where he was? These were grounds for suspicion; my conviction came from my feeling that somehow Xan merited Lai's revenge.

I could not read Lai as I could read Xan. I could see no guilt in him, in his reaction to the story that I told him the next weekend when he came to Kornu. His horror at what had happened, his grief at Xan's death, his sympathy for me appeared all they should have been. But what is guilt? It doesn't show like leprosy, eating away the flesh. Can one tell the state of another's soul, as Xenia claimed? She has nothing to hide, perhaps, so she can believe that. I know it is possible to live a lifetime with the past hidden, smoothed over, like the soil over the child's bones, and nobody any the wiser. Once I had reached England, I hid my past as completely as I could. Only the outline remained, the details were obliterated. And what details; husband, child, lover, all erased. So why should I have expected to see guilt in Lai?

I said nothing, but my certainty of his betrayal lay beneath everything. I made no accusations, for I needed Lai and indeed was to need his particular skills scarcely a month later when my son was born.

I had been relying with the complete carelessness of youth on the experience of the maids to assist me at the birth. Maris had had three illegitimate children; the gardener's wife had a family of seven of her own and five grandchildren. Everyone else managed, I reasoned, so why shouldn't I, especially with such experienced help at hand. In fact, to my indignation, the process was much less easy and natural (or perhaps it was too natural) than I had believed and only Lai's presence saved Alek's life. For that act of preserving the son I forgave him for ever for destroying the father. If I had ever loved Xan, and I had, passionately and wholeheartedly, for a long time without hope, it was nothing to what I felt for Alek from the moment he was placed in my arms.

He was born on his father's birthday, 7th July 1941, less than a month after Xan's death. Setting aside his troublesome arrival, he was the easiest and happiest baby in the world. He had a long oval head with enormous eyes that had turned grey like Xan's by the time he was one. His hair was dark when he was born but lightened to brown as he grew older. His fingers were disproportionately long and I shall never forget the first time I uncoiled his minute mottled fist like the tendril of a new frond of fern to put my finger in his reflexive grasp. I think it was the happiest moment I have ever known.

Part Nine

ZITA

Chapter Eighteen

Zita was at a concert with two of her quintet friends. Normally, she found that music had the power to eradicate the quotidian and to transport her to a world of pattern and harmony. This evening the effect was absent. Her mind moved restlessly, distracted by one sense or another, by memory, by the ever-intrusive Oliver, while the music could only thread through her fretful thoughts. She observed the curious acoustics of the little gothic church in which she was sitting between Gerald and Georgina Orr. It was narrow, truncated, inordinately high for its ground plan, so that the voices of the singers were funnelled upwards to hang in the upper air of the clerestory. (Oliver, Oliver, Oliver.) She lowered her eyes to take in the red linen of her skirt, the satisfyingly tight texture of its web, slightly scratchy to the finger tips, palpable to the eyes. She must ring her dressmaker to see if her new black dress was ready. (Oliver, Oliver, Oliver.) His name was like the rhythm of the wheels of a train, drumming along a track without a destination. (Oliver, Oliver, Oliver.) Tom had been a real pig this evening. She had hoped that the concert would soothe and compose her after a day of frustration in which she had tried to undertake two new resolutions.

The first was to pay more attention to Tom. She did not like to admit to herself that her mother's visit had shown her how little time she actually spent with her son. Nevertheless, it had been the unexpected sight of Valentina wheeling her grandson about, maintaining a constant flow of conversation with him, that had jolted Zita into recognition of her neglect. Her life might be organized on the basis of his needs, but she did not really do very much with him. She lacked Lynne's patience and empathy, her quick understanding of what his groping, dribbling, headbanging and rages were about.

Her second resolution was action against Stevens. It occurred to her that there might have been a well-known story which would explain the discovery of the skeleton, a story, that is, that was well documented in its time but which had simply been forgotten. This was the reasoning that had led her, with Tom, to the library that Saturday morning.

As it was a fine day, she had decided to walk. She strapped Tom into his wheel chair. It was very upright, holding him in position, with a head rest that came around the sides of his skull, like earphones. As she knelt down to buckle the belt around his waist she looked into his hazel eyes, very pale, greeny brown this morning, just like Oliver's. They were like spirit levels, she thought; she must concentrate on his eyes; they remained faithful to his understanding when everything else about him was out of true. Today they were full of life and interest.

"There. Are you comfortable, now?" He cast up his eyes to say yes. "We're going to the library and we're not going in the van, so I can't take your computer. You'll have to look at a book when we get there. OK?" As they walked towards the centre of town, jolting over the kerbs and uneven pavements, she kept up a monologue about what they could see as they passed: a cat perched on a wall turning its head to watch them with insolent eyes; a car parked across the edge of the pavement so that they had to make a detour round it. Tom seemed to enjoy this. He listened and she could sense his concentration even from her view of the top of his head. Then her own attention slipped. It was impossible for her to comment endlessly on the cars and gardens that ran past her moving gaze and her mind turned back to the child's skeleton. There were several oddities about Stevens and his enquiry. The first was that he was very senior for such an unimportant investigation. She thought it very likely that normally a much younger and more junior officer would have been placed in charge of a few old bones. Stevens had taken over the case from the start and had given it its momentum. She also suspected that he was running two enquiries, official and unofficial, one from the incident room at Broad Woodham police station, another in his head.

At the library she had rung for assistance to get Tom up the imposing nineteenth-century steps into the building and had taken him straight to the children's section where she selected a book at speed. With this to act as a distraction for her son, she took him to the lift to the reference section on the first floor. Tom was pleased by the novelty. He was watching everything with his attentive look rather than his sullen one. She parked him, opened his book and began to scan the local history section. Some thirty minutes later, she had, with the help of the librarian, assembled a number of volumes on her desk and was ready to read them, when Tom signalled that he was bored. His book fell to the floor. Zita picked it up and opened it again. He closed his eyes, to indicate he did not want to look at it. Although he could not talk, Tom could make a range of extraordinary sounds, which Lynne alone could interpret with finesse. Now, he was gurgling gently in the back of his throat, raising the volume slightly until Zita abandoned her book and turned to him. She mopped the saliva from his chin and turned his head so he would look at her.

"Be quiet, Tom," she hissed. Already hostile glances were being cast at them by the smelly old men reading the racing pages who always seem to occupy the chairs in public libraries. He closed his eyes again.

"Look, take one of mine if you don't like yours." She put a picture book of local beauty spots in front of him and turned the pages for him every few minutes, as she attempted to examine the indexes of the other works on her pile. Tom read well for a seven-year-old, but his lack of control of his limbs meant that turning pages was a source of enormous frustration, as he needed an attendant to help him when he eye-pointed his readiness for the next page. His computer was much more successful as he could scroll down using the head switches on his wheel chair. Zita, dividing her attention between her books and her son, was almost as frustrated as he. There was plenty of local history of the Queen Elizabeth slept here variety; very little that was recent and relevant. She allowed herself to be distracted into reading some amusing and interesting facts or fictions about the town's history without gaining any information to explain why poor Yorick lay in Yevgenia's garden.

She leaned over to display a new picture for Tom. She had given him a book of old photographs of the town and the strange familiarity of some of the pictures may have been what held his attention for slightly longer than usual on each page. As she smoothed the central partition of the pages her hand, drawing itself over the right-hand photograph, revealed St Michael's Square in which a corner of Asshe House was clearly recognizable. *St Michael's Square after the V2 in 1945,* read the caption.

"Do you see," she said, "that's Yevgenia's old house and there's the churchyard in 1945. It looks very dilapidated then."

Tom was no longer interested. The gurgling started again; this time he made it rhythmical, stopping just at the moment when he sounded as if he were about to choke and beginning again.

Zita gave up. Research was an utterly thankless and time-wasting task. She would not be surprised to learn that historians made up most of their facts because of the impossibility of being able to discover anything of interest. She had learned nothing and infuriated Tom.

That evening at the concert as she sat trying to concentrate on the music, she wondered why her first efforts had not been directed at the papers in her own keeping, the deeds of Asshe House, which she recalled seeing among Yevgenia's files when she had been doing the conveyancing for her new house. She had brought them out in case Yevgenia wanted to transfer the ownership into Marcus's name, something that she still had not done. Zita had pointed out that she should do so in order to minimize liability to inheritance tax. Like many elderly people, Yevgenia was capable of behaving with great generosity in

handing over her possessions for use by the younger generation, but she was reluctant to give up ultimate control of what
was hers. She had listened to what Zita had said and then
waved a dismissive hand.

"Too late for that. I shan't survive long enough, so there's
no point."

"Yevgenia, you're only seventy-five, you're good for another fifteen years," Zita had responded robustly. "I really advise
you to think about this. Anyway," she added practically, "it
works on a sliding scale; seven years isn't the once for all cut-
off point." Yevgenia had not been convinced.

She could visualize the deeds now, a squarish bundle
secured with pink tape, containing the thick legal papers of a
century earlier, folded, sealed, stamped. She had not examined
them at all. She suddenly longed to open out the packages of
paper to read the names of former owners and tenants, as if
one of them would suddenly reveal himself as a child murderer
by the combination of letters on a page. The decision was taken
in the concert. After dinner, farewells said, she set the car on
the road to Broad Woodham, but when she reached the outskirts of the town, instead of taking the by-pass towards home,
she drove into the town centre to her office. She parked in her
usual space in the empty car park and let herself in by the back
door. She deactivated the alarm, but, in order not to alert
patrolling policemen, she did not turn on the lights as she
mounted the fine staircase to the archives on the fourth floor.
The street lights from the square and the floodlighting of the
church lit up the familiar space in an unfamiliar way. She
moved along the passages between the metal racks until she
reached L. She was able to identify by touch the parcel of old
documents which included the deeds to Asshe House.

The church clock struck the half-hour and she glanced
automatically out of the window to check the time on the
tower. As she did so, she saw a light go on in one of the ground-
floor rooms of Asshe House on the north side of the square. A
second later it was extinguished.

She stared at the house, wondering if she had really seen

what she knew she had seen. The windows, glazed with builders' dust inside, like eyes with cataracts, stared blankly back at her, reflecting the street lights, revealing nothing of what was within. A burglary? But there was nothing inside to steal, at least, nothing that could be taken without a removal van. Furniture that Yevgenia had allocated to Ivo, Rosie or Marcus and Naomi was stacked in the first-floor drawing room; but there was nothing there to interest a casual thief, no money, silver, small objects, electrical gadgets.

Later, when she came to look back on the events of the summer, Zita was to observe a growing tendency within herself to act in opposition to her reason, or rather to act simultaneously in reasonable and unreasonable ways. The first example was her persistence beyond the call of duty in pursuing the identity of the skeleton child. Her behaviour this evening was another. She reacted immediately as a responsible citizen. She ran rapidly down to her own room, obtained an outside line and dialled the local police station. Even as she did so, however, she knew that she could not leave it there. She reported what she had observed to the officer on duty, replaced the receiver and, carrying the parcel of deeds by their pink strings, she relocked her office. On the ground floor in the secretaries' office she opened a small cabinet and selected a bunch of keys. She carefully reset the alarm and let herself out of the building, by the front door onto the square this time. Her progress across the cobbles in her high heels (an old and favoured pair of red leather with an open toe) was necessarily slow and gave her plenty of time to notice the paradox of her lawyerly precautions with locks and alarms and the recklessness of what she was about to do. On the face of it, she was about to act in such a way that if her own corpse turned up in Asshe House garden she would not have the right to be surprised. She was able to hold this knowledge in her head at the same time as a conviction that she was not going to find a burglar.

Without attempting to silence her movements or conceal her presence she walked up to the front door and inserted the large, old-fashioned key. She opened the door which fell back slowly on its hinges under its own majestic weight, and put her hand out to turn on the light.

Yevgenia's chandelier, an absurd confection of bronze flower petals and tear-shaped drops, had been taken down and a single harsh bulb illuminated a scene of builders' devastation. One floor board had been lifted and a tangle of wires was exposed, like guts in a slashed belly. The formerly smoothly polished parquet was encrusted with dust onto which splashes of water or plaster had fallen like a blood trail from a wounded animal. Allowing her footsteps to sound on the boards, she walked firmly to the foot of the stairs and turned on more lights. She hesitated a moment. Her impulse had propelled her thus far; it slackened sufficiently for recognition of her recklessness to return. She listened attentively: only silence.

She was more cautious now as she turned towards Yevgenia's old sitting room, from where she judged the light to have come, moving as quietly as she could. She placed her hand on the door knob, turning it silently, easing the mechanism out of its groove as she applied the pressure of her arm to open the door inwards. The room showed only the same scene of building works: the plaster stripped off the wall under the window, more floor boards up, narrow-bore pipes lying along the skirting board, a pile of tool boxes and, on top of them, a pair of discarded dungarees. This was where the light had come from: the light switch turned on and off for a moment for someone to orientate himself. Zita looked around for the sign of a presence. There were footprints in the dust, but whether they were the workmen's or the intruder's it was impossible to judge.

She slipped off the high-heeled shoes and made her way back across the hall barefoot, feeling the gravelly dust under her soles. She stopped again at the foot of the stairs. She could hear nothing. The police would arrive soon and she would be able to tell them herself that she had wasted their time. She entered the old study which looked out over the garden, and went over to the window; cupping her hand against the glass, she peered out into the darkness.

Suddenly, above her head, she heard very distinctly the sound of a heel on the wooden floor.

She first found her shoes. It was a mistake to face an intruder without them; shoeless, she was defenceless. Then she walked up the stairs, without attempt at concealment, and opened the drawing-room door. She was not surprised to see him there when she turned on the light. She had already, instantaneously, recognized his form as a bulk in the darkness; indeed, she was expecting him, for who else was as interested as she in Asshe House?

"Are you a cat, Superintendent? Can you see in the dark?"

He was standing looking out at the garden and only half-turned as she came in, as if he, too, had known who it was moving around in the empty house at almost one in the morning.

"How did you get in?" she asked.

"As you did, with a key."

"Mine," she said tartly, "is a legitimate one. I should like to know where yours comes from."

"From Wilson, the builder."

"So what are you doing here, entering if not breaking, without permission, at a totally bizarre time?"

"I could ask you the same thing."

"So you could, and I have a very good explanation which I have ready to give to the police when they arrive to investigate the presence of an intruder which I reported to them about fifteen minutes ago."

"You did? Not very speedy, are they? The phone's downstairs; I'll let them know there's no need to come."

Zita stood aside to let him pass. He lumbered down the stairs and she heard him talking in Yevgenia's sitting room. His voice, rapid and authoritative, spoke briefly. She turned off the light and walked slowly down to the ground floor, disconcerted by his lack of embarrassment. From the sitting room she heard the surge of an electric kettle and found him squatting beside the clutter of tools, his back to her.

"Tea?" he asked. "It's all they've got. Not even Nescafé."

"All right." She was annoyed to hear that her voice betrayed irritation and discomposure in contrast with his calm. "All right. I'll have some tea. And you can tell me what the bloody hell you're doing here."

The kettle clicked; the steam clouded the air behind the stooped figure. "It'll have to be Russian tea. No milk, no lemon, only sugar if you want it."

"No thanks." She refused to let herself be diverted by the disparaging way he described the tea. He fished the tea bag out of a mug and put it on a stained saucer. "The mug's clean. Now, you tell me first what you are doing here."

"I was in my office when I saw a light go on in here. Naturally, thinking there had been a break in, I rang the police."

"And equally naturally, thinking it was a break in, you decided to walk over to see who was doing it."

Zita said nothing. She had noticed before how quick he was to focus on the weak point in a story. "And you?" she said. "What were you doing? Don't tell me, let me guess. You were on duty, coming back from some little incident of domestic violence or late-night mugging when you passed Asshe House and, happening to have a key in your pocket, you decided to get out your magnifying glass and do a quick check for any clues left from thirty years ago."

Propped up on the carpenter's work bench, he sipped his tea. "Well, more or less, that's right."

"And the key? Why the key? You could have got in any day when the workmen were here and you still wouldn't have had to ask the owner's permission."

"I could have done, of course. But I preferred to be here without them. I just wanted to have a look around on my own."

"And I spoiled your plan."

"No, no, it's quite all right. I'd been here long enough before you arrived."

"Just what is it about this case?" she said, her voice rising in frustration.

"We need some certainty," Stevens said. "We're looking for the proof."

"Proof that it was Eddie Cresacre that was buried out there?"

"Yes, and if it is, it'll prove what I always knew. Petre didn't do it. I was sure he didn't do it. The whole thing was a travesty. He gave himself up, you know, Petre; it wasn't the police who found him. He confessed; then he withdrew his confession, claimed it had been beaten out of him." He stood up and turned towards the grimy sheen of the window; the darkness repelled the eye. "He was beaten up, but it was after he confessed, not before. You couldn't blame them. They thought he was a child-killer. But he wasn't. He was completely cracked, Petre; you could see it. But he wasn't a murderer, you could see that too. I could see it, at any rate."

"And now you can see Jean Loftus is?"

"I saw her right at the start."

"But what evidence is there? At the moment you look, not to mince words, as much of a nutter as Petre. You're convinced, without evidence, that the skeleton is Eddie Cresacre's. You're convinced, without proof, that my client is..." Zita could not bring herself to say that Yevgenia was a murderer. "...is involved. You break into her house at night. This isn't reasonable behaviour. As far as I can gather, the only firmly based accusation you have against her is that she is Russian by birth. All this seems to suggest a lack of balance in your judgements, to say the least."

Stevens was not put out by Zita's analysis; there was none of the fury with which he had reacted to her suggestion at the station that he had been upset by his youthful involvement in the Cresacre case. He simply commented, "Your own actions this evening have been about on a par with mine, I'd say, as far as common sense was concerned."

"I knew it wasn't a burglar here. I knew it would be you."

"You knew it, did you? On what basis? You were working a hunch, were you? As far as evidence goes, I can do much better than hunches for Mrs Loftus. She knew Eddie Cresacre very well. A middle-aged childless woman, she made friends with a number of local kids, was very kind to them. He was one of them. She had no way of accounting for herself for the time of his disappearance. She claimed to be at home, but we had another witness who saw her, or someone very like her, walking her dog by the river where Eddie Cresacre's bicycle was eventually found."

"You're struggling, Superintendent. You must have had half a dozen people with similar vague connexions with the child who could not produce alibis."

Stevens shrugged. It was clear he intended to argue no further.

Zita put down her mug. "Well, even if you find the Cresacres you've a long way to go to prove that Jean Loftus did it. You've got to produce more than a mad fixation to reopen the case." She patted her jacket pocket to locate the keys. "Now, if you've finished your empathizing with events thirty years ago, if that's what you were doing, I'd like to go home to bed and to leave my client's property secured before I go."

Chapter Nineteen

For the next few days there was a lull. Zita heard nothing more from Stevens, either in explanation or apology for his behaviour on Saturday night. She had hardly expected it as he had evidently seen nothing exceptionable in what he had done. She rang Reskimer about the bones, several times. He was always out of his office, lecturing, administering, digging, whatever it was that professors of archaeology did. Her persistence was only rewarded with a message delivered by the departmental secretary that the bones were looking younger rather than older at the moment, which she did not wish to hear. She decided to pursue him no further for the time being.

From the old leases, conveyancing documents and an estate rent book she composed a list of Yevgenia's predecessors as owners and occupiers of Asshe House. She had taken as her starting point the purchase of the house in the mid-1860s by a family called Hibberdine, who had occupied it for some twenty years and then, in 1885, had given it on a sixty-year lease to a certain Geoffrey Gamble, who had been mayor of Woodham at the time. This dignity did not last long. After about ten years the Gambles moved out and, although they retained the head lease, they had sublet and it appeared that the house had even fallen into multiple ownership for a time. The Hibberdines had sold the freehold after the First World War to a family called Juxon, who apparently had never lived in it. During their ownership the house had deteriorated even further, both materially and socially. It had been let on a series of short leases until, in

1938, it had been taken by a family called Dryburn. They had left in 1945 when the head lease had expired and the house had lain empty, unlet and for sale, until Yevgenia bought it and renovated it four years later. Simply having a list of names of owners and tenants was, Zita felt, an achievement, which she summed up on one side of paper.

Owners	Tenants
1864 - 1890: Simon Hibberdine	1885 - 1896: Geoffrey Gamble
1890 - 1912: John Hibberdine	1896 - 1897: James Whimster
	1897 - 1898: Paul Woodruff
	1898 - 1901: Arthur Morris
	1901 - 1907: Mitchell/Winchester
	1907 - 1912: Selwyn Allan
1912 - 1921: Maurice Hibberdine	1912 - 1922: Gavin Peel
1921 - 1949: Daniel Juxon	1912 - 1922: John Jump
	1922 - 1928: Clive Peerless
	1928 - 1938: Charles Crane
	1938 - 1945: Matthew Dryburn
1949 - 1992: Jean Loftus	

She concentrated particularly on the names of the tenants, which was depressingly long. Given the range of scientific estimates of the age of the skeleton, any one of them, from Geoffrey Gamble onwards, could have been involved, or at least in residence, at the time of the burial. She had been hoping for a non-English name somewhere on the list. Pigot had said that the skull's shape was Caucasian, but not necessarily English, in type. There was no help from the surnames. If the wives or grandparents of the owners or tenants had supplied the genetic characteristics noted by Pigot, the legal documents gave no hint.

It occurred to her as she studied her list that there might be information on either owners or tenants in the files of her own practice and in the lunch hour one day took herself up to the archives room again. She tackled the job alphabetically. No Allans with an A; no Cranes. She was passing on to Gamble when the name Cresacre leapt out at her from the stacks. This was not what she was looking for, not what she wanted to find, but she could not pass it by. She took off her shoes (imitation crocodile today) to stand on the wobbly booster stool to reach the Cresacre box. Then she sat on the stool to lift off the lid and look at the spare pile of its contents. On the first paper she opened she saw a vigorous signature, K. Loftus, witness. This must be the right family. Reluctantly, she sifted through what she had found until she came upon what Stevens needed: an address.

There was no real conflict in her mind about what she should do. The address was thirty years old and most likely no longer valid, but it must be handed on to the police straightaway. She could under no circumstances withhold information. However, she thought as she slid her shoes on again and carried the box downstairs to her office, she did not see why she might not make Stevens pay for it. When she gave her name, she was put through to him at once.

"Have you found the Cresacres?" she asked without preamble. She was not sure whether there was a moment's hesitation before he spoke or whether the gap was caused by his naturally calm manner. His reply when it came was as frank as her question. There was an assumption of a shared enquiry.

"No, nor the Gillings."

Zita was wondering how long DNA testing would take and whether the Cresacres might refuse to be involved. Their willingness to co-operate would depend entirely on their attitude to the police and to the death of their child. They might want to leave their grief in the past.

"I might have something to help you. I was pursuing my own enquiries when I came across an address for the Cresacres when they left Woodham."

There was another pause, more pronounced this time. "That's...fortunate. What's the date of the new address?"

"It's 1962, so it's not exactly hot. But it could be a start for you."

"It could," he agreed. "It is very public-spirited of you to hand it on."

"You wouldn't have expected less. But if it is..."

"If it is what?"

"If it is your Cresacres, I want to meet them."

"Go ahead. You're the one with the address."

"I haven't any status," Zita said bluntly.

"And I have?"

"Precisely."

"This is unorthodox."

"It's co-operative. This is the address: 22 Baxendine Drive, Crawley."

She heard him move a sheet of paper as he received her dictation and then he said, "Right, I'll get back to you."

He rang her that evening at home. "This is unofficial."

"OK."

"If you were to make a visit, unannounced, on your Cresacres at three tomorrow afternoon, by a curious coincidence you would find me about to go in. They're expecting me."

"OK. Well, thanks. I'll be there."

The following morning she rearranged her day and then rang the local paper. Did they keep back numbers she wanted to know. The archivist referred her to the library; they had no room at the paper's offices for more than ten years' worth of bound volumes, he affirmed, but the local studies room at the library had copies going back to 1720. What period was she interested in? Zita rang the library and asked if she could see the volumes of the local paper for 1960 and 1961 that morning. If she was to meet the Cresacres, she was going to find out what she could about the case.

Zita drove to Crawley thinking about the papers she had skimmed over in the library earlier that day. There had been pages about the case of Eddie Cresacre, his disappearance, the arrest of Petre and, later, the trial. The parents, however, had featured little. There had been a photograph of them in one of the earliest articles, their heads together, turning as if to avoid the camera flash. They did not look young, even then.

She stopped several times to consult her map and finally turned into a street of prim, pre-war bungalows, its invitingly straight length cut by the humps of sleeping policemen. She identified the house and drew up in front of it. An elderly

Fiesta was parked outside a small garage; a curving path led up to the porch between the neat grass of a flowerless front garden. A little farther up the road was an unmarked black car which must be Stevens'. His door opened as she got out. She had wondered if they would put on a show of surprise at seeing one another, but he did not bother. He led the way down the path with no more than a nod of greeting.

The door was opened to them promptly by a gaunt figure dressed in old flannels and a neatly buttoned cardigan and they were led through the hall to the sitting room at the back, looking onto another green patch.

Mr and Mrs Cresacre settled themselves in armchairs on either side of the fireplace containing an electric log fire. This forced Stevens and Zita to sit awkwardly side by side on the hard bench-like sofa, between them. The parents of the murdered child were by now over seventy, Zita judged, much older than she expected. Eddie Cresacre remained fixed at seven years old, his round face polished like an apple for the school photograph which had been used time and again in the newspaper reports, and in her mind his parents had remained at the age they would have been in 1960. So it was a shock to be reminded that although Eddie would always be seven, his parents were now a generation older, of grandparental age. They were both thin and pallid, with a bloodless, fragile air. They spoke little. There was no rush of words of welcome, or of curiosity. This seemed to be due less to wariness than to habitual reserve. The house had an atmosphere of passivity and silence about it. Everything was very tidy. Although the signs of the clutter of everyday life were there: newspapers beside the chairs, letters and circulars on the table near the window, each pile was ranged with an obsessive neatness.

They sat attentively, without showing emotion, as Stevens explained about the discovery of a child's skeleton in Broad Woodham and his belief that it might be their son's body. When he had finished speaking, Freda Cresacre turned her gaze from Stevens to her husband, not to see what his reaction would be, but as if confident that he would express her thoughts for her without her having to speak.

"That's very interesting, Mr Stevens. And it's very good of you to come all this way to tell us about it. But from our point of view, it doesn't really make much difference. We know his soul is with Jesus, so where his body lies doesn't matter. Isn't that so, Mother?"

She nodded. "There was a time, straight afterwards, when I wanted a grave to decorate, to visit every week. But we came through that. And I don't want it any more." She corrected herself. "Of course, if it were him—Eddie—we would have to see he got a proper burial. I suppose that's what you've come about. But I'm so used to thinking of him above, I don't think of him needing a grave any more."

Stevens was about to speak when Jim Cresacre said, "And how can we know it is him? I can't see how, after all this time, you can tell. He wouldn't be recognizable, I imagine. He'd be all eaten away."

"Oh, Jim." His wife's cry of distress was involuntary.

"This is very painful for you, I know," Stevens said, "which is why I wanted to come myself. It's now possible to identify people from their remains, even after thirty, thirty-two years. It's called DNA profiling and they've got techniques of finding minute bits of genetic material in the bones and blowing them up until they can read the genetic code." Jim Cresacre sat listening and nodding at what Stevens was saying, as if, Zita thought, he was already thoroughly familiar with the principle that was being described. He probably was, from having watched some science programme on television. "But, and this is where I would need your help, you have to have something to compare it with, a relative's DNA. They can't say who the dead person is, they can only say this dead person was or was not, most likely, related to this living one. So, if we took a blood sample of yours, Mr Cresacre, we could find out if the child was Eddie, and then, if it were, we would be able to release the remains to you for Christian burial."

Zita noted Stevens' cunning use of the epithet "Christian". But the old couple, who had begun the meeting with perfect composure, were now showing signs of unease.

"It's the same principle as a paternity test," Stevens was explaining, "except with this new technique you can do it over many generations, to discover if a skeleton belonged to your great-grandfather."

Freda Cresacre was leaning forward in her chair now. "Oh, I don't think we want any tests done, like that. It's quite unnecessary. I think it isn't Eddie's body. Who knows what that man did with it. Do you remember how he said he had left him in the Whitham Woods and they spent three days going through them, walking in lines to and fro? And again on the Guildford road and somewhere else too. I shall never forget that. Somehow I thought then if I got his body it would be getting Eddie back. It was mad. What difference does a body make? No, I don't think we want tests."

"Well, Mrs Cresacre, I appreciate that for you, after all these years, finding the body doesn't have the meaning it once did and brings up all kinds of unpleasant memories. But it would help us, you see. It would be a kind of elimination. If it is Eddie, then it's not someone else. If it is not Eddie, who is it? Why is it there?"

"I might have known. It's not for us that you bothered to come."

Jim Cresacre spoke over the top of his wife's bitterness. "Why is it there? How would Petre have buried the body in someone else's garden? It can't be Eddie, it stands to reason."

"It would help us greatly in our enquiries if you could see your way to help us to eliminate Eddie."

They had reached a stand off. Stevens had clearly thought at the start that the finding of their son's body would be pleasing to the Cresacres; once he had understood their position, he spoke of "elimination" of Eddie from the enquiries. The conversation began to turn in circles. Freda Cresacre repeated her belief that her son was "above", rather than on earth; Stevens patiently reiterated his need for their assistance.

Zita glanced round the room which was dim in comparison with the brilliance of the sun on the grass outside. No books were displayed in the alcoves, no photographs. A few small ornaments of little animals, their cuddly, furry aspects coldly rendered in ceramic, were ranged, widely spaced, on the lower shelves. In one corner were two telephone directories, and on top of them a compact, solid volume, unmistakably a Bible.

Stevens was now trying a different tack, emphasizing how easy the test was. "Just a pin prick of blood would be all that's necessary," he was saying. "There's no need to go anywhere special, to the doctor or a laboratory. Somebody would come and take a little drop from your thumb. It's not complicated or painful. It's a very common one nowadays, the paternity test, and they're so good at it they can do it on Egyptian mummies."

The agitation in Freda Cresacre became more pronounced. "No," she said. "Dad won't do it. Why should he? He doesn't like injections."

"It doesn't have to be a blood test," said Stevens, sounding a bit desperate by now. "Just a little swab around the mouth with cotton wool. For some reason the scientists prefer blood, but saliva'll do."

Zita leaned forward, towards Mrs Cresacre. "Would *you* rather take the test?" she asked. Both Cresacres looked at her for their first time. They had clearly registered her as some kind of junior assistant, a secretary possibly, and her initiative seemed to surprise them. There was a long pause, which Stevens did not break.

"I don't know," Mrs Cresacre replied at last. "Would it work, then, for me?"

"Of course. And I would have said that it was a better idea myself. After all, you are his mother and that is a much more certain relationship than paternity."

Her comment was a statement of impersonal scientific fact. It was aimed, obliquely, at Stevens for his concentration on Mr Cresacre, his ignoring of the wife. As she was speaking she regretted what she was saying, which might be misunderstood by two people who were probably very literal-minded. The reaction she received was astonishing. Mrs Cresacre leaned back in her chair, her hands gripping the ends of the arms, her eyes closed. Her face was contorting to such a degree that Zita thought that she might be about to have an epileptic fit.

"The sins of the past rise up and cry out against me. There's no cheating God. You can live a righteous life for very nearly forty years—Eddie would have been thirty-nine this year—but the sins of your past come back to haunt you. You try to forget…"

Her husband lurched forward from his chair, trying to release the grip of her hands, stroking her forehead. "There's no crying out against you, Freda. You can do the test, if they insist. There's no need to go through all that again. The past is dead and buried."

It was an hour later when Zita and Stevens got back into their cars. As the front door had closed on them he had said, "Let's go somewhere for some tea." She had nodded in agreement. He led the way and she saw he was taking them back to Woodham. She followed docilely, thankful for a period of isolation in her car after an afternoon of emotion.

They were approaching the outskirts of the town. Stevens turned off the ring road one roundabout early into an estate of modern houses whose unfenced front gardens gave the area an American atmosphere, as if the inhabitants were all saying, we have nothing to hide, no secrets here, we're all upfront. He swung the car into a driveway in front of a double garage.

"We really need a drink after all that," he said as he waited for her to join him. "But it's too early and I've still got work to do. So it'll have to be tea. Come in." He unlocked the glass front door and waved at the room straight ahead. "Go on in," he said. "I'll bring it through."

Zita had made no protest, not even a conventional one; she was curious to see him at home. Houses concealed as much as they revealed: her own said that she had a handicapped son and not much more. Yet there was something to be learned, nonetheless. This one was arranged for ease and comfort over elegance or style. It was tidy without the obsessiveness of the Cresacres. There were books in a bookcase against one wall interspersed with a run of CDs and another of videos. It defined itself openly as middle of everything, middle class, middle aged, middle brow. Yet there were incongruities that jarred, not violently but insistently, with the bland surface. The flowers on the coffee table were a huge arching bunch of white scented lilies. On a side table, under a lamp, was a gathering of photographs, not the family snapshots that might have been expected, but stiff, signed black and white portraits, dating from the twenties or thirties, of the kind that are seen standing on the cashmere shawl thrown over a grand piano in a great house. There was a woman in a trim little suit and a hat with a feather, again in a white ballgown; an army officer wearing jodhpurs and a curious little forage cap; a be-medalled old buffer with mustachios and white hair cut *en brosse*. Zita had only time to glance at them before Stevens came in carrying a tray with a pot of tea, two mugs and a plate of chocolate digestives.

"Well," he said, after a moment or two. "I'll have you sit in on an interview, any time. You really know how to punch below the belt."

"You got what you wanted, didn't you?" Zita said disagreeably. "She's going to do the test for you."

"I told you they beat up Petre, didn't I? No names were ever mentioned, but we all knew who'd done it. It wasn't just the lads, the PCs. One of them was my boss. He wasn't much good as a CID officer. He had no understanding of psychology at all. But, by God, he could kick your head in with the best around. You remind me of him."

"Don't tell me that you saw it all, understood it all, and had decided to say nothing," Zita said furiously, "because I bloody won't believe you." She never swore; she never found it necessary to swear. What was happening to her? "I said it as a statement of fact. I didn't know the result it would produce."

"So that's it now. No skill involved, just chance. No admiration required."

"Well, did you guess?"

"No. That's why I was speaking to him. I thought in these old-fashioned godly families, it's the man who is in charge.

You can't undermine him by addressing the wife. I hadn't even worked out that it really had to be the mother who had to take the test."

In the face of this admission, Zita said, "I suppose I guessed something when they were both so anxious for him not to take the test, but I spoke before I had time to work out the implications. Oh hell." She put the heels of her hands into her eyes, to blank out what she had seen. "What a mentality. Thirty years of thinking a child died as punishment for your sin. And if I understood properly from all that self-abasement, it was one drunken, adulterous fling."

Throughout the hour of painful, unstoppable confession that Zita and Stevens had endured, Freda Cresacre had paradoxically never lost control. She had raved, tugged at her own hair, literally beaten her narrow chest with her fists. Yet all the time Zita had the impression that she willed her behaviour. She wanted to confess and she was determined to do so. She may have played the same part on several previous occasions. Certainly, her husband had known that Eddie was not his child before the disappearance. Afterwards, she had become convinced that the child's death was a punishment for what she had done; her self-reproach must have reached the proportions of near-madness. To have precipitated and witnessed such an outburst had left Zita ashamed and depressed, angry with Stevens and with her own success. She did not altogether want the test done. Even if it were Eddie Cresacre, Stevens would be a long way from arresting Yevgenia for murder, but things would look a great deal worse for her.

"How long will it take, the test?" Zita asked.

"Not long. The old one used to take about six weeks, but they've got a new one now which is still under trial. It amplifies the DNA from the old bones. You really need marrow and there's not much of that left after thirty years, but they can now isolate DNA from the smallest scraps and enlarge it. The difficulty is with the old stuff, of course, not the new. It's not as precise as the old test, but it'll certainly tell us if the body was Freda Cresacre's son."

"Then what? If it is Eddie Cresacre?"

"We shall interview the Russian woman again, since she was the owner and occupier of the house at the time of Eddie Cresacre's death. She'll still have a lot of questions to answer. Peter Gilling, for example."

"Why do you call her the Russian woman all the time? How did you know she was Russian? Even I didn't know she was Russian until this summer. She is always known as Jean Loftus."

He did not reply at first, absorbed in pouring tea. Finally he said, "That kind of thing is routine. Name-age-address-date-and-place-of-birth. I must have written it all down. I was taking the record. We sat in that room of hers, overlooking the garden. And all the time the child was lying there beneath our noses. I try to remember whether the garden was recently dug, what it looked like. But it must have been well hidden. We would have noticed if there were obvious signs of digging."

"What's her being Russian got to do with it?"

Stevens paused as if he had never thought of it before.

"Nothing, I suppose. It just stuck in my mind she was Russian. And I always think of them as very cruel people, harsh and cruel."

"Do you? I think of them as emotional, sentimental people. We can't both be right. National stereotypes are hardly the best ways to categorize individuals." She put down her mug. It was odd how, with Stevens, she passed so quickly from antagonism to amicability, and back again. "What about the test?"

"I'll get someone round there to take blood from Mrs Cresacre tomorrow, the sooner the better. Then it goes to the Met's laboratory in London."

"And how much is all this going to cost? I can't believe technology like that comes cheap."

"My budget will stretch to it, don't worry. But you're right. Six hundred pounds? Eight hundred? It depends how difficult the bones are."

Chapter Twenty

Stevens' remarks about Russians made Zita think about Valentina, who was due back from Milan at the end of the week. She was guiltily aware that she had done nothing about her promise to arrange a visit to a concert or a play for her mother. As so often happens, the reactivation of her mother in her mind presaged a phone call. Zita had a sudden vision of Valentina's white helmet and manic dark eyes as she picked up the receiver.

"Zita? I wondered if I would get your crazy girl."

"Mama, she's not crazy. She is marvellous with Tom. You mustn't..."

"Of course she's crazy. Tom needs someone much more intelligent, a mathematician. But that's not what I was calling about. The conference has been very interesting and stimulating. I'm very pleased I came." Zita hunched her shoulder to hold the telephone against her ear and began to tear open a bag of salad and divide it between two plates; Yevgenia was coming to dinner. "And I bought you a handbag."

"Mama, how sweet of you. I know you think I'm frivolous for liking clothes so much."

"And a belt," Valentina went on relentlessly. "I bought waist sixty-six centimetres to make you lose a kilo or two."

"What's the point, Mama. I'm happy as I am. Keep the belt yourself. It'll fit you." She was cutting smoked halibut into pieces and draping them over black bread.

"No. I shall bring them over to you when I get back. But

that won't be immediately. So you'll have to cancel the tickets you've got for us. Or go with someone else. Invite a man. What about Marcus's son, the chef? He would suit you ideally, two greedy people."

"I've never even met Ivo, at least since we were children."

"Well, take that boorish inspector you told me about. He's the only man you know who hasn't got a wife. Forget Oliver."

"Mama. Anyway, he must have a wife." Had he? The house had showed signs of a woman, in the flowers for example, while at the same time its atmosphere was solitary.

"OK, honey, leave it. Now, I'm not coming back immediately because I met some interesting people at the conference and I'm going on with him to Leningrad."

"Leningrad?" Zita said in astonishment.

"They call it St Petersburg now," Valentina said, as if Zita did not know where Leningrad was. "There's a consulate general here and I've had the Russian Academy of Sciences fax me an invitation and my visa should be ready tomorrow or the next day and then we'll go."

"Mama, I'm...Well, I'm amazed. You've always said you would never go back."

"Of course, I couldn't go back before, but now I think I will. So I'm going to Rome once my visa's through and I'll get a flight from there direct to St Petersburg and back in about ten days. I may try to go back to Moscow too. I'll phone you before I leave and from Russia, if they have telephones that work there."

"Right, Mama."

"Goodbye, Zita. Kisses to Tom. Forget the bastard."

There was much in this conversation for Zita to think about as she set the table, put out the cheese and opened the wine. If Valentina had been twenty years younger she would have thought it was a mid-life crisis. Her mother had always been so contemptuous of her native country, in both large and small things. Russians were so inefficient, so pusillanimous, she always said. They submitted to tyranny and were slaves even in their minds: invalid science and grotesque art was the result. During Zita's childhood Valentina had been as English as she could make herself, which was not very. Since John Guilfoyle's death and her move to America she had transformed herself again. She had clearly been meant to be a Californian from the start. So what this sudden return to her roots presaged Zita could not understand.

Zita asked Yevgenia about it as they sat at the kitchen table later that evening.

"Something or someone will have raised a question, a reminder of the past," Yevgenia said authoritatively. "So she will have had to go back. And much better she should go now, while she's able to, than put it off for twenty years and then not be able to manage it. If you have made breaks in your life, as your mother or I did, you have to face the past sooner or later. If you don't go and deal with it of your own accord, it rises up of its own will, as it has done with me."

"That reminds me. Stevens has found the Cresacres. They are going to do a DNA test to find out whether the skeleton is Eddie Cresacre."

Yevgenia looked so vague for a moment that it was clear that she had not followed Zita's train of thought. Then she said, "Yes, that too, I suppose. That is the past literally rising up in accusation."

"How can it be in accusation? The skeleton must surely predate your ownership of the house. How could Petre possibly have buried a child in your garden when you were living there? Could you have been away on holiday?"

"I forget now what was happening to us at the time. I only remember the unpleasantness of the police interviews."

"Interviews? There was more than one?"

"Oh, yes, the police came back several times. But the significance is this: the finger of the child points at other deaths."

"What do you mean?"

Yevgenia did not reply. Zita turned to the more practical line of approach which she had decided to follow.

"Did you know the people you bought Asshe House from?" she asked. "The Juxons?"

Yevgenia submitted to her questioning without protest,

although it was evident in her expression that she thought it pointless. "No, I don't remember meeting anyone. I think someone had died and that was why the house was for sale. And it hadn't been inhabited since the end of the war. It was in an appalling state. I did to it everything that Naomi is redoing now. I was so proud of my modern kitchen. I felt I had come so far from Maris and our scullery at Kornu with a hand pump over the sink and the great wood-burning range."

Zita was afraid that the old woman was going to wander off into a welter of reminiscences about her childhood home, but Yevgenia suddenly reverted to the subject of Asshe House. "There had been some tragedy, I think. No one told me what it was. Kenward probably knew, but he kept it from me. It was the kind of thing that local people gossip about, whatever it was. I had a char who had worked for the previous people, they must have been the tenants, not the owners..."

"The Dryburns," Zita put in.

"Is that what they were called? They had left long before I came. But the char used to talk about them cryptically sometimes. She called them 'funny folk'. Though she probably said that about me, too, because as far as I could see their funniness lay in the fact that the wife was a foreigner—a Pole or a Czech—and had an odd religion, Catholic perhaps. So I was just as funny, in those terms."

"But perhaps she didn't realize it in your case, that you were Russian and Orthodox."

"No," Yevgenia said slowly. "She didn't, of course. I hid it very well in those days."

"What was she called, the char?"

"Oh goodness knows. You're not seriously going to look for her, Zita?"

"Why not? But not if you can't remember her name."

"I can. I may be getting on but I can still remember some things. She was called Hovell, Mrs Hovell. I never knew her Christian name. I loved what I saw as democratic politeness in respectfully addressing my cleaner as Mrs Hovell. And talking of cleaning ladies, I have agreed to have Xenia from next week when Lucia goes to Switzerland."

Zita allowed the conversation to be turned. She was sure that Yevgenia had nothing to do with the skeleton; it was her business to be convinced of it. To admit otherwise raised a series of horrendous pictures: Yevgenia and Petre; Yevgenia and her husband; Yevgenia alone. And then to live with the body blooming each year in the roses, to see every June the dark flowers of Tuscany Superb blossoming over the bones. She preferred not to imagine it. It seemed to her such a combination of wickedness and sickness that she could not see that anyone could live out their normal life like that. Then she would remember the concentration camp guards who put behind them a long episode of unimaginable cruelty to settle down to life at home or in exile as loyal husbands and devoted fathers, dog lovers and worthy citizens. No. No. Better to think of that odd girl, Xenia.

"Rosie rang me yesterday and begged me to have her," Yevgenia was saying.

"I thought you were not at all keen, originally. Why does Rosie want her to come?"

Yevgenia cut herself another slice of cheese. "She didn't say precisely. She simply begged me to let her come here. I told Marcus yesterday that I wouldn't take her. But I can't refuse Rosie anything and when she appealed to me like that, of course I said I'd have her. I don't know whether she just finds the competition intolerable in Gayton Street or whether there's more to it. I suspect…"

"What do you suspect?"

"I don't like her, you know. She's both too Russian, and not Russian enough. She is of a generation which has grown up under communism, shifty, saying what they think you want to hear."

"That seems a bit hard," Zita said tolerantly.

"I saw her with Marcus when we went to Glyndebourne. She was like a spider; she had very delicately wrapped him up and swathed him in silk. He was at her mercy."

"Marcus? Yevgenia, you're exaggerating."

"No, no. There's no fool like a middle-aged man with a pretty girl younger than his own daughter."

"You don't mean she's sleeping with him?"

"No, I don't think I do. I mean something much more powerful which perhaps you rarely see these days: that is, not sleeping with him. So when Rosie phoned I suspected a problem with Al."

"You're turning her into a seductress of epic talents. She's not even a pretty girl. She seemed to me to be struggling to cope and finding it a bit hard. She had the enterprise to get herself here; she's obviously very adaptable, just a bit bewildered by everything she sees around her. Do you think she is from your family, by the way, or was that just an excuse to get here?"

"No, she's not one of my Chornoroukys: she's sly."

"But that's not a reason, Yevgenia."

"No, and the problem is that she's Xenia Alexandrovna; her father's patronymic was Alexandrovich: he was Alexander Alexandrovich Chornorouky." The words on Yevgenia's tongue rolled with the heavy Russian stress.

"Yes?"

"Well, they're very common names. Every second Russian is Sasha Alexandrovich, so it proves nothing. But I had a cousin who was Alexander Alexandrovich."

"Could she be..."

"No, no absolutely not. He died during the war. He was shot by the NKVD. No, I just meant that it was a Chornorouky name. And Xenia too."

"Yes?"

"I had a great-grandmother called Xenia. I never knew her, of course. She died young, I think. She was Xenia Vassilievna Orlova. She hated the Russian climate and lived all her life at a villa in the Crimea, leaving for Egypt or France or Rome in the winter. She had an extraordinary collection of rubies. No wonder there was a revolution. You cannot imagine the pleasure of being innocent English middle class."

"So Xenia is transferred to your care, or you to hers. Perhaps you'll become fond of her while she's living with you."

Yevgenia depressed the corners of her mouth sceptically. "Anyway, she's not like you and Valentina, she's going back to her own country."

"I doubt it," said Yevgenia.

Zita volunteered to collect Xenia from the station on the day of her arrival. Yevgenia had tried to brush away her offer. "Let her take a taxi," she said. Zita, who had not seen Xenia since the lunch two months earlier when she had seemed a very forlorn creature, had insisted and was surprised at the new Xenia who walked out of the station carrying her shabby Russian suitcase. Her appearance was different, certainly; the slim girl in jeans, T shirt and long cardigan was not any smarter in any conventional way than the skinny creature in a nylon skirt who had radiated a sharp, hostile scent, yet she was so changed that she was almost unrecognizable. It was as if she had gathered up the fragmented pieces of herself into an intensely hard missile that she was about to launch at some objective. What that might be Zita could not guess. She could only wonder what effect this new personality would have on Yevgenia. She no longer thought it likely that the old woman would become fond of her guest and helper. Yevgenia did not give her approval or friendship easily. Zita hoped that Xenia would make herself as adaptable and agreeable in Broad Woodham as she had in Hampstead, but it was certainly a difficult task. Not only was Yevgenia suspicious of her, Xenia had the additional disadvantage of having Rosie's dislike. Yevgenia was not demonstrative; she had controlled that Russian trait, if she had ever had it, in her assumption of Englishness; but she was, Zita knew, devoted to Rosie, much more so than to Ivo. Ivo's brilliance of personality and success in his career made him an admired grandson; Rosie's less showy character (Zita assumed Ivo to be showy from his television appearances) made her the beloved one.

"I hope you won't find Broad Woodham too quiet after London," Zita said to the silent girl beside her in the car.

"Not at all," Xenia replied politely. Her English had come a long way in two months. "I shall do different things from what I did in Hampstead. Naomi said there is a bicycle I can ride to see things. And I believe I have more defined duties, so many hours a week to work. At Naomi's, I really did not have to do anything. I hope, too, you will recommend me to your friends for baby-sitting. I must work, you know, to earn money."

Part Ten

XENIA

Chapter Twenty-one

As the date for her departure came into view, five weeks away now, Xenia had the sense that she was walking up a mountain path with a sheer drop on one side, her left. The track was stony, precipitous and progressively narrowing. She could not see whether it was going to take her, at last, to the invisible cliff top that must be somewhere above her, or whether it would eventually peter out in front of a smooth and featureless rock face. Only very careful control of where she placed her feet, intense concentration on the path, prevented her from lurching over the edge.

For the first time, on her last afternoon in Hampstead, after they had drunk their tiny cups of syrupy black coffee in the garden, she had led Al silently upstairs to her attic room. She had paused three steps below the first landing, placed her finger on her lips, and moved with exaggerated caution past Naomi's door.

"Yes," Naomi's voice spoke with her habitual calm, encouraging tones, "so how did you feel when that happened?"

They ran up the next flights, stifling laughter, and shut Xenia's door crisply behind them, to stand staring at one another. Like many initial encounters, it had been too rapidly and explosively successful. However, Xenia had not been dissatisfied with the outcome which was renewed desire. She could only hope that telephone calls and occasional meetings would sustain and increase it. She was resolved both to maintain her hold over Al and to exploit the opportunities that offered in her exile to Broad Woodham.

She found at first that she faced a much harder task in her second objective than she expected. She had known from the start that Yevgenia resented and distrusted her. She wanted to find out why and to turn the dislike into its opposite, if she could. She was concerned to find that the evidence of hostility was very strong and hard to live with. Naomi and Marcus had been easy for her, she now realized; they had busy lives and were well disposed towards her. During the few hours of the day that they were all three of them together it was not difficult to please them. Yevgenia, on the other hand, was at home all day long, watching her as Xenia herself had watched her hosts in Hampstead, so that she could not take over the house with the same ease as at Gayton Street.

Yevgenia was, too, often in pain which could make her fractious, even though she concealed it. It was lucky, Xenia thought, that she had had long practice of coping with an alcoholic father, as she waited, without betraying impatience, for the old woman to stalk from one room to the next on her two sticks. She never allowed herself to succumb to an impulse to retort on Yevgenia's brusqueness, which often amounted to rudeness. She noticed that the old woman did not like to look at her; she knew this signified her dislike. She concentrated at first on making herself both as useful and as unobtrusive as possible. In rendering herself almost invisible, she was able to observe the rooms and routines of the house. Although Yevgenia still had sharp hearing, Xenia, once she had installed her in her chair in the drawing room, could move around on bare feet at the far end of the house. She gradually reconnoitred Yevgenia's bedroom and bathroom. Late at night she explored in the dark by touch the kitchen cupboards, the interior of the fridge, the study and the drawing room.

In the first week of her move to Broad Woodham she was impelled, during her afternoon explorations of the town, to take a blue and white sponge bag from Boots, which she left in a neighbouring department store; a paperback of Man Ray's photographs which she left on a bench in the park by the church, after caressingly turning the pages and admiring the images. A number of items ended up in dustbins, as it was impossible to add to the sparse contents of an old lady's shelves in the same way as to the crammed cupboards of the Hampstead house. She longed to rid herself of the obsessive search for the ideal object and at four o'clock when she returned from her walk she vomited furiously in her bathroom. Each day, while she was out, she telephoned Al and only the evidence of the phone picked up at the second ring kept her from despair. The mountain path be-came steeper and narrower.

One evening in Xenia's second week in Woodham, Zita had called in on her way home from work to see how Yevgenia was and, as she was leaving, said with mock severity, in Russian, *"No, shto,* what are you doing to Xenia? She is losing weight; she looks like a scarecrow."

Yevgenia, who until then had only spoken in English to Xenia, replied in Russian, "Is she thinner? Let me see you, child."

Zita took her by the shoulders and turned her to face Yevgenia. "Look how thin she is. It is most unRussian." She pulled at the loose top of Xenia's jeans. "Even my mother would think it has gone too far. Did I tell you she called from St Petersburg last night? She has decided to extend her visa and go to Moscow. She wants to visit the block of flats where she lived as a child and to trace her mother's older sister. I can't imagine what is happening to her. She said she now realized that I had the perfect Russian figure."

Xenia pulled away from Zita's hands. "But why would she say that? You're beautiful," she said. She spoke with evident sincerity.

"Oh dear, oh dear," Zita said. "I've made you cry. Are you homesick, thinking of Moscow?"

Xenia sniffed and flicked at the corners of her eyes with her finger tips. "Of course not," she said.

"Yevgenia," Zita's voice resumed its imitation of her mother's scolding tone, "you must take more care of Xenia. Feed her up. You'd better come to me this evening, so I can nourish you both."

Xenia escaped from them before Zita left, agreeing to accompany Yevgenia to dine next door that evening. After dinner, she complained of tiredness and returned home, leaving Yevgenia with Zita. She was about to go to her own room, when, passing the open door to the drawing room, she glanced in at the empty chair with its little table beside it, arrayed with Yevgenia's books and papers. Xenia had never yet had the opportunity of freely examining the room without its owner somewhere nearby. She walked in slowly, sniffing the air like an animal. It smelled faintly of old lady, a talcum-powdery odour of roses. She sat down in the high-cushioned wing-chair and began to pick up the objects from the table, turning them over in her hands to look at them from every side. She ruffled the leaves of a pad of lists, opened a biography of Churchill and glanced at the postcard which functioned as a book mark. It was from Ivo, from Madrid, showing Eve placidly holding the apple that she had just plucked, while a concupiscent Adam stood behind her, caressing her right nipple. An extraordinary card to send your grandmother, Xenia thought. She put Yevgenia's reading glasses on her own nose and looked out at the lights beyond the hedge, then removed them abruptly as the other woman's vision hurt her eyes. She moved in the chair and encountered a small rectangular object tucked down the side of the cushion. As she slid her hand down to remove it Yevgenia said to her, "Let me trace the death of Alexander Alexandrovich Chornorouky."

Xenia leapt out of the chair with a terrible cry, whirling round to face the door. There was no one there. Fortunately for her, no one had seen that her face was bloodless. Her eyes, which normally appeared as pale as water, were dark and staring, the pupils enlarged almost to envelop the yellow-grey irises. She realized at once that no one had seen her involuntary self-betrayal. She put her hand to her chest. Her heart was lurching and pounding with overwhelming force that only gradually diminished sufficiently to allow her to hear the gentle hissing of revolving spools. She reached back into the chair and drew out the tiny palm-sized tape recorder. She touched the rewind button and waited until the light clunk indicated the beginning of the tape had been reached. She sat down again in Yevgenia's place to press the play button.

"Finding the Chornorouky money was as extraordinary and fortuitous as meeting Kenward and getting myself out of Germany. At the time that I came to England I had no idea that there was anything much here. Certainly it played no part in my wanting to come. I came in flight; I was running as far as I could from Kornu, from Xan, from Lai, from everything that had happened since the beginning of the war. Not even when I was once here, did I think of Prince Yegor. It was not until Kenward was divorced, not an easy or quick process in those days, and we were married, that somehow the memory came back to me. No one had told me anything directly. Aunt Zoya just before her death had told Xan that his grandfather had left an English will and there might be something for us in London. Xan had reported what she had said to me, without details, and almost in parenthesis. He had mentioned the English will, only to dismiss its importance. There might be money in England, but he did not intend to go there: Sweden and America were his goals and anything in London would have to wait for the unimaginable future after the war. If there was a written record in Latvia among Aunt Zoya's or Xan's papers, it was left behind when Alek and Lai and I began our trek to the West in 1944.

"How do you find the legacy of a great-uncle who died more than twenty years ago in another country? At first I thought it was hopeless, that whatever was here was lost with everything else my family had once owned, one item in the trail of fortunes seized from them over the previous three decades, estates in Russia, the Ukraine, the Crimea, palaces in Moscow and St Petersburg, villas by the sea, country houses, all of them crammed with furniture, jewels, pictures, sculptures, none of which I had ever seen. I was entirely wrong. It was all so easy. Such an amazing contrast to come from Kornu, walking westward through devastated landscapes and a collapsed society, to arrive in England where administration had never broken down, where, even through a world war, all the aspects of civil life remained in place.

"I went to Somerset House and obtained a copy of my great-uncle's will, dated 1923. A solicitor in Queen Anne's Gate, still there, still working in the same office, had drawn it up, was the executor. Everything was in order; the will proved; the money invested; the key to the safe deposit in Coutts waiting for me. The arrangements were all very simple: everything was to be divided between Xan and me, the last of the Chornoroukys. The money was not a great fortune, though it had been prudently invested for twenty-five years. The real legacy was an afterthought, discovered in the safe deposit. I can remember opening it one afternoon, with Kenward. It was with a complete lack of excitement, without any anticipation of treasure trove, that we unwrapped a brown paper parcel containing an album, three rolled canvases and a casually scribbled note from Prince Yegor. It was addressed to Xan and stated that he had bought the album at auction in 1910 and for some reason it had been left in London throughout the war. One canvas, *An Old Man,* was being cleaned in 1914 and Prince Yegor had forgotten about it until a few months before his return to Kornu to die. The other two pictures had a special value for me. They had been ordered by my grandfather, Yuri Alexandrovich, for his daughter while they were in France in 1912. Prince Yegor had collected them for his brother from the artist in Cannes after the war and for some reason not transported them farther than London. His note to Xan finished, *You and Genya must share these oddments one day as mementos of our past."*

There was so long a pause on the tape that Xenia thought that Yevgenia must have broken off her account at that point. She was about to turn the machine off when Yevgenia said, "The flotsam of the Chornoroukys, cast up in London, by chance, in 1914 at the start of the war, consisted of about forty pages of drawings by Leonardo da Vinci. The *Old Man* was a Rembrandt. The two paintings which my grandfather had ordered for my mother on their travels together in Europe before her marriage, were by Matisse. They are called *Sea* and *Sky* and can, I believe, be seen nowadays at the Museum of Modern Art in New York. My mother had interested my grandfather in modern painters. From what Aunt Zoya used to tell me, I know that my mother particularly loved Paris and from the time of her earliest visits had bought paintings there. Her first purchase, as a teenager, had been a little oil of a pile of fruit by Cezanne, which had hung in the bedroom where she had been killed. I remember it was salvaged from my father's house and brought to Kornu. I had it in my school room and used to sit at a battered pitch pine table, chewing the end of a pencil, looking at its acid greens and oranges. But that is by the way."

Xenia stopped the tape. She suddenly imagined the small Yevgenia of the 1920s, kicking her legs against her old chair, gazing at Cezanne's fruit chosen by her mother. Was that painting one whose impersonal beauty Xenia had studied on the walls of the Pushkin Museum in Moscow? She thought of the postcards of admired images that she used to stick on the wall by her bed in the *obshezhitiye.* There was an immediate wash of envy and desire, as real as the fear that she had experienced a few minutes earlier. She would have the real one, not the imitation.

"I sold them all, the album and the three paintings. No feeling for the past, for my mother's love of art, held me back. Such possessions are appropriate for Russian princes, not for the English bourgeoisie. I could not sell them all at once, and that was another piece of luck for me, for the delay only increased the money I received. Half of everything belonged to Xan. The will was the kind of document made by people who see their families going on and on; there is no assumption that their world may come to an end and the dinosaurs and the dodos die out. So Prince Yegor had envisaged every case he could think of, my death or Xan's, the birth of our children and our grand-children. As I was the survivor, it all came to me; I only had to prove Xan's death. I knew Xan was dead, clubbed and then shot on the platform of Riga Station as he was loaded onto the cattle trucks to Siberia, but they do not deliver death certificates in circumstances like that. I thought that this would mean that Xan's half would stay in limbo and I was not unhappy that it should be so. It gave me some sense of his presence in the idea that his half of our inheritance remained separate, discrete. But this was something that was impossible to explain to Kenward who had not even known of Xan's existence before this. He set in motion the legal machine which, although it moves very slowly, eventually produces what is required. Applications were made to the Soviet authorities to trace the death of Alexander Alexandrovich Chornorouky of Kornu in the Latvian Soviet Socialist Republic. I too wrote, for the first time, to Inna at Jamala, asking her to try to get news of Xan from the authorities in Riga. Months passed and even years. I can't remember which came through first, the formal legal notification of his death at Riga on 14th June 1941, or the letter from Inna, enclosing the statement she had received of Xan's death at Krasnoyarsk in Siberia in 1944.

"The inconsistency did not worry me. I knew Xan was dead. I had never believed in his being alive since the moment I had found the signs of the raid on the woodcutters' hut. Now, looking back, I marvel at my faith in his death. You read of women who cling to their belief in the existence of their husbands, lovers, children, in the face of all the evidence and no evidence, and, years later, their loyalty is rewarded and the dead ones rise again, crawl out of the gulag to return home to them. I never believed. At the time, I knew that Lai had killed him; Lai had willed his death. Now, I think that I did it. If I had believed, if I had remained in Kornu with Alek throughout everything, would I have got Xan back? Would he have been released from the camps with the others in the 1950s and come home to Kornu, expecting to find me and Alek waiting for him? If I had believed enough, would he have survived?"

Xenia turned off the tape recorder. The room was dark now and Yevgenia would soon be back, assisted by Zita; she would hear their voices speaking Russian with their odd accents, as they unlocked the door and entered the house. But still she did not move, but held the face of the machine against her cheek. An idea, germinating in her head since listening to Naomi before she left Hampstead, suddenly burst out fully grown, like a speeded up film of a developing plant seed. Those dead bones must be made to live.

She went to her room and waited for the sounds of Yevgenia's return; she counted her slow movement towards her bedroom, the sloth-like placing of stick, foot, stick, foot. She listened to the soft, night-time noises of running water and closing cupboards, checking the passage of time every fifteen minutes on her bedside clock until she dared to get out of bed and silently cross the hall to the drawing room again. She was sure there was more; she needed more. Without turning on any of the lights she knelt down by Yevgenia's chair and placed her palms on the objects on the little table. Moving them around gently, she identified a box of tapes. She picked it up and crawled to the window, so that by the light of the moon she could examine them. They were only marked by numbers in Yevgenia's clumsy arthritic hand. She took the first and slipped it into the machine. Holding it against her ear, still crouched on the floor, she turned it on.

"I was born in Petrograd in 1917 in the last days of the Russian empire..."

Xenia listened to Yevgenia's childhood for hours, then and on succeeding nights, sometimes sitting by the sliding doors, looking into the garden, sometimes in her own bed with the recorder tucked under her pillow below her ear. Her reactions to what she heard were complex. The ability to put herself in someone else's place did not come naturally to her and she was usually too busy with her own emotions to make an effort to identify with another's. No such effort was required of her in listening to the tapes. Yevgenia was Xenia; Xenia was Yevgenia. Somehow Yevgenia had managed to escape that doomed

Latvian paradise and to reach England. Xenia listened to each tape in the hope of learning how it was done, but found nothing. Yevgenia had not told her story in chronological order. Although she had begun at the beginning, her mind had swung backwards and forwards across the years of her childhood and youth, picking out incidents and anecdotes, beginning each new recording session at a new point speaking Russian or English as her feelings or the subject dictated. Not that she thought that the same ploy that had worked for Yevgenia would work for her: Yevgenia herself had told her that at the opera. The interest lay in the parallel which she would make work for her, along with the name of her father. Was he the Alexander Alexandrovich Chornorouky, Yevgenia's cousin and husband? Xenia was not sure. Her father had been born in 1915. He had been over seventy when he was consumed in the burning flat in Siberia. But how old would Xan have been? He was a few years older than Yevgenia, already in the care of Aunt Zoya when she was born. His age was roughly right. But there was no other link that could connect her father with Xan Chornorouky. He had never spoken of an idyllic Latvian childhood, of a girl cousin, of his great-aunt who brought him up, of his grandfather and great-uncle who had died when he was a child. He had never spoken about his childhood at all. Her knowledge of his life went back only to the camps. His past was all bitterness and wrong, but his fuddled conversations with himself had only rehearsed in detail the injustices he had suffered.

Xenia wished now that she had paid more attention to those hours of drunken ramblings, instead of deliberately shutting her ears to them and filling her heart with hatred for him. His evenings had usually been spent in solitary drinking and sometimes the vodka did not speak. He would slip rapidly into unconsciousness before he had drunk so much that he was incapable of working the next day. Drunkenness was everywhere habitual in Novoleninsk and his pallid and tremulous appearance in the mornings was not remarkable. Only occasionally did the alcohol fail to deliver oblivion, and then he would remain awake, alive, and suddenly vocal. She always listened for the first sound of his voice. On those nights she did not come out of the minute kitchen where she sat over her homework to set up her camp bed in the hall at ten o'clock. Instead, she wedged the kitchen chair under the handle of the door and spent the night on the kitchen floor. She had suffered too much as a child, to risk facing him on those nights. Her suffering at first had been indirect, as a witness of her loved mother's; only later when her mother had fled, had she herself become the target of his rage. So, even though she had been only eight when her mother disappeared one night, never to return, she could not blame her for her abandonment. It was, after all, so much less than what Xenia had finally done.

The connexion between her father and Yevgenia's cousin and husband was, in the end, immaterial, for she was going to recreate the past, so that the relationship was what she wanted it to be. As she had listened to Yevgenia's tapes, hotch potch, she had only gradually come to an understanding of the links between the characters, of blood and emotion. Only when she came across the account of Yevgenia's marriage to her cousin did she realize the significance of the first tape she had heard. Yevgenia had married Kenward Loftus as soon as his divorce was arranged. There was no mention of the dissolution of her own marriage. If you have had your husband snatched from his hiding place in the woods, if you have heard accounts of his being clubbed and shot on Riga Station, you are not likely to regard him an impediment to a second marriage, six years later. Yet, it seemed that it was not until she was trying to get hold of her share of her great-uncle's property, long after she was married to her second husband, that she had bothered to obtain an official statement of her first husband's death. Xenia began to suspect that Xan had been wiped out of Yevgenia's life during that blank period at the end of the war that saw her transported from Latvia to England, transformed from an impoverished aristocrat in a remote corner of Europe to the wealthy wife of an English country doctor. Xenia felt a complete understanding. If the existence of a previous husband, now dead but unofficially so, could prevent your marriage and your new life, who would not forget him? Remembering him would not bring him back; burying him deep in the past and in your memory would enable you to live again. The knowledge of how easily you can erase someone came from her own experience. She did not resurrect the memory of the flames that had consumed their tiny apartment on the fifteenth floor; she simply recognized the process by which Xan had been made to disappear.

But supposing he had not died? Supposing he had been thrown into the cattle truck and survived his beating, the journey to Siberia and fifteen years in the gulag? It was not easy to imagine, but there were those who outlived all these experiences, her own father, for example. Supposing he had been released in the mid-fifties to work as a clerk in a lumber camp, as her father had done, until he finally reached Novoleninsk and found a job teaching languages in the Technical High School. If he had done that, which he could have done, what would Yevgenia's reaction be to hearing such news?

It meant, of course, that Yevgenia had never been legally married in England. Xenia could not see that mattered to anyone now. She had no thought of blackmail, for who cared if Yevgenia had lived for thirty years as the bigamous wife of Kenward Loftus, even though the bigamy was unknowing or, at the very most, wilfully unknowing. That aspect was of no importance. What was significant about this story was to lay Xenia's own claims. Yevgenia might or might not like her; what Xenia had to do was to demand justice, not liking. Who had the greater right to Yevgenia's money, the child of Alexander Alexandrovich Chornorouky who had lived out his life in Siberia, or the granddaughter of Kenward Loftus who had somehow rescued Yevgenia from the chaos of the aftermath of the war in eastern Germany?

A few days later Zita reported that Naomi had phoned from Tuscany with urgent questions about the building work at Asshe House. She was going round there. Would Xenia like to see it? Xenia accepted the suggestion with every show of pleasure. She was wary of Zita's efforts to be kind, for she could see no reason for them; they lacked the element of power-seeking which explained Naomi's benevolence. Xenia had heard from Naomi the story of Zita's disastrous marriage and this was a comfort to her, making her feel more in control of her own life and feelings.

It was early evening and the workmen had gone. Zita went around the house making notes of the answers to Naomi's questions, leaving Xenia to wander from room to room by herself. When she had finished her task she found Xenia on the ground floor and said, "Shall I show you round? I thought you might be interested to see it, because it is a fine example of late seventeenth-century architecture and anyway it is so nice poking about in other people's houses, don't you think?"

They climbed the stairs and went into the drawing room, Zita pointing out the details of the fireplace, the moulding of the ceiling and the plastering of the walls.

"Who is going to live here?" Xenia asked. "Has Mrs Loftus given it away?"

"She has given the use of the house to Marcus and Naomi and they are making all these changes, but whether they intend to live here permanently, I doubt. Rosie said she didn't think they would leave Hampstead in the near future. She couldn't live in it herself. Perhaps Ivo will. Or perhaps it will just be a weekend place for them."

Xenia made a little face to indicate her astonishment that anyone could have such a large house on such a basis. All she said was, "Ivo?"

"Rosie's brother. You didn't meet him when you were staying with Marcus and Naomi?"

"No. I know he is Rosie's brother. I meant he doesn't seem much part of the family."

"No, it's odd isn't it? I've known Yevgenia for years, well, six or seven, and my mother has known Naomi and Marcus for ever and yet I've never met Ivo, or at least not since I was five years old in Cambridge."

They were walking up the stairs now with the fine curved panels on their left. "I think for a time they were rather ashamed of him. He ran away from Bedales and refused to go to university."

Ivo had been a failure, for Naomi and Marcus as much as himself, a sign of a flaw in a perfect household. He had so conspicuously refused to follow in his parents' footsteps, to take on their academic and social values, that they simply blotted him out of their conversation. Now he was so successful they had, with diffidence and embarrassment, begun to talk about him again. Xenia had evidently assumed the Hampstead attitude to the black sheep.

"He is a cook, I think," she said condescendingly.

"Yes," said Zita, opening a bedroom door. "Look, this will be the main bedroom. I would adore a bedroom with a fireplace in it. But a very smart cook. Naomi and Marcus are terribly proud of him. Have you ever seen him on television?"

"No."

"I must show you a video. I don't think he's been on while you've been here. I love his cooking. This will be the dressing room and bathroom, though I have to admit it is rather hard to imagine at the moment."

"In Siberia, our whole flat was the size of one of these rooms."

Zita turned to her a face so full of interest and sympathy that Xenia immediately saw her opportunity. "What was it like? The way we live must seem like madness in comparison."

"Oh, no, the madness is there, not here. So our flat was on the fifteenth floor and the lift was never working. Our front door was padded. I have not seen that anywhere here. You come in here and there is a little hall with a box for our shoes, because immediately you change your shoes for slippers. No one does that here. Then, here is the loo, here is the bathroom, like this." She stretched out one arm to indicate its confines. "Then the kitchen in which we have a stove, a sink, a little table with one chair. I always sat on a stool, kept under the table. There was not space for two chairs. Then our living room. So it would have been smaller than this, in fact."

"But where were the bedrooms?"

"There are no bedrooms in Russian flats. My father slept in the living room and I in the hall. There was just room to put up my bed for the night."

Zita was looking out of the window at the garden. "My mother once told me about the communal flat where she grew up in Moscow in an old apartment block. Do you think yours was an improvement on that?"

"Moscow," Xenia said contemptuously. "In Moscow they don't know they are well off. Even if the flats are bad, they have transport, films, theatre, music, shops. In Moscow life is paradise in comparison with Novoleninsk. It was particularly bad," she went on, "for my father. He was an old man; he would be in his seventies now, if he were alive. He had grown up in Latvia before the war. He had known different things."

"How did he come to live in Siberia?"

"Oh, he was in the camps for many years and even when he was freed, he was not given a permit to return to Latvia. He had to remain in Siberia."

"Did he ever talk to you about life in the camps?"

"No, never. It was something that you hid and did not speak about. Until a few years ago it was something shameful in your past and in your family's past. Even though people knew that under Stalin you could be sent to the camps for no reason, they still thought that there was something wrong with an ex-camp inmate, a sort of contamination. It is only now that you can admit it."

"Do you know why he was there? I mean, was it a casual round up or was it for some particular professional or regional causes?"

Xenia shrugged. "I don't know. My father never told me about it. But I think the name Chornorouky was enough." They were walking back downstairs now. Zita was holding the house keys in her palm. She was thoughtful, absorbed.

"My mother has just gone back to Moscow and St Petersburg," she was saying. "I wonder how she will react. She has always been rabidly anti-Soviet and anti-Russian."

Xenia, walking a step behind, did not reply. She was pleased with her evening's work. She was sure that within the next few days what she had said would be reported to Yevgenia. The information about her father's youth in Latvia, about his age, would be all the more convincing for being expressed in Zita's mouth. The mistrust that Yevgenia felt for her, Xenia, would thereby be disarmed.

As she locked up, Zita said, "It's Tom's birthday on Wednesday next week and he wants to go to the cinema with two friends. Would you be free to join us? I shall need some help, you see, as they are all in wheel chairs."

Xenia felt a surge of happiness and power. She suddenly saw how to clinch it, how to make Yevgenia see she was Xan's daughter. She would have to do some careful research; she must get her information right. If she were wrong, even by a day, she would ruin everything. If she was right, she could win.

"Of course," she replied. "It will be a pleasure."

"I'm so glad you're free. Tom asked for you particularly."

Part Eleven

ZITA

Chapter Twenty-two

Zita had heard nothing from Stevens since their visit to the Cresacres. She assumed that, as planned, a police surgeon had visited them in Crawley to take a blood sample and that the DNA testing of the bones was going ahead in the Met laboratories. She had turned her attention to Mrs Hovell, the char mentioned by Yevgenia as the woman who had worked for her in the early fifties, who had previously worked for the tenants of Asshe House during the war. Fortunately, it was not a common name. If she had had to telephone every Smith in Broad Woodham, she might have abandoned her search before she began. As it was, the phone book yielded only five Hovells, three of them in Woodham. Two listened to her request for help with interest and one made co-operative, indeed enthusiastic, suggestions about how the search might be pursued. Neither produced success. The third number rang unanswered.

On Friday, on her way to her quintet evening, when she turned down a road which was familiar in itself, although she had never before observed its name, she saw the street sign, Hastings Road. At the same moment she visualized the address in the small print of the telephone directory of the last Hovell, whom she had not been able to contact. She slowed down until she came to a halt opposite number sixteen, a thirties house with an arched, keyhole entrance.

She got out and locked her car door, thinking as she did so, this is stupid. She would be late for her music and irritate Georgina Orr, who kept time in everything. The house looked unoccupied and she rang the bell only to confirm that there was no one at home. She was surprised when the door opened so promptly as to imply that someone had been watching her from the moment of her arrival.

"Mrs Hovell?" she said tentatively. The woman facing her was square, a solid pile of cubes of different dimensions culminating in a square face, highly coloured, contrasting with her jet hair, evidently dyed for the face below it was not young. Zita put her in her early sixties.

"Yes?" The reply was both affirmation and question.

Zita stated her name and went on, "I'm looking for a Mrs Hovell who worked at Asshe House in St Michael's Square during the war and in the fifties. I wonder..."

For a moment she was full of hope. The age was right, or at least within the range of possibility.

Mrs Hovell shook her head. "No, dear," she said, "not me." Then she added, "At least not during the war. In the fifties, perhaps. When were you thinking of? I qualified in 1952 and I began work in Woodham in March 1953, so I could have. I mean, I went to so many houses. In those days there were lots of home births." She saw Zita's look of disappointment. "What sort of work were you meaning? I was a midwife."

"No," said Zita, "I am looking for someone who was a cleaning lady for a Mrs Loftus and, before her, for a family called Dryburn. And it was over quite a long period, about fifteen years I should say. It's stupid of me. I can see that you are much too young."

This remark had a warming effect. Mrs Hovell released the edge of her door and said, "Why don't you come in for a moment? It could be my mother-in-law you're thinking of. I didn't marry until June 1958 and she wasn't working then, but she had been before that." Zita hadn't asked Yevgenia about the age of her char. She could now see that she could have been a middle aged woman in the 1950s and so, in all probability, dead and beyond her reach now.

"That would make more sense," she said. "It might have been her. I don't suppose she's still alive?" The idea of a sixty-year-old having a mother-in-law seemed rather far-fetched.

"Oh, she's still going strong. Eighty-four she is now. What do you want her for? Do you want to come in?"

Zita hesitated, looking at her watch, and stepped inside. "It's a bit gruesome," she said. "You may have read in the papers about a skeleton found at Asshe House. I'm the solicitor of the owners. I'm trying to find people connected with the house a long time ago who might know about its history, its past owners, any stories about it."

Mrs Hovell led the way into the sitting room, before answering. "Well, if that's what you want, you'll have a job. Alzheimer's. You could have a go. I mean, she remembers some things, especially the past. In fact, she lives in the past." She sat herself down with the solidity of someone expecting a good chat. Zita followed suit more tentatively, placing herself on the edge of the chintz-covered sofa. "And it's very funny what she does remember," Mrs Hovell went on. "Often it's little things, and the really important things have all gone. Last time I went to see her, Sunday afternoon it was, she'd forgotten her husband. Well, I mean. We were talking about her old house up at Hinton, you know, up on the hill; it's really part of Woodham now. She lived there for forty years. I said to her, 'You know, Mum, you lived there with Brian,' that was her husband, and do you know what she said? She goes, 'Brian?' as if she'd never heard of him before. She'd blotted him right out of her past. Can you imagine someone forgetting her husband, father of her children? Memory's a funny thing. And she thinks *I'm* *her* grandmother. Well."

"Do you think she might be the person I'm looking for?"

"Could be. She worked more like a maid. She didn't go to lots of different people's houses. She went every day to one house, regular hours. She always wore a blue overall and a white apron over it. Like a uniform. It might have been the house you mean. I could ask my husband."

Zita looked at her watch again and took out her card.

"Would you mind? I wouldn't want to disturb her if she didn't work there, but if she did, who knows? She might remember something. So, if you could just check with your husband."

Georgina was vexed at Zita's lateness, grumbling acidly that if Zita wanted to remain part of the group she must cultivate greater punctuality. She was eventually soothed by Gerald and by two hours of music-making which enabled her to say goodbye to Zita with better humour. Zita too was tranquillized by the music.

Yevgenia had been baby-sitting for her, as it was Lynne's night at the pub and Xenia was already employed for the evening. The two of them drank a cup of tisane together on Zita's return. Zita wanted to soften Yevgenia towards Xenia, and began to tell her about the Russian girl's account of her home in Siberia.

"According to Naomi," Zita said, "she would hardly say a word about Russia or about her past when she was in London."

"Perhaps it's you, my dear," Yevgenia said, "I would rather confide in you than in a professional receiver of secrets, like Naomi. What did she say about her father?"

"He died about three years ago. What happened to her mother, I don't know; she doesn't feature at all. The father was an alcoholic and elderly, in his seventies, she said. He spent years in the gulag, though she didn't know much about his time there. She said he never spoke about it and she clearly didn't know what he was in for, except that he was a political."

Yevgenia was struggling out of her chair with the aid of her two sticks. "I can't bear it," she said. "That country. I'm not like your mother, reviling it. I just can't think about it. The sum of the horror there this century, the injustice, the misery, the individual grief, is unimaginable, unmeasurable. If I thought about it, I would weep."

"She said he was never able to go back to where he came from, Latvia, I think. The system of internal passports meant that you were chained to your assigned place like a serf. Extraordinary really."

"So, he couldn't go back. I must go back, I must go back now. Good night, my dear."

Looking back, much later, Zita was to think that had been the moment when her role as the accomplice, albeit unwitting at first, had begun and that Yevgenia's cryptic remark, which she had dismissed at the time as a reflection of the painful business of remembering was, in fact, the point of Yevgenia's conversion to belief in Xenia.

Mrs Hovell the younger was evidently one of those busy, efficient, interfering people who, once they have undertaken a task and become part of a project, do not rest until their own part is done and so is everyone else's. She was on the phone the following day to report that her mother-in-law had worked at Asshe House for about eighteen years from the start of the war.

"You'll want to have a word with her," she said. "I could take you up to see her one afternoon. She's in a home, of course. I'd better come with you to introduce you, like. Not that it makes any difference to her, but the people running the place like to know who's going in and out."

Zita met her the following day outside the Rose Bank Residential Home, a suburban villa with a modern extension built on at the back, which doubled its size. Its old front garden had been tarmacked to provide parking for staff and visitors, and everything else that could be considered non-utilitarian had been stripped away. The entrance hall held a faint undercurrent of odour in its air, tainted and sinister, composed of urine and rancid cooking fat. In a lounge on their right Zita could see a row of old women arrayed in chairs along one wall. They looked like a shelf of second-hand books, untidily propping one another up. One of them was talking, but without addressing anyone in particular, and none of the others gave any appearance of attention or even of understanding what was being said.

Mrs Hovell glanced inside and then made for the lift. "She's not downstairs today. They usually bring her down. It does her good to be with the others, they say." On the third floor she led Zita through heavy fire doors, along a narrow featureless corridor, stiflingly hot from the lights that burned twenty-four hours a day. She reached the last door and waited a moment for Zita to catch up with her.

"I'll leave you alone with her for a while. I've got a bit of shopping to do, so I'll just come in to say hello."

She had been speaking in a conspiratorial whisper; once she had opened the door she raised her voice to the self-conscious tone used for children, the handicapped and the elderly. "Hello, Mother. How are you now?"

From behind Mrs Hovell's bulk Zita could see a wispy figure sitting in a chair gazing out of the window. She turned, regarding them with cloudy blue eyes. Her white hair was parted on one side and held on the other with a blue plastic clip in the shape of a bow. Her expression was childlike, but no child, apart from Tom, would have had such a blank, unrecognizing stare. Her daughter-in-law bustled in the tiny space, making Zita edge round her to sit down on the other side of the window. When she left a silence fell on the room. Old Mrs Hovell looked placidly back at Zita. Perhaps she thought she was a new doctor, a nurse, a carer; perhaps she made no explanation to herself to account for a stranger's presence; perhaps everyone was a stranger, however often they came.

As Zita stated as clearly as she could what she wanted to know, Mrs Hovell watched her wonderingly. When, at last, she began to speak, her words had nothing whatsoever to do with what had come before. She had failed to take in any meaning from what had been said to her.

"My mother always said that people with yellow eyes couldn't be trusted. She meant those very pale eyes, like a glass of water. And she's right; that new girl's no good, I'm sure of it."

"One of your nurses?" Zita asked. She decided that she would accept Mrs Hovell's own topics, rather than impose her own.

"A nurse? Oh, no, I wouldn't have thought she was a nurse. She was a land girl, as far as I remember. They were always very flighty pieces. She came from London. Funny to be a land girl and come from London. You wouldn't have thought she'd've known a cow's tits from its tail, but the truth was that she was a very good worker. That's what my mother said. But she got around, I'll say that for her. Her...her..." The word would not come. She made vague circular movements with one hand, looking appealingly at her visitor.

Zita realized that she was looking at someone who was a witness to a past which was as deeply buried in her mind as the skeleton had been buried in the earth. None of the normal conventions for the exchange of information applied here. No offer of lunch or a drink, no thought of reciprocation, no idea of helpfulness or duty could persuade Mrs Hovell to part with information that she no longer knew she had. She must, Zita thought, have been a very chatty cleaning woman. One whose work was simply an opportunity for conversation. She was still talking now. For her the past was the present, infinitely repeating itself. Here it had its revenge at last. It was no longer ruthlessly mastered as Valentina mastered her own history, nor suppressed as Yevgenia had suppressed hers for almost fifty years; the past lived again in random replay. The bliss, she thought. No need to struggle to abolish Oliver: he would always be there in her mind, which would have shed the painful reality of his absence.

Mrs Hovell had fallen silent, for a moment, pondering. Zita had given up all hope of learning anything from her by questioning her. What she needed was some sort of stimulus to memory which would induce Mrs Hovell to give up her information without realizing it. A photograph of Asshe House was the best thing she could think of; she would have to come again with one. She looked around for something to direct the old woman's attention. On the chest of drawers were a few snaps tucked into the frame of the mirror. They were all in colour, modern. Zita picked up one of a young woman and a baby and held it out for Mrs Hovell to see.

"Is this your granddaughter?" she asked.

Mrs Hovell took the photograph and admired it without recognition. "Very nice," she said. She put it back on top of the chest. Her eye fell on a small metallic disc stamped with a head lying on the surface closer to Zita than to her. She reached for it; Zita pushed it towards her. Mrs Hovell smiled and nodded, holding out her hand. Zita placed the medal in the cupped palm. The old woman looked at the disc for a moment and caressed it with the tips of her fingers. The feel rather than the sight evoked a response.

"I lived and the child died; that I never understood, never understood." She held the medal between her fingers face out-wards as though the sight of it would ward off a threat, gorgon-like, turning it to stone.

"The child died?" Zita repeated.

"I lived and the child died." She muttered the phrase again counterbalancing the two halves of the sentence. "The...killed him and saved me." She could not say what it was that had killed her child. Lacking any knowledge, Zita could not supply the understanding with which her family would have filled up the lacuna. This time Mrs Hovell seemed aware of the failure of communication.

"I know what it is," she said. "It's just the name won't come. The..." She was making gestures, as if scooping some-thing out of her lap and throwing it in the air. "It made a...a hole." Zita gazed back at her blankly. Then, abruptly, she knew who the child must have been, without proof, as surely as Stevens knew that Yevgenia was guilty. The intrusion of the thought of Stevens reminded her that she knew nothing.

The younger Mrs Hovell entered as the mother-in-law was repeating her actions, still muttering the first half of her incan-tation. "I lived...I lived...I lived."

Zita looked for help. "Something that makes holes," she said, as if it were a cross-word puzzle.

"A road digger?" the daughter-in-law suggested helpfully. "I must take Mrs Daunsey away now, Mum," she went on with-out waiting to see if she had solved the riddle. "I'll be back to see you at the weekend, then. So, look after yourself. Take care, goodbye, goodbye." She led the way out briskly.

Zita said, "There was a medallion on her chest of drawers. She wanted to talk about it but couldn't find the words."

"That happens sometimes. She's got the idea in her head but the words for it won't come. Well, it happens to all of us sometimes, doesn't it? The medallion? She was very superstitious, was Mother. You wouldn't believe the things she fussed about. She didn't like green in the house. I think that medal thing brought her luck. Anyway, she likes to have it around."

They were in the lift descending to the ground floor. "No good asking if she could tell you anything you needed to know. It was one of her bad days. I could tell as soon as we saw her. She has good times and bad times and when it's bad she talks a lot but doesn't get anywhere. Well, you could always try again, another time. Or see if my husband can help. He was in his teens in the 1940s. He might remember something that would be useful to you."

It was almost funny, she thought, driving home afterwards. It was funny. It would certainly be funny if she had anyone to recount it to. Her independent witness turned out to be senile, whose memory could not be tapped and most of whose random remarks were masterpieces of irrelevance, but who, nevertheless, had made her understand what could have happened. Stevens was not the man to whom to tell her story. He would take her effort seriously and pour scorn on it. She might have told Yevgenia. Until recently she had often done so; now Yevgenia was so absorbed by her own past that she would not respond to Zita's anecdote. It only belatedly occurred to her that she had not thought of Oliver. Not that Oliver was there to listen, or would have been interested even if he were. That was the point. His absence had always been the first thing she noticed at that moment, which arrived daily, when she wanted to share amusement. It was odd she had not thought of him at first.

This was a time of year when he was usually especially present, or absent. Wednesday was Tom's birthday and the punctual arrival of cards and gifts despatched by Shobana according to the notes transferred from her diary year by year always threw into relief the lack of anything actually chosen by Oliver himself. The birthday this year was to consist of a visit to a cinema to see a Walt Disney film, followed by tea at home, to which two of his friends from the Centre had been invited, with Lynne, Xenia and Yevgenia. The cinema was a new experience and one to which Tom was looking forward with great intensity. No video seen at home could compare with a film seen in a cinema. It had taken Zita several weeks of persuasion and organization to get the manager to agree that three wheel chairs would not contravene the fire regulations, as he had at first insisted. Tom's invitations to his friends were also a new departure. Birthdays had hitherto been celebrated only with his mother and Lynne. With Xenia's help and that of Lynne, Zita had one able-bodied adult for each wheel chair in the cinema. Before the expedition started she had already decided that there was never to be a repetition: it was all too difficult. However, the afternoon passed off well and the children's delight in everything, the film, the visit to an ordinary cinema, the tea, was so great and so evident that at the end she felt that, as long as the numbers did not grow and nothing more ambitious was attempted, she would certainly do it again.

Finally the party broke up. Tom's friends had been taken home and Lynne was putting Tom to bed. Zita begged Yevgenia and Xenia to have a drink with her before they left.

"Sit down again. And, Xenia, I must pay you for your help this afternoon. You were marvellous with them."

"No, you must not pay me. I thought I was a guest today, invited as Tom's friend."

"Of course, you were. But still I must pay you. If you had only been a guest you would have come just for tea, like Yevgenia."

"The birthday is something serious in England," Xenia remarked as Zita handed her a glass of wine.

"It's true. Often children have extraordinarily elaborate parties, magicians, films, outings. I think it's particularly guilty working mothers who put on these performances."

Xenia was less interested in learning about English children's birthdays than in talking about her own family's.

"In Russia we celebrated a birthday by trying to buy something special to eat. When I was little, you could sometimes find caviar, the red if not the black, in our town. And there was a certain kind of cake, like a chocolate wafer, that I would get for my father's birthday. But in recent years, during perestroika, you did not often find caviar or even cake. His birthday was St John's Day, 7th July, and when I was a child, when my mother still lived with us, we had wonderful feasts of soup and caviar and blinis, a whole special meal for his day."

"Tom-Tom will have to wait until he is grown up before he can demand caviar for his birthday party," Zita commented. "For the moment a Thomas the Tank Engine cake will have to do." Then she said, "St John's Day is 24th June in the West, isn't it, Yevgenia? Midsummer's day."

"Yes," Yevgenia replied. "That's right; 24th June, Old Style."

"How confusing," said Zita. "It's as much as I can do to cope with birthdays in one calendar without muddling it up with another. In spite of the fact that she is in Russia, Valentina remembered Tom's birthday this year, which she never normally does. He got a card this morning from St Petersburg."

Yevgenia was getting up as Zita spoke. "Xenia, my dear, I think I must go back. But you stay with Zita, there is no need for you to come." Zita, seeing she was determined to go, accompanied her to the front door. "It was very sweet of Tom to ask me to his party. I enjoyed it very much. Delicious cake, Zita. Forgive me for leaving like this. I want to sit down with my tape recorder for an hour or so. I have the worst bit yet to do, the most painful confession to make."

"I hope it won't be that bad," Zita heard herself saying, in the same tone that Mrs Hovell had used to her mother-in-law, the tone with which the young humour the old. It was not clear whether she meant the emotion or the text.

Yevgenia set off, leaning forward on her sticks. "By the way," she said. "May I make an official appointment for next week. I want to make some changes in my legal arrangements."

"Of course. Would you like to come to the office, or shall I come to you?"

"I'll come to the office, I think. You've got a lift, so I can reach your room. It will be an outing for me. I'll ring your secretary tomorrow."

Part Twelve

YEVGENIA

Chapter Twenty-three

I think he was the happiest time of my life: I had almost
four years of Alek's company. Because of him, I have forgotten
the terrors and difficulties of the war years; that is, I remember
the facts, but I do not feel them; they have no residual pain.

In June 1941, just after Xan was killed, and just before
Alek was born, the Germans invaded Russia. They swept for-
ward on a huge front, one army group curling north to take the
Baltic States. The Russians retreated, disappearing into the
East, driving their prisoners before them like cattle. The
Germans took over the Russians' control of the country and
their methods, but their violence was directed at different peo-
ple, or the same people for different reasons.

When we were told, after the war, that ordinary people in
Germany had not known what was going on, I know it wasn't
true. I lived out the years of the war on a farm in Latvia, about
as remote as you can get, and we knew what was happening.
It's impossible to do the sorts of things that were being done
without people knowing; to round up one group of the population of a small town with the utmost brutality, to march them
out to the woods, to make them dig their own graves, then
shoot them, all of them, men and women and children, so that
they fall into the pit they have just dug; or to load them onto
cattle trucks and ship them off to a place from which they
never return. We knew what it meant when the Soviets did it
to intellectuals, aristocrats, capitalists; it meant labour camp
and death somewhere in Siberia. We knew what it meant when

the Germans did it to the Jews; it meant labour camp and death somewhere much closer than Siberia. I don't think I had heard the name of Auschwitz before the end of the war. I didn't know about Zyklon B and the gas chambers. But I knew in essence, if not in detail, what was happening. In the villages all around us the Jews who had been the artisans, the traders, the travelling packmen, the loggers, were rounded up and sent to live in ghettos in the towns where they worked as forced labourers. Sometimes they were just paraded and shot. We all knew about it. I knew about it, and I did nothing. I saved no one, except the man whom I believed was responsible for my husband's death, because I had Alek, because I was afraid. So, like many others in Latvia, I stood between the bully and the victim, an unwilling accomplice.

For me the arrival of the Germans at first made life better. Lai told me to start calling myself von Korff again, rather than Chornoroukaya. As a Baltic German and an aristocrat, I fell into two categories which, if not honoured, were more favourably regarded by the Nazi authorities than by either the Soviets or the Latvians. So I was able to live at Kornu unmolested. Life was not bad; it went on much as usual. We had always lived very simply; we still had the farm and the difficulties of supply faced by people in the city were much less for us.

So I was able to live in my paradise with my son. It seems to me that women have two childhoods; the first is their own, and no sooner have they emerged from that than they are plunged again into a second with their children. I lived in a child's world with Alek: his discovery of the world was mine too; his toys, books, games, were mine. Nothing outside Alek and Kornu counted for anything. Naturally, I cared about what was happening in the war. I listened secretly to the BBC. I listened to German propaganda about the eastern front; I even heard Russian radio and followed the siege of my birthplace, Leningrad. But these things only mattered in so far as they might affect Alek. And while the Germans pressed forward into Russia, that meant they did not matter at all.

For Lai it was different. For a time he tried to go on as he had under the Russians, training as a doctor in Riga, secretly doing what he could to undermine the occupiers of his country. He came to see me and Alek very frequently, almost every week, taking a train from Riga, cycling from the station on a bike which he left in the stationmaster's keeping. It was after about nine or ten months of German occupation that he decided to do more. It was sometime at the end of winter in 1942; Alek was at the stage of sitting up and beginning to creep around the room holding onto furniture, pulling things down on top of him. One afternoon I had put him on a little sleigh and towed him over the snow to the lake which was starting to melt, water lapping through the ice, when I saw Lai coming towards us. He had a bag on his back and he was walking. He had decided to join the partisans, and had come to say goodbye. He could no longer stand the ambiguities of trying to live a normal life under the Nazis.

What was happening to the Jews was intolerable to watch, Lai said. He had told me, week by week, about events in Riga during that winter just as the previous year he had told me what the Soviets were doing. The Jews of the region had been rounded up and forced to live in a crowded and squalid ghetto area in the town. Conditions got worse and worse as transports of Jews, deported from the Reich, arrived from the West. Dealing with overcrowding with their own appalling logic, the Nazis had taken thousands from the ghetto into the woods and shot them. More and more German Jews came; over and over again they and the Latvian Jews who were left were taken out into the forest and killed, thousands and thousands of people. Later, in the spring when the thaw came, the earth groaned and tossed as if uneasy sleepers lay beneath. Sometimes the ground gaped and an arm would be thrust up through the soil. The peasants, who were superstitious enough at the best of times, were terrified by the thought of the vengeful spirits that must haunt the woods.

"Evil can't be hidden," Maris told me when she whispered these tales. "*We* can't do anything. How can we stop them? But the time will come when the earth will open and their deeds will

be revealed." She used to tell her stories with a kind of incanta-
tory tone and portentous vocabulary which somehow removed
what was happening from the present. At first I did not believe
what I was told, until Lai explained to me that the gases from
the huge numbers of decomposing bodies really did cause the
earth to heave. The scale of the slaughter was unimaginable; I
could not imagine it. Lai did not need to do so; he saw the bar-
barities every day. The effect of living with evil was subtle and
corrosive. The Nazis worked on Latvian hatred of the Russians
and Jews to recruit them for their worst work. Under the
Russians, the Latvians had been victims; now they were bullies.
He couldn't stand it any longer; he was going to run away.

It sounded, the way he explained it at the time, as if it was
a decision of principle. Only later did I hear the story of what
had happened in Riga that week and realize that he was in danger of arrest. Lai had witnessed a small incident in the street.
A work gang of Jews from the ghetto doing forced labour
under the supervision of a soldier was being taunted by two or
three Latvian youths. It was nothing, a feather in the balance
of horrors; but it was enough to make Lai decide to go. The
fact that they were Latvians, the soldier and the youths,
enraged him. He had attacked them, started a brawl, fled
home. He knew that he would be marked out for what he had
done, so he packed at once and left Riga. He spent two days
with me before disappearing into the forest.

Of course, I slept with him before he left. Now, looking
back on that other person who was Yevgenia Chornoroukaya
all those years ago, I can see reasons for these things. Lai was
going to fight. The instinct to love when confronted with death
is primeval; if nothing else, it is, I suppose, natural for men to
say, one last woman before I die. And as for me, the same
instinct, to love in the face of death, is felt by every widow. I
still missed Xan and wept for him when I woke in the night.
But the body fights against grief, and resists the call of the dead
from the grave. What's more, I needed Lai, that is, I needed a
man. I was a woman alone with a young child and I needed or
would need help. The cunning of instinct tells you to bind your

helpers to you in whatever way you may, and so I did. Cynicism, a life's experience, tell me that these were the reasons for what happened.

But if this was really the explanation, why did I not find a German officer to protect me? They were there, in Riga; it would not have been hard to find one who was more or less acceptable. If Lai needed a woman, there was no shortage. Yet I knew then and I know now more than an instinct for survival brought us together. I loved Lai. I sometimes wonder if I had not loved him more than Xan all along. Yet I never stopped believing he was responsible for Xan's arrest and death. How can you love two people at once? How can you believe the worst of someone and still love them?

Lying beside him during those two days before he left for the forests, I silently compared him with Xan, the ultimate disloyalty of the faithless wife. I knew I ought to love Xan best, every standard that I had been brought up by told me so. But I had to recognize then that I did not. I recalled those agonizing minutes beside the lake when Xan had mocked him and I had said nothing. I was Xan's accomplice then; now I lay beside my husband's murderer. I stroked Lai's skin, like silk, I can almost feel it now. I grieved for Xan, but I loved Lai. I can remember, even though I am so old and I have not allowed myself to think of it for forty years and more, how I yearned for him, how I wanted more, with that unassuageable love that can never be satisfied, even by the presence of the beloved.

I find it strange how the memory selects the emotions that belong to the past. Those last years at Kornu were terrible, terrifying. I know I lived in fear all the time: fear for Xan, then fear for Lai, fear for Alek. At Kornu it was not a question of waiting for a knock on the door. The arrival of strangers was announced by the dogs. Anyone coming could be seen from the verandah, making his way along the road beyond the lake, turning the curve at the little temple and then beginning the climb to the house. I had Maris's youngest son stationed much of the time in the garden at the front, in order to keep an eye on the approaches in case someone, a detachment of the Red

Army, the NKVD, later the German Army or the Gestapo, should come, so that I could prepare myself to meet them. At Kornu then my fear was open, in England it was secret. In Latvia everyone dreaded the authorities with their arbitrary powers to force you out of the house, to shoot you in the garden, to drag you off to the trains that carried you away to your death. When they came in 1960 to Asshe House it was so politely. They interviewed me in my own drawing room. They were offered, and accepted, cups of tea. They probably ate home-made biscuits. But they were just as unpleasant. All the fear I had felt twenty years earlier returned. As I answered their questions, my mouth was dry, my hands sweated.

Where was I on such an evening? At home.

Was there anyone else with me? No. My husband was out on a call; it was Mrs Huxford's afternoon off.

Had I spoken to anyone? No.

Made any telephone calls? No.

Was there any way I could prove where I was? No.

The older one was coarse, a bully, the kind of man who has an instinctive recognition of fear, who cannot be stopped from exercising his power, even when it would be in his interest to conceal it. The other said nothing. He was subtler. He wrote down the answers and watched craftily, waiting for me to contradict myself. When they had gone I wept. When Kenward came back he found me crying. I could not stop. In the end he gave me some sleeping pills and put me to bed. I could not explain why I was weeping.

Lai said goodbye, but not for good; he came back from time to time during the next two years. The partisans lived in the forests. They were not going anywhere: there was nowhere for them to go. They were simply living outside the control of the German conquerors, whom they harassed when they could. The band Lai joined was a mixed group: some Latvians, some Jews, some Lithuanians, some Poles, some Russians. There were many tensions among them which sometimes erupted into fights, the Russians against the Latvians, the Poles against the Lithuanians, any of them against the Jews. There were desertions; a small faction would disappear in the night, taking with them precious food or weapons. However, they all hated the Germans and that basic enmity held them together in a fragile, mobile unity. It was, Lai used to say, a microcosm of the making of society. Each of them was Rousseau's or Hobbes's man in a state of nature who is forced to unite with others in order to live, to survive and to protect himself and so the sharp prejudices which each member brought from his origins had to be sheathed in order that the group could function. Lai's band was a fighting unit. It consisted of between twenty and fifty men, ranging in age from fifteen to fifty. They occasionally had a woman or two who joined them for a time, but only as fighters. There were other bands in the woods, Lai told me, that had old people, women and children. Usually they were Jews who had fled from the ghettos in the towns. Such groups were particularly vulnerable in the winter time when the choice for the frail was between returning to a ghetto which would soon mean a place on the transports or the loan of a shovel to dig their own graves, or remaining in the woods to die of cold, hunger or disease.

Even at Kornu those winters were cold. I would stare out of the window of my stove-warmed room and think of Lai in his encampment in the woods and shudder. Winter was a dangerous time for the partisans. They lost the cover of the foliage and the snow insidiously betrayed their tracks to any scouting aircraft or soldiers. The Germans would, every so often, turn their attention from their systematic rounding up and killing in the villages to hunting down the partisans. It must have been a sport for them, like a shooting expedition, a recreation from the drudgery of murder. They would force the peasants to reveal their knowledge of a band's whereabouts and then go in with a few armoured cars and machine guns to clean up the area, retreating to their warm barracks after a couple of days out in the forest. Lai's band used to break up in January and February, dividing into smaller units, going to ground and hiding in isolated farmsteads and hamlets. There were individual peasants and some whole villages who would help; though only their own kind. Our villagers would help the Latvians but not the Russians or the Lithuanians; some would sometimes help their own Jews, but not the ones who spoke Russian or German or Polish. During these months Lai would come and hide with me at Kornu, as Xan had done, with this difference: the servants, who were all Latvians, knew he was there and never betrayed him.

During a winter attack, in 1943, Lai lost his left arm. He was wounded, not very seriously, by a gunshot, a bullet passing through his lower arm and breaking one of the bones. In the six days that it took him to reach Kornu, gangrene had set in. Our local horse doctor amputated his arm above the elbow in the kitchen in Kornu, in conditions like an eighteenth-century battlefield. I watched the operation and thought I was witnessing my lover's death. But it was too early for that. Lai was extraordinarily strong and within weeks he was planning his return to the band. His arm had healed up very well, leaving an abrupt, puckered stump just above the elbow. He let me construct a protection for it out of some old silk underclothes of Aunt Zoya's, to prevent the chafing of the scars by the knotted sleeve of his woollen shirt.

All this time, from when Xan died on Riga station in June 1941 to the spring of 1942 when Lai ran away to the partisans, until the summer of 1944, I knew that what had happened to them would one day happen to me. I was given a temporary reprieve because I counted as German, and I knew I must take every second of respite in order to let Alek grow up. But it could not last. I am not sure whether I really thought Germany would be defeated, but I was certain that in the long run Russia would push back and Latvia would be conquered again from the east. Lai hoped for an allied victory and for renewed independence for Latvia. For him everything was different. In the last resort he was Latvian and could find a home among his own people. But I was of no nationality. As a Baltic German I was not welcome in Latvia; I had no home in Germany and indeed did not want one there. As an aristocrat, I was an enemy of the people in Russia. So I knew that one day, sooner or later, I would be on the run, living like Lai in the forests. I had no plan except that, as I knew my camouflage worked best among Germans, I intended to run west rather than east. America, Xan's goal, became mine. I dreamed of crossing the Baltic to Sweden, a paradise of neutrality. Lai disabused me of that hope very early on. There could be nothing more unrealistic than any thought of bribing a fisherman and making a secret crossing of the Baltic or fleeing across the Gulf of Finland, dressed in white furs, as Russian aristocrats had done in the winter of 1918.

I began to make preparations quite early, from at least 1942 when Lai joined the partisans. I cut down an old fur coat, there were plenty of those at Kornu, for Alek. I sewed several pearl necklaces into the hem of my own fur coat like curtain weights and kept a box in my room of the smallest, most portable, most valuable things I could find: diamond rings, a Fabergé egg, gold roubles and sovereigns. We had been hoarding as much food as we could in any case. In the cellar beneath the kitchen we kept honey, flour, salt, lard, bacon, dried beans. Anything we could preserve, we did. We boarded up the steps into the cellar and left only a trap door over which we placed a table. We only went down to add to our store at night.

The moment I had been waiting for arrived in the summer of 1944. The news from the BBC and Radio Moscow had made us aware that the Russians were no longer simply holding off the Germans, they were pushing back. The front was advancing westward and, although the main impetus was the thrust towards Minsk, Warsaw and Berlin, we knew that even our backwater of Latvia would be scoured clean of Germans as the Russians moved on and tidied up behind their lines.

The Russian advance broke up Lai's band. Their last exploit, which had taken place several days' march to the north-east of Kornu, had been the sabotage of the trucks and armoured cars of retreating German forces, an enterprise performed in co-ordination by radio with the commander of the nearest advancing Russian corps. The group was about to be overtaken by real soldiers and this fractured the guerrilla band into two: those who looked forward joyfully to rejoining a proper army, to being assigned a uniform, rations, orders, and those for whom the Russians were at least as much to be feared as the now receding Germans. Lai was among these last.

He had seen the Russians in Latvia in '40 and '41 and had no illusions about what their return would mean for his country. If what the optimists urged came true, that at the peace conference after the war the West would see that Latvia was re-established, as it had been at Versailles in 1919, then he would be able to return in peace. Until then he would leave. I knew that I had nothing to hope for from the Russians, so when Lai arrived at Kornu in July with the news that the Soviets had reached Minsk, I knew we would have to go.

It was not an easy decision. It seems strange to say so now. At the time, from the perspective of Kornu, it was not clear that the war would end soon and with an allied victory. We were moving, Alek and I, from the only home I had ever known, my only possession, and going, where? Into Germany, with no clear idea of where or what we would do when we got there, with no means of support. For Lai, it was going into the heartlands of the people he had been fighting for two years. But for both of us the Russians were worse, and so we began our trek earlier than many others. The Germans of East Prussia did not start their flight westward until the middle of the winter; ours at least began in summer weather.

This first stage in the late summer of 1944 was comparatively easy, although I found it terrifying at the time. It was to be a journey far longer and far worse than anything experienced by my parents on their escape with me in their arms from St Petersburg to Kornu. Although I had papers that were acceptable to the German authorities, Lai was a renegade. I had no influence, but I had the means to bribe, so before we began, we had to turn him into a German. He disappeared to Riga with a ring of Aunt Zoya's and returned a few days later with papers describing him as Nicolas von Korff. His empty sleeve explained on sight why he was not in uniform; his flaxen hair made him look as Aryan as necessary.

We departed with suitcases, as if we were real von Korffs of the old days, en route for the Riviera. When I think of how we began our trek, I laugh at our optimism. Two suitcases contained our fur coats in the heat of August, extra shoes, some food. We set off in style, by train. It was not an easy matter to get on a train. Civilian traffic had low priority and it took some time and some payments, under as well as over the counter, in order to obtain the necessary permits. Where were we going, setting off into the hostile unknown? What did we intend to do? I keep asking myself that. There must have been some plan, some rational view of the future in our minds. It would have been destroyed by the events that overtook us, but to have had it would have been a sign that we still thought we had some control over our futures. But I don't think we had a plan. We were already refugees when we left Kornu, after sitting for a while in silence on the verandah, Russian fashion, kissing the maids goodbye and then picking up our bags and walking down the steps. Our only purpose was to survive, to wait for better times and, each day, to find something to eat, somewhere to sleep, the two fundamental priorities.

Our first destination was Danzig. Not far from the city was the estate of an elderly cousin of my father's. It took us a week to get there. We waited at stations for trains without timetables. We sat in darkened carriages, stationary amid the trees. We were forced off a train, and had to wait twenty-four hours for another. When we reached Danzig, we had to walk the fifty kilometres to my cousin's estate, carrying Alek, only occasionally managing to beg a ride from a peasant with a cart, returning from the fields. That part took us three days and two nights, one of which we spent in a barn, another at an inn. We were the first refugees that they had seen in that part of Pomerania. Later they were to become familiar with the miserable stream of humanity pushing carts, motor cycles, bicycles, prams, wheel barrows, hand carts, sledges, piled with bundles, children, old people. Then they were to become part of the stream themselves.

When we arrived, we found that Baron von Uxkull had abandoned his estate and was living in rooms in his market town, looked after by a housekeeper. He did not want us, had barely room for us. However, family duty told him he must make room for us and so he did. His chief worry was Nikolai who would not fit into the Almanach de Gotha of his family and all its connexions that he carried in his head. Who was his father, he kept asking me. He might have asked the same question about Alek, though he never did, perhaps fearing to hear the answer. He clearly assumed I was travelling with my lover and illegitimate child, which was not so wildly short of the mark. I kept Alek and Lai out of his way as much as possible and waited to see what would happen next.

Lai, with nothing to do but listen to the wireless, kept day by day a chart of the Russian advance, comparing Radio Moscow with the German news bulletins, contrasting the boasts and the claims with the silences and evasions, to plot what was happening. He had already said that we would have to move on again in the autumn, that the Russians were not going to stop until they reached Berlin or beyond and there was no hope that the western allies were going to get to the capital, let alone to Pomerania, before them. We were safe during the rains, he said, up until Christmas. No one could move during that period, but once the ground froze hard in December, for the next three months, the Russians would be unstoppable until it started to thaw in March. The problem was where to go next. My impetus was exhausted by this first stage; I was reluctant to move on, while Lai fretted at our indecision. My only concern was where I could take Alek for safety. Lai thought that somewhere west of Berlin we would meet the Americans and British who would save us from the Russians. By January we saw the first of the columns in flight from the East and heard the first stories about the Red Army. Forgetting the Russians of 1940 and moved by some atavistic loyalty to my mother's people, I refused to believe what I heard. The soldiers pillaged wherever they went, it was said. Not just the towns or the great houses, even the peasants' houses in the villages were torn apart; their tiny hoards of honey or lard, saved against the worst that could happen, were seized and destroyed, wantonly tipped into the muck. Women were raped, men killed, shot, bayoneted, hanged, according to the level of drunkenness and fury of the Russian soldiers. Lai for a while allowed me my protests, until one day he said, "It's true. It's not just stories made up by people running from an unknown terror. It'll be deliberate. The officers will have given permission, or at least will be turning a blind eye. It's revenge for all they've suffered."

And still we did not join the westward stream. Alek had fallen ill just before Christmas and I would not move until he was better. There was no chance of moving by train this time. When we set out we would have to go on foot and I could not risk carrying a delirious child in temperatures well below zero with no certainty each day of where we would sleep the night. We would take our chance, and I begged Lai to leave ahead of me. He would not go and so he stayed and worried, his attention divided between the advancing Russian front and Alek's slow recovery, without medication. Eventually the day came at the end of January 1945 when I agreed that Alek was well enough and that we could leave.

Part Thirteen

ZITA

Chapter Twenty-four

Zita had put Tom to bed and was making herself a dish of pasta. The phone kept ringing and interrupting the grating of the Parmesan, the peeling of the tomatoes, the tearing of the basil, all of which should have been simple and rapid tasks. The third call began with a crackling silence, giving her time to prepare herself for her mother's voice. Valentina was in St Petersburg and just ringing, she said, to find out how her daughter was.

"I'm fine, we're fine, all of us, Mama. What about you?"

"I'm very well. I've been amazed at everything I've seen here. Really, it's astonishing we ever thought they were a great power. They can't manage to make anything, even kitchen knives, that are fit for their purpose."

"They had nuclear weapons, Mama, that's why we were afraid of them."

"Their theoretical science is excellent. But they have nothing, nothing; they need so much. Anyway, I am now going on holiday. We're going to a dacha near Lake Ladoga for a few days before I come home."

"We?"

"Didn't I tell you that I met one of my old classmates from university at the Milan conference? It was he who persuaded me to come back here."

Zita absorbed this information. How strange her mother was, she thought; a man took her away from Russia all those years ago and another one takes her back now. It was as if her mother's attitude to her country was on a circuit that had no reference to her work, or reason, an emotional loop that was somehow self-contained. She was not sure what she was supposed to say, whether Valentina required some kind of emotional reaction. If she did, she was not going to get it.

"No, you didn't say. Well, send a postcard. The one you sent of the Winter Palace has just arrived. Tom loved it."

"I shall. Though I shall probably be back before he gets it. I'm booked on a flight next week sometime."

Zita replaced the receiver, marvelling at the rewinding of her mother's past. She poured the sauce she had just made over the pasta and sat down at the kitchen table. She cut herself a piece of bread and was about to lift the first forkful to her mouth when the phone rang again. It was Stevens. He did not identify himself, beginning abruptly, "I'm sorry, you're eating."

"No, no. Well, yes, actually, but it doesn't matter."

"I won't keep you. Can you meet me tomorrow morning?"

"Yes, I should think so."

"What about 11.15 at that coffee bar on the other side of the square." He only waited for her to agree before ringing off. Zita wondered briefly what he had to tell her that could not be stated over the phone; then put him out of her mind for the evening. As she ate she found herself recalling old Mrs Hovell, and the flickering replays of the past that ran in her mind. She had known Asshe House in the 1940s and 50s when she would have been in her forties herself. Her son, the midwife's husband would have been in his teens, so although he was not a direct witness, he had presumably been around when his mother was working for the Dryburns and Yevgenia.

On an impulse, before she had even cleared away her plates, she took the phone and, leafing through her notebook to find the number, she dialled the Hovells. Please don't let it be Mrs Hovell, she thought. It was embarrassing being so persistent, going back over the ground again and again. Mrs Hovell had enjoyed the attention at first; by now she might become irritated by it. Zita was in luck; the voice that answered was an elderly, masculine one. She introduced herself, mentioning her visit to his mother. Then she said, "I hope this isn't going to be painful for you. It's a very long shot as far as I am concerned. Your mother was a bit confused when I saw her, as you can imagine, and she kept saying, 'I lived and the child died,' and I wondered whether you knew what she was referring to?"

Mr Hovell was a ponderous man, Zita could tell. She interrupted his inconsequential half sentences to give him some ideas. "You didn't have a brother or sister who died, for example?"

"No, nothing like that, not that I know of, that is. There was just me and my sister. She's in Australia, now. She married in, when would it have been? Well, say around 1950, and went to Adelaide with her husband. No, I don't think it's that. I mean, even if you didn't talk about that kind of thing, there would have been a grave to visit, you know. No, it's not that."

Zita left a pause to allow him to suggest his own theory, but nothing came. Then he said, "I'll think about it. I do think about the things that Mother says. It's not madness. It's all sense as she sees it. It's just she's living in another time, different to ours."

Zita thanked him and began to clear up. She was making no progress. Perhaps Stevens, with all the high technology of the Met's lab at his disposal, had greater success to report. Tomorrow he would be crowing over her.

Stevens was, in fact, not in a mood for crowing when Zita found him already waiting for her in the churchyard as she made her way to the café. She had dressed with care, unexceptionable black court shoes that could have no bad repercussions, she thought, even though they were suede and very high in the heel. His face was set in an expression of even heavier gloom than usual, but the shoes had their subliminal effect. He smiled as she arrived.

He said, "I should have suggested lunch, but I've got an appointment at two. You probably wouldn't have been free either."

"Ah, well." In her book lunching was a business activity rather than a social or nutritional one and she as the one with more to gain from pumping Stevens than he had from anything she could tell him, should have been offering lunch. Perhaps it was a hint that she owed him something for being permitted to meet the Cresacres with him.

The coffee room was only half full, mainly with middle-aged women with shopping bags propped around their legs. Right at the back was a small alcove with a semi-circular bench. Stevens led the way there directly, ignoring other free tables, suggesting that he had often used this position, with its view over the café and out into the square. She wondered if he interviewed police narks here, incongruously surrounded by lumpy women eating slices of cheesecake with forks and exchanging scandalized comments about the latest doings of their daughters-in-law. He ordered an espresso, Zita a cappuccino. She looked at him expectantly; he was in no hurry to impart any information, pouring sugar into his coffee, stirring it vigorously, then swallowing most of it at once. She sipped her froth slowly, waiting for him to begin.

"Is she worried?" he asked at last, as though he had come because he needed her knowledge.

"Who?" Zita asked. Her mind was on old Mrs Hovell, who was worried by nothing now.

"The Russian woman, your client, Mrs Loftus."

"Worried? No, not especially. What about?"

He sighed exasperatedly at her deliberate obtuseness. He assumed that they were carrying on a conversation that they had begun some time ago and which she ought to remember. "Did you tell her, then, that we were testing the bones to find out whether they were Eddie Cresacre's?"

She tried to remember whether she had or not. "Of course," she said confidently to cover the gap in her memory.

"Did she react at all? Show any signs of nervousness?"

"No, certainly not."

"It must be Peter Gilling then. She knows it. That's why she wasn't nervous about the tests on the Cresacres."

Zita had now understood. "The bones are not Eddie Cresacre's?"

"No. I got the report yesterday. They definitely can't belong to a child of Mrs Cresacre. Now I'll have to tell them. Oh God." He groaned softly.

Zita said nothing. The Cresacres' newly stirred emotions had now to be put to rest again; she did not particularly wish to be involved in that interview. She was thinking, too, what the news meant for her and Yevgenia. If the skeleton had been the Cresacre child, Stevens would have been able to attack Yevgenia much more directly, something that, for a reason she still had not understood, he was determined to do. Eddie's disappearance was still not accounted for and the discovery of his body in the garden would be a good enough reason for arresting and charging the occupier of the time. Yevgenia had escaped that fate for the moment. Zita's sense of frustration at the lack of progress in her own searches increased. What she needed was a complete and self-contained explanation which would entirely exclude the possibility of Yevgenia's involvement. Such certainty was unlikely ever to be forthcoming.

"We're still looking for the Gillings. That is, I shan't make the same mistake again, we're looking for Peter Gilling's mother. But we've got nowhere. She's probably remarried and moved to Australia, knowing my luck."

There was a terrible personal animus there, Zita thought. Every set-back was directed at him by malign Fate, or Furies working for the other side. Could he really react to every case like this? Why did this one inspire such violent and personalized emotion?

He put down his cup and said, "I need to start at the other end. I'll have to talk to her. I must see if I can get something out of her."

"Go ahead," she said calmly. "Your people saw her right at the beginning of all this, to ask about the garden and when the roses were planted and that sort of thing. But you can ask to interview her again any time you like. It won't do you any good. She doesn't know anything about the body. She's always at home, she can't escape you. You've only got to ask for an appointment."

A mulish, angry expression lay on Stevens' face, as if Zita were taunting him and he was determined to bear it.

"She still remembers your original meeting in 1960. It was obviously a powerfully hostile encounter that you both recall it so clearly more than thirty years later."

"It was."

Zita looked at the smudge of coffee at the bottom of her cup and gestured to the girl who served them. She picked up the chit of paper and handed it back with a note. Stevens' need to see her was at the moment greater than hers to see him. Nevertheless, it was worth keeping the upper hand by being faster than he was with her wallet, even for a cup of coffee. He paid no attention to what was going on, appearing immersed in his thoughts, only realizing what was happening when Zita pushed the table aside to get out.

"Don't go yet."

"I must. But," she added, "I should like to know what develops about the skeleton. So I'll keep in touch."

"It's not finished yet."

She left him still sitting in his place, feeling his eyes on her back until the door closed behind her. She wondered whether his remark was intended as a reinforcement of his own purpose or a threat to her.

She felt more cheerful as she made her way back to her office. This might be the point at which the skeleton could be forgotten. Other more important and more urgent matters would arise to take up police time and with no evidence as to whose the body might have been, the case would become a statistic on the list of unsolved crimes. Or perhaps, with a little cunning with definitions, it would not count at all, for it was not certain a crime had been committed. Stevens' demeanour had affected her mood more than his words. He had spoken of his determination to go on; his expression had shown that he did not know which direction to take. The building work at Asshe House was continuing and had now reached such a point that order was beginning to be glimpsed through the chaos created by the workmen. The little pool had been lined; flagstones were being laid around it. Soon all reminders of the grisly find under the roses would be erased in the new vision of the house. She would allow the skeleton to slip from her mind.

A day or so later, she was entering her office on her way back from the County Court when she found an elderly man pulling at the door that had to be pushed. He turned out to be Mr Hovell, reluctantly sent in by his wife to find her. He was sheepish and obviously uncomfortable, regarding what he had to say of such minimal importance that it was not worth doing.

"She said you might like to know. Well, you might; but I don't know if it's worth anything."

Zita took him up to her office and sat him down, offering coffee or tea. She looked at him encouragingly. "What was it that your wife thought you ought to tell me?" she asked.

"It's about what Mother was saying. I didn't make the connexion at first. It was only when Mrs Hovell mentioned the medallion I knew who she might be meaning. She always believed the medallion was lucky; she said it saved her life. It was during the war. Those bombs right at the end. Not the Blitz but the flying bombs, V2s they were called. One of those fell on Woodham. It hit the corner of the square here, over where the post office is now. Well, Mother was out with the child of the people she worked for at Asshe House..."

"The Dryburns?"

"Was that their name? They were funny people. It must have been at the beginning of 1945, Mother and the child were caught in it, knocked down by falling debris. They weren't trapped for long but Mother used to say that you don't need long to be killed. She was very upset about it at the time. She must have been very fond of the kid. I don't think I ever knew him, but I remember how shocked she was when he died. I remember that at the time she kept saying, 'It's the wrong way round when the young are taken and the old are left.' "

Zita was rolling a pen beneath her fingers as if she were rolling out pastry with a rolling pin, smoothing, stretching. She was recalling the picture under her fingers as she smoothed open the page for Tom in the library, of St Michael's Square in a state of ruin. "I'm very glad you did decide it was worth dropping in to tell me. You don't recall the child's age, whether it was a boy or a girl, its name?"

He was looking more relaxed now, relieved at the reception his trivial memory had received. "Oh, it was a boy. It's a bit hard if you're only going on what she said and you never saw him. She used to talk about him the way you talk about…a boy, if you know what I mean. Not a baby, not a teenager, a little boy. Say between five and eight." He fumbled in his breast pocket and pulled out a photograph. "I found this photo and I think, though I can't be sure, that's him." He held out a black and white snapshot, not much bigger than a credit card, its edges nicked and creased. It showed three characters, layered one on top of the other. A crouching woman was holding a child, a small boy with a fringe, standing within her arms, against her right shoulder. He in turn held a teddy bear under his left arm. The eyes of all three, the woman's blurred, the child's wide, the toy's sharp, button-like, stared at Zita from 1944.

"I remember his first name. Ezra, funny name. But they were a funny family, very strange."

"In what way strange?"

"Religious. One of those funny religions. Christian, but not regular church goers, if you follow me."

"Ah." She waited. If she was patient with him, something more might emerge from his memory. But now he had reached the end of what he could recall. There was nothing more to come. She thanked him, encouraging him to contact her again if anything more came back to him. When he had gone she sat at her desk looking at her oblique view of Asshe House, thinking about the strange family who lived there during the war. She could see who he was now quite clearly. She was as sure of her answer as Stevens was of his, and now the proof was starting to come in. She would set about the acts of confirmation at once, although they would be done not for herself: she was sure she was right. She would do it for Stevens, to show him he was wrong.

She began by ringing Reskimer. He was at a conference in Manchester, she was told, and would be back next week. She made a note in her diary to phone him as soon as he was back. "Reskimer", she wrote, "eye-buttons".

The impulse to tell Stevens was strong. On her way back from the quintet that evening she dropped the violin-playing art teacher at her home and found herself at the end of a street which she suddenly recognized as his. She drew up outside his house, hesitating, glancing at her watch. There were lights on inside; a little Peugeot car was parked in front of the garage. She rang the bell and found herself looking at a small woman, with a spray of orange hair above a pale, much-creased face dominated by a pair of brilliant blue eyes.

"Is Mr Stevens in?" she asked, so startled by this apparition that she forgot his official title.

"No, not at the moment."

She was too old to be his wife; no other relationship suggested itself immediately. She was as interested in Zita as the latter was in her, gazing at her with a frankness of examination that was almost childlike.

"Ah." Zita was turning away indecisively.

"...But he won't be long. I've been expecting him back for the last hour or more." She spoke with a precision that suggested that she was not English. "Would you like to come in and wait for him?"

Zita hesitated again. "I can't really stay long and it isn't anything important. I can ring him sometime."

"It was important enough for you to stop in the first place. Come in for a few minutes. If he's not back immediately you can try again."

Zita stepped inside. "I'm Zita Daunsey," she said.

The woman spoke over her shoulder as she led the way to the living room. "And I'm Barbara Przedziecka." She turned to indicate a seat to her guest. "His mother."

Zita looked rather than spoke her enquiry.

"He was Przedziecki when he was born, but he changed his name. Bruno Szczepan Przedziecki: it was not just Conrad who found the inability of Anglo-Saxons to pronounce foreign names too maddening to be borne. Now, let me get you a drink. No? Well, I'm not going to wait any longer; I shall have something."

She poured herself some whisky and disappeared into the kitchen for water and ice. While she was out of the room, Zita got up quickly and bent over the photographs she had seen last time she was here. She was holding the picture of the officer in jodhpurs and forage cap, when Mrs Przedziecka returned.

"You've spotted my husband," she said, extending her hand for Zita to pass her the little silver frame. She looked into it dispassionately. "Odd to think he has been dead for more than fifty years now. I was only married to him for two years, but I still go around talking about my husband. He disappeared in 1939 and I didn't know whether he was alive or dead. You can see, he was in the Polish Army: the cavalry. It's quite true they still had their horses and their sabres in 1939. But my husband knew that the Germans would fight with aircraft and bombs and he sent me to England in August 1939, with Bruno. We got one of the last flights out of Warsaw. No sooner had I arrived here than war broke out and I never heard a word from him again." She sipped her whisky thoughtfully. "I don't know why I'm telling you this. You've probably heard it all from Bruno. God knows, it's obsessed him all his life, totally dominated his existence, ruined his marriage. And he was a baby at the time and didn't know what was going on. I've managed to forget it, why can't he?"

"I don't know anything about it," Zita said. "He's never mentioned his father." She did not explain that they had never met in circumstances that made such confidences likely. "Do tell me. What obsesses him? The war?"

"No, not the war, his father, or rather his father's disappearance. A very bad thing, you know, for a boy not to have a father. I should have married again. But, well, that's easier said than done, especially if you're poor, don't speak English well and have a child. Are you married?"

"I was."

"Children?"

"One son."

"Just like me. Single parents they call us now. My advice is: find a man and marry him as soon as you can. Much better for your boy." She sipped her whisky, thinking through the implications of her own advice. "And for you too. But don't choose Bruno, for heaven's sake."

Zita was feeling uncomfortable with Mrs Przedziecka's assumptions about her relations with Stevens. "What happened to your husband?" she asked, to move the conversation back to the safer past.

"About three and a half years after the outbreak of war, it was in the winter of 1943, the Germans discovered a mass grave in the forest at Katyn in what had been Poland. And then we knew what had happened to him."

"How awful."

"You know about Katyn? It means something to you?"

"Of course."

"You know that the Russians split our country with the Nazis in 1939. My husband's corps was in the Russian zone. He was captured and put in a prisoner of war camp in eastern Poland. He and everybody else there was taken out into the forest and murdered. Their greatcoats were tied over their heads and their arms twisted up to their shoulder blades and they were shot at the back of the skull. Then huge pits were dug and they were thrown in face-down, layer upon layer."

When you are faced with authentic accounts of horrors, even when they are told in the unemotional tone used by Mrs Przedziecka, there is nothing that you can say, Zita thought, that is not trivial in the face of enormity.

"And for years the Russians tried to pretend that the Germans did it." Mrs Przedziecka put the photograph face-down on a little table beside her. "Barbarians, the Russians."

"It's been accepted now, I think, hasn't it? that it was done by Stalin."

"Yes. They fought for ages, the Poles in exile, to get the

truth accepted. Of course, the Poles in Poland knew very well, but they weren't allowed to say. It's odd." Her voice was reflective, as it had been throughout her account. "I could never get worked up about it. I mean, about getting other people to acknowledge the truth. In some ways I was lucky in knowing, quite quickly, what had happened to him. And *we* knew who had done it. After the war the question went away for a time, but the Poles never forgot. He was one of the worst, Bruno, I mean. Not that he could remember because he was only a baby when it happened, and he never knew his father. But sometime in his teens, it started to become an obsession. He wrote a book about it, you know, proving that it was the Russians who did it."

"But he still changed his name?"

"That was just practical. You try spelling Przedziecki every time you make an appointment. Later it was quite convenient for him. A book written by Bruno Stevens looks less partisan than one written by Bruno Przedziecki."

"So he is a man with his ambition fulfilled?"

"Yes, you could say so. And not just over Katyn. The collapse of communism has been a wonderful time for him: the Russians themselves are allowed to speak and now we know that the old estimates of deaths from the famine in the Ukraine and the purges of the 1930s are far too low. Everybody knows what happened in the gulags. In the old days no one would believe Bruno's research. He was thought to be a bit of a madman with a bee in his bonnet about Russians. And he was, of course. The more he discovered about them, the more he interviewed emigres who knew about the terror and torture, the more he hated them."

Zita looked at her watch. "I really think I shall have to get back. I have a baby-sitter waiting."

Mrs Przedziecka put down her glass. "You never know when he's going to come in. I shan't wait around myself much longer. I try to look after him a bit, fill his fridge, put out flowers, but I doubt if he notices. He needs a wife, yet he drove his last one mad. She couldn't stand it, living with the horrors of the past, so she left him."

Chapter Twenty-five

Zita drove quickly home, her mind turning over the revelations of Stevens' garrulous mother. When she had said goodbye to Lynne, she went to see what could be made out of the contents of her fridge. She was ravenous. Ignoring Tom's purées and yoghurts and Lynne's hamburgers and pies, she found a coil of black pudding. She took a couple of apples from the fruit bowl, peeled them and put them with some butter in a pan. She had just finished the preparations and was about to assemble the sausage and the apples on her plate, with some salad and cheese in front of her as the final stages of her meal, when the door bell rang. Frowning with irritation, she turned off the gas and went to the door. She could see a masculine shape which revealed itself as Stevens'.

He blundered in without waiting for her invitation or explaining why he was there. She saw that he was looking distracted, barely aware of where he was. He began taking off his mackintosh. Why do policemen wear mackintoshes, Zita thought, even when it isn't raining?

"You're back," he said. "I called earlier, but you were out and your girl didn't know when you'd get in."

"It's my quintet evening." They looked at one another for a moment. "You'd better come and join me. I know you haven't had anything to eat yet. I called on you on my way home."

He was not taking in what she was saying, entirely absorbed in processing something else. He made none of the usual disclaiming sounds at her offer of food, sitting down, automatically, waiting to be served. Zita resignedly divided what there was in two. He began to eat immediately.

"Why did you call on me?"

"I wanted to tell you something about the skeleton. I met your mother and she invited me in to wait for a bit. That's why I wasn't here. And you? Why did you call? Not just on the off chance of some black pudding and apple?"

"What? Oh, no." He looked at his fork as if he were only now aware of what it was he was eating. "Why did I come in the first place? I can't remember; there was something...But you weren't in, so I went next door."

"To see Jean? Had you made an appointment?"

"No. It was on the spur of the moment. Since I was here and she was just there, I went round." There was a long pause. He pushed away the plate. Zita saw, to her annoyance, that he had left at least half of what she had given him. "She did it. She as good as said she did it. But I'll never be able to prove it."

"Did it? Did what? What are you talking about?"

"She killed the child, Peter Gilling, or whoever it is. She said so, I heard her say so."

"You're wrong. She could not have said any such thing because it is not true. She could not kill a child. It is impossible."

"I heard her."

"This is mad. You heard her? You mean you asked her and she admitted it?"

He was so adamant that Zita suddenly thought she was wrong. She had been wrong all the time, in her instinct and in her gradual building up of proof. The skeleton was Peter Gilling and Yevgenia had killed him. It was possible for her to have killed a child. It was possible to kill a child. Tom lay like a corpse under his sheet and she was free. Why had she fought so hard to insist that Yevgenia could not have killed those children, Eddie Cresacre, Peter Gilling, when she had no proof, not even a simple denial? Now she came to think of it, she had never asked Yevgenia directly, how could she? And Yevgenia had never rejected Stevens' unspoken accusation. She had worked on an instinctive belief in a person, and she had been wrong.

"No, it wasn't like that."

"So what was it like? What do you mean?"

"I walked up the path to her door and I knocked and waited. There was no reply, so I walked round the side of the house into the garden at the back."

"You were snooping," Zita said. "I don't believe you ever knocked."

He didn't contradict her. "I came round into the garden and everything was quiet, then I saw that one of the sliding doors into the house was open. I was just going towards it, to see if she was there, when I heard a voice. She was talking. At first, I thought she was with someone, they were chatting together, so, naturally, I stopped to see what I would be interrupting."

"Naturally," Zita repeated. He did not observe, or chose to ignore, the irony of her tone.

"The voice went on and on. I kept waiting for a reply. Then I went closer, because I couldn't hear what she was saying. She was talking to herself, thinking aloud, or something. I suppose it's old age."

He had not originally intended to spy, simply to look around at the Russian woman's new place, just to stand at the gate and think of her inside. The blankness of the house had tempted him, even though he knew she was unlikely to be out. The garden was green yet somehow barren, as though grass were grown to inhibit other plants, to deny them their life and to cover over with its sharp green fur all the shards of the past hidden below. He moved quietly, easily, over this suppressing carpet, not approaching the house like a normal visitor, skirting it, to come at it from behind. The murmur of a voice from within the house had made him hesitate, then drawn him on. Nothing he could say to Zita could convey the effect of that dry, elderly voice. It was rather low, rasping, the vocal cords frayed by a lifetime's nicotine.

"What did she say?" Zita was hostile.

"She said…she said that she held the child against her. It's funny; I can't give you her exact words, they've gone already, but as she spoke I could see what she was doing. She pressed the child to her. She'd come up behind him, grabbed him, then she put her hand over his mouth and held it there while he struggled and tried to cry out and when the movement stopped she let him go. Then she stopped. She wasn't talking all the time, you see. There were long pauses. Then she said that— about the child. And she began to laugh. Or perhaps she was crying. Great, hacking gasps. She sounded mad."

Zita waited, but he was now reabsorbed in his thoughts. She got up abruptly and began to pile the plates with a deliberate, domestic clashing of china.

"This is nonsense," she said, loudly. "This is complete fantasy. She didn't say all this. You're making it up. You simply want something to be so and now you have reached the stage of fabricating evidence." He did not protest, sitting quietly under her accusations. "You aren't the sort of man that beats up witnesses; you create the evidence you need in your own head. It's sick. You're sick, obsessed."

"And you, you won't believe when you're told the truth because your mind is closed. You think no woman could kill a child, because she's a woman, so you won't hear of anything that suggests that she killed a child."

"A closed mind. *Mine* is a closed mind." Zita heard her own voice rise almost to a shriek.

"I'm telling you what I heard less than an hour ago and you won't believe me because your mind is fixed." He was shouting.

"Will you keep your voice down. My son is asleep." She was hissing now. All pretence of civilized behaviour had broken down. "You couldn't have heard it because it didn't happen." She was making coffee. The familiar actions helped to contain her rage. She measured coffee into the cafetière, noticing it was not decaffeinated. Who cared, she would not sleep anyway. "What child are we talking about anyway? We know it wasn't Eddie Cresacre. And the child found in the garden was not suffocated. It was hit on the back of the head. Or are you going to tell me that you now remember that she said that after suffocating him she threw him face-down on the ground and hit him?"

If at that moment she had been more prepared to be just, she would have realized that his expression as she spoke was evidence of his truthfulness, at least as he saw or heard the truth. He was trying to fit the new material with what he already had. He had been so convinced by what he had heard that he had failed to put it alongside other information about the dead child. As it was, filled with rage, she could only see his puzzlement as a sign of her victory.

"No," he said slowly, "it's not Eddie Cresacre. That is, not the child in the garden. It could have been Eddie Cresacre she was talking about, who was suffocated."

"It could have been, it could have been. What does that mean? It wasn't. Eddie Cresacre, poor child, has gone. We're not dealing with him; he's out of it. The child in the garden." She stopped for a moment. "I think I know who he was and how he got there."

"Oh yes? You've been doing your own detective work, have you, snooping too?"

Zita had intended earlier that evening to share with him her hypothesis about the skeleton. She had been expecting to meet the amenable Stevens of recent days. This implacable Stevens enraged her. She looked at her feet. She was wearing her Turkish mules with the turned-up toes. "When I have proof, I'll tell you."

"So you haven't any evidence, you admit it. At least I have proof now. I know what I heard and that's good enough for me, the evidence of my own ears, even if it can't be used. You're as prejudiced as you say I am. More so. You won't allow me what I heard and yet you're going to find your own proof, make it, make it up."

"Of course I'm not." Zita's voice was rising again and she dropped it abruptly on the last word. Tom, waking to hear raised voices, a man shouting, would be terrified.

"Yes, you are. You've taken up a fixed position and everything you discover is going to be moulded to fit. You've discounted everything I've said or suggested all along, first on the grounds that policemen are all thick, right-wing thugs without the education or the cultivation of a person like you. Secondly, on the grounds that I'm a man. All men are stupid and violent and terrorize women. In every one of our dealings, everything you have said and done has shown it. You can't deny it."

"What *is* this? Now, we're into an examination of all those bits of my personality which don't please you. Who are you to say what I do and don't think? Talk about terrorizing women. This is a perfect example of male crassness and arrogance."

Zita's fury was fuelled by the accuracy of Stevens' perceptions. She recognized their justice at the same time that she denied them. She did not think that he was thick or imperceptive; she had early on observed the shrewdness of his judgements. But she did think he was authoritarian, illiberal, ungenerous, someone whose range of references were not the same as hers.

"What's more," she went on furiously, "all this persecution of Jean is entirely because she's Russian and for no other reason." She felt a momentary triumphant pleasure in catching him by surprise. "Don't look so astonished. You must have enough self-knowledge to realize that right from the start you were convinced she was a murderer because she was Russian and Russians in your book are all savages. Civilization ends on the Bug, beyond that the barbarians."

"What have the fucking Russians to do with all this? Anyway, they are barbarians. Are you trying to pretend that they haven't murdered sixty million of their own citizens in the last seventy years? You're like these people who say the Holocaust didn't happen. Stalin was dear old Uncle Joe and a few deaths are necessary on the way to socialist heaven."

"Of course I'm not saying anything of the kind. What I'm saying is...I'm Russian."

"*You're* Russian." She could see he was horrified.

"Yes."

"You speak Russian?"

"Yes. Do you speak Polish?"

The atmosphere had lost all its vehemence. He got up. "I don't know how we got into this. I'm going."

The phone pierced the silence. Zita looked at it for a moment in surprise that ordinary life still had the power to impinge; then picked it up.

"*Eta ti,* Zita?"

"*Da,* Mama, *minutchka...*" But he had already gone. She heard the front door close behind him.

"Zita, you sound very tired. What's the matter? Has Tom being playing up?"

"No, no. It's my quintet night. It's been a long evening."

Part Fourteen

YEVGENIA

Chapter Twenty-six

I came to England because I wanted to be safe. I wanted to escape from the horrors and dangers and cruelty that I had seen in Latvia and Germany. I would've done anything to get here; just as I suspect Xenia will do anything to stay. And once I was here I was grateful, to Kenward, to his family, to the whole country. But underneath all my admiration and gratitude, I resented them. I chose to live in a little town and not to buy a country house. I could not bear the English petty gentry and their pretensions to an aristocratic way of life. I preferred to be a bourgeois, limited, safe. But from time to time I felt, what do they know? Nothing. What was their war? The jolly camaraderie of the Blitz, then sitting tight for four years until they got the Americans to help them invade France. In the meantime the Russians endured the siege of Leningrad, defeated the Germans at Stalingrad and pushed them back to Berlin, losing millions of lives in the struggle. I never said any of this. I became more English than they were, more patriotic. But when they made a fuss about what they went through in the war, or when the whole town was in a state of mass hysteria about the disappearance of a child, I thought, don't they know that children died by the tens of thousands, shot and gassed and hacked to death not twenty years ago? Don't they know that? Why should I care that one child goes missing? I lost my child. I searched for him, weeping, even though I knew quite well what had happened to him. Every mother knows that "lost" means "dead" and she is responsible for that death.

When we took to the road the second time we joined thousands of people moving west. It was the very last gasp of the war. The German army of the east had fallen back to Berlin, the Russians were advancing like a wind which blows before it a tattered whirl of leaves, sticks and debris, anything that is not tied down. We were all desperate to reach somewhere, we were not sure where, before the Russians caught up with us. Some had a destination in mind, a cousin in Frankfurt, or Hamburg, a brother in Bavaria or the Pfalz. Our hope of escape in the short run, that is, escape from the rape, pillage and murder of the conquering Russians, was illusory. When Lai and I had set out the previous summer, we had only had German bureaucracy to impede us. The Russians then were holding themselves back deliberately, waiting for the Germans to destroy the Poles of the Home Army who had risen in Warsaw. By the new year the Red Army was moving westward fast and we, travelling on foot, had no hope of reaching the protection of the American or British in western Germany before the Russians in their armoured cars and tanks overtook us.

The refugees from further east already on the road told us stories of the arrival of the barbarians. One woman, pushing a pram containing all she had in the world, said that the Russians had hanged all the young men in her village from the tree in the square. They had dangled from every branch to make a giant gamekeeper's gibbet as a warning to others. The women had been herded into the church and raped for two days. She walked as if she did not know where she was or where she was going, moving forward because she still could. I couldn't bear to ask about the pram.

I wonder now if we had stayed on with my cousin, resisting his feeble hints and only half-hidden dislike of the invasion of his apartment, whether things would have been different, if Lai would have survived, and Alek too. This is another of the alternative lives I might have lived. The price we would have paid, I suppose, would have been a lifetime in East Germany under the communists. I can't do that sort of sum; the calculation of relative values and exchange rates, the market in futures, of real lives, is beyond me.

Now I am going to try to say what happened to us. This is something I have never spoken of before. Kenward never knew that Alek even existed, nor Lai. He knew of Xan only as the cousin who should have shared my inheritance, but was killed by the NKVD. I could not speak of it because to tell was an acknowledgement that it had happened. If it wasn't said, and above all, wasn't shared, if it did not exist for the people who surrounded me, I could pretend that the past did not exist. Or I could try, because if I cancelled out Alek, Lai and Xan, what was left of my life before I came to England? Nothing at all. Mention of any part of my childhood and youth led round from Xan and Lai to Alek. I could not really forget, of course. In the beginning, when I was still in Germany, it was easier not to remember. I was young and the will to live is inextinguishable. The struggle to achieve safety took so much of my energy that I was really able to forget, to pretend the past had not happened. Until I came to England, that is. Once I was here, there was time and peace. Life in the late forties was hard here, but the hardships were nothing, nothing, in comparison with what it had been like in Germany at the end of the war. And I found my great-uncle Yegor's money and I had to prove that Xan was dead. So I learned you cannot go on without the past. It demands its due. And that I gave it, but nothing more; no thought of Lai or Alek. Still, I used to wake in the night. I didn't dream of the events themselves. I woke at the instant it was over, when I knew what had happened. I knew that the minute could not come back, could never be cancelled, and I would live with the knowledge of what I had done for the rest of my life.

We set out, the three of us, Alek well wrapped up in his little fur coat, perched on the sledge that I had found in my cousin's cellar store, sitting on top of those possessions, mostly food, that we had decided to take with us. I think now of how adorable he was, his little face peaky with illness under his *shapka* with its earflaps tied down. It might have been an after-noon's walk from Kornu, he looked so happy and excited.

We went out into a very harsh world, and not only in terms of the climate. You might think that in extreme conditions common misery and common humanity would unite strangers: a little community of refugees, supporting one another. Not at all. The first rule is every man for himself and women and children last. You can trust no one except your own family and perhaps not them. If you are alone, you are desperately vulnerable. If you are a group, at least one of you can keep watch while the others sleep. For the danger comes not just from the approaching army, but also from your fellow refugees. The army will rape and kill; the refugees will steal: food first of all, then money, papers, valuables. Everyone is desperate, everyone's need is supreme, no one acknowledges any rules or laws or conventions of ethical behaviour. No one can delay to help the elderly who are slow and weak, or women with young children. The young and fit move ahead. To stay to help makes you likely to share their fate and the very fact they are there, to take the first brunt of the oncoming marauders, makes your own escape more likely. Survival is all. We were young, well fed, fit, but burdened with a sick child; we watched others overtake us.

The moment comes nearer and nearer. When was it? Days after we left my cousin's house. Where? A village on a small road, a speck on the flat and featureless north German plain, certainly not marked on the old map I had brought with us from Kornu. We had deliberately tried to keep to small roads; there were fewer refugees and we thought that the Russians, who were going to overtake us soon, might pass us by, rolling on the big roads in their tanks and armoured cars.

It was late afternoon. We had not made good progress that day. The little roads inevitably are longer, indirect; they turn away from the direction in which you want to go. We had met a group of about a dozen travellers at a crossroads. Some wanted to continue on the road, even though it would be dark in an hour or so. Others, including me, wanted to approach the mayor or a big farmer in the village to ask for shelter, in a barn, a church, a school. Some places on the routes into the Reich were so used to refugees by then that they ran a soup kitchen to give hot food in the evening, had a dormitory set up in some public building. In the end more than half of the group walked on, the rest of us went into the village that we could see a kilometre or so ahead.

The mayor was not welcoming. We trailed along the straight, blank street and found an abandoned shop which had been used by refugees before. The lock on the door was broken and we were told that we would be permitted to use it. It was bitterly cold, minus ten or fifteen, and to shelter from the cold, to light a fire seemed to me at first the only thing in the world I wanted to do. We went inside and at once I smelled a terrible odour, not strong but pervasive, there was no escaping it. It smelled of death. I insisted to Lai that we could not stay there. I was determined to leave in spite of the time and the temperature, because I suddenly had a powerful premonition of death, a terrible foreboding about that place, so that I could not stay there. I knew it must have been a Jewish shop; I could imagine what had become of its owners. I could not explain my feeling to Lai who would certainly have had no patience with such fantasies, so I said that I thought that it was unhealthy, contaminated, and that I could not bear to be there with Alek. This was persuasive enough for Lai and we left the others there and went on out of the village with the idea of finding a barn in the fields. We were, it appeared, luckier than that, because we saw smoke rising from behind a sheltering belt of trees, and as we drew nearer we discovered a farmstead. The large house and the arrangement of the farm buildings suggested that it was a German rather than a Polish one, whose owners might be more sympathetic to us than the glowering Poles.

The peasants welcomed us with great kindness. The paterfamilias was an old man with a tangled white beard; he must have been very old, for his son was well over fifty. The son's wife and her two daughters, huge and powerful women with red faces and blonde hair, fussed over Alek. They had helped other refugees and showed us the outbuilding across the courtyard from the main house where we could stay. They gave us fuel to burn in the fireplace and sacks of straw that had already been made up for earlier travellers to sleep on. They invited us to share their evening soup. I crouched by the fire and Alek played beside me on the floor clutching his mousie, a toy he had held in his fist for comfort since he was a baby. That night we slept on the floor near the fire, Alek between Lai and me, his warmth warming us both.

We had often heard the sound of guns in the distance behind us, which had hurried us forward. This time we heard nothing until they reached the village which we had left the night before. In the early morning there were gunshots and Lai, after consultation with the farmer, went out to investigate. He returned an hour or so later to report that he had seen four Russian armoured cars, a small detachment, who had evidently raided some liquor store, either in the village or in a nearby great house, for they were already drunk and still drinking. They were banging on the villagers' doors with their rifle butts, shouting, rounding people up. For us, some distance from where all this was going on, the question was whether to stay or to go. The farmer would not hear of our leaving. We might only cover a few kilometres before the Russians came across us, we would be on the road with nowhere to hide. We must stay with them and with any luck the detachment would pass on during the day and we could set off again tomorrow. He insisted on our staying in the house with his family and we spent the morning beside the stove in the kitchen, receiving reports from time to time from Lai, from the farmer and his son, of what they could see or hear from the village. The firing of the abandoned house where our fellow refugees had spent the night convinced me that my premonition had been correct and we had been right to leave. We could only hope that the occupants had been evacuated before the building went up in smoke and that they were not burned alive, as I feared they might be.

That afternoon another Russian detachment was spotted moving along the road towards the village from the north.

Immediately the farmer's daughter-in-law and her daughters got ready to hide. They had their places well prepared and with methodical speed lifted floor boards to step down into the cellars. The farmer led us along a corridor into a little storeroom. Here he raised a trap door and showed us a shallow storage hole, no more than a couple of feet deep, rather like the one we had constructed at Kornu to keep our extra preserves hidden under the floor in one of the outhouses. I jumped in first and inserted my feet and legs under the floor, reaching up to take Alek whom Lai handed down to me. He then followed us and with a combination of deliberation and haste the farmer lowered the planks on top of us. I could hear him scuffing the dusty floor to conceal our tracks and moving some bundles on top of the loose boards.

My premonitions which had been so active the previous day should have told me that we were being shut in a grave, but they did not. My fear was so great that I felt instead like an animal in its burrow, safe and hidden and enclosed. We lay as we had lain that night, with Alek between us, tightly packed like plums in a jar. Alek's back lay along my body; he was facing Lai's shoulder blades. He lay quietly, relaxed. For a long time there was no sound and he fell asleep; I could feel the gentle rhythm of his breathing. I leaned across him, my lower arm being the only part of my body that I could move, to touch Lai. I found his hand against his side and held it.

I think I may have dozed, for the first sounds of the Russians sprang on me without warning. There were shouts and shots, cries and inexplicable silences. I had no idea what the farmer and his son intended to do, whether they planned to hide themselves and let the marauding Russians take anything they wanted, or whether they intended to defend their property. It became evident that, even if they had hidden, they had been found, for there were renewed screams, shouts, banging and the sound of heavy boots. I moved my arm with difficulty from holding Lai's hand and put it over Alek's ear to try to shield him from the noise of alarm and pain.

They came nearer and burst into the room where we were

hiding. The noise now resounded over our heads; there was no need to see to understand what was going on above us. A heavy body was flung down on the wooden floor, but she was not dead. She rolled and squirmed above our heads, her heels hammering the floor. The animal sounds of struggle and protest told us she must be gagged. She was being held down by several men. I pressed my hand more firmly over Alek's ear, wishing you could close off sound as you close off sight. The obligation to hear was horrible; the lack of words even worse. One man was forcing himself on her. The violent banging of her head on the floor, the stamping of the boots of the watchers in time to the penetration, the parody of a bayonet thrust or the entry of a bullet, the bestial breathing were unmistakable. Finally, the gag must have worked itself loose and the repeated act was accompanied by smothered groans, over and over again, over and over again. The horror for us was to lie and do nothing. I could feel the tension in Lai. We couldn't help. Nothing we could do would stop the violence and the rape, but to be a witness was to be an accomplice. As I lay there, I thought of my mother and of how I must have heard this once before. But then I hadn't understood, and I prayed that Alek didn't understand. Perhaps I had slept, as he seemed to sleep.

Then he woke up. The noise was too great for me to protect him from the brutal sounds above our heads and he began to whimper. I don't know whether he actually emitted a cry or whether, in my anxious anticipation, I just felt him preparing to sob. I put my hand with difficulty between Lai's back and Alek's face and pressed my hand over his mouth to stifle his moans. Above us was just piston-pounding, humping, groaning. The woman fell silent, as if she had lost consciousness, could no longer fight or even feel. Perhaps she was dead. The tiny thread of Alek's cry pierced the brutish sounds above like a child soprano through a mechanical digger.

I held him closer, the back of his skull ground into my chest; I crushed his mouth with the palm of my hand. For a moment he resisted, turning his head against me in protest.

Then he seemed to submit and lie still. But still I didn't take my hand away.

I wanted to envelop him, to take him back within me and so protect him from what was happening above us. I don't think it was so much the danger to us that concerned me at the time. I didn't want him to be a witness. The row above went on and on, but Alek's will to cry left him. He lay against me quietly. I didn't dare to move my hand and so we lay as still as corpses in a mass grave. We were there for hours. Many men took their turn above us and all the noises were the same. After a time it was like a night in a storm which denies you sleep. You go into a waking dream in which consciousness is removed so far from the actual that the reality only impinges as an incoherent nightmare.

But I didn't sleep. I already knew. I must have known the instant it happened that Alek was dead. The warm dampness of his breath on my fingers failed. The flicker of his heart under my hand had stopped. But I didn't believe it. It was impossible that it should happen. We lay there for hours and he didn't move; there was no whimper, no movement, and when we rose from the grave, when at last it was over, I carried out Alek's body.

Part Fifteen

ZITA

Chapter Twenty-seven

"**W**hen do you go back to Moscow?" Zita asked Xenia. They were standing in Yevgenia's drawing room on the edge of departure. Only Yevgenia sat, as usual, in her chair, looking out over the garden. Even Tom, strapped in his chair, was turning his head restlessly to indicate his desire to be off. Xenia was leaving the room as Zita spoke and did not reply until she returned from the kitchen with two pills on a saucer and a glass of water which she offered to Yevgenia.

"In a month," she said.

"Two weeks," Yevgenia corrected her.

"Two weeks? Yes, it is. I had not realized how long I had been in Woodham already." She shook a jar of pills which she held in her hand. "We shall have to order some more of these next week, but there are enough of them for now." She put them down on the little side table. "I'll leave them there for you."

Zita watched Xenia making preparations to leave for the day, arranging things within Yevgenia's reach with an impatient briskness. It was evident she was longing to go. Yet their little exchange about returning to Moscow suggested it was Yevgenia rather than Xenia who was waiting most eagerly for the moment of final departure.

"What time are they coming?" Yevgenia asked. "Xenia is going out for the day with Al and Rosie," she said in explanation to Zita. "Will they have time to come in for some coffee? What will you do about lunch?"

"I expect we go to a pub," said Xenia. She was kneeling down to look Tom in the face, blotting the drool of saliva from his chin, so she avoided Yevgenia's eyes. "But it's just Al. Rosie couldn't come."

"Rosie won't be with you?"

Xenia did not reply, concentrating on Tom. From outside came the sound of a car door slamming. Before the bell rang, Xenia had already risen and left the room.

Zita stroked Tom's silken head before taking the handles of the wheel chair. "Is there anything else?" she asked. "Apart from the books to be collected from the bookshop?"

"Yes, Zita, my dear. Will you wait for a moment? I think Xenia will just be going." From the hall they could hear little exclamations from Xenia, Al's voice mumbling in reply. Xenia reappeared in the doorway.

"We're going then, Mrs Loftus, goodbye."

Yevgenia spoke, not turning her head, "Where is Al? Is he not coming to say good morning?"

Xenia laughed. "I think he was hoping you would not ask to see him." She sounded unaffectedly amused, unguilty. Zita had sensed the disapproval in Yevgenia when she had understood that Xenia's expedition was to be undertaken without Rosie and immediately assumed that Al's reluctance to present himself stemmed from a consciousness of guilt. When Al entered she realized she had been reading too much into the situation. Al's embarrassment was explained at once by his appearance.

Yevgenia did not turn, waiting for Al to move forward into her view. Zita was astonished into silence and only Tom reacted at first, the contortions of his face and hacking laugh startling Yevgenia into turning her head.

"Al," she said. Then, seeing him, "Good lord, whatever have you done?"

"He has cut his hair; he has cut his hair," Xenia's voice was gleeful.

The women all gazed at him.

Al said crossly, "There's no need for you to laugh like that, Tom."

"I'm sorry, Al," Yevgenia said. "It is most unfair of us. I can quite see why you wanted to escape with Xenia, unseen."

"You look very fine, Al," Xenia said. "Much better."

"Better?" said Yevgenia. "Very fine, perhaps, not necessarily better. I was always very admiring of your mane of hair, Al. Now we must stop discussing your appearance. It is very bad form. If you were a woman, of course, it would be different; you would enjoy it."

Far from enjoying the admiration and commentary, Al was looking sheepish. His thick tail tied back with a twisted strand had gone and his hair was cut short all over his head. Zita, looking at the pale vulnerable skin at the back of his neck beneath the sharp edge of the newly shorn hair, saw that it had been very expertly and expensively cut. This was not a sudden impulse; or if it had been it had been an impulse to have the hair cut properly, not to hack it off with nail scissors.

"What does Rosie think of it?" Zita asked. "No, don't tell me. Yevgenia is right. We have talked too much about your hair. Yes, yes, Tom, we're going very shortly."

Xenia and Al left, Xenia calling out as she closed the door, "I shall be late, Mrs Loftus, so I shall see you in the morning."

The sound of Rosie's car manoeuvring in the drive filled the silence between Yevgenia and Zita when they had gone. The car reversed, moved forward, reversed again. There was a grinding of gears. Tom was shaken with laughter again. The air was filled with comments that neither could make now Al was no longer there. Yevgenia reached down for a large envelope propped against the legs of her chair.

"Zita, I want you to take charge of this. You know I have been making tapes of my memories of my life before I married. I wish I could have written it down because writing makes you form your thoughts better. When you speak, your mind just jumps from one thing to the next without any proper framework. But with hands like mine I couldn't hope to write. I have finished saying what I can and now I want to give it away. Will you keep it for me?"

"Surely. I'll put it with all your records in the office. What do you want done with it?"

"You mean when I'm dead? I'm not sure. I don't want anyone to hear them for the time being. When I've gone, you can listen to them, if you think they would be interesting. It has to be you, because they're partly in Russian."

Zita spent the rest of the day with Tom. She pushed him into town to the toyshop, where he spent some birthday money from Valentina, and then on to the bookshop where she collected the biographies that Yevgenia had ordered and Tom chose a book on dinosaurs. She made Tom's lunch and the two of them endured the long and troublesome process of feeding. Tom resisted food, particularly Zita's, and her lovingly created concoctions were regularly spat onto the floor or ejected in a stream over his chin. Zita lacked Lynne's careless skill in spooning something in when Tom was least expecting it and in catching what he spurted out. They needed a rest from one another after this. Zita put Tom in his chair, semi-reclined, in the garden to have a nap. Although he rarely slept in the afternoons, he was willing to spend an hour watching the leaves against the sky or listening to the small sounds of the garden or absorbed in whatever went on inside his head in those long periods when no one provided amusement or activity for him.

Zita sat down at her desk for an hour's domestic administration. At the back of her mind was the thought of Yevgenia's tapes which might hold the explanation of many things, but which were not to be heard until she was dead. Later, she went out to collect Tom and to prepare for swimming at the Centre. She found him lying intently watching the hedge between her garden and Yevgenia's.

"What have you been looking at, Tom?" she asked. Conversation with Tom was one-sided if he did not have his computer and its synthetic voice with him. You supplied the answers to your own questions and carried on as if Tom had replied. He eye-pointed the hedge.

"Did you see squirrels today? The big one with the ratty

tail?" She waited for him to cast his eyes upwards which was his normal method of affirmation. Instead he closed his lids.

"What about the big pigeon, you know, the fat pigeon who eats all the bird seed in the winter. Was he here today?" He closed his eyes again. In denial his delicate, distorted face always looked as if he were exasperated at the stupidity of the world that could not follow his silent, incommunicable reasoning. She knelt down on the grass beside him. "OK, it's a quiz; I have to guess what you saw. You saw the blackbirds, father, mother and grown-up-daughter-still-living-at-home, hunting worms. No? I'm doing my best. It was Hector." This was a neighbour's cat who fastidiously chose other people's gardens in which to deposit his faeces. "No, all right. You'll have to give me a clue."

Tom opened his mouth to produce a jerky braying. Lynne was much better than Zita at interpreting the sounds that he made. "A person?" she said doubtfully. "Good lord, did someone come? I didn't hear anything. Really?"

Tom was enjoying himself. He cast up his eyes and brayed again. Zita looked even more surprised. "Running? Then it couldn't have been Yevgenia in her garden. Did Lynne come? Then I give up. I can't possibly guess. You'll have to tell me when you're in your chair."

She took him inside and transferred him to his electric-powered wheel chair and pushed it out to the minivan. He was working the head switches on his computer, but she did not look at what he was writing. She had just settled in the driving seat, started the engine and was turning the minivan into the road, when Tom's voice simulator, a huge bass voice like the Commandatore from the last act of *Don Giovanni,* blasted out, "Xenia."

"Tom, don't do that when I'm driving," Zita shrieked irritably. "Or switch to one of your other voices; you know that one always gives me a horrible fright. I could have driven off the road."

For a Saturday afternoon in August the pool at the Centre was curiously empty. Everyone must be on holiday, Zita thought. Tom, as always, loved the pool; buoyed up by his rubber ring, he could propel himself forward and the feeling of lightness and freedom bestowed by the water always pleased him. In the evening he was tired and happy, falling asleep over his supper and allowing himself to be put to bed early.

Zita still had the books which she had collected to deliver to Yevgenia and now with Tom asleep she picked them up from the table in the hall and let herself out of the house. A suburban peace hung over her as she walked from her own garden to Yevgenia's. It was so quiet that, although it was not yet fully dark, all the inhabitants of the area might have been already in bed and asleep, or dead. It was an elderly neighbourhood. No children shouted from the nearby gardens; no battered sports cars revved in the driveways. Faintly, from some distance, she could hear the whirr of a mower. There was no car in Yevgenia's drive and no lights visible within the house. Xenia must still be out with Al, for if she were back she would have turned them on. What had Tom meant by blaring out Xenia's name in the car?

Zita rang the bell in case Xenia was in and to warn Yevgenia she was there, then tried the handle of the front door. It was locked. She walked round the house to the back garden and saw that Yevgenia must be sitting in the dark: no light lay over the terrace from the drawing room. The last rays of the sun shone on the great sliding panes of glass, not penetrating, making a broad, flaming foil sheet out of them. She walked to the corner of the terrace to try to push back the doors; then, as she peered in, she saw that she still could not see. It was as if she were looking into the murky waters of an uncleaned aquarium in which a faint current carried the turbid liquid in a light, smoky movement.

Smoke, smoke. She tore at the doors. The handle which released the catch would not move; it was locked from within. She ran from the terrace towards the kitchen door; it, too, resisted her. She ran back down the drive towards her own house to find Yevgenia's keys. She scrabbled in the drawer of the table in the hall, telling herself that Yevgenia was certainly out; she must be out. But she did not wait to telephone for help from home; she raced back as fast as she could. As soon as she unlocked the front door an acrid smell filled her nostrils, burning her throat. She pushed open the door of the drawing room and, like a wall of water from a broken dam, a black wave engulfed her, blinding her, gagging her. As she staggered back, she saw little red crocus flowers springing up on the ground through the black mist.

Chapter Twenty-eight

Tom, normally so sensitive to light and dark, noise and silence, emotion of every kind, slept tranquilly through everything, the sirens and the flashing lights in the road, the arrival of the ambulance, of Dr Flowers, of Lynne, of Xenia, of the stretcher bearers. Neither the telephone calls nor the strange voices within the house made any impression on him that night. Zita, switching in and out of consciousness as if someone else was in charge of the remote control and was manically and arbitrarily swapping from channel to channel, kept repeating his name, "Tom, Tom, Tom, Tom."

"*He's* all right," she was told. "Don't worry. *He's* all right. Lynne's here. Xenia's here. He'll be all right."

Tom was her first thought as she struggled back to life next day. Light filtered through her half-open lids and with it memory. Without moving, she opened her eyes; she could see the carpet of her own bedroom and a pair of thin knees: Xenia.

"Tom?" she said.

"He's all right. Lynne's taking him for a walk. How are you?"

"Yevgenia?"

"No."

"What happened?"

"I think they are going to ask you that."

"No, to me."

"Smoke inhalation. Is that what they call it? Dr Flowers

tried to take you to hospital, but there was no bed. So he left you here. He's coming now. He said you would be all right."

Zita closed her eyes. "I'd like to see Tom."

"I'll get Lynne to bring him to you as soon as they are back."

Dr Flowers came first. Zita was already up and dressed, brushing her hair in front of the mirror, when he came in.

"I'm later than I meant to be. I had to drop Laura at church. You're all right then? How do you feel?"

He was a small, slight man, looking at all times rather like a tough Irish jockey, even more so in his Sunday dress of tight yellow corduroy trousers worn with a green jacket and waistcoat. Thick fine hair, now going grey, stuck straight out from his forehead like a boy's fringe and beneath it his long wispy eyebrows quivered like antennae, sensitive to every feeling released into the atmosphere by the pain and distress around him. They knew each other well. Zita, never sick herself, consulted him constantly about Tom.

"My chest hurts a bit."

"That's normal after what you breathed in."

"My hair smells disgusting, of smoke. I must wash it. Was it a cigarette?"

"Must have been. The fire brigade are next door again now. They think a lighted cigarette fell down into her chair and smouldered there for hours. She must have fallen asleep. She'll have died from smoke inhalation. She'll have known nothing; no pain." Dr Flowers broke off his account to examine her. Zita obediently breathed in and out on command while she absorbed this news.

"By the way," he said as he put away his stethoscope. "Have you got the son's phone number in Italy? Xenia told us last night that he was away on holiday. So the family hasn't been informed yet."

"I can get it. I'll let them know. I'll have to speak to Marcus in any case. Let's go and find some coffee. I feel drugged."

"You are, or you were. I gave you something last night. You were still trying to organize the world from a state of semi-consciousness. So I put you out and called Lynne. Then Xenia came home, and I brought her round here."

In the kitchen she saw that someone—Xenia, undoubtedly, for Lynne would never have thought of it—had laid breakfast for her, a cloth, with a plate, a bowl, a cup and saucer. No wonder Naomi and Marcus adored having her with them.

"And when I opened the door, the flames..."

"They probably burst out for the first time at that moment, with the rush of oxygen."

"So I did the worst possible thing?" Her head ached. She poured out their coffee. Xenia had found a honeycomb, butter, yoghurt, a loaf, but Zita could not eat.

"The police'll want to speak to you. It's all very straightforward, but I imagine there'll be an inquest." Zita leaned her head on one hand. "You're lucky it isn't a double inquest. How you managed to escape serious burns yourself, I don't know."

She looked at the palms of her hands in surprise that she had been at risk.

"I threw the rug on the flames. I didn't go near them myself."

"Then you picked Yevgenia up and carried her out."

"I'm used to picking people up." But pulling Yevgenia out of her chair hadn't been like picking Tom up. She was a tall woman, though not heavily built. Zita had put her hands in her armpits, in the way that she lifted Tom, and once she had pulled her forward the point of balance had shifted so violently that they had toppled together to the floor. The fall had probably saved them—her—for there was enough air at floor level to allow her to breathe, choking and gasping, as she crawled backwards, pulling Yevgenia's body by the armpits as she went. They had reached the fresh air and, leaving Yevgenia on the ground by the front door, she had returned within, this time making for the kitchen and shutting the door behind her. The air here was tainted but not consumed by smoke and she was able to call for an ambulance and the fire brigade, before the fumes overwhelmed her. So they had come and rescued her and not Yevgenia, who was already safe in death.

"I'm ashamed," she said. "I did everything wrong. I'm afraid one doesn't think clearly at such a time."

"No harm came of it. The firemen said you should have phoned and waited for them to come. But I can't see you standing outside for fifteen minutes when you know there is someone inside a burning house."

"But I didn't..."

The first doubt came into her mind. For she remembered that she hadn't known that Yevgenia was there. She had been hoping that she was not, that the drawing room would reveal itself as empty. It had been just before she had unlocked the front door and gone into the swirling sea of smoke that she had suddenly understood why Tom had blared out "Xenia" to her in the car. It had been the answer to the quiz, to the guessing game about whom he had seen. Perhaps Xenia had been there and taken Yevgenia for dinner with Al. So her actions in going into the smoke-filled house were even less rational than he realized. She would say nothing more about her motives.

"If only I had gone over an hour earlier. If only Xenia had not been out."

"It is useless to say 'if only'. Don't think like that. I must go and collect Laura who should have finished praying for me by now. You're all right, I'm glad to see. And Tom? He's over that last infection?"

Zita accompanied him to the door; as she watched him drive off, she saw Xenia returning from next door and waited for her.

"I went to find some clothes and things," Xenia said. She put an arm tentatively on Zita's shoulder. "How are you now?"

"Oh, I'm OK. What's it like over there?"

"The fire people are there to see how it started. It's terrible, black everywhere, even in the bedrooms and the drawing room is like, like hell. They said the police will come later, and the insurance people."

"Oh, what a nightmare. At what stage did you get back last night?"

"I don't know the time. I was at a film in Woodham, so not very late. The fire brigade was here already and Dr Flowers and Lynne. It was terrible because they were carrying you on a stretcher to your house. I thought it was you who was dead."

"Poor Yevgenia; poor, poor Yevgenia. She was all right in the afternoon, presumably, when you saw her?" Xenia looked at her blankly. "I must phone Rosie and let her know what has happened. She must have Marcus's and Naomi's phone number in Italy and Ivo's." They had turned inside the house. "You must move in here. Bring over all your stuff."

Lynne and Tom returned from their walk at that moment and Zita was distracted from her intended task for a while. Only sometime later did she dial the number of Rosie's flat. Why, she asked herself, did Rosie not know already? Al could have told her. Al would have brought Xenia home. Why had Xenia made no reference to Al? Zita did not waste time in the usual introductory rituals when Al answered; she simply asked for Rosie.

"She's gone out to get the papers," Al said. "Shall I get her to call you back?"

"Yes, please. Can you warn her, Al, that something awful has happened. Yevgenia died last night, rather horribly. She set fire to her chair with a cigarette, at least that's what we think. She must have been overcome by the smoke. It was that awful acrid smoke that killed her, apparently. She wasn't really burned because the flames didn't get going until I opened the door. Oh dear, why am I telling you all these horrible details?"

Al sounded appropriately shocked, concerned for Zita. "Do you need Rosie? Do you want her to come down to Woodham?" He sounded reluctant; there was no rushing to be on the spot to help.

"No, no." Zita might have welcomed seeing them if there had been any eagerness to come. "It's not necessary. But could Rosie phone Marcus and Naomi, and her brother and do that sort of thing. If she could get Marcus to phone me, he can tell me what he would like me to do about things."

"Rosie'll want to speak to you first, to hear about it. She'll be terribly upset. I'll get her to call you in the next quarter of an hour."

He was about to put the phone down when she asked, "What time did you bring Xenia back last night, Al?"

There was a moment's embarrassed pause.

"I didn't."

"What do you mean?"

"I didn't bring her back. She went home on her own."

It was Zita who now let the silence grow. Eventually when neither of them rang off, Al said, "We had a disagreement." There was another pause. "Basically we had a row. Xenia went off. I came back to London. I got back here about eight, I suppose."

Yevgenia's house was remarkably little damaged by the fire. Only her chair was calcified by the intense heat of the smouldering upholstery. The Persian rug that Zita had seized from the floor in the hall and used to put out the flames was charred. For the rest the whole of the interior of the house was covered in a thick black soot which, as Xenia had said, had penetrated even the rooms farthest from the fire, and painted them an ashy grey. The drawing room itself was horribly blackened and the air was still poisoned with the sharp dry odour which had overwhelmed Zita the night before. She found a man standing beside the corpse of Yevgenia's chair.

"You're the neighbour?" he said. "I was just going to bring the key back to you. I've finished here." He had a cropped head and muscular arms and thighs that seemed about to burst out of his clothes. "The insurance people might want to look at it. You'd better be in touch with them tomorrow."

"But it's clear what happened?"

"Clear? That's a laugh looking at this mess. Yes, it's clear. Cigarette dropped on this side, left-handed was she? between the cushion and the frame. Not enough oxygen to make a flame, just smoke. Lucky it wasn't one of those modern chairs that go up like a torch. Much more painful death. She might have been drowsy: an afternoon nap? a little drink? and didn't notice. Probably fell asleep holding the cigarette. Anyway, she wasn't going to make a quick get away if she used those." With his foot he nudged Yevgenia's sticks one against the other; a brown pill bottle rolled out from under the chair. He picked it up and shook it and dropped it again, wiping his hands on the sides of his trousers. "Empty," he said.

They went out into the hall together, where they met Xenia carrying her thin Russian suitcase.

"I've got everything now," she said. They left the house and locked it behind them.

"The smell hangs on everything," said Zita. "You'll want to wash all your clothes."

Xenia walked slowly, leaning away from the weight of her case. "Let me help you," Zita said.

"No, I can manage. Did Al say...?"

"Say what?" Zita did not want teenage confidences.

"About yesterday."

"He said he didn't bring you back."

"No. I left him. I went to see a film in Woodham by myself. I didn't say before because I did not want to embarrass him. I decided to leave because, well, he is Rosie's boyfriend, after all."

She stopped to change hands. Zita put out her hand to help. "What on earth have you got in here?"

They reached Zita's door and put down the suitcase. Suddenly Xenia's pale face creased, comically, like a clown's or a child's, the corners of her eyes and mouth turning down. "It was so awful; yesterday was so awful," she wailed. Tears spurted rather than rolled from her eyes, projected by passion. She was sobbing hysterically. Zita put her arm over her shoulder and led her inside.

"What's the matter with *her,*" Lynne asked unsympathetically.

"She's upset. It's all been a bit much." The telephone began to ring. "Oh, that'll be Rosie, or Naomi," Zita said. "Xenia, go and sit down. I'll make some coffee in a moment." A long moment if it was Naomi. She picked up the receiver in the kitchen, preparing herself to rehearse all the details at length. She was surprised to hear her mother's voice.

"Zita."

"Mama, where are you? Are you in Oxford?" She knew at once she was not by the echo, the gap between speaking and reply, giving an uncharacteristic note of hesitation to Valentina's speech.

"No, I'm not back. In fact, I shall not be back until next week now."

"You're enjoying Russia." She said it, a statement rather than a question, to fill in the pause which seemed to be greater than just the time lag on the line. "What are you doing now?"

"Zitushenka."

"Yes?"

"Zita, I am going to get married."

"Mama."

"What?" The pauses throbbed with electronic noise; they rushed to fill the space and their voices overlapped and interrupted one another.

"You must stop calling me Mama, Zita. You're too old."

"All right, all right. Mama, he's Russian. Who is he?" Zita felt faint again, faint and furious. She looked behind her for a kitchen stool and sat down. "What is this, Mama?"

Valentina's voice was firmer, now that the news had been told. "He is an old classmate. We were together at university and at the Institute. His name is Boris Andreevich Zurin. I met him again at Milan and he invited me back to Russia."

Zita did not comment, so Valentina went on. "I am making arrangements to get married in a month's time. He has to apply for a passport and an exit visa again. I have to get him visas for England and the States. There is so much bureaucracy, you cannot imagine."

"So he's coming to live with you in the West? You're not planning to set up home in Moscow?"

"St Petersburg. He's now in St Petersburg. We may commute. We shall raise some money for his Institute. Or he'll come to the West, if he can find a job he likes. Zita, are you still there?"

"Yes, Mama. So Russia is not so bad after all?"

"Did I ever say it was bad? Anyway it'll be a very good chance for you to see for yourself, when we get married here in the Palace of Weddings. It will be such a joke." Humour had never been Valentina's strong point, Zita reflected, sourly.

"Zita," Valentina was cajoling. "Have you got over the shock now?"

Her daughter's eyes filled with tears. "I'm ashamed," she said. "I haven't wished you every happiness, Mama. When shall I meet Boris? When will you come back?"

"You'll meet him at the wedding. You'll come with Tom and your crazy girl, if necessary."

"Valentina, I hope you will be very, very happy. It sounds so romantic, to meet a lover from the past, to be carried off by him to Russia, to plan a new life."

"It is romantic. I can't tell you, Zasha, what it is like to be in love again. It is so extraordinary. Everything is filled with light and life. Everything is beautiful. Russia is beautiful. I see everything like new, with a new meaning."

Zita made a supreme effort. "Send my warm good wishes to Boris. Tell him I look forward to meeting him. Send photographs. I hope you have taken masses of photos, of everything, of Moscow, of St Petersburg, the spire of the Peter-Paul fortress, the onion domes, the birch trees, the river, Boris..."

"Zitya, I am going now. I shall call you later."

Zita slowly replaced the receiver. Xenia and Lynne came into the kitchen pushing Tom between them.

"Was that Naomi?" asked Xenia.

"No," said Zita abstractedly. "No. If the phone rings it'll be her next time, so you take it, Xenia. I can't face making lunch. You two girls can produce whatever you like. I'm going into the garden."

Outside the world was dusty and tired; the grass was unkempt and scuffed like an old carpet; the encircling hedges made the air stuffy, closing round her like her office walls. Valentina was right. Why did she live like this, not, as her mother meant, a narrow suburban, provincial life, but inside her head a narrow one-track existence like a commuter train, travelling to and fro on its tracks, never looking at what lay outside, never getting out to explore what was beyond?

She had walked the circumference of her garden, she discovered, tracked round the circle. She went back through the kitchen where Tom made gagging noises to attract her attention. She ignored him and continued her route into the garage, where she pulled open the Oliver trunk. She stuffed bundles of papers and photographs into a plastic bag, without looking at them. In the kitchen she found some matches and took them with the bag out into the garden. At the side of the house, by the garden shed, was an incinerator, an aluminium dustbin with holes in the bottom and a chimney in the lid. It was part of the kit for playing at gardening which houses such as hers are equipped with, but which she had never had time to use. She emptied a few handfuls of paper into the incinerator, then struck a match. The first one went out as she was lowering it inside to reach the paper at the bottom. She applied the second one, as soon as it flared, to a single photograph, allowing it to catch, before she dropped it on the pile below. She fed the flame with fragment after fragment, waiting patiently until the last was well alight before adding the next. She could hear a voice, Xenia's, calling her name from within the house, but took no notice.

A few moments later footsteps approached and she turned with some irritation to find Stevens standing behind her.

"What are you up to?" he said. "Burning the evidence?"

He had evidently decided to forget that they had been shouting at one another two days earlier. Perhaps such exchanges were so common among the police that you did not even have to choose to forget them; or perhaps having shouted and sworn at one another they had entered into a new relationship. For the first time she allowed herself to look at what she was about to place on the flames. It was a self-important photograph with a thick mount, one of the formal groups taken at her wedding. She looked at the former Zita and the previous Oliver in the centre of their families: Valentina and

John Guilfoyle on one side, Oliver's parents on the other, the rest of his family all around them. Oliver had wanted the whole works and, although it was not how Guilfoyles usually did things, he got them. Her father looked vaguely bewildered, every bit a professor; Valentina, a larger Valentina than today, looked determined; the will that had decided everything in her own life was there in the fierce gaze. Oliver's parents—strange to think of Oliver's having parents, he seemed a man ready formed, without need of nurture—looked not dissatisfied with what their idolized son had committed himself to. And in the midst of them all, the bride. Zita gazed at herself. In the past, in her secret orgies of regret, looking at these mementos, such a photograph produced fruitless rage for what might have been and wasn't.

She found she had no such feelings now: the pathos of vanished love did not strike her. It was like looking at the ancient photograph of an unknown group that you might come across when clearing up after someone who had died; you could laugh at the dated clothes, the odd expressions, because the scene was without emotional resonance.

She handed it to Stevens, saying casually, "Exactly. When you've got that sort of thing in the case against you, what can you do but burn it?"

He looked at it briefly, without interest. "Who is it?" He dropped it on the bonfire.

"Not like that, you'll put the fire out." She poked it into position. "Me, of course. What did you think I meant?"

"Didn't look like you."

"No, well, I was someone else then." She fed another folder of photos in without bothering to open them. "And what are you doing?"

"I came to see what had happened there," he jerked his bald head back at Yevgenia's ruined house. The air currents shifted direction slightly. Zita moved round the incinerator to avoid the smoke. Now it wavered in a fine veil between them. "You'll have to agree now," he said.

"Agree on what? I agree nothing."

"That I was right."

"Right?"

"It looks like suicide to me."

"What are you talking about?"

"One day she confesses to a murder, to herself if no one else; then the next she dies. There must be some connexion."

"There's no connexion at all." Zita bent down and began to drop in more paper, one sheet after another. "So you're going to hound her even beyond her death, are you?"

"No. No, you're right, too, that's really what I came to tell you. They've called it off, closed it down, the investigation into your poor Yorick. There was a planning meeting, to review current cases, their progress, what to do about them. I had managed to keep it going, but now that the lab reports on the Cresacres are negative, it was felt that we were getting nowhere. The file's left open; if anything more comes up in the future, it can all be started up again."

Zita emptied the last papers in her carrier bag into the incinerator. The flames died down and dark grey smoke rose in a column. She drew back blinking. "So you've been forced by circumstances, by unco-operative superiors to put it on one side again. But you know what really happened and you'll wait another twenty years hoping to prove it."

He shrugged. "Yes, I know what happened, more or less. I haven't worked out the details. And now she's gone I don't suppose I'll get proof. But I know what I heard."

Zita folded her arms. She no longer felt the rage at his obtuseness, at his refusal to see or understand, that she had on Friday evening. Yevgenia's death made it all seem pointless now.

"Poor Yorick was the son of the previous tenants, who lived in the house before Jean bought the place. They were called Dryburn and belonged to some obscure puritanical sect. The child was killed on 6th March 1945 by a flying bomb which fell on the corner of the square. He was called Ezra; he had a teddy bear which was put in the grave with him in the crook of his left arm. I imagine that the parents buried him in the garden with permission from the local authorities. I haven't had time to check that yet, but it is perfectly legal. They usually ask to be assured that there is no spring, stream or well in the garden. I suppose the grave should have been marked on the deeds, but it seems not to have been, or I missed it. The oddity is putting him in the ground without a coffin; I suppose that was part of their cranky beliefs."

"You're making all this up."

"No, I'm not."

"Where did you get it from?"

"The cleaning woman who worked there at the time."

"In 1945? How old is she, for Christ's sake? Aged ninety and gaga, obviously."

"She has got Alzheimer's, but her grasp of the past is perfectly good. She just doesn't present it in the way you'd expect."

He laughed, unbelieving. "The word of a senile old woman reveals all," he said, sceptically.

Zita went back to the garage with her carrier bag and Stevens on her heels. She squatted in front of the trunk. Some things were unburnable: they would have to go into the dustbin. Or perhaps she would take them direct to the dump. She began to sort them. Stevens propped himself comfortably against the seat of a bicycle. She picked out a sealed parcel which contained the letters Oliver had written to her when she went to America just after they met. They were not love letters; they hadn't got that far. They had just been witty accounts of what he was doing every day, of the people he met. She had never, even in her worst moments, had the courage to reread them. His biographer was going to have to do without them.

"Don't you see," Stevens was saying, "even if poor Yorick is your child, whatever his name is, it still doesn't explain what happened to Eddie Cresacre and Peter Gilling." He was running his hand upwards over the suede skin of his naked head that Zita had always longed to touch.

She sat back. "Bruno, listen. I can't account for every dead child and nor can you. You've got to give it up. Take these."

Obediently he held out his arms for the parcel of letters, folders of papers about the decoration of their house in Islington, endless other rubbish. "Anyway, we have an explanation for those other children, a legal explanation. You just don't agree with it."

The fire in the incinerator had died down to a heap of charred flakes.

"Do you want this to go? You'll need one of those firelighters." He relit the new fire, which flared up, licking round the brown paper. "It's either true but you can't prove it, or it's a fantasy you have created. Either way, it drives you mad," he said sadly.

"No one is going to give you an answer. There is no answer, or there are several," she replied. She watched the letters transfigured into layers of flame.

"The thing is," he went on, "as I see it, if it's true and you do nothing about it, you're sharing in the crime. You're an accomplice."

"And if it's a fantasy, you're persecuting an innocent woman. You have to live with it. You have to live with not knowing."

They stood together in silence, the differences unresolved, until the papers were all burned. He shrugged his shoulders, as if pushing something out of his mind.

"You're right, of course. There's no evidence, at the moment. But remember Katyn." Without saying goodbye, he turned and disappeared round the side of the house.

Part Sixteen

XENIA

Chapter Twenty-nine

Xenia spent the time between Yevgenia's death and funeral in a state of trembling anticipation. She was waiting for something to intervene, to prevent her return to Russia. Al rang several times, but even when she was alone in Zita's house she pretended that there was someone with her so that she was excused from any intimate conversation. She was confident that in spite of their row on the day of Yevgenia's death, he was still attached to her, on the end of an unbreakable thread which just at the moment she allowed to lie slack. If she needed to, she could tighten it at will. Would she need to? Sometimes she thought that she had lost everything and that she would be trying to escape once more from Moscow, captured as closely by lack of money as by political repression in the old days. Sometimes she was filled with a certainty of success, that her plans had worked and she would not need Al.

One day, picking up the phone on the extension in the kitchen at the same time that Zita had answered it in her study, she overheard a conversation with Naomi who had at last arrived with Marcus from Tuscany, having declined to cut short their holiday.

"It was much the best thing to do," Naomi was saying. "All the business with the insurance assessors is over already, so poor Marcus won't have to be involved with that. If he'd been in England, he'd have had to rush down to Woodham to organize everything which would have been too much. So, I am very glad we decided to stay. It's done him so much good."

Xenia could not suppress a smile, for she knew that it was Zita who had dealt with the insurance company and everything else as well.

"And Asshe House must be ready by now. Have the builders finished, do you know?"

"Not quite," Zita said. "I still see their van in the mornings, but the skip has gone and all the digging is finished." There was a pause. When she resumed, Zita's voice was uneasy. "But the situation with Asshe House is quite complicated now that Yevgenia's dead. I wondered if she had spoken to Marcus recently about it."

"I don't know."

"She didn't write or phone while you were away?"

"No, not that I know of."

"You didn't find a letter waiting for you when you got back?"

"No, of course not. A letter from beyond the grave? What a horrible idea. You can talk to Marcus about everything when we come down for the funeral. We can all meet at Asshe House afterwards. She's being buried next to Kenward, isn't she? At St Michael's? I remember her getting quite excited when they closed the graveyard and turned it into a park ten years ago. She insisted on getting confirmation that she could still be buried there."

"Yes, I've gone into all that; there's no problem there."

"Well, I can't see there would have been a problem in any case. If she had to be buried somewhere else, what would it matter? I can't see the point of being buried next to your husband. She didn't really think they would reach out underground to hold one another's hands in the grave, did she? I'm going to be scattered when I'm dead. Burned and scattered."

Xenia noticed the constraint in Zita's voice as she said, in response to Naomi's public-spiritedness, "Everyone wants different things; it's a way of supervising your death when you're no longer there to exercise control. I'm just the legal instrument of her wishes and what Yevgenia wanted she is going to get."

"I just meant the family would not have made a fuss, if there had been a problem."

Xenia let Zita ring off before she delicately replaced the handset. She was looking out into the garden, crouching in a chair set in the position in which Yevgenia's had always been in the house next door. She spent much of her day there. She no longer roamed the town, neurotically collecting items from the shelves of the shops and depositing them in rubbish bins. She seemed to live in a dream, like Tom, watching the movement of the leaves in the hedge that enclosed her view, or the clouds that moved from right to left across the sky.

On the day of the funeral she accompanied Zita to the church and sat with her in the second pew, opposite the Loftuses. She could sense the tension in the large form beside her, something more than the grief which Zita, more than anyone, evidently felt, though had never communicated. The coffin was placed in the centre of the aisle, just in front of the communion rail. Xenia gazed at it abstractedly. She was the last true Chornorouky left. Now there was no way of contradicting that assertion; unless one day Yevgenia was exhumed and DNA tests performed, and that surely would never come about.

She looked across at Naomi and Marcus, Rosie and Al, judging their states of mind from the lines of their backs. The energy that emanated from Naomi's fidgety movements contrasted with the stillness of Rosie's upright neck. Naomi was anticipating the busyness of clearing up Yevgenia's life, and the interest she would find in the task. Rosie must be feeling real sorrow at the loss of someone who had loved her, and was perhaps worried about another love and another loss. Marcus sat immobile. He should be pondering his mortality, Xenia thought. He was the oldest in the family now; his generation would be the next to go. Al, farthest from her, was only just visible. His thin neck still looked naked, pleading.

Just as the vicar was entering the chancel someone strode

down the aisle. He glanced at the Loftuses in the front pew on the right and, judging there to be insufficient room in spite of Naomi's beckoning, he sat down in the empty row immediately in front of Xenia and Zita. The words that were intoned had no resonance for Xenia. She held her service sheet up and studied the newcomer's back. He was tall, very thin, dark hair already greying, pale-skinned. He was obviously Ivo at last.

When the service was completed there followed a brief period of greeting and parting in the park. Now the burial was over, the spirits of the survivors rebounded. The atmosphere was almost festive, and the sun shone with a dark, late summer radiance. Xenia could feel herself what she observed in others, in their unforced smiles, excited pleasure, as old friends, only reunited at weddings and funerals, met one another. Death had got one of them, she thought; he might be placated now, absorbed in his prey for a while, and those left could enjoy life, which suddenly, for a moment, seemed more sharply worth living. This was the limit of the celebration of grief; there was to be no wake and eventually the party broke up, leaving only the family with Zita and Xenia.

They stood in an uncertain huddle as if wondering what was to happen next. Zita was talking to Marcus. "I need to speak to you about Jean's will, Marcus. Could we do it now?"

Naomi, standing beside him said, "Shall we go to Asshe House? We could sit in the garden. I could see what has been done while we were away and you two can have your chat. Rosie, Al, why don't you come too. And Ivo, you haven't seen it at all. Ivo, you do *know* Zita, don't you? Have you two ever met? Oh and Xenia too."

She put her hand on her stepson's shoulder to turn him from his conversation with Al. He was closest to Xenia, shook hands with her first, before looking at Zita. Naomi was already shepherding the family towards Asshe House. Only Xenia watched Zita and Ivo.

"Yes," said Ivo. "We've not met recently. But I knew you at once, of course." Zita's face lost the frowning concentration with which she usually confronted the world.

"Ah, yes, the chef," she said.

Naomi was by now almost out of the park. She stopped and called, "Xenia, you must come as well. You're family too." Xenia turned and left Ivo and Zita still shaking hands.

The front door of Asshe House, newly painted an authentic Georgian blue, was already unlocked and from somewhere above came the sound of whistling as some final touches were made.

"Into the garden," Naomi directed them. "You'll see a lot of changes."

The child's grave was now a pool, reflecting the gothic arches of the summer-house. The flagstones that surrounded it looked as if they had been there since the gazebo was constructed. Amid the pots of bay trees there were wooden benches and chairs.

"I'm having cushions made." Naomi settled herself in the sun. "It'll make these less hard on the bum. I'll just hear what you have to say, Zita, then I'll leave you to talk to Marcus about the details."

Marcus and Zita sat in chairs on either side of her. Naomi patted the hard wooden bench. "Ivo, you come here. Xeni, Al, Rosie, sit down for a moment and admire my new garden. It's a change from Hampstead, you have to admit. Now, Zita..." She looked across at her expectantly. "No great surprises, I imagine."

Zita opened her bag slowly. "I brought a copy of Jean's will along with me. Whether it is a surprise or not depends on whether she told you about it. Marcus?"

"She gave me an outline of what she planned to do a number of years ago, and again last year when she decided she couldn't cope with Asshe House any more. She didn't mention the sums involved, but the global division, as it were."

There was a silence. Finally, Zita said, "She didn't speak to you when you were in Italy?"

"In Italy, you mean just now? No."

Disquiet had crept into the air. Xenia could see that Zita was unhappy; she had been cornered into a formal reading of the will, a scene with which Xenia was familiar from her reading of nineteenth-century novels.

"Then it will be a surprise." Zita spoke flatly. "I told Jean at the time that she should speak to you, Marcus. However, she was adamant that she wanted certain changes made and she would not agree to wait to discuss them with you when you got back."

"Quite right too," Marcus said. His voice was calm, unsurprised. If his assumption had been for the last two weeks since hearing of Yevgenia's death that he had inherited certain money and property, he showed no emotion at these indications that they had been snatched away from him. "Jean's money was her own; it was not my father's. We have no claim, moral or legal. I had understood that she intended to leave it principally to Rosie and Ivo, with Asshe House and a bit of money to me."

"You mean she *changed* her will?" Naomi's voice betrayed all the indignation of disappointed expectations that Marcus's had concealed. "Why? What happened? What's been going on? She seemed perfectly normal when we left. She was a bit ratty when we went to Glyndebourne, but..."

"Naomi, let's just hear what Zita has to tell us."

Xenia was sitting on the stone edge of a raised bed between Naomi and Zita. Although she could not see Ivo's face, the rest of them were open to her, all manifesting degrees of interest, distress, concern. She felt her own stomach clench with excitement.

This was the moment, the culmination. She hoped that her expression was as impassive as Marcus's. Certainly, she would never show her feelings with Naomi's directness; Rosie's face was tense. She, thought Xenia, was alert to danger. She had thought she was winning, but that depended on whether Xenia let her win; Rosie's stake was Al, not her grandmother's money. Xenia looked at him. Like her, an outsider, he was sitting not on one of Naomi's new teak chairs, but on the stone edging of the border, a little apart. He was half-turned away, gazing at the house, as if to signal his lack of personal interest in what was going on; but he, too, was sensitive to every motion and emotion. Xenia could feel his intense concentration focused on her, willing her to see him. She glanced for a moment at his knife-like profile, exposed now his hair was a thick, conventional cap. The excitement gave her a sensation of power. She might have Al, too, she thought. It really depended on how everything went now. She might have to abandon him to Rosie. Seemliness, a need to diminish confrontation with the Loftuses, might demand it. But she might not do so; she might take everything.

Zita had unfolded the stiff legal paper she held in her hands and was smoothing it out. "I am going to tell you about the arrangements Yevgenia made about three weeks ago. Why she did it, I do not know for certain, because she did not tell me explicitly. However, I have some idea, for she left a long tape recording about her life. She gave it to me just before she died and I have listened to it subsequently."

"All right, Zita, just tell us, will you."

"Rosie!"

"Sorry. I won't drag it out with explanations. Jean has left the bungalow to you and Naomi, Marcus."

"The bungalow?" Naomi's voice had fallen to a whisper.

"She has left certain items of jewellery which I understand were given to her by her husband to you, Rosie. All his grandfather's books and some of his personal possessions, his desk and certain pieces of furniture, she left to Ivo. Everything else, which she says came from her Russian family, that is Asshe House, most of its contents and her money, she willed to Xenia."

Xenia was glad it had happened like this. She had rehearsed how she would react when she was told. She knew what to do. She had imagined playing the scene to Zita, to Marcus, to Naomi. Now she had all of them at once to witness her two quiet words.

"To—me?"

No one seeing her face could doubt that she was simply amazed. All the Loftuses looked at her. She looked at Zita, whose eyes were lowered.

"But why?" Rosie's tone was hard and calm. She was not reclaiming her lost inheritance; she was asking for the explanation that had been cut off earlier.

"Something, this summer, I'm not sure exactly what, made Jean think of her past, her childhood. It may have been Xenia coming; it might even have been Valentina; it might have been something earlier that set her on this course. She began to dictate an account of her youth onto a tape recorder. As she began to relive the past, Jean became convinced that Xenia's father was her cousin, who was also her first husband. She had believed he had died during the war. She never told anyone that she had been previously married, that she had had a son, both of whom died during the war. Then she discovered that her husband had been alive all the time, for many years in a camp in Siberia. She had escaped from Germany and claimed her family's money. I think if you put those two ideas together: that he was in Siberia, while she was in England living on their family money, the reason for her will becomes apparent."

No one moved or spoke. Xenia could control herself no longer. "Does this mean I can stay in England?" she asked.

Zita turned her head to look at her directly for the first time. "Oh yes," she said. "There should be no difficulty about that now. You will be well able to support yourself."

As Zita looked at her, Xenia was shocked by the scepticism of her regard. Among the people to be managed and orchestrated, she had never listed Zita, who was of peripheral importance to her, a mechanism only. She suspects something, she thought. Her conviction of power ebbed and she felt the dissolving sensation of fear. She dropped her eyes.

"How strange," she said. "When I wrote I had no idea..."

"No, how could you have had?" Naomi was now recovered. She was consoling to Xenia as if her shock were worse than her own. "It is the most extraordinary story. Jean didn't say anything to you? No, of course not, you were as surprised as any of us. Well." She got up rather heavily. "We must get back to London. No point in looking at the tiling in the bathrooms now. Zita, you're executor, aren't you? You'll sort everything out."

"With Marcus. But, yes, I'll do everything for you."

They were all rising, moving towards the house in an uneasy bunch, checking their belongings with the subdued air of people who have escaped uninjured from a terrible car crash and are thanking God for the miracle of remaining alive amid the wreckage. Xenia watched them go. They had all behaved very well, even Naomi, especially Naomi. No tears, no recriminations; they were above all that. This was a family which had always had everything and whose creed was to deny the importance of money and possessions. They would cope. She heard them beginning to talk about other things as they went through the garden door into the back hall. Zita had followed them and Xenia was left for a moment in solitary possession of the garden. The door banged and Al ran back across the flags.

"Xeni, I'm sorry about Saturday. What are you going to do? Can I see you before you go?"

I might give him back, Xenia thought. Rosie can have him. "Of course," she said. "I might not be returning anyway, if I can get an extension to my visa. I'll let you know. I'm staying with Zita, so you can ring me there."

Al took her arm and kissed her. His fingers pressed urgently into her flesh; then he turned, picked up a service sheet from the ground where he had been sitting and ran back into the house.

Part Seventeen

ZITA

Chapter Thirty

So, in the end, Zita, not Xenia, packed to go to Russia. Valentina's wedding was to take place in St Petersburg in a week's time and she had arranged for her daughter to come with Tom to join a huge party of friends from England and America staying at the Europeiski for the occasion. Tom was in a state of high excitement. His suitcase had already been packed by Lynne and he was now sitting in his wheel chair blocking Zita's progress around her bedroom and using his American little girl voice to comment on her clothes as she laid them out on her bed. Valentina appeared to be as excited as her grandson. She phoned at least three times a day to check arrangements and to ask Zita to bring some small and essential item that could easily be fitted into her baggage.

"Tom-Tom, move, will you." Zita was getting out yet more shoes and putting them beside the ten pairs already lined up on the floor at the bottom of her bed.

Xenia was not going back. Zita had always suspected that there was a powerful energy behind the docile teenager trailed around during the summer by Naomi. She had still been surprised by the demonic organization demonstrated by Xenia in the days after Yevgenia's funeral. She had first found herself a place at London University through the UCAS clearing system and obtained the necessary financial guarantees from Zita herself. With this documentation, she had had no difficulty in obtaining a change in her visa, allowing her to stay on as a student.

"I shall get right of residence and a British passport later," she told Zita. She had already rented somewhere to live in London. "I'll probably buy a flat in the end," she went on. "I have taken this place just until all the business of the will is settled. It's in Hampstead, because that's the only area I know. But I shan't buy there. It reminds me of the Lenin Hills where I lived in the *obshezhitiye*. I shall go somewhere near the river when I buy, Chelsea or Kensington, perhaps."

Zita concealed her alarm at this display of decisiveness. "What will you do with Asshe House?" she asked. "Have you made up your mind yet?" They were seated in Zita's office, for there were legal papers to deal with. She could feel the regard of Asshe House's façade, blank and unoccupied, obliquely, through her windows. Invisible behind the church was Yevgenia's grave.

"Oh, I'll sell it. It has no sentimental value for me. Why would I want to live in the middle of a town like Woodham?"

Why, indeed, thought Zita. "Well, that's for later. We can put it on the market when the will is proved. Now let me take down some details for all these papers that have to be prepared. Xenia Alexandrovna Chornoroukaya. Place of birth: Novoleninsk, Siberia, Russia. Date of birth?"

"Twenty-three, oh-two, seventy-one," Xenia said automatically.

"Mother's name?"

"Yelena Petrovna Danilova."

"Date of birth?"

"Twenty-one, oh-eight, forty-five."

"Father's name?"

"Alexander Alexandrovich Chornorouky; twelve, twelve, fifteen."

Zita made her notes and later, after work, took Xenia, who had already moved into her flat in Hampstead, to the station.

She was not sorry that Xenia had acted with such rapidity to sort out her new life and to remove herself from Woodham. She had felt uncomfortable, having her in the house. She had an invisible, cat-like presence which was quite different from the untidy self-assertion imposed by Lynne. She felt embarrassed, too (though why should she, she asked herself every time), when each evening the phone rang and Xenia seized it. Whom was she expecting to call, Zita wondered. Al? Marcus? She had inherited Yevgenia's suspicions. Then Xenia would hand the receiver to Zita, or shout to her in Tom's room, "Zita, it's for you. Ivo."

She was glad to see her go also, because she could not rid herself of the unease which she had felt from the moment she recovered consciousness after Yevgenia's death. The explanation of what had decided Yevgenia to act as she did, that she had given to the Loftuses, was clear enough, accepted by everyone. But tiny fragments of observation still nagged her and made her wary in Xenia's company.

She rejected one of the pairs of shoes, low-heeled slingbacks. It was September, so what she would need in St Petersburg would be a good pair of leather boots, fur-lined, rubber-soled. She looked doubtfully at her ankle boots with their frail soles and neat laces. The only answer was to buy another pair in Russia. She got up from the floor and moved back towards the cupboard where her shoes were stacked to the ceiling.

Tom read her mind and his Betty Boop voice said, mockingly, "I need a new pair of shoes." He manoeuvred his chair into her path, so that his left wheel almost ran over her foot.

"Tom, go away. You're being a real pain. Listen to a tape or something and let me pack in peace."

"No tape machine." It was the Commandatore this time.

"Damn, I've packed it. You've got to do something." She remembered seeing Yevgenia's tape recorder in a carrier bag in the coat cupboard in the hall. "I'll find you another and you can listen to Roald Dahl in your room."

She found the bag on the shelf above the coats. The tapes were in her office waiting to be delivered to or collected by Marcus, who had showed no interest in them at all. She extracted the recorder and flicked it open as she walked towards Tom's room. A tape still lay in the machine. She took it out ready to replace it with *Charlie and the Chocolate Factory* and saw that it was unmarked, apparently new, but that the spools were half wound on. With a slight frown of irritation, she put it back.

Hearing Yevgenia's story had been harrowing in the extreme. Sitting in her office she had listened to the accounts of Kornu, of Xan's charm and Lai's devotion. The death of Alek she had found unbearable, her own nightmare, or dream, of Tom's death come true. Only the impersonal surroundings had prevented her from breaking down and she could not stop herself from crying when she began to tell Ivo what she had heard. He had listened with attention, not eating the lamb with juniper that she had cooked.

At length he had said, "You mustn't take it all so personally. You're sad because Jean's dead. You miss her. But treat her story like a novel or a film. You must detach yourself."

"But it's *so sad.*" Zita snivelled and blew her nose. "She thought he was dead and he was alive all the time. She loved someone else anyway, but she thought he had betrayed them, and he died too. She lost her son. She killed him. Can you imagine anything worse? It's *so sad.*" Her tears flowed afresh.

"Nonsense," Ivo was eating again. "This is really excellent, this garlic purée. Jean had a very good life. She was rich; she was loved; she had people to love. She survived, for God's sake. Her story is just one of millions of that period; she was one of the lucky ones."

Zita did not want, now, to listen to more. Yet with the precision of lawyerly duty, just to finish the job, she replaced the tape and pressed the rewind button. She heard the sound of Tom's hacking laughter and realized that he was playing a game on his computer. He had forgotten about the tape. She sat down on the second step of the stairs and pressed, Play. Yevgenia spoke this time in Russian.

What happened after Alek died? I hardly know, for I think I was mad. The farmer had survived, much beaten; his son and one of his granddaughters were dead. They were all buried in the cemetery attached to the church in the village with others who had been killed that day. It was a terrible job to dig even a shallow pit in that frozen earth and there were no coffins. Alek was laid alongside the woman whose sufferings he had heard, wearing his fur coat like a barbaric princeling. Mousie was tucked under his hand. I didn't cry out or weep. I was like an automaton.

I haven't allowed myself to remember this for almost fifty years. I never made up an alternative life to fill in the hole, I just erased the journey from Kornu to Berlin from my mind. I cancelled out the war years at Kornu; Xan, Lai and Alek, all went. Sometimes I would wake on the edge of remembering them, some vision of a lake, like the lake at Kornu, a dream of light through tall trees, like the forest at Kornu, would jolt me into consciousness. But I never allowed myself to recall anything, anything at all. Now it has forced its way to the light, grubbed up by Naomi's workmen and Xenia's arrival.

Somewhere between that nameless place and the refugee camp where Kenward found me, I lost Lai, too. I had no purpose any longer. I did not care if I lived or died. I was, as I said, a bit mad. I remember waking once, I think we were in Berlin then, getting up to search for Alek, even though I knew that he was dead and I would never find him. I stumbled about in the dark looking for a way to dig up the ground. I scrabbled with my hands amid the rubble in the street, convinced that I could find Alek's body and release him from his grave. Lai looked after me through all this time when I would have been very glad if a ricochet, a falling brick from a bomb-damaged building, anything, had killed me. He led me as if I were an animal on a leash that he could not let go in case it ran away. Unlike me, he still had his wits about him and he got us to where we wanted to be. I don't know, I never knew, the stratagems he used to reach Berlin and from Berlin Hamburg in the British sector. I did not care where we went or what became of us. Lai, whom I often felt I hated, was the only person I could bear to be with.

The war had already ended when Lai died. It was a stupid, unheroic death, some form of food poisoning that killed him. We were always desperately hungry. We ate anything, the most extraordinary things, if we ate at all. I never cared whether I ate or not and Lai had to beg me to eat what he found, and very often I would not. Partly because I wasn't interested in food, but partly because I wanted him to have more. That wish must have been the first sign of a return to some kind of normality, the recognition of someone else's needs. It was certainly something that he ate which I had refused, I who wanted to die, which produced violent vomiting. His death was horribly quick. I could not believe that when we had survived so much and reached the West at last Lai could be taken too. It was like the death of Alek, when I knew, but could not believe, that such a thing could happen. I had forgotten the fundamental rule of life taught me by Aunt Zoya and the Princes: *Everything Gets Worse.* Like Alek, he died in my arms, in fact in almost the same position. He lay on his back between my legs with his head on my chest. My arms were round him, a trail of vomited water trickling over us both.

I've never mourned for Lai until now. I have never done justice to how much he did for me, or how much I loved him. I grieved for Xan and was crazed with sorrow for Alek, but when Lai went I had no time to miss him. I had to die or start to look after myself, and I found dying harder than I thought. Standing in a queue a few days later, I fainted for lack of food. I was taken to hospital and there I met Kenward. My life began again.

Alek died; Lai died; Xan did not die. I now believe that. My lack of faith didn't kill him, for he was alive all the time, until three years ago, in Novoleninsk in Siberia. I suppose I suspected this since I first received the letter from Xenia. The little pieces of evidence accumulated all through the summer, but I resisted them. Now, suddenly, an alternative life has turned out to have been there, running alongside mine in Woodham. Xan alive, in the camps in the forties, released in the fifties, then married, teaching, father of a child. It is all too incredible not to be true.

So, if Xan was alive, perhaps Lai was innocent. Everything I have believed of them up till now is wrong.

But none of that changes what happened to Alek. Alek died in Germany. I killed him. Nothing that Xenia can tell me can alter that.

I have done what I can to put things right. I can ask Xan's memory for forgiveness for my lack of belief in his existence. I can ask Lai's memory for forgiveness for my belief in his betrayal. I can repay to Xenia everything that her grandfather left us. She is the last Chornorouky, so she must have everything.

I told her this morning that I knew that her father must be my cousin, long thought dead. She was reluctant to believe it. She said she knew very little about her family; that her father never talked about his past, which was evidently something to be concealed. She didn't even know anything about her grandfather, though she thought he might have been called Alexander Yegorovich. I told her that even the little she did know fitted exactly with my family. Alexander Yegorovich was indeed his name. He was my mother's cousin and had been killed fighting in the army of General Denikin in the Caucasus in 1920. The moment of proof for me, I told her, was Tom's birthday, when she described the special food prepared for her father's birthday. I remember so well Xan's birthday parties on 7th July at Kornu when we were children. We did not have caviar, of course; we had lamb for St John's Day, and a cake, and we sang "Happy Birthday" in English. She agreed, then, that they must be the same person. I asked her about Xan, but there was little I could recognize. Is that surprising? Who from Kornu would recognize Yevgenia von Korff in Jean Loftus? He was a kind man, she said. A loving father. She had hated her mother for running away with another man and had chosen herself at the age of eight to stay with her father. He spoke English and French and German, though he had only taught her English and French. He was a gifted teacher, beloved by his students. Then, with tears in her eyes, she told me about his death. She spoke about it with difficulty. It was a horrible death. So strange to think that

Xan endured the transports and the camps only to die at last, smothered by the smoke of a fire in their apartment as he lay asleep. "He did not suffer," she kept saying.

Zita snapped off the tape. Her heart was beating so fast that she thought she might be sick. She put her hands over her mouth, to her cheeks, to her forehead. Her movements were unconscious ones, to calm her own distress. All the minute fragments which had made her uneasy formed themselves into a rose window in a kaleidoscope: the Commandatore's voice saying "Xenia"; the empty tablet bottle rolling out from under the burned chair; Xenia's surprise, which was no surprise, in Asshe House garden; the date of birth, stated automatically, twelve, twelve, fifteen.

Xenia had made Yevgenia think she was her cousin's child. She must have known that Yevgenia had changed her will. She had returned from her day out with Al, drugged Yevgenia, set fire to her chair.

No, it was impossible. It was impossible to believe it; no one would believe it. Why would she have killed Yevgenia?

So that she would not have to go back to Russia. So that Naomi and Marcus or Rosie would not change Yevgenia's mind again. So that no evidence that Alexander Alexandrovich Chornorouky of Novoleninsk was not Xan Chornorouky of Kornu could have time to emerge.

Did she kill her father? She had not spoken of him with any tone of affection on the one occasion she had mentioned him to Zita. "A drunk," she had said. The coincidence of the smoke-filled flat in Siberia and the fire in Yevgenia's house was too great.

Zita's hands clasped one another in her lap; she was washing them, waterlessly. No, that was too much. She could not believe what her mind had created. She could not bear to believe any of it. It could not be true. If it were true, what evidence could she show? She sat weighing the tape recorder in her hands, passing it from left to right. Would she fight the past or become its accomplice?

She thought of Stevens. *It's either true, but you can't prove it, or it's a fantasy you have created. Either way, it drives you mad.*

She sat, still now. This would drive her mad, she thought. This must have been how Stevens had felt about Yevgenia, about Katyn, knowing but not knowing. But she would not allow it to obsess her; she would put it right out of her mind. Yevgenia had in the end wanted to believe that Xenia was Xan's daughter. She wanted to repay the past. Why should Zita tamper with her wishes?

If it's true and you do nothing about it, you're sharing in the crime. You're an accomplice.

She did not move. Stevens was right, after all. She could not live with not knowing, as she had so wisely counselled him. She would have to put that series of coincidences, dates, observations, to someone else, to begin a process of enquiry. There was only one person she could tell.

She stood up at last and walked towards the phone in her study, glancing through the open bedroom door at Tom as she went.